MIKE CAVALLARO's

NICO BRAVO

AND THE CELLAR DWELLERS

:01

First Second
NEW YORK

First Second

Copyright © 2020 by Mike Cavallaro

Published by First Second
First Second is an imprint of Roaring Brook Press,
a division of Holtzbrinck Publishing Holdings Limited Partnership
120 Broadway, New York, NY 10271

Don't miss your next favorite book from First Second!
For the latest updates go to firstsecondnewsletter.com and sign up for our enewsletter.

Library of Congress Control Number: 2019948196
Hardback ISBN: 978-1-250-22037-0
Paperback ISBN: 978-1-250-21886-5

Our books may be purchased in bulk for promotional, educational, or business use.
Please contact your local bookseller or the Macmillan Corporate and Premium Sales Department
at (800) 221-7945 ext. 5442 or by email at MacmillanSpecialMarkets@macmillan.com.

FIRST

EDITION

First edition, 2020

Edited by Mark Siegel and Kiara Valdez
Cover design by Kirk Benshoff
Series design by Andrew Arnold
Interior design by Mike Cavallaro
Printed in China by 1010 Printing International Limited, North Point, Hong Kong

This book was written and drawn on park benches and kitchen tables, aboard trains,
and in cafés and bars, on an iPad Pro using Clip Studio Paint, and colored in Adobe Photoshop.

Paperback: 10 9 8 7 6 5 4 3 2 1
Hardcover: 10 9 8 7 6 5 4 3 2 1

TO PAOLO & AURORA

PART 1:
SCRATCHING
THE SURFACE.

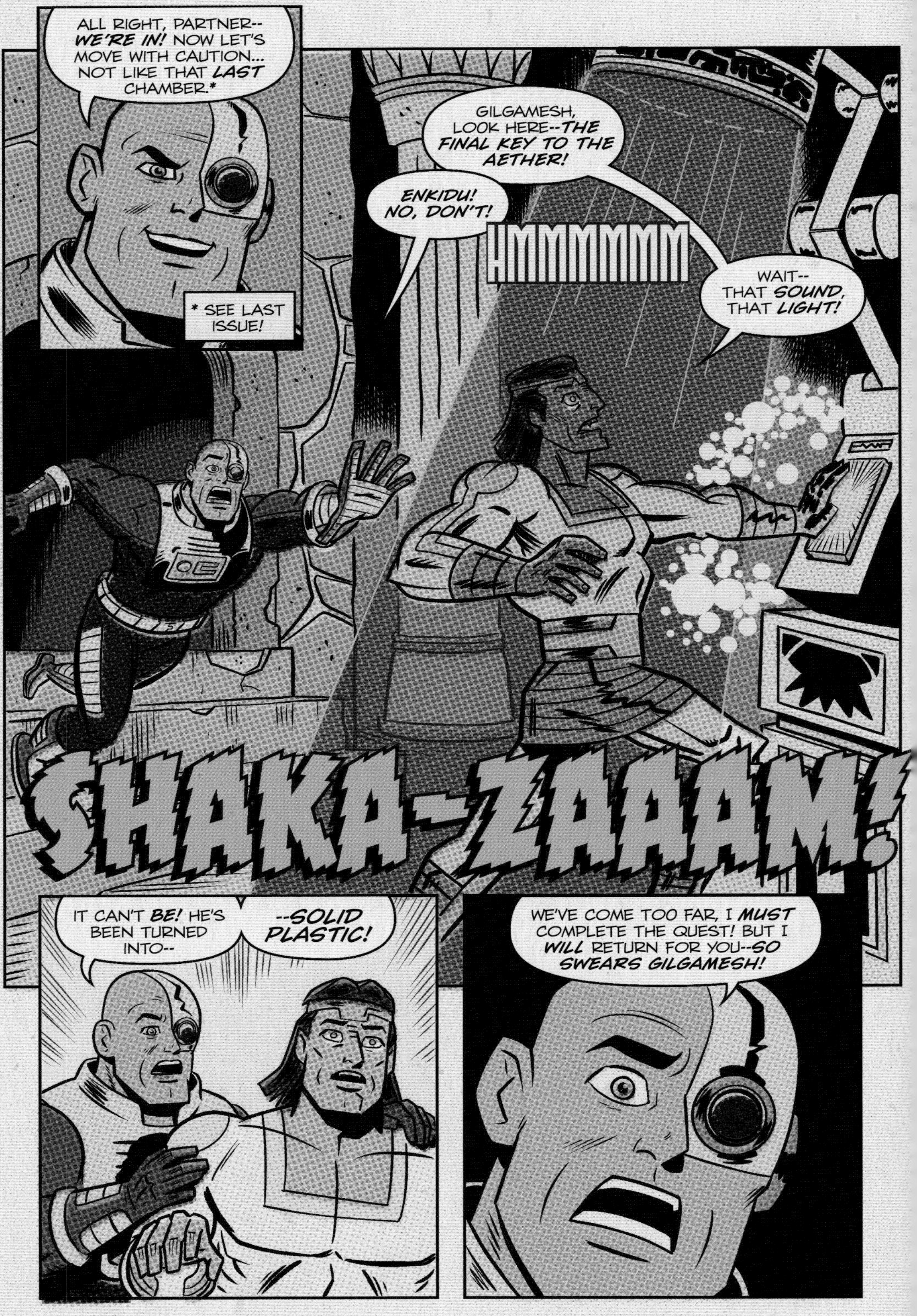
ALL RIGHT, PARTNER-- WE'RE IN! NOW LET'S MOVE WITH CAUTION... NOT LIKE THAT LAST CHAMBER.*
* SEE LAST ISSUE!
GILGAMESH, LOOK HERE--THE FINAL KEY TO THE AETHER!
ENKIDU! NO, DON'T!
HMMMMMM
WAIT-- THAT SOUND, THAT LIGHT!
SHAKA-ZAAAM!
IT CAN'T BE! HE'S BEEN TURNED INTO--
--SOLID PLASTIC!
WE'VE COME TOO FAR, I MUST COMPLETE THE QUEST! BUT I WILL RETURN FOR YOU--SO SWEARS GILGAMESH!

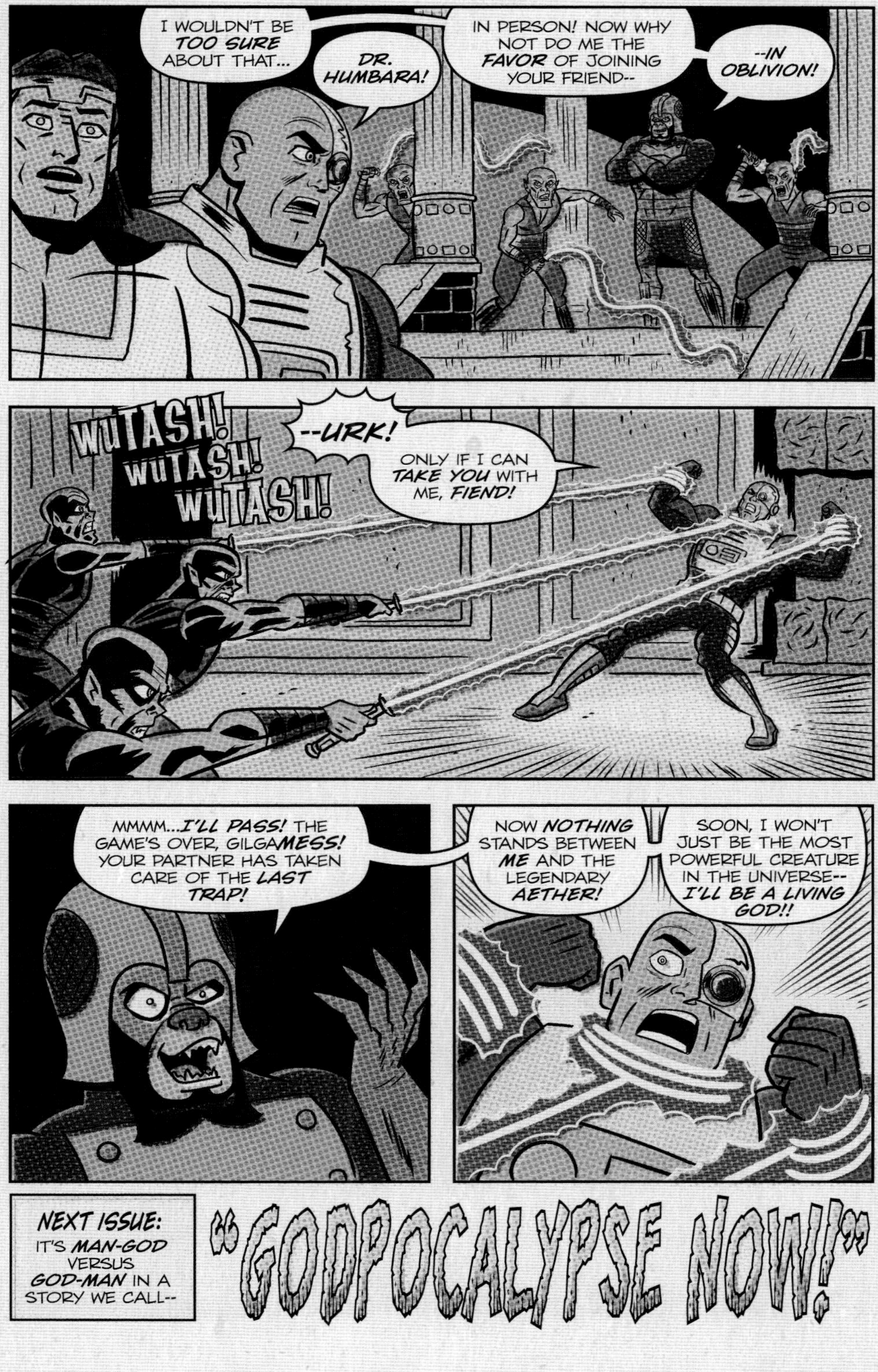
I WOULDN'T BE TOO SURE ABOUT THAT...
DR. HUMBARA!
IN PERSON! NOW WHY NOT DO ME THE FAVOR OF JOINING YOUR FRIEND--
--IN OBLIVION!
WuTASH! WuTASH! WuTASH!
--URK!
ONLY IF I CAN TAKE YOU WITH ME, FIEND!
MMMM...I'LL PASS! THE GAME'S OVER, GILGAMESS! YOUR PARTNER HAS TAKEN CARE OF THE LAST TRAP!
NOW NOTHING STANDS BETWEEN ME AND THE LEGENDARY AETHER!
SOON, I WON'T JUST BE THE MOST POWERFUL CREATURE IN THE UNIVERSE-- I'LL BE A LIVING GOD!!
NEXT ISSUE: IT'S MAN-GOD VERSUS GOD-MAN IN A STORY WE CALL--
"GODPOCALYPSE NOW!"

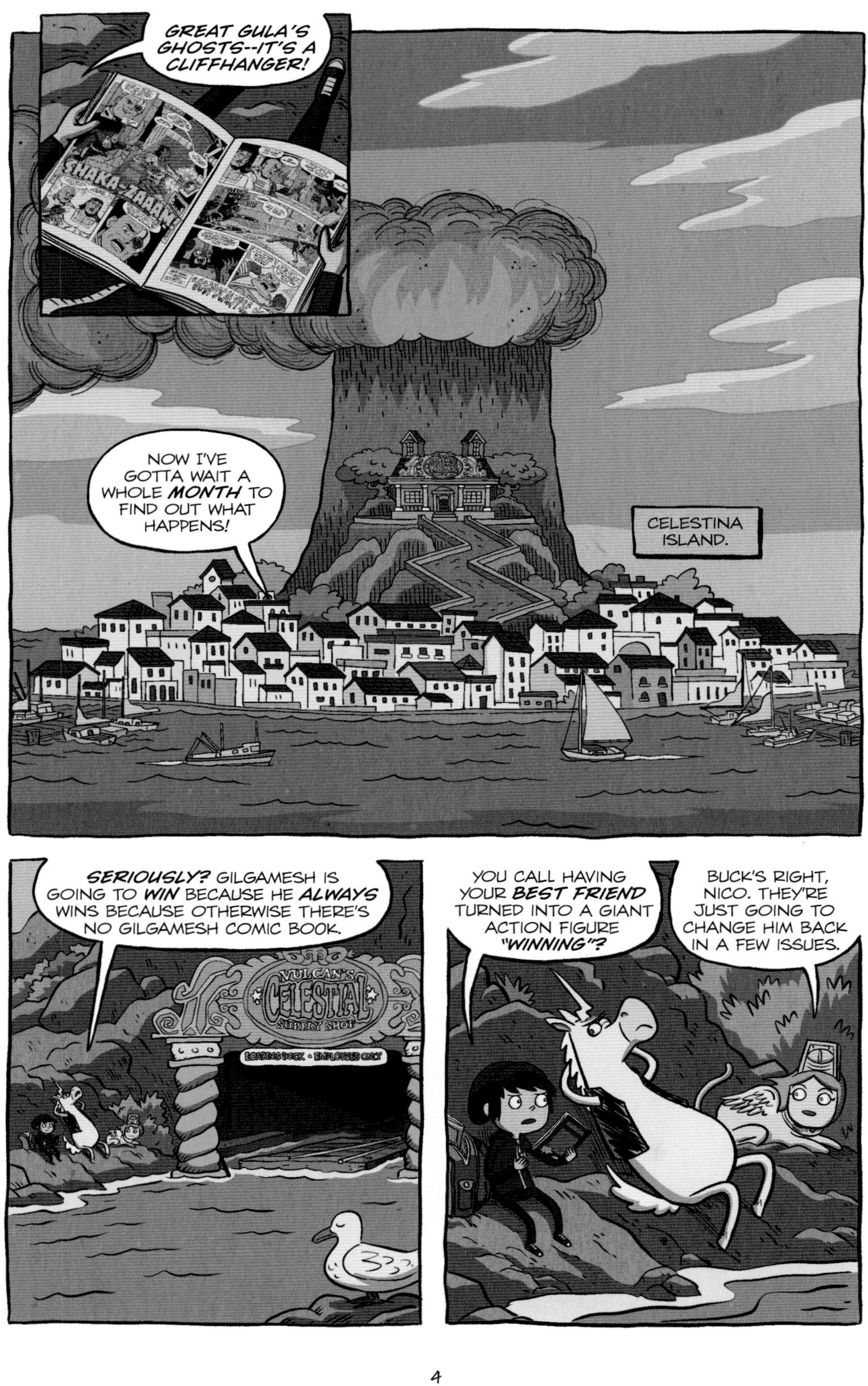

GREAT GULA'S GHOSTS--IT'S A CLIFFHANGER!
SHAKA-ZAAAM
NOW I'VE GOTTA WAIT A WHOLE ***MONTH*** TO FIND OUT WHAT HAPPENS!
CELESTINA ISLAND.
SERIOUSLY? GILGAMESH IS GOING TO ***WIN*** BECAUSE HE ***ALWAYS*** WINS BECAUSE OTHERWISE THERE'S NO GILGAMESH COMIC BOOK.
VULCAN'S CELESTIAL SUPPLY SHOP
LOADING DOCK • EMPLOYEES ONLY
YOU CALL HAVING YOUR ***BEST FRIEND*** TURNED INTO A GIANT ACTION FIGURE ***"WINNING"?***
BUCK'S RIGHT, NICO. THEY'RE JUST GOING TO CHANGE HIM BACK IN A FEW ISSUES.

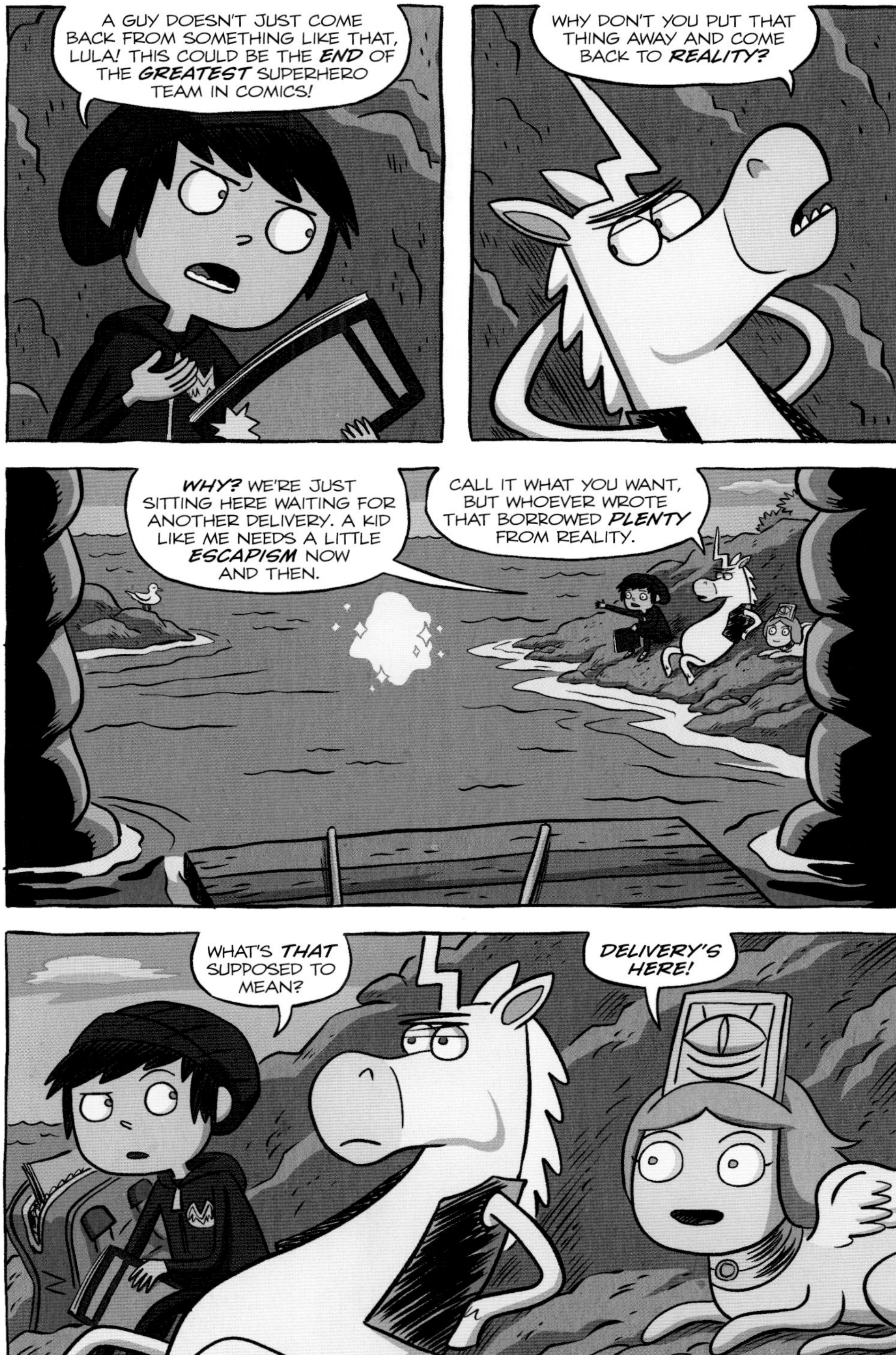
A GUY DOESN'T JUST COME BACK FROM SOMETHING LIKE THAT, LULA! THIS COULD BE THE END OF THE GREATEST SUPERHERO TEAM IN COMICS!
WHY DON'T YOU PUT THAT THING AWAY AND COME BACK TO REALITY?
WHY? WE'RE JUST SITTING HERE WAITING FOR ANOTHER DELIVERY. A KID LIKE ME NEEDS A LITTLE ESCAPISM NOW AND THEN.
CALL IT WHAT YOU WANT, BUT WHOEVER WROTE THAT BORROWED PLENTY FROM REALITY.
WHAT'S THAT SUPPOSED TO MEAN?
DELIVERY'S HERE!

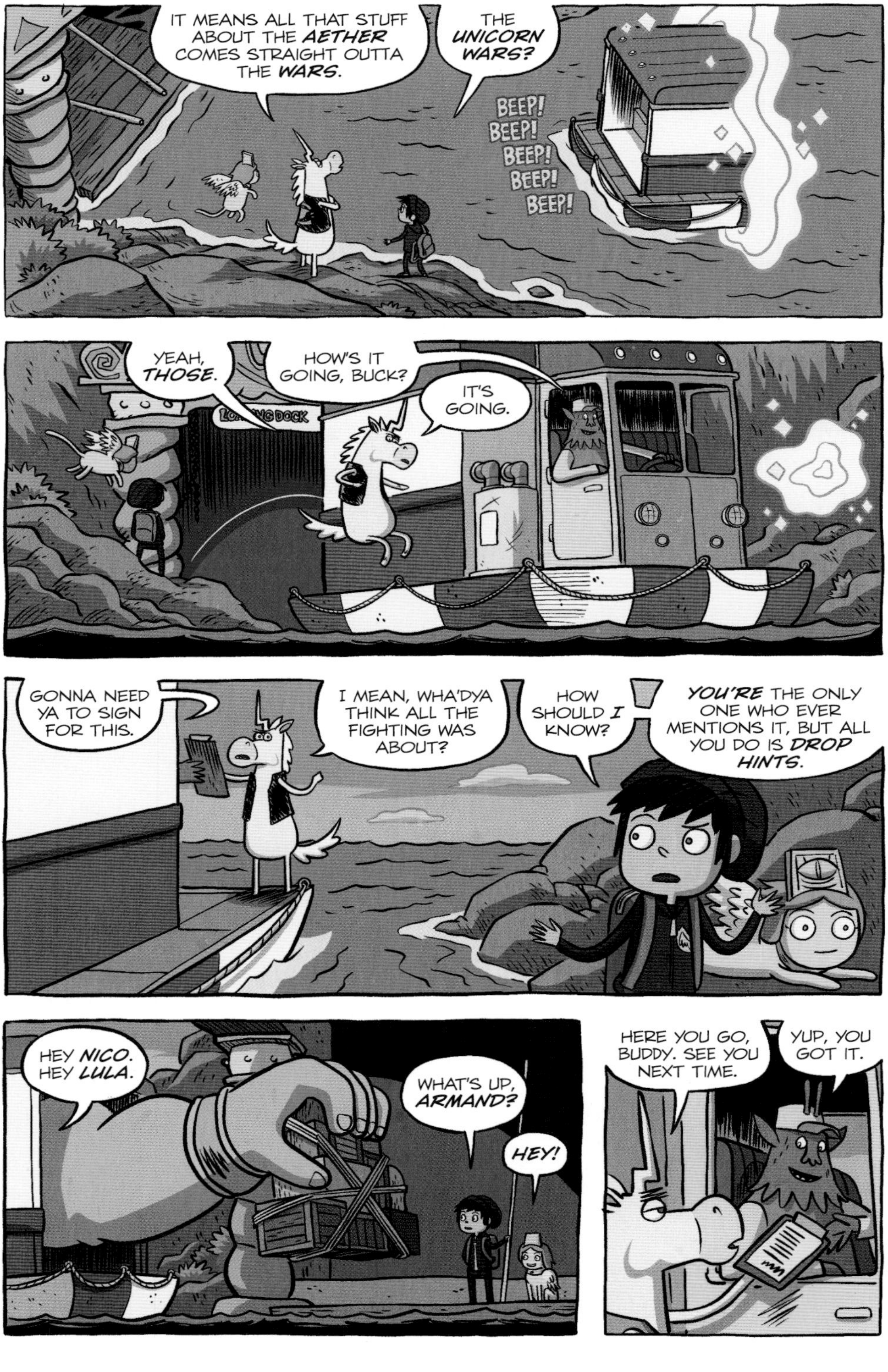
IT MEANS ALL THAT STUFF ABOUT THE AETHER COMES STRAIGHT OUTTA THE WARS.
THE UNICORN WARS?
BEEP! BEEP! BEEP! BEEP! BEEP!
YEAH, THOSE.
HOW'S IT GOING, BUCK?
IT'S GOING.
GONNA NEED YA TO SIGN FOR THIS.
I MEAN, WHA'DYA THINK ALL THE FIGHTING WAS ABOUT?
HOW SHOULD I KNOW?
YOU'RE THE ONLY ONE WHO EVER MENTIONS IT, BUT ALL YOU DO IS DROP HINTS.
HEY NICO. HEY LULA.
WHAT'S UP, ARMAND?
HEY!
HERE YOU GO, BUDDY. SEE YOU NEXT TIME.
YUP, YOU GOT IT.

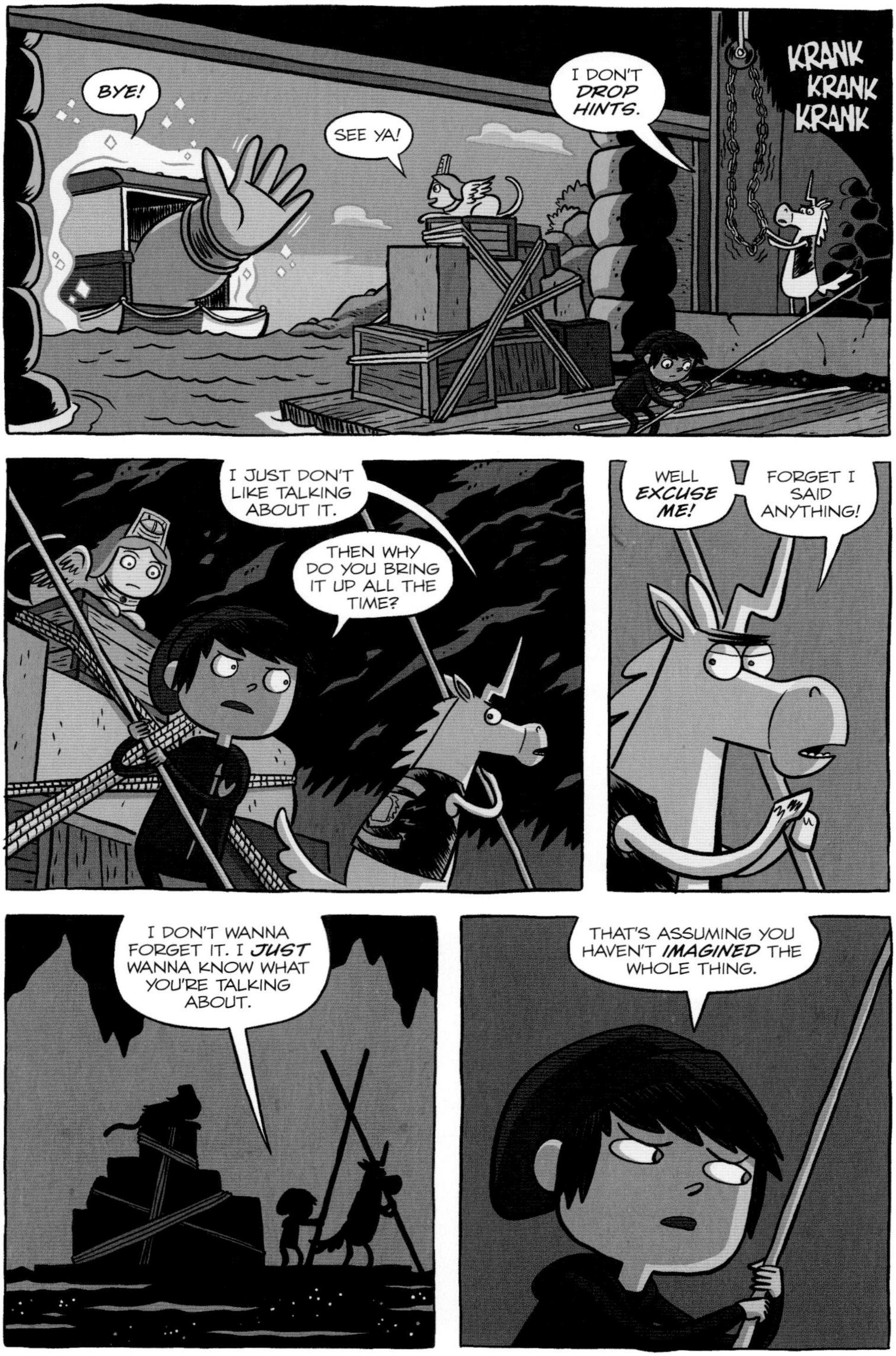
BYE!
SEE YA!
I DON'T *DROP HINTS*.
KRANK KRANK KRANK
I JUST DON'T LIKE TALKING ABOUT IT.
THEN WHY DO YOU BRING IT UP ALL THE TIME?
WELL *EXCUSE ME!*
FORGET I SAID ANYTHING!
I DON'T WANNA FORGET IT. I *JUST* WANNA KNOW WHAT YOU'RE TALKING ABOUT.
THAT'S ASSUMING YOU HAVEN'T *IMAGINED* THE WHOLE THING.

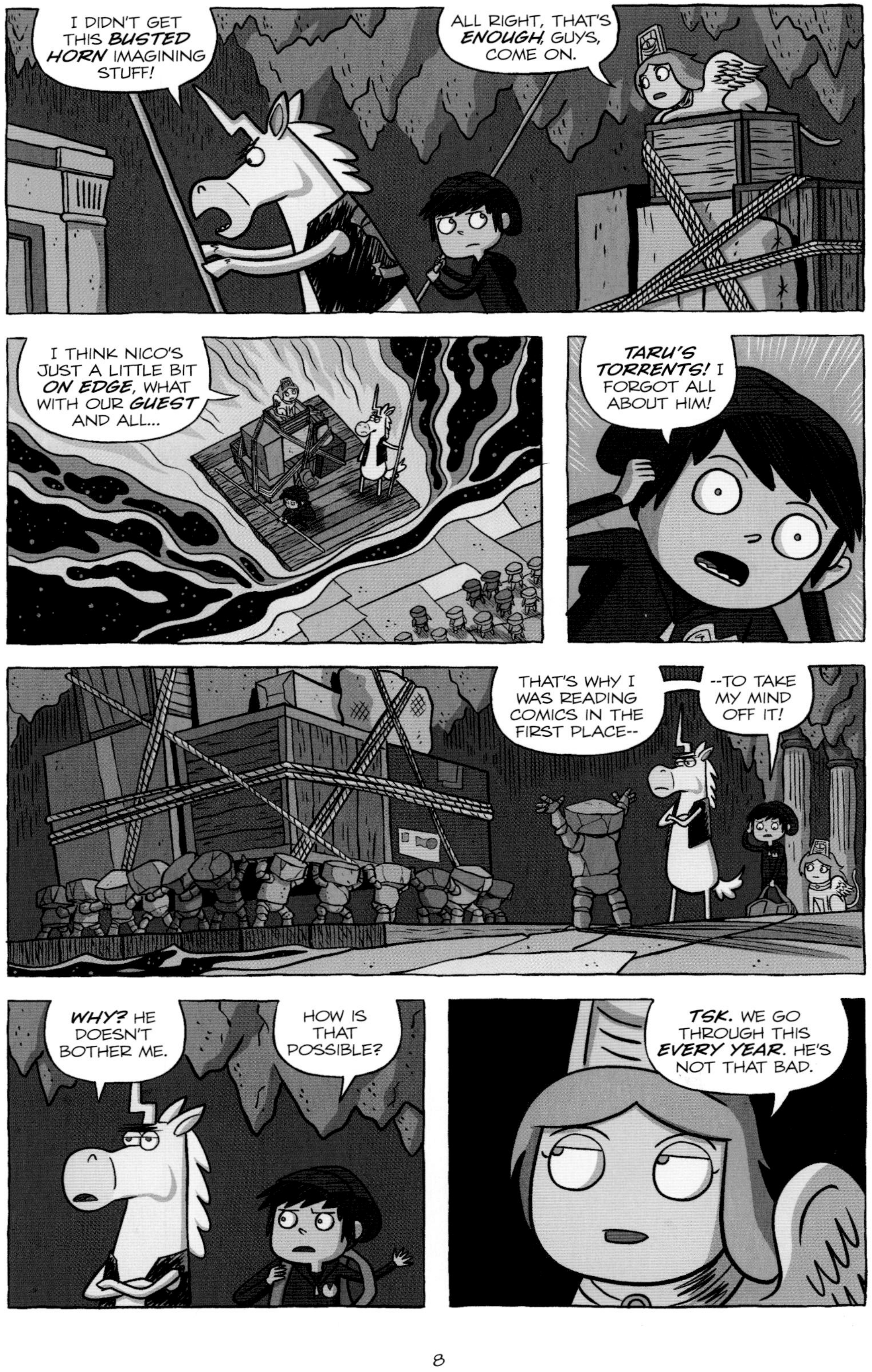
I DIDN'T GET THIS BUSTED HORN IMAGINING STUFF!
ALL RIGHT, THAT'S ENOUGH, GUYS, COME ON.
I THINK NICO'S JUST A LITTLE BIT ON EDGE, WHAT WITH OUR GUEST AND ALL...
TARU'S TORRENTS! I FORGOT ALL ABOUT HIM!
THAT'S WHY I WAS READING COMICS IN THE FIRST PLACE--
--TO TAKE MY MIND OFF IT!
WHY? HE DOESN'T BOTHER ME.
HOW IS THAT POSSIBLE?
TSK. WE GO THROUGH THIS EVERY YEAR. HE'S NOT THAT BAD.

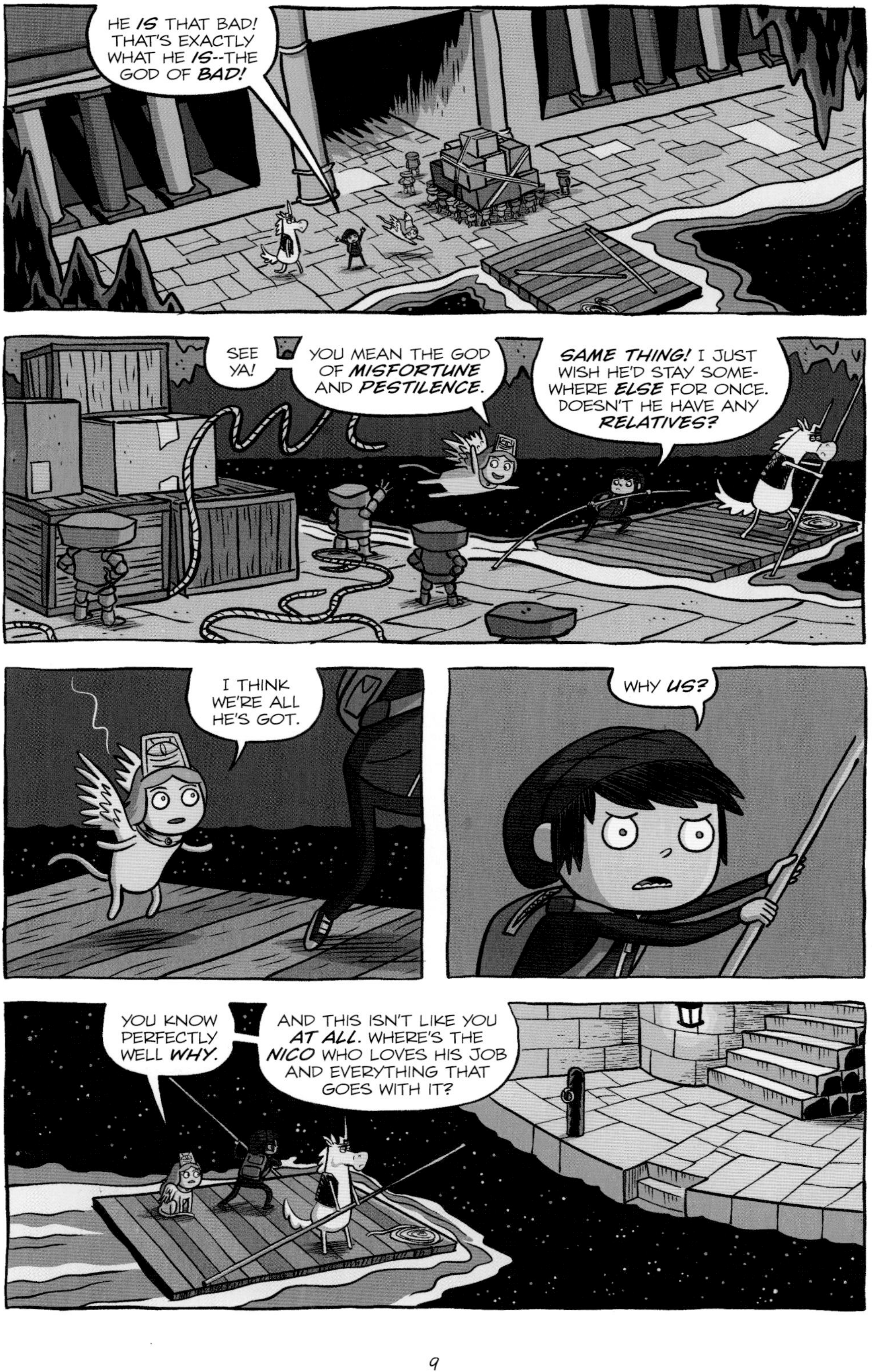
HE IS THAT BAD! THAT'S EXACTLY WHAT HE IS--THE GOD OF BAD!
SEE YA!
YOU MEAN THE GOD OF MISFORTUNE AND PESTILENCE.
SAME THING! I JUST WISH HE'D STAY SOMEWHERE ELSE FOR ONCE. DOESN'T HE HAVE ANY RELATIVES?
I THINK WE'RE ALL HE'S GOT.
WHY US?
YOU KNOW PERFECTLY WELL WHY.
AND THIS ISN'T LIKE YOU AT ALL. WHERE'S THE NICO WHO LOVES HIS JOB AND EVERYTHING THAT GOES WITH IT?

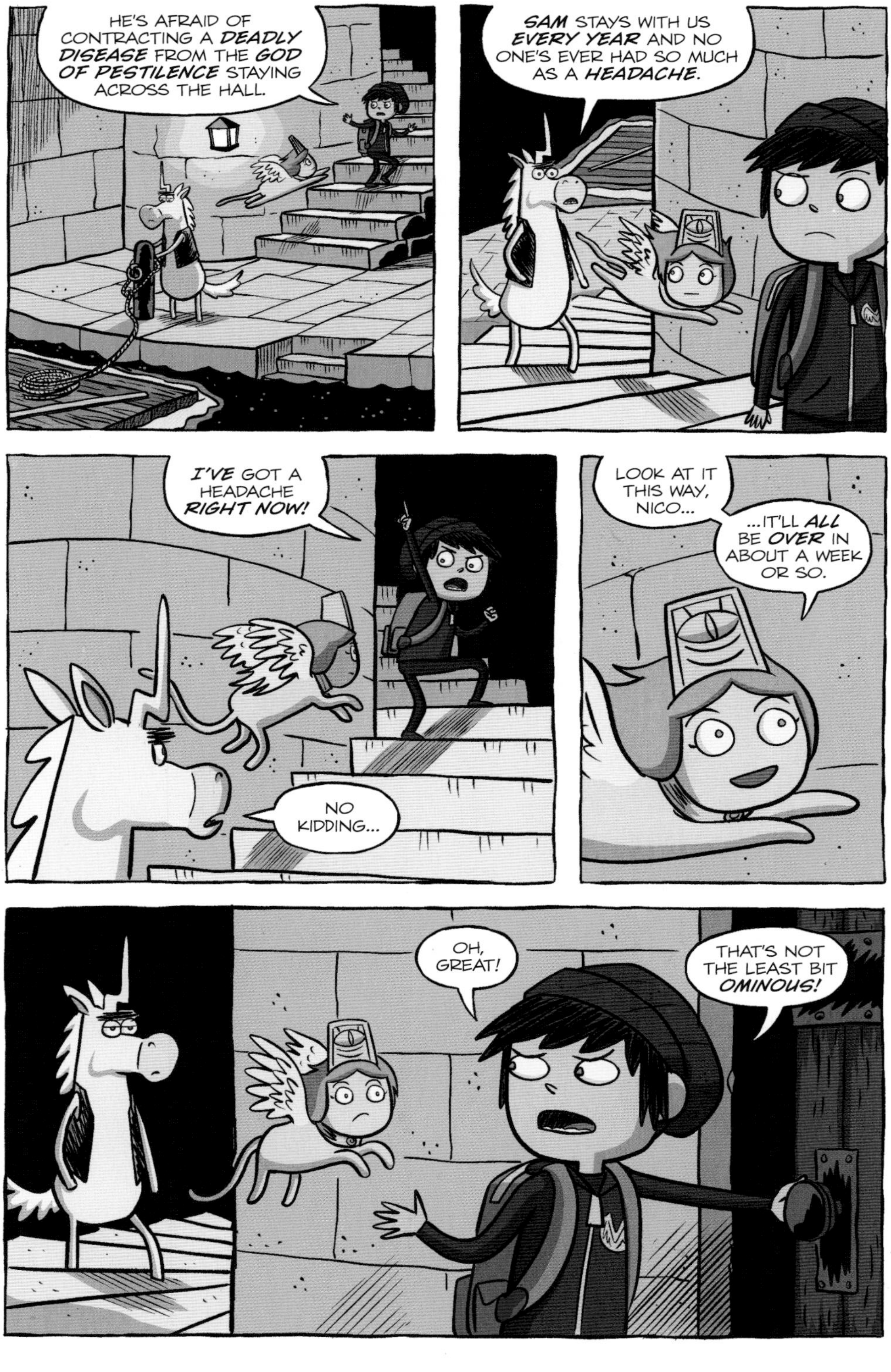
HE'S AFRAID OF CONTRACTING A DEADLY DISEASE FROM THE GOD OF PESTILENCE STAYING ACROSS THE HALL.
SAM STAYS WITH US EVERY YEAR AND NO ONE'S EVER HAD SO MUCH AS A HEADACHE.
I'VE GOT A HEADACHE RIGHT NOW!
NO KIDDING...
LOOK AT IT THIS WAY, NICO...
...IT'LL ALL BE OVER IN ABOUT A WEEK OR SO.
OH, GREAT!
THAT'S NOT THE LEAST BIT OMINOUS!

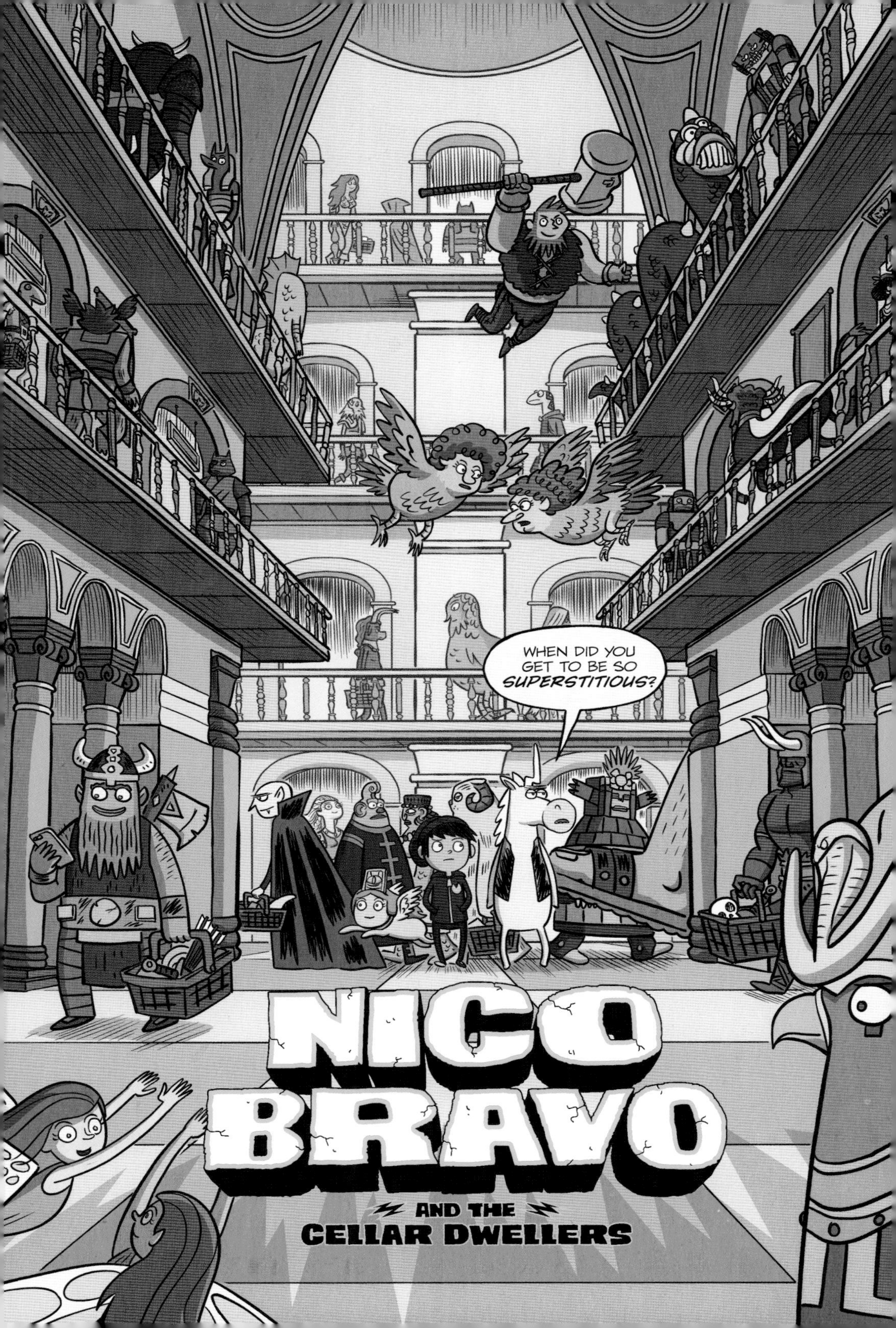
WHEN DID YOU GET TO BE SO SUPERSTITIOUS?
NICO BRAVO
AND THE CELLAR DWELLERS

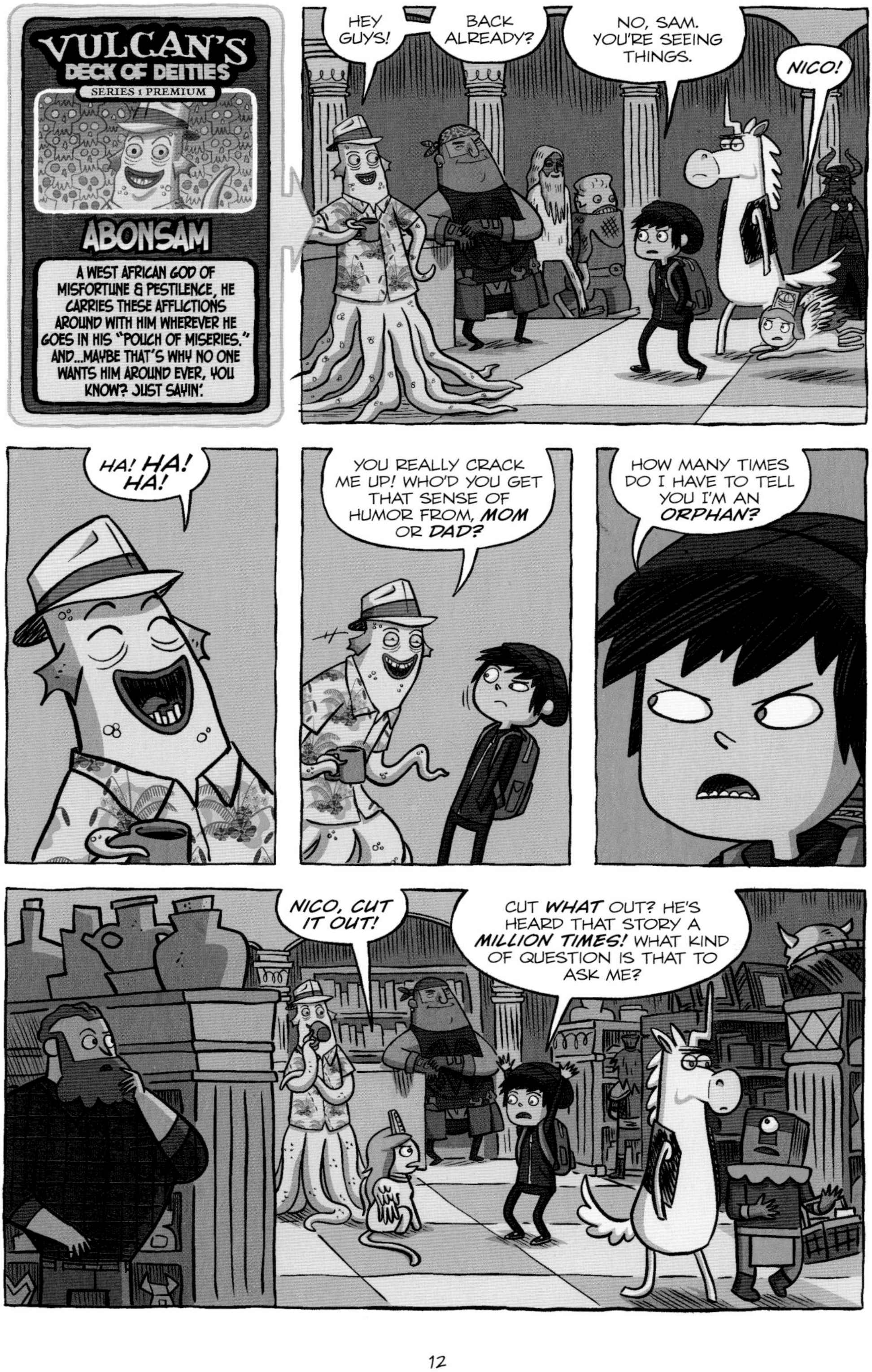
VULCAN'S DECK OF DEITIES
SERIES 1 PREMIUM
ABONSAM
A WEST AFRICAN GOD OF MISFORTUNE & PESTILENCE, HE CARRIES THESE AFFLICTIONS AROUND WITH HIM WHEREVER HE GOES IN HIS "POUCH OF MISERIES." AND...MAYBE THAT'S WHY NO ONE WANTS HIM AROUND EVER, YOU KNOW? JUST SAYIN'.
HEY GUYS!
BACK ALREADY?
NO, SAM. YOU'RE SEEING THINGS.
NICO!
HA! HA! HA!
YOU REALLY CRACK ME UP! WHO'D YOU GET THAT SENSE OF HUMOR FROM, MOM OR DAD?
HOW MANY TIMES DO I HAVE TO TELL YOU I'M AN ORPHAN?
NICO, CUT IT OUT!
CUT WHAT OUT? HE'S HEARD THAT STORY A MILLION TIMES! WHAT KIND OF QUESTION IS THAT TO ASK ME?

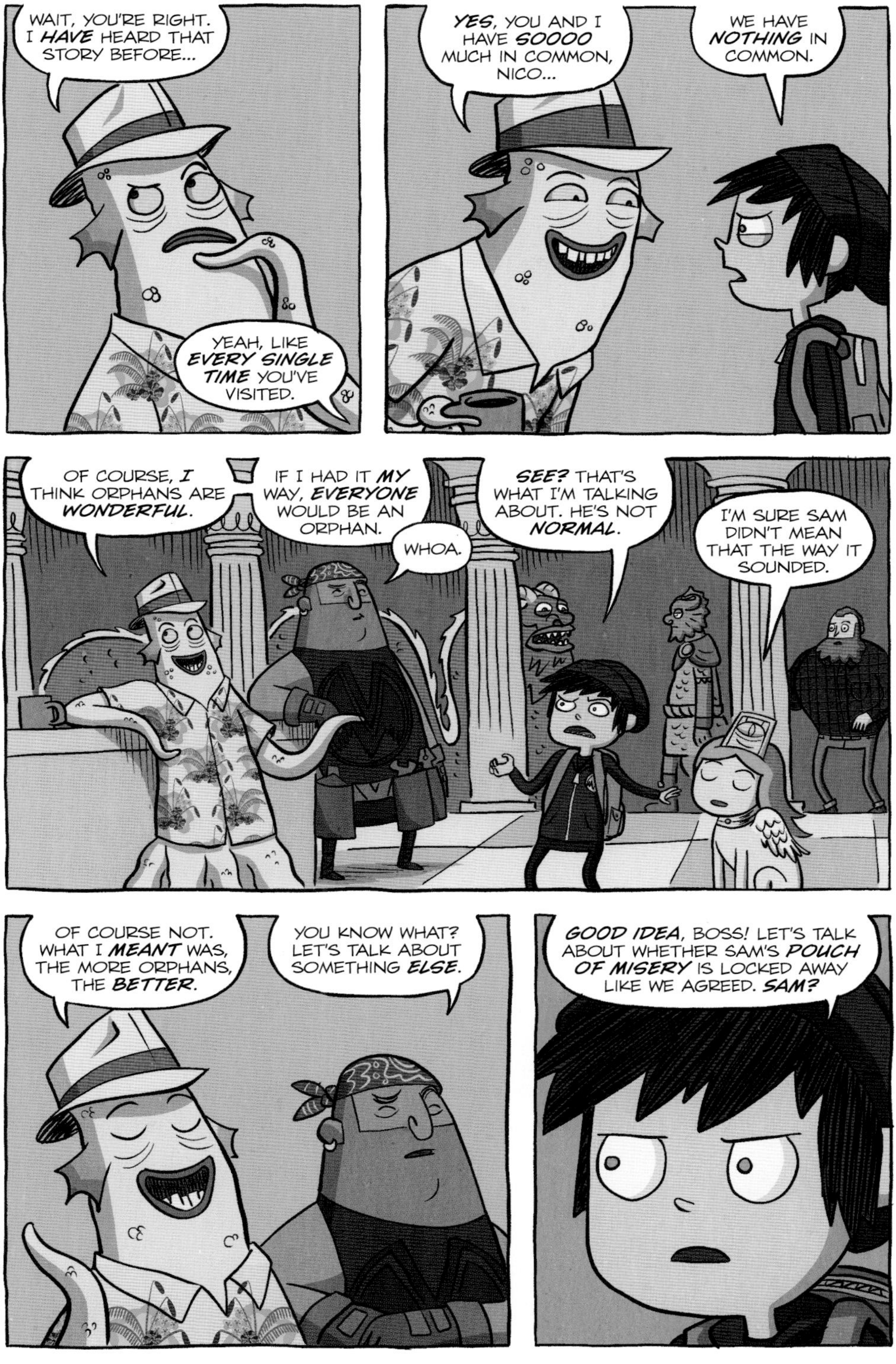
WAIT, YOU'RE RIGHT. I **HAVE** HEARD THAT STORY BEFORE...
YEAH, LIKE **EVERY SINGLE TIME** YOU'VE VISITED.
YES, YOU AND I HAVE **SOOOO** MUCH IN COMMON, NICO...
WE HAVE **NOTHING** IN COMMON.
OF COURSE, **I** THINK ORPHANS ARE **WONDERFUL**.
IF I HAD IT **MY** WAY, **EVERYONE** WOULD BE AN ORPHAN.
WHOA.
SEE? THAT'S WHAT I'M TALKING ABOUT. HE'S NOT **NORMAL**.
I'M SURE SAM DIDN'T MEAN THAT THE WAY IT SOUNDED.
OF COURSE NOT. WHAT I **MEANT** WAS, THE MORE ORPHANS, THE **BETTER**.
YOU KNOW WHAT? LET'S TALK ABOUT SOMETHING **ELSE**.
GOOD IDEA, BOSS! LET'S TALK ABOUT WHETHER SAM'S **POUCH OF MISERY** IS LOCKED AWAY LIKE WE AGREED. **SAM?**

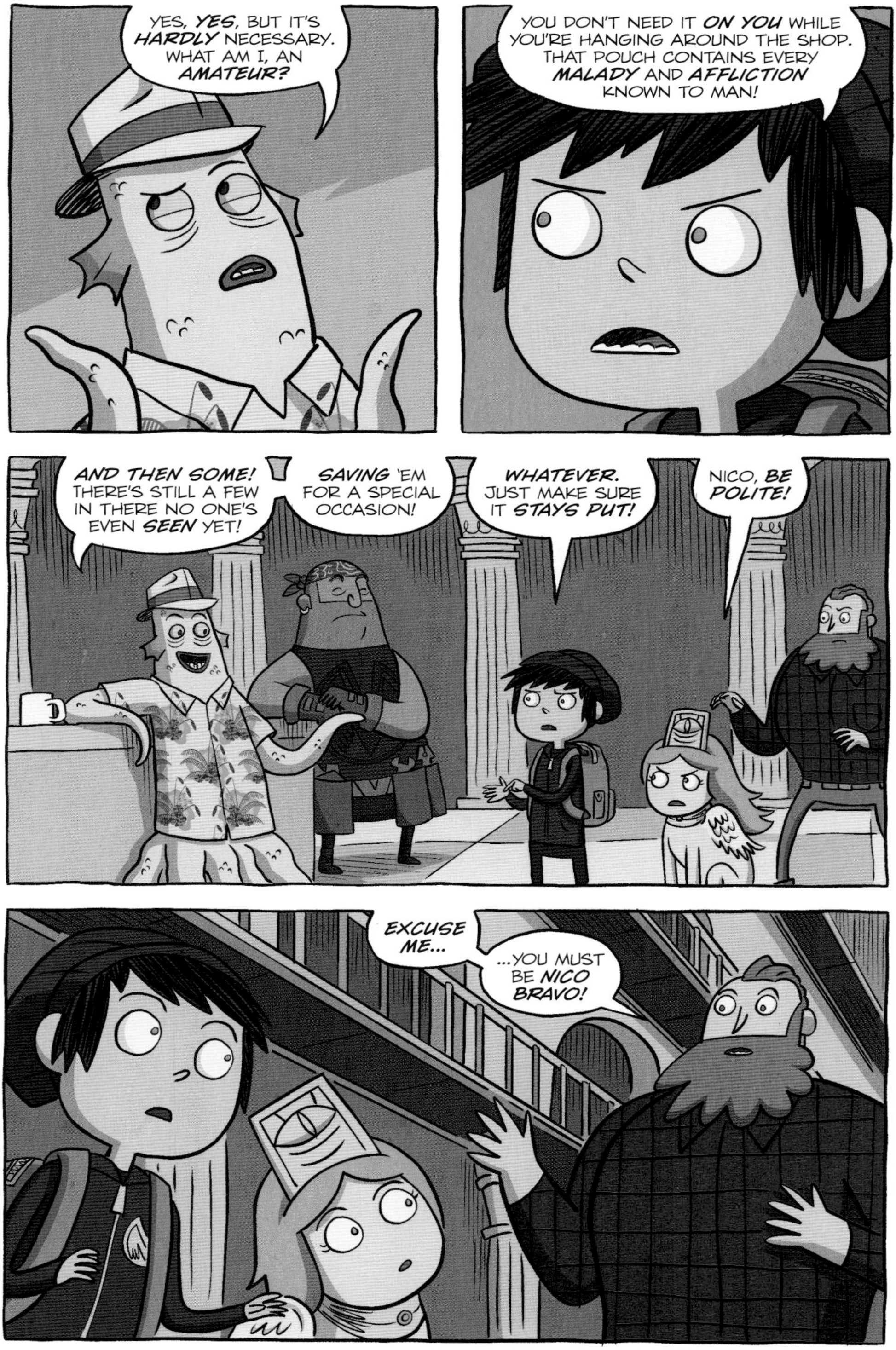
YES, YES, BUT IT'S HARDLY NECESSARY. WHAT AM I, AN AMATEUR?
YOU DON'T NEED IT ON YOU WHILE YOU'RE HANGING AROUND THE SHOP. THAT POUCH CONTAINS EVERY MALADY AND AFFLICTION KNOWN TO MAN!
AND THEN SOME! THERE'S STILL A FEW IN THERE NO ONE'S EVEN SEEN YET!
SAVING 'EM FOR A SPECIAL OCCASION!
WHATEVER. JUST MAKE SURE IT STAYS PUT!
NICO, BE POLITE!
EXCUSE ME...
...YOU MUST BE NICO BRAVO!

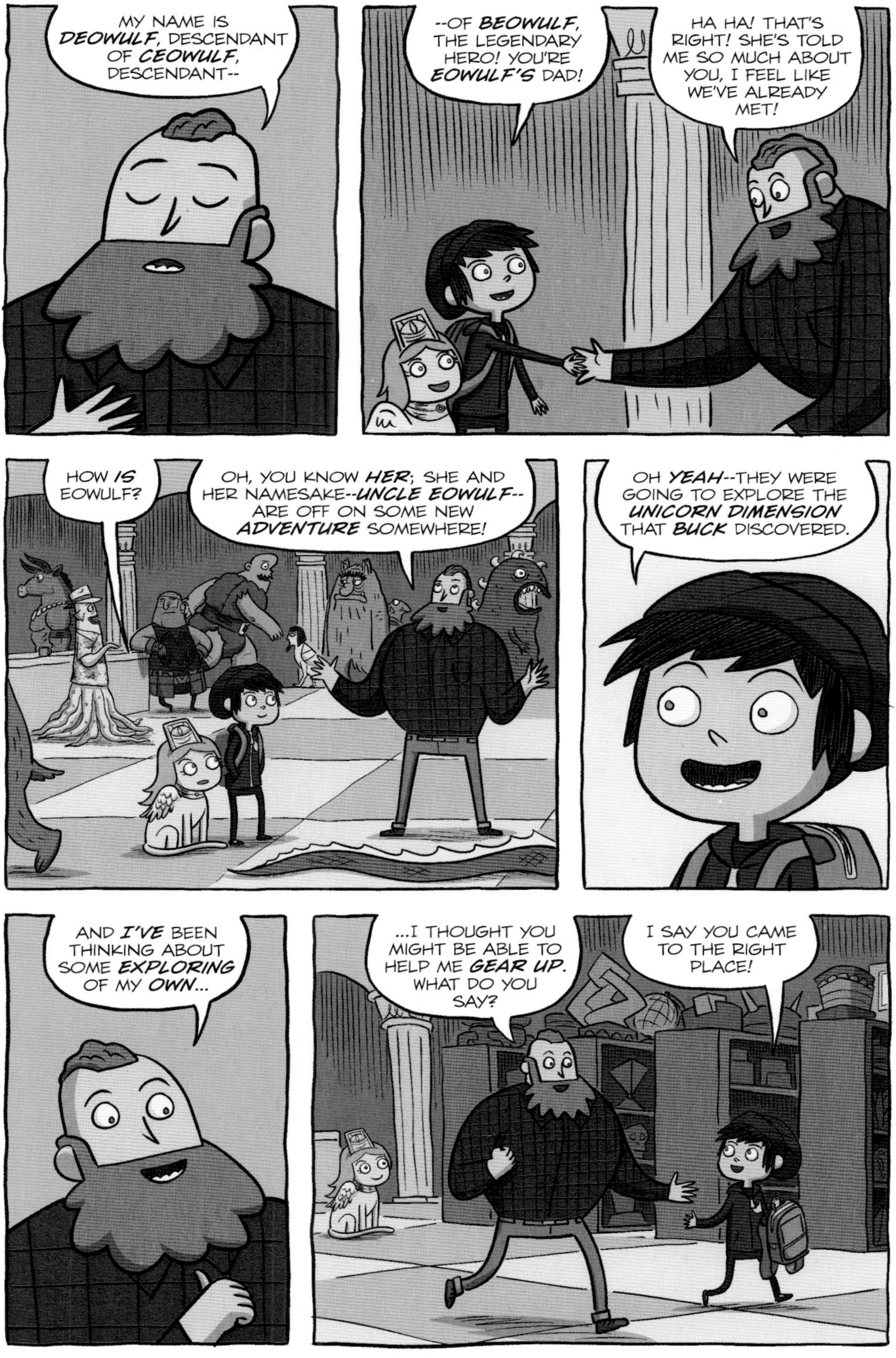
MY NAME IS DEOWULF, DESCENDANT OF CEOWULF, DESCENDANT--
--OF BEOWULF, THE LEGENDARY HERO! YOU'RE EOWULF'S DAD!
HA HA! THAT'S RIGHT! SHE'S TOLD ME SO MUCH ABOUT YOU, I FEEL LIKE WE'VE ALREADY MET!
HOW IS EOWULF?
OH, YOU KNOW HER; SHE AND HER NAMESAKE--UNCLE EOWULF--ARE OFF ON SOME NEW ADVENTURE SOMEWHERE!
OH YEAH--THEY WERE GOING TO EXPLORE THE UNICORN DIMENSION THAT BUCK DISCOVERED.
AND I'VE BEEN THINKING ABOUT SOME EXPLORING OF MY OWN...
...I THOUGHT YOU MIGHT BE ABLE TO HELP ME GEAR UP. WHAT DO YOU SAY?
I SAY YOU CAME TO THE RIGHT PLACE!

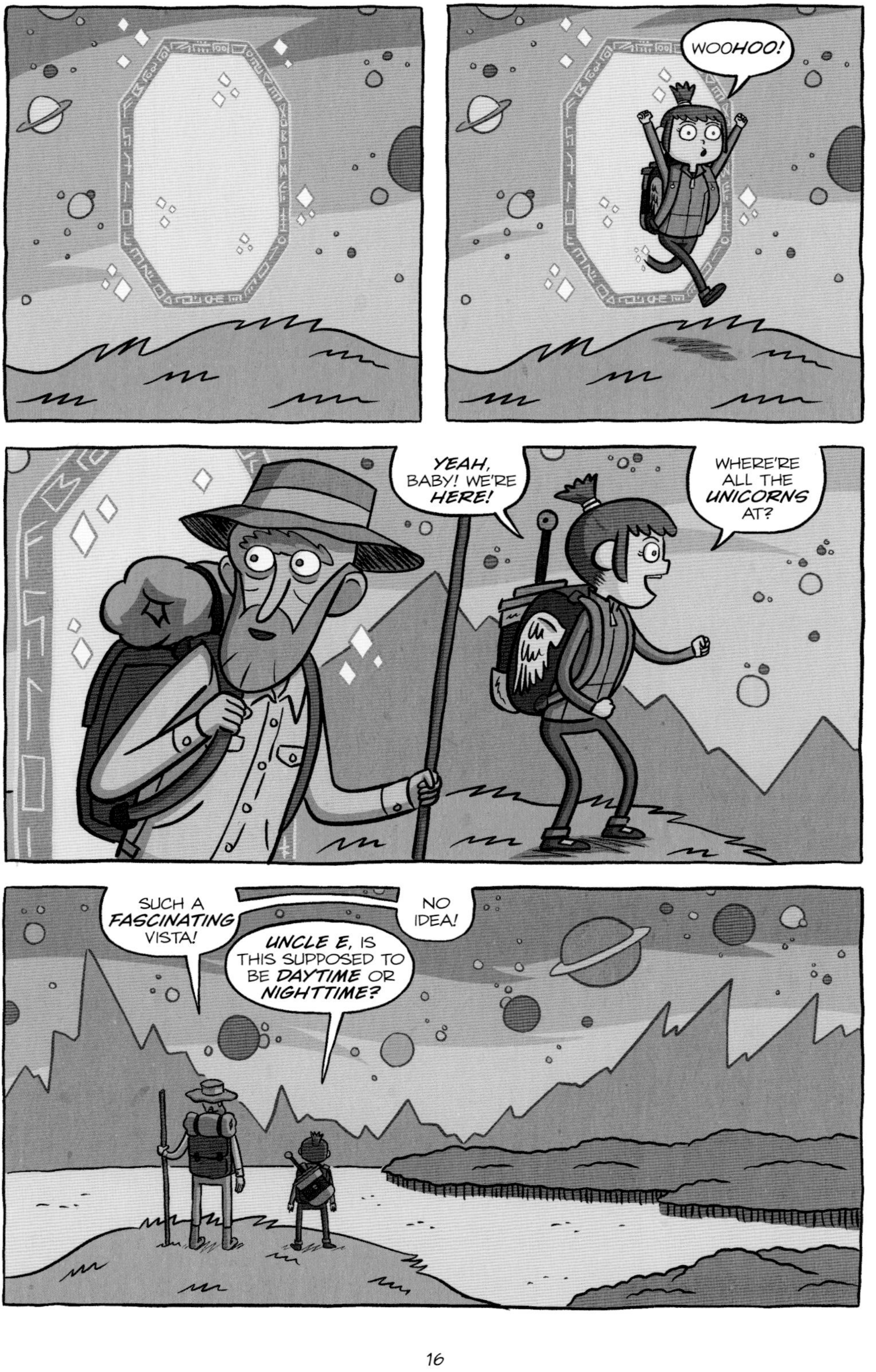
WOOHOO!
YEAH, BABY! WE'RE HERE!
WHERE'RE ALL THE UNICORNS AT?
SUCH A FASCINATING VISTA!
UNCLE E, IS THIS SUPPOSED TO BE DAYTIME OR NIGHTTIME?
NO IDEA!

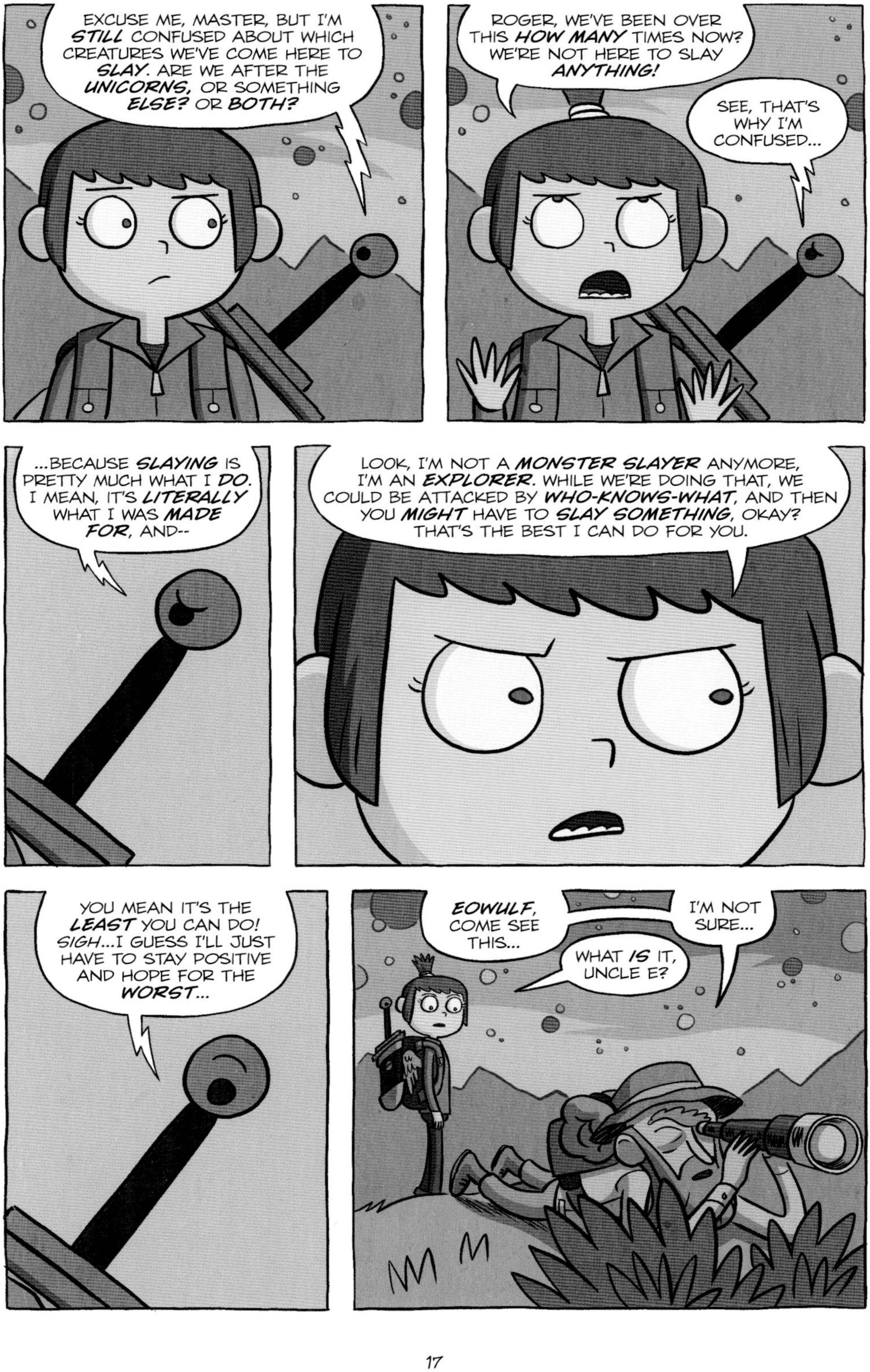
EXCUSE ME, MASTER, BUT I'M STILL CONFUSED ABOUT WHICH CREATURES WE'VE COME HERE TO SLAY. ARE WE AFTER THE UNICORNS, OR SOMETHING ELSE? OR BOTH?
ROGER, WE'VE BEEN OVER THIS HOW MANY TIMES NOW? WE'RE NOT HERE TO SLAY ANYTHING!
SEE, THAT'S WHY I'M CONFUSED...
...BECAUSE SLAYING IS PRETTY MUCH WHAT I DO. I MEAN, IT'S LITERALLY WHAT I WAS MADE FOR, AND--
LOOK, I'M NOT A MONSTER SLAYER ANYMORE, I'M AN EXPLORER. WHILE WE'RE DOING THAT, WE COULD BE ATTACKED BY WHO-KNOWS-WHAT, AND THEN YOU MIGHT HAVE TO SLAY SOMETHING, OKAY? THAT'S THE BEST I CAN DO FOR YOU.
YOU MEAN IT'S THE LEAST YOU CAN DO! SIGH...I GUESS I'LL JUST HAVE TO STAY POSITIVE AND HOPE FOR THE WORST...
EOWULF, COME SEE THIS...
WHAT IS IT, UNCLE E?
I'M NOT SURE...

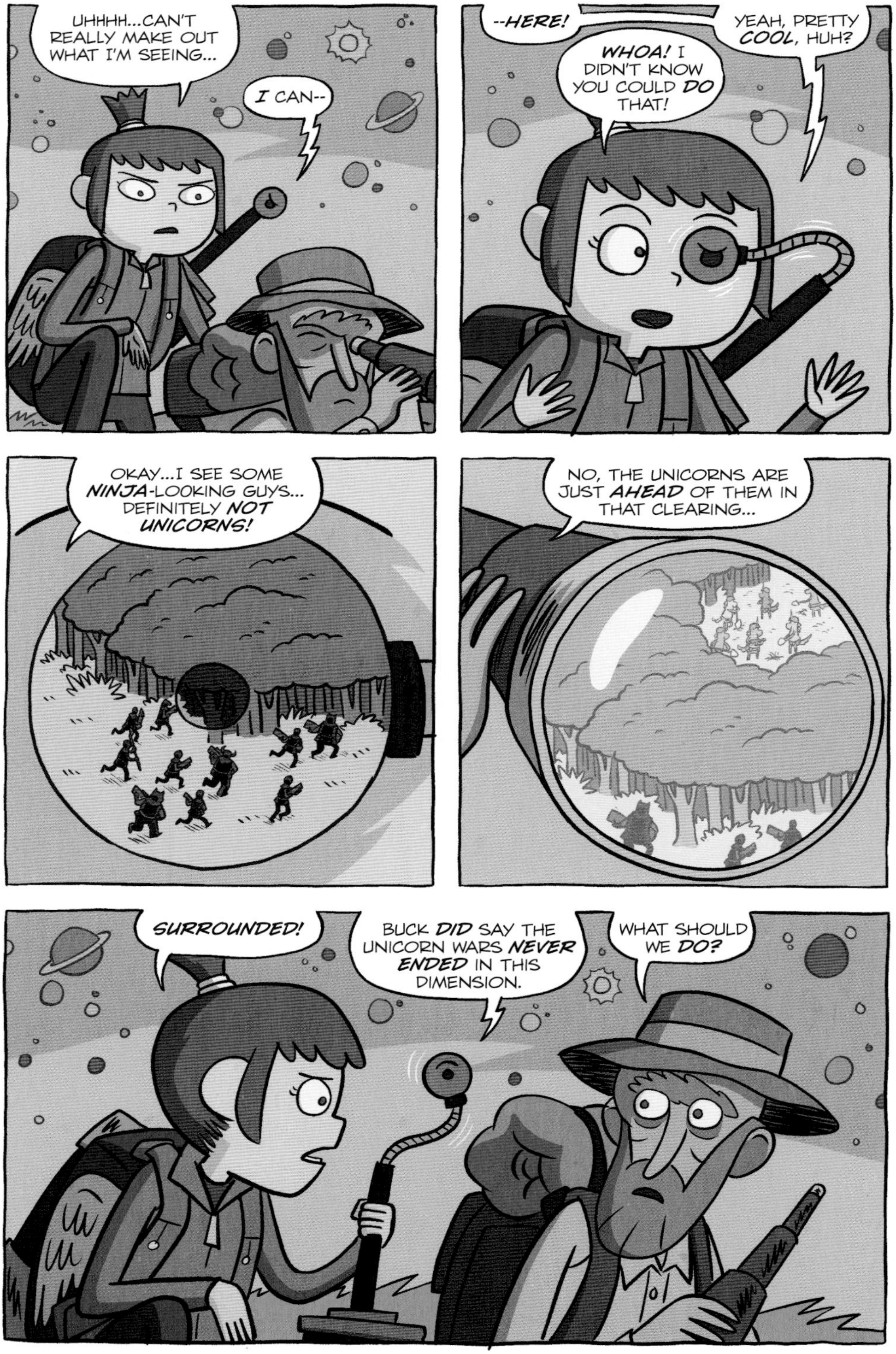
UHHHH...CAN'T REALLY MAKE OUT WHAT I'M SEEING...
I CAN--
--HERE!
WHOA! I DIDN'T KNOW YOU COULD DO THAT!
YEAH, PRETTY COOL, HUH?
OKAY...I SEE SOME NINJA-LOOKING GUYS... DEFINITELY NOT UNICORNS!
NO, THE UNICORNS ARE JUST AHEAD OF THEM IN THAT CLEARING...
SURROUNDED!
BUCK DID SAY THE UNICORN WARS NEVER ENDED IN THIS DIMENSION.
WHAT SHOULD WE DO?

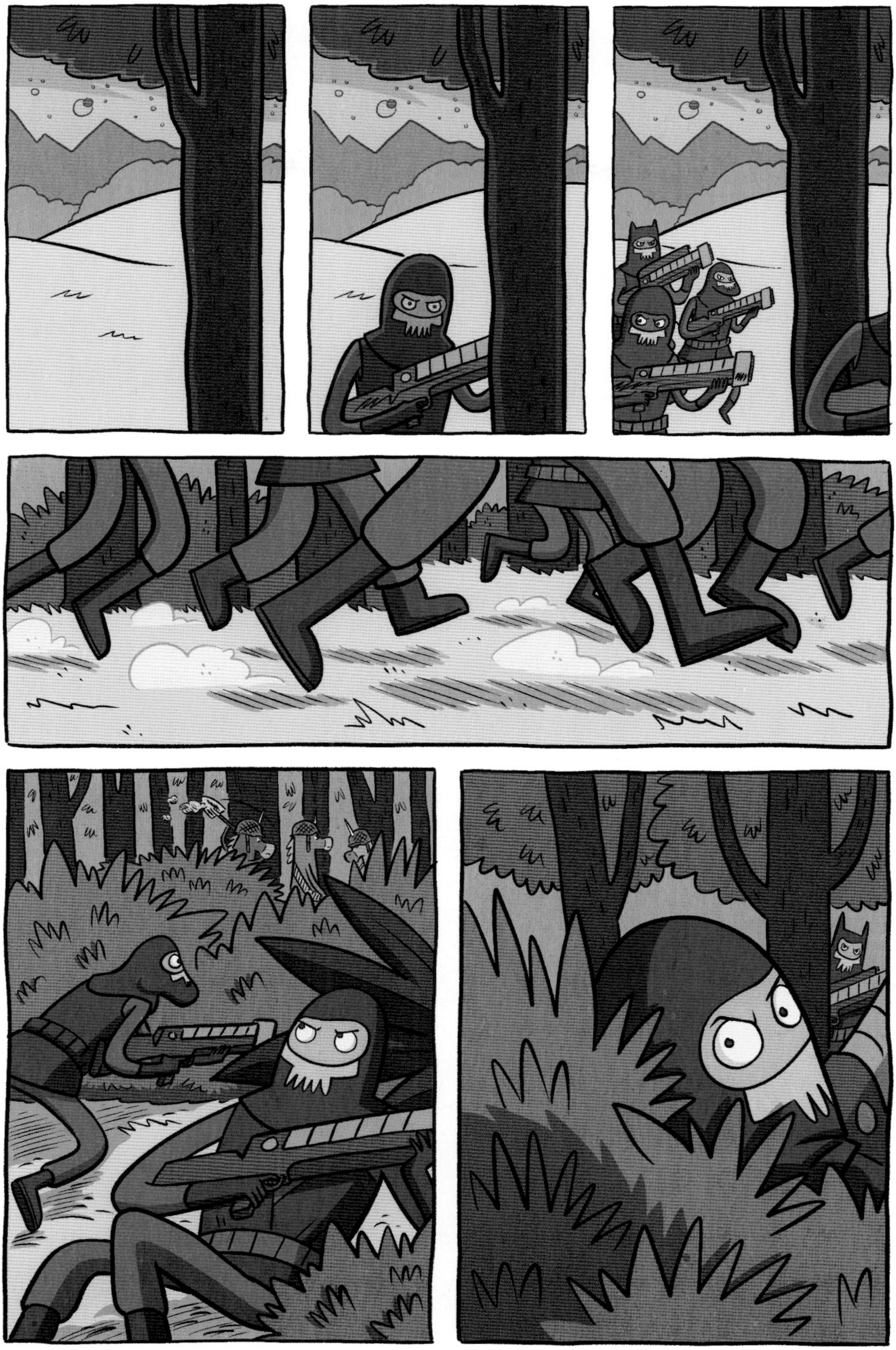

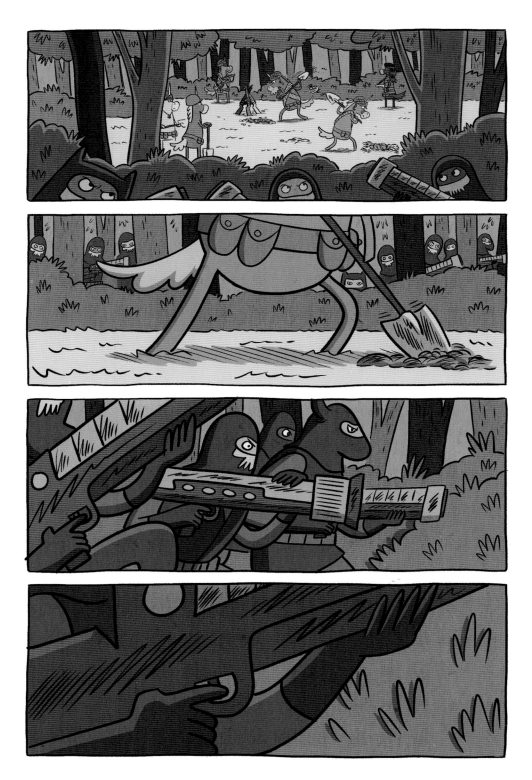

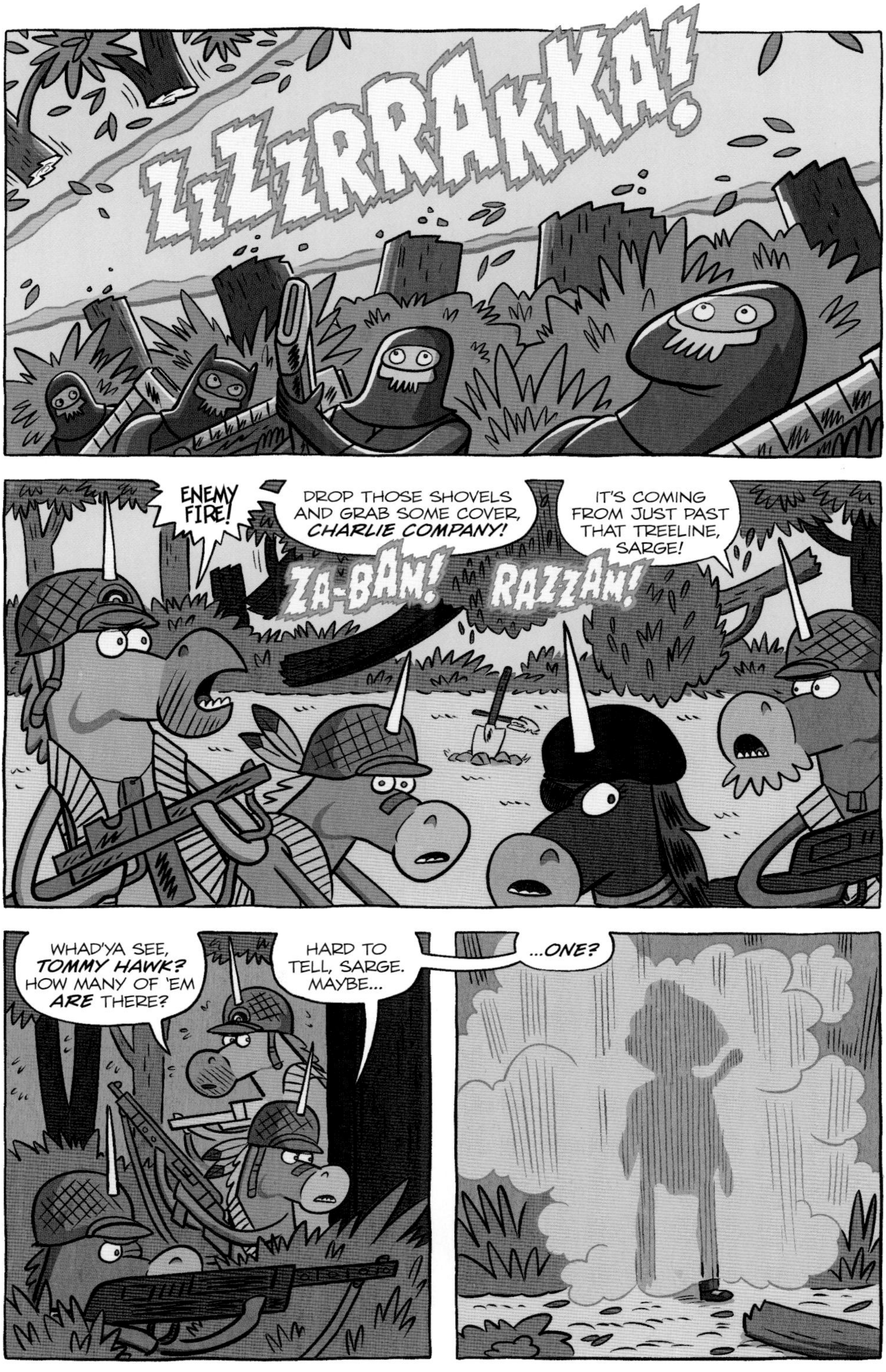
ZzZZRRAKKA!
ENEMY FIRE!
DROP THOSE SHOVELS AND GRAB SOME COVER, CHARLIE COMPANY!
IT'S COMING FROM JUST PAST THAT TREELINE, SARGE!
ZA-BAM! RAZZAM!
WHAD'YA SEE, TOMMY HAWK? HOW MANY OF 'EM ARE THERE?
HARD TO TELL, SARGE. MAYBE...
...ONE?

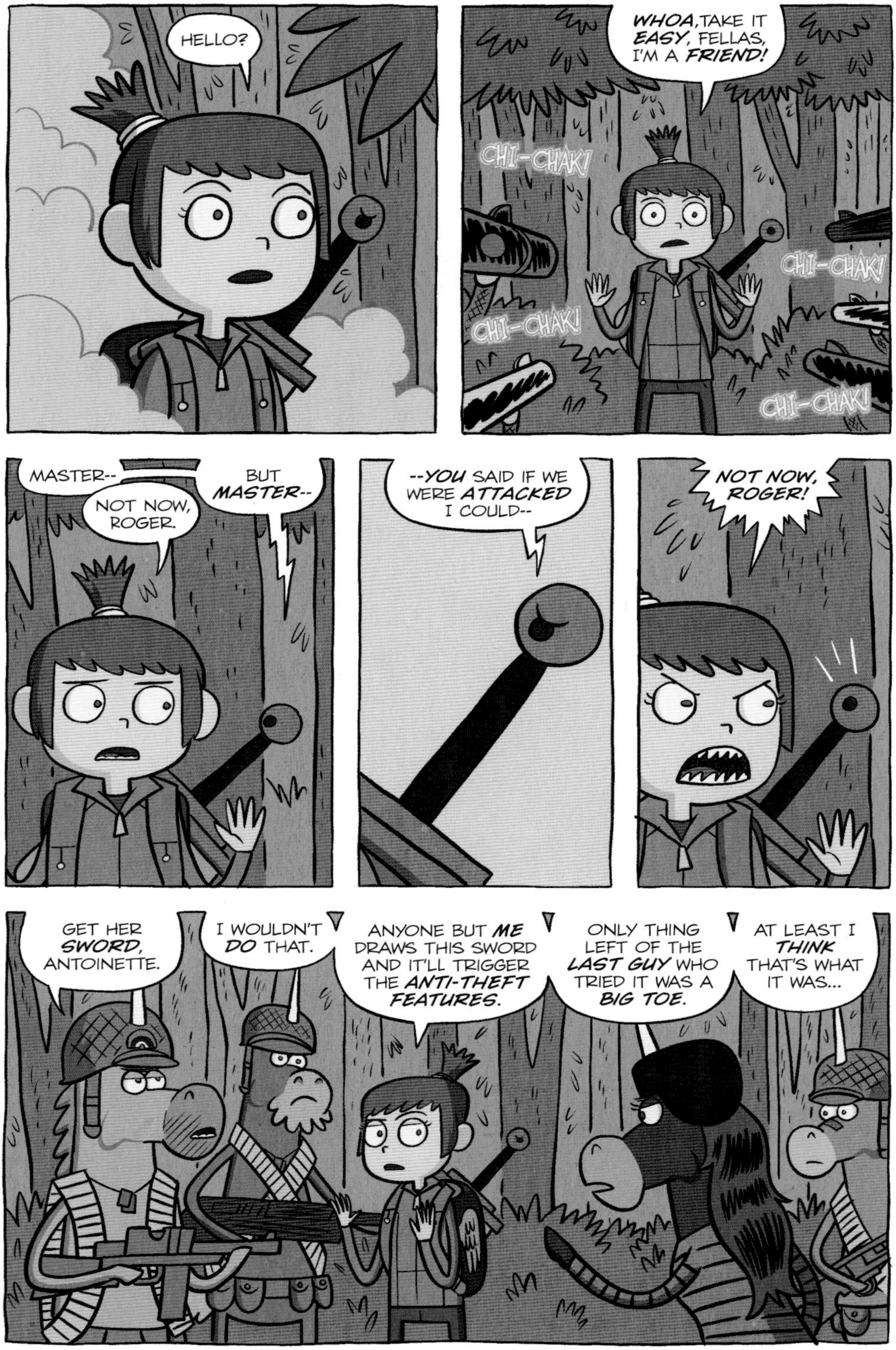
HELLO?
WHOA, TAKE IT EASY, FELLAS, I'M A FRIEND!
CHI-CHAK!
CHI-CHAK!
CHI-CHAK!
CHI-CHAK!
MASTER--
NOT NOW, ROGER.
BUT MASTER--
--YOU SAID IF WE WERE ATTACKED I COULD--
NOT NOW, ROGER!
GET HER SWORD, ANTOINETTE.
I WOULDN'T DO THAT.
ANYONE BUT ME DRAWS THIS SWORD AND IT'LL TRIGGER THE ANTI-THEFT FEATURES.
ONLY THING LEFT OF THE LAST GUY WHO TRIED IT WAS A BIG TOE.
AT LEAST I THINK THAT'S WHAT IT WAS...

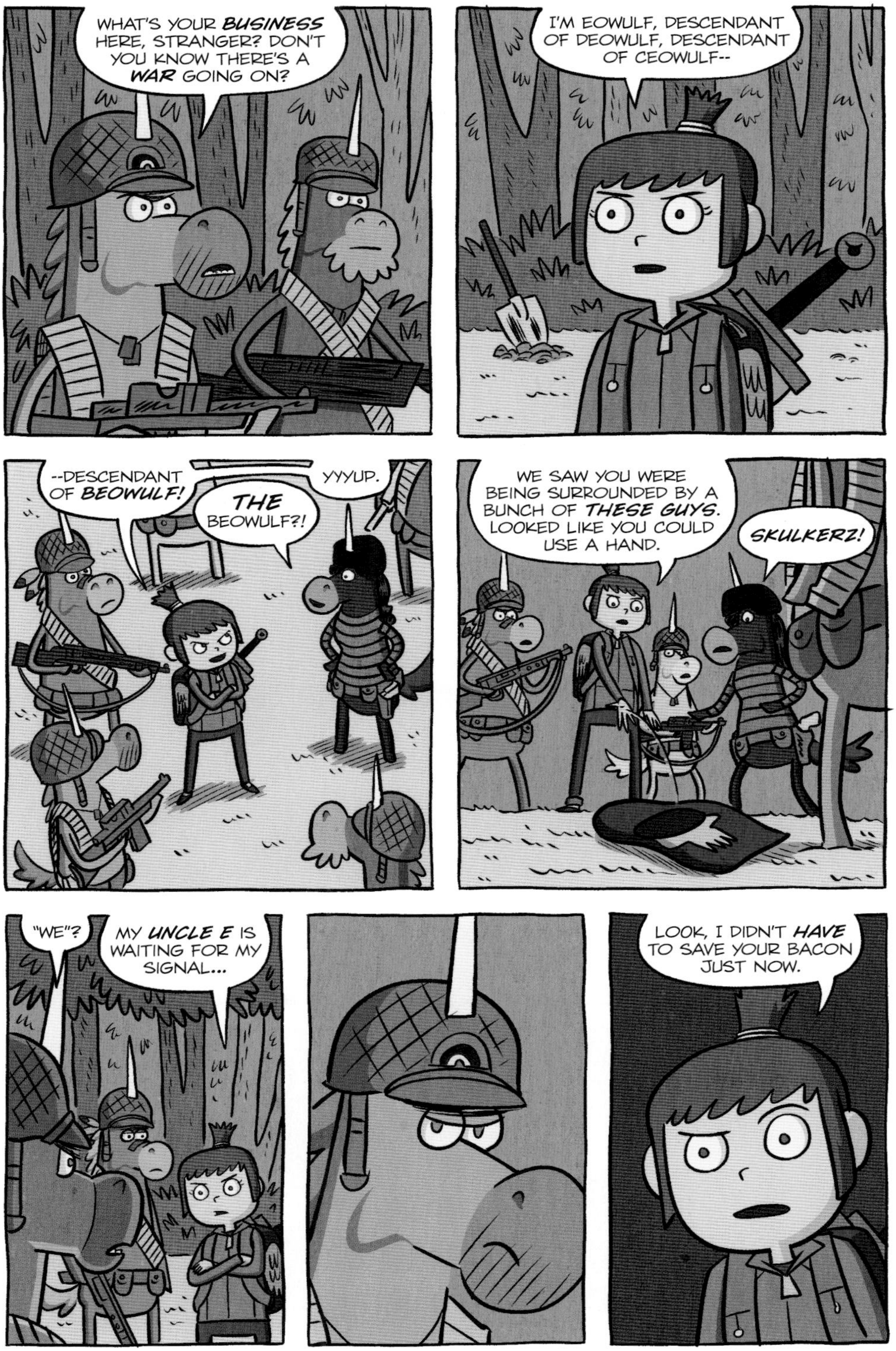
WHAT'S YOUR BUSINESS HERE, STRANGER? DON'T YOU KNOW THERE'S A WAR GOING ON?
I'M EOWULF, DESCENDANT OF DEOWULF, DESCENDANT OF CEOWULF--
--DESCENDANT OF BEOWULF!
THE BEOWULF?!
YYYUP.
WE SAW YOU WERE BEING SURROUNDED BY A BUNCH OF THESE GUYS. LOOKED LIKE YOU COULD USE A HAND.
SKULKERZ!
"WE"?
MY UNCLE E IS WAITING FOR MY SIGNAL...
LOOK, I DIDN'T HAVE TO SAVE YOUR BACON JUST NOW.

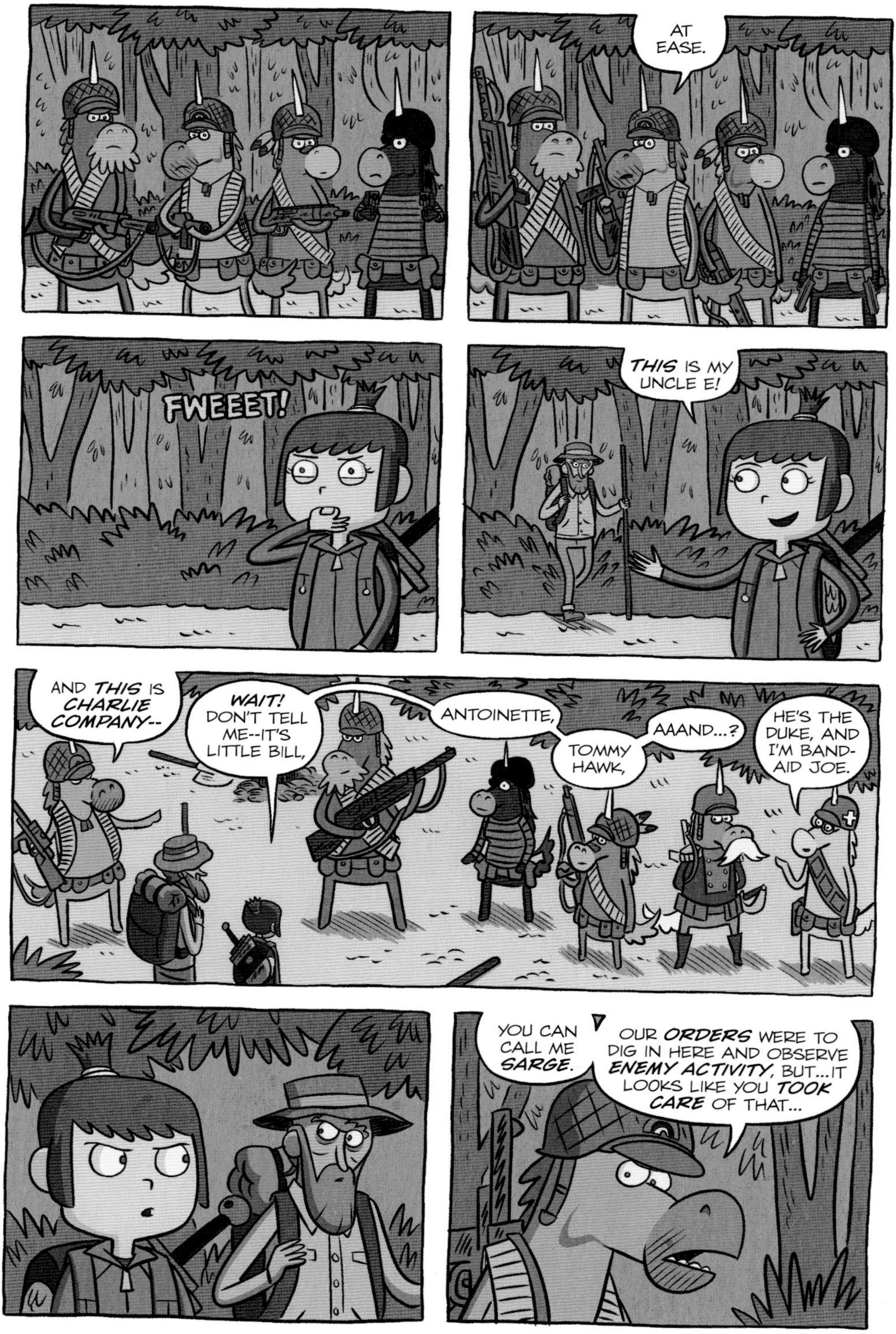
AT EASE.
FWEEEET!
THIS IS MY UNCLE E!
AND THIS IS CHARLIE COMPANY--
WAIT! DON'T TELL ME--IT'S LITTLE BILL,
ANTOINETTE,
TOMMY HAWK,
AAAND...?
HE'S THE DUKE, AND I'M BAND-AID JOE.
YOU CAN CALL ME SARGE.
OUR ORDERS WERE TO DIG IN HERE AND OBSERVE ENEMY ACTIVITY, BUT...IT LOOKS LIKE YOU TOOK CARE OF THAT...

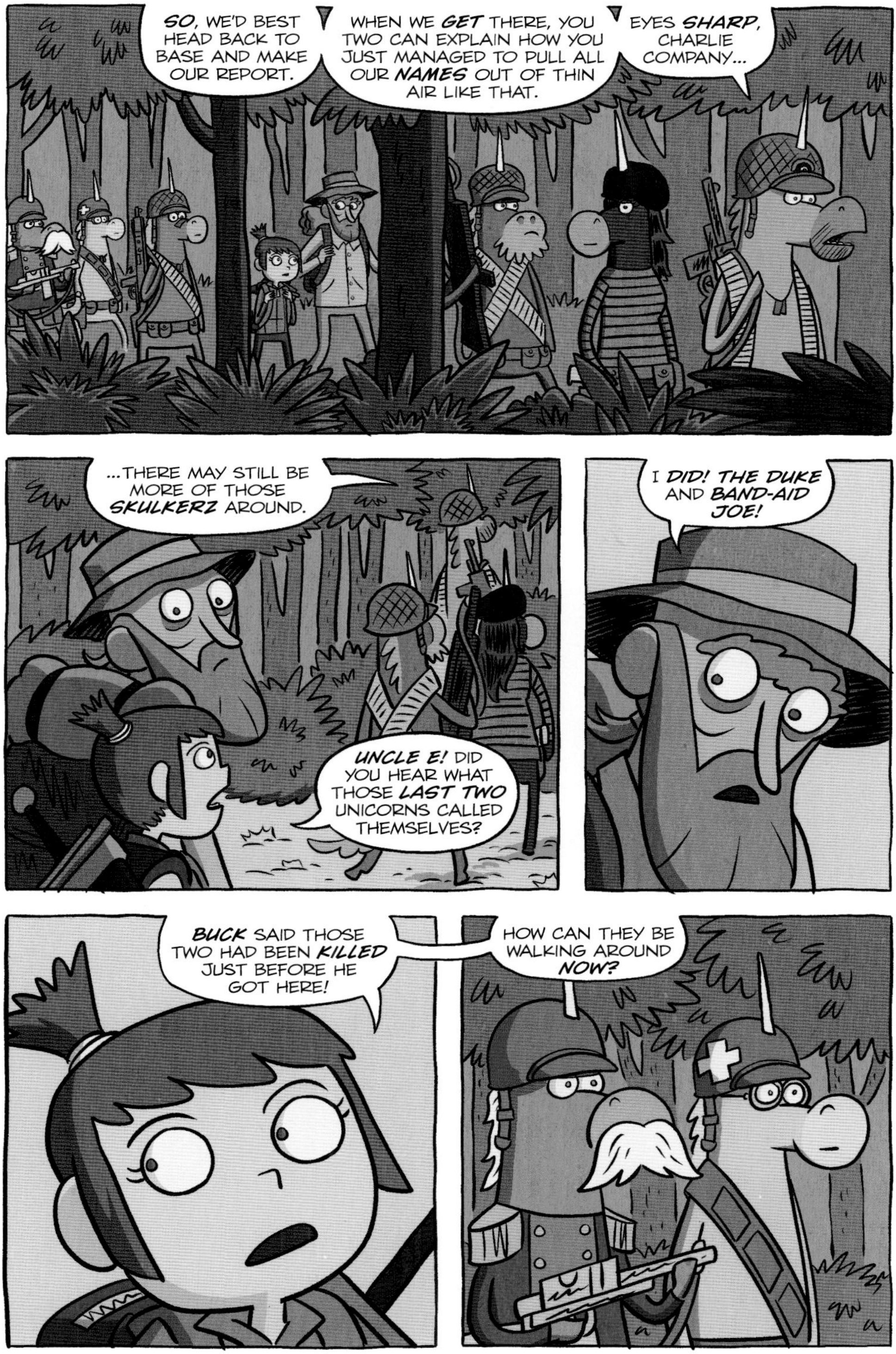

SO, WE'D BEST HEAD BACK TO BASE AND MAKE OUR REPORT.
WHEN WE GET THERE, YOU TWO CAN EXPLAIN HOW YOU JUST MANAGED TO PULL ALL OUR NAMES OUT OF THIN AIR LIKE THAT.
EYES SHARP, CHARLIE COMPANY...
...THERE MAY STILL BE MORE OF THOSE SKULKERZ AROUND.
UNCLE E! DID YOU HEAR WHAT THOSE LAST TWO UNICORNS CALLED THEMSELVES?
I DID! THE DUKE AND BAND-AID JOE!
BUCK SAID THOSE TWO HAD BEEN KILLED JUST BEFORE HE GOT HERE!
HOW CAN THEY BE WALKING AROUND NOW?

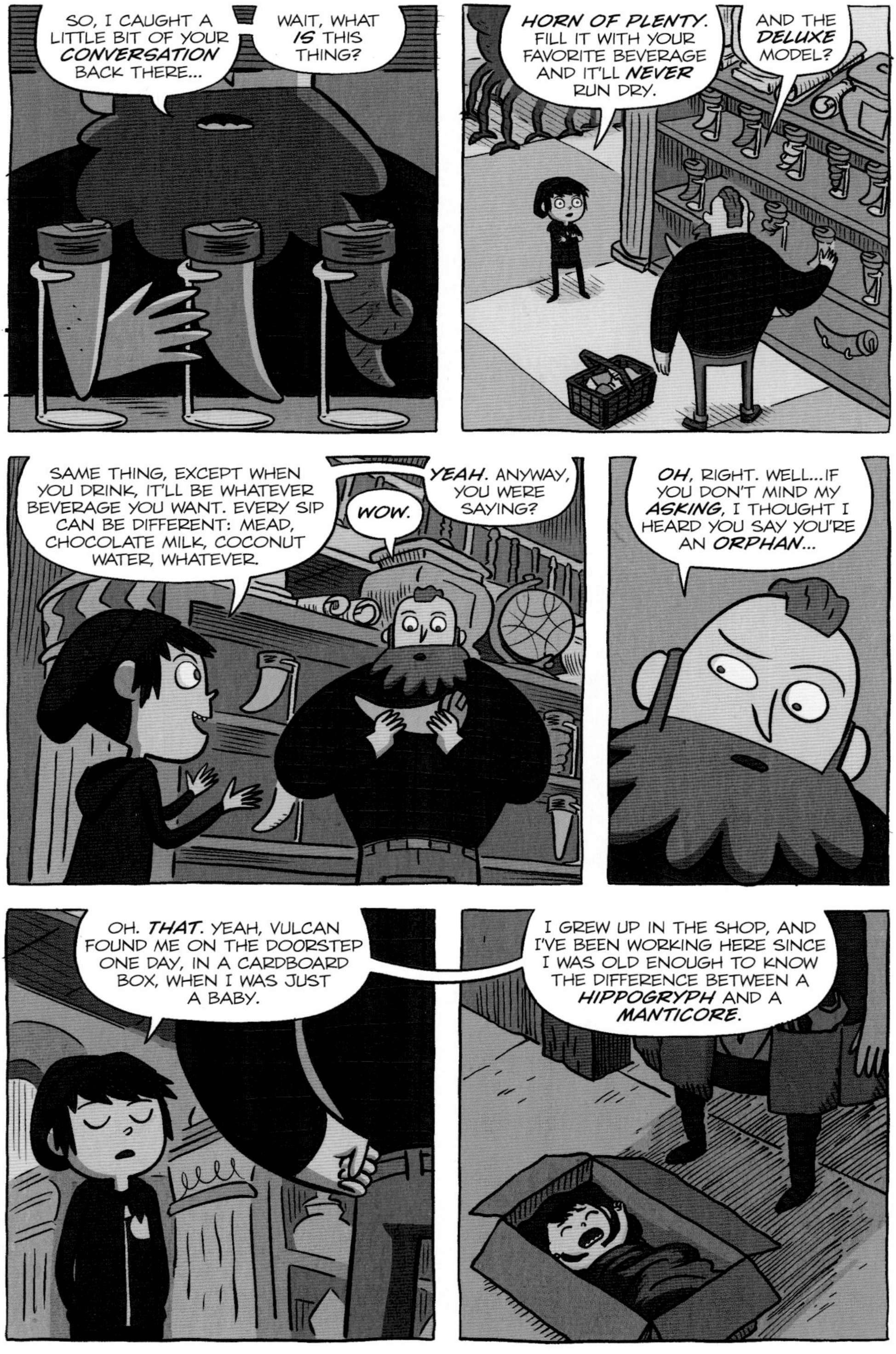
SO, I CAUGHT A LITTLE BIT OF YOUR CONVERSATION BACK THERE...
WAIT, WHAT IS THIS THING?
HORN OF PLENTY. FILL IT WITH YOUR FAVORITE BEVERAGE AND IT'LL NEVER RUN DRY.
AND THE DELUXE MODEL?
SAME THING, EXCEPT WHEN YOU DRINK, IT'LL BE WHATEVER BEVERAGE YOU WANT. EVERY SIP CAN BE DIFFERENT: MEAD, CHOCOLATE MILK, COCONUT WATER, WHATEVER.
WOW.
YEAH. ANYWAY, YOU WERE SAYING?
OH, RIGHT. WELL...IF YOU DON'T MIND MY ASKING, I THOUGHT I HEARD YOU SAY YOU'RE AN ORPHAN...
OH. THAT. YEAH, VULCAN FOUND ME ON THE DOORSTEP ONE DAY, IN A CARDBOARD BOX, WHEN I WAS JUST A BABY.
I GREW UP IN THE SHOP, AND I'VE BEEN WORKING HERE SINCE I WAS OLD ENOUGH TO KNOW THE DIFFERENCE BETWEEN A HIPPOGRYPH AND A MANTICORE.

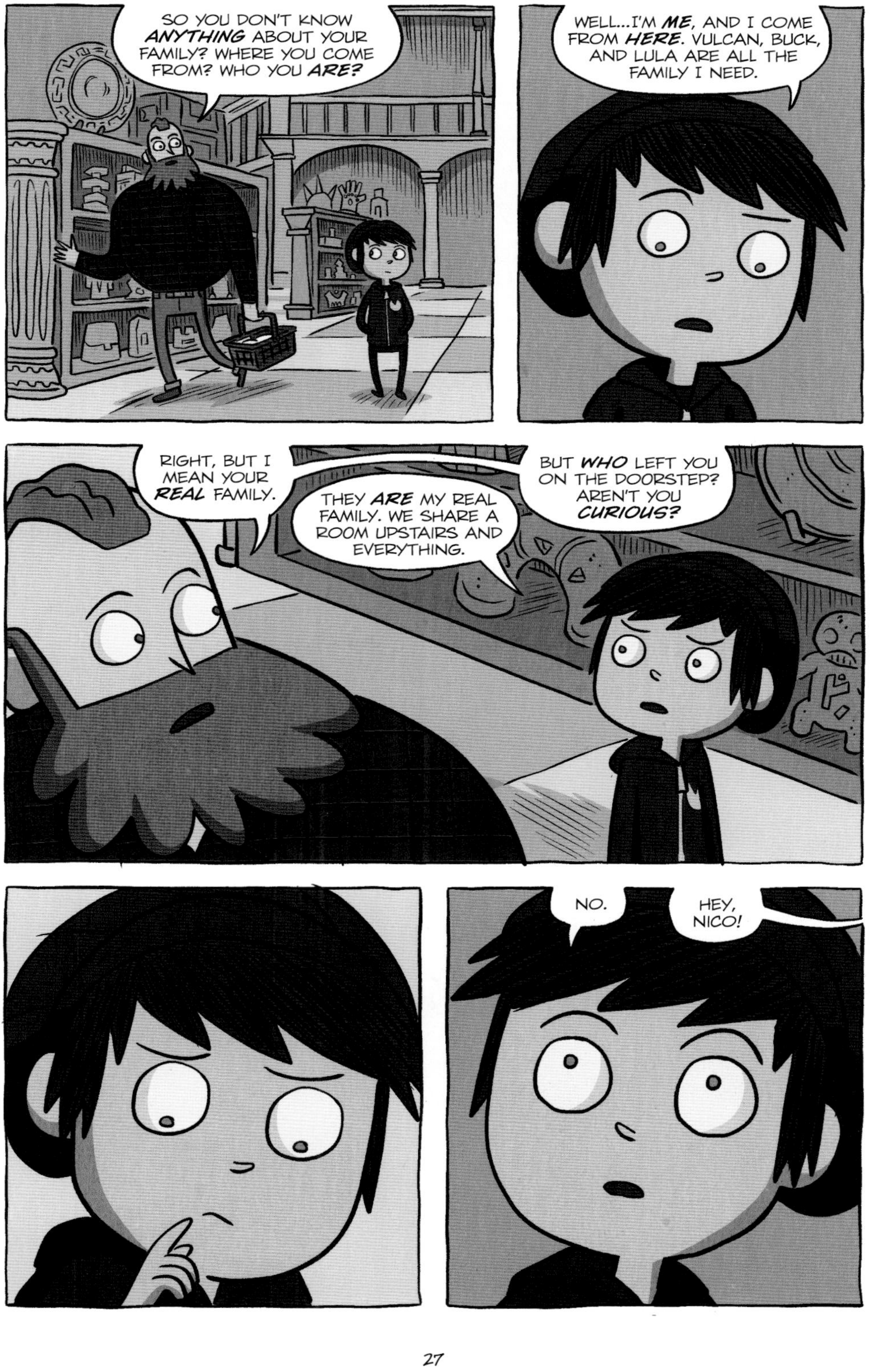
SO YOU DON'T KNOW ANYTHING ABOUT YOUR FAMILY? WHERE YOU COME FROM? WHO YOU ARE?
WELL...I'M ME, AND I COME FROM HERE. VULCAN, BUCK, AND LULA ARE ALL THE FAMILY I NEED.
RIGHT, BUT I MEAN YOUR REAL FAMILY.
THEY ARE MY REAL FAMILY. WE SHARE A ROOM UPSTAIRS AND EVERYTHING.
BUT WHO LEFT YOU ON THE DOORSTEP? AREN'T YOU CURIOUS?
NO.
HEY, NICO!

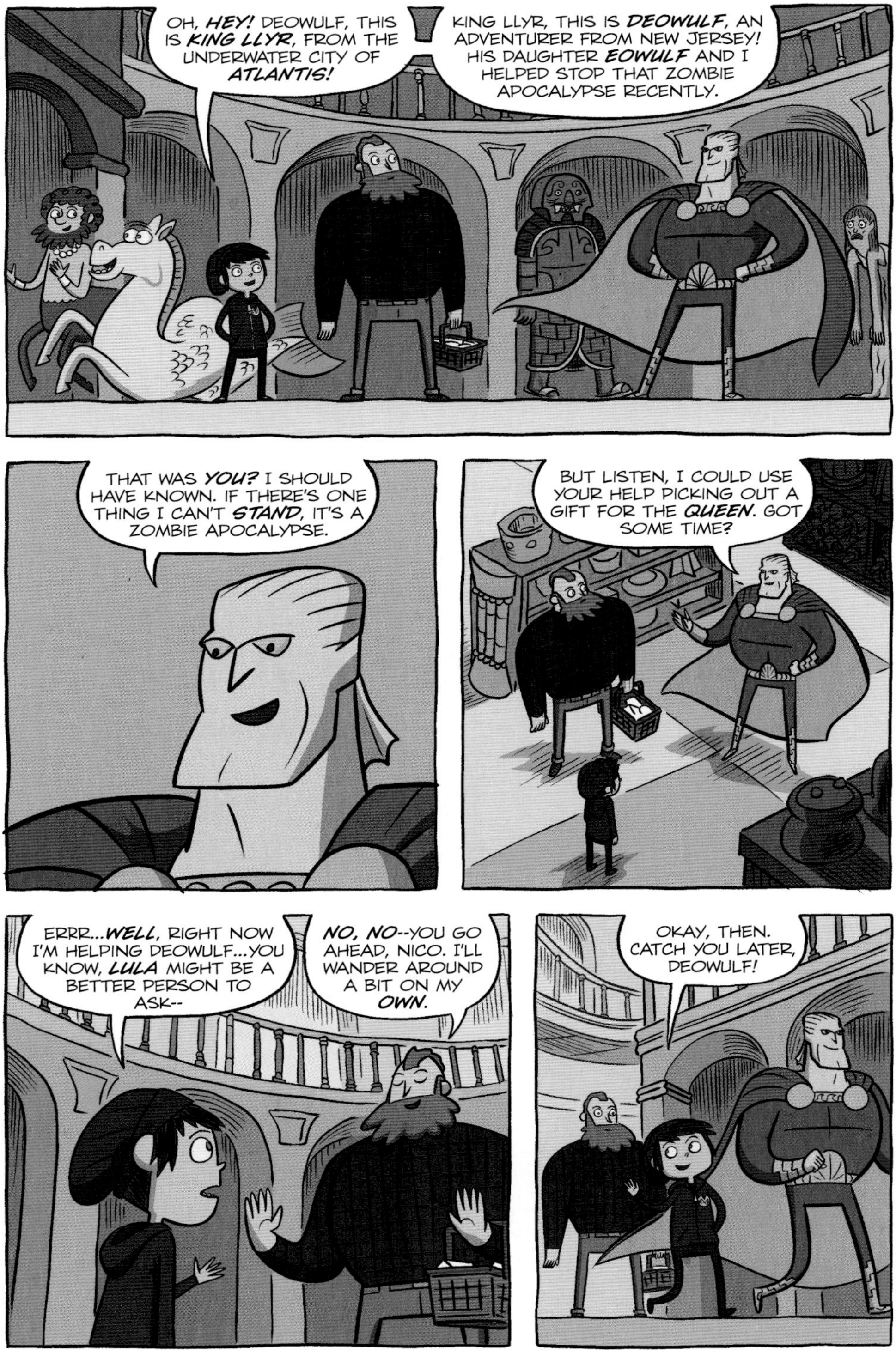
OH, HEY! DEOWULF, THIS IS KING LLYR, FROM THE UNDERWATER CITY OF ATLANTIS!
KING LLYR, THIS IS DEOWULF, AN ADVENTURER FROM NEW JERSEY! HIS DAUGHTER EOWULF AND I HELPED STOP THAT ZOMBIE APOCALYPSE RECENTLY.
THAT WAS YOU? I SHOULD HAVE KNOWN. IF THERE'S ONE THING I CAN'T STAND, IT'S A ZOMBIE APOCALYPSE.
BUT LISTEN, I COULD USE YOUR HELP PICKING OUT A GIFT FOR THE QUEEN. GOT SOME TIME?
ERRR...WELL, RIGHT NOW I'M HELPING DEOWULF...YOU KNOW, LULA MIGHT BE A BETTER PERSON TO ASK--
NO, NO--YOU GO AHEAD, NICO. I'LL WANDER AROUND A BIT ON MY OWN.
OKAY, THEN. CATCH YOU LATER, DEOWULF!

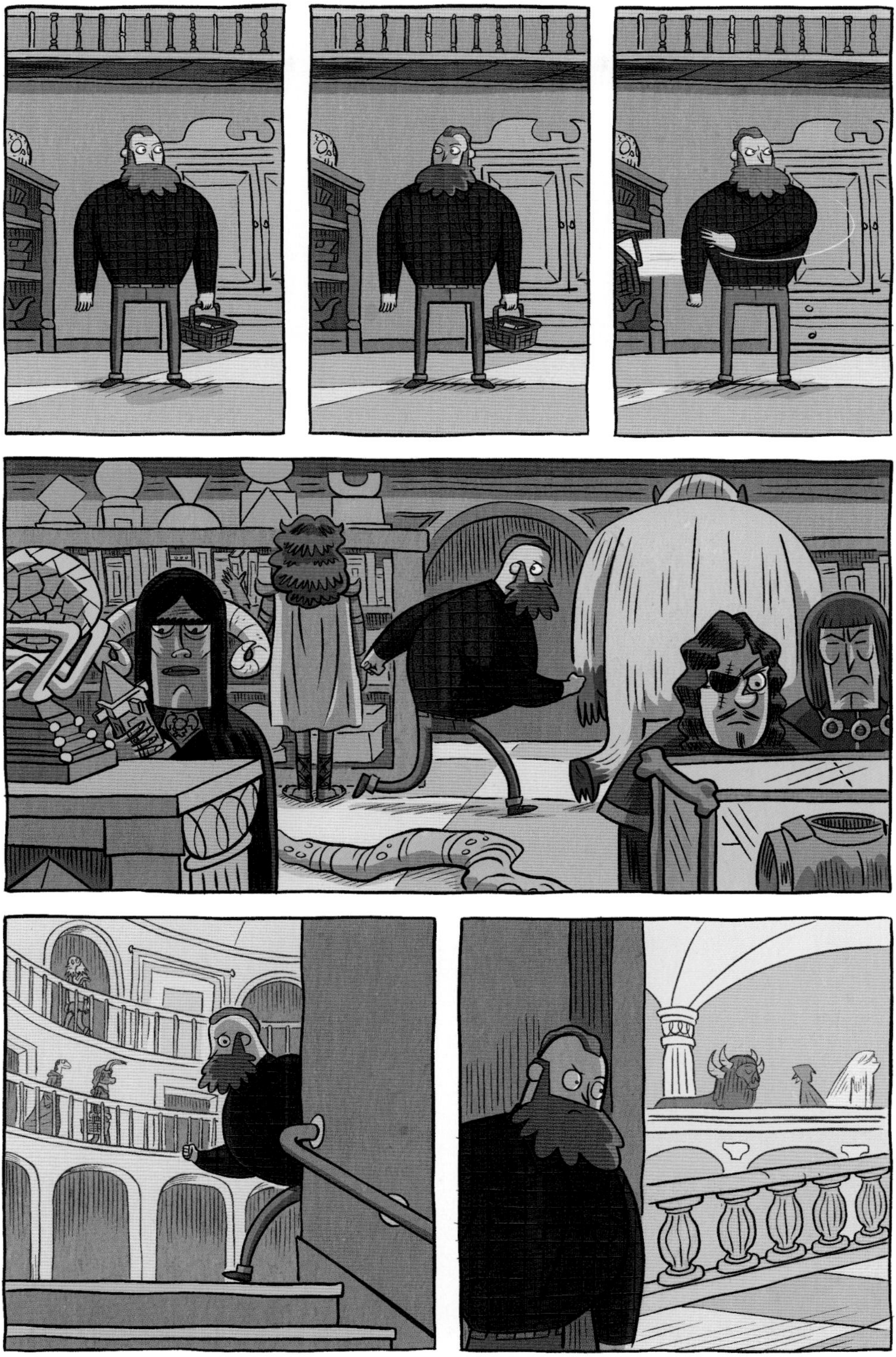

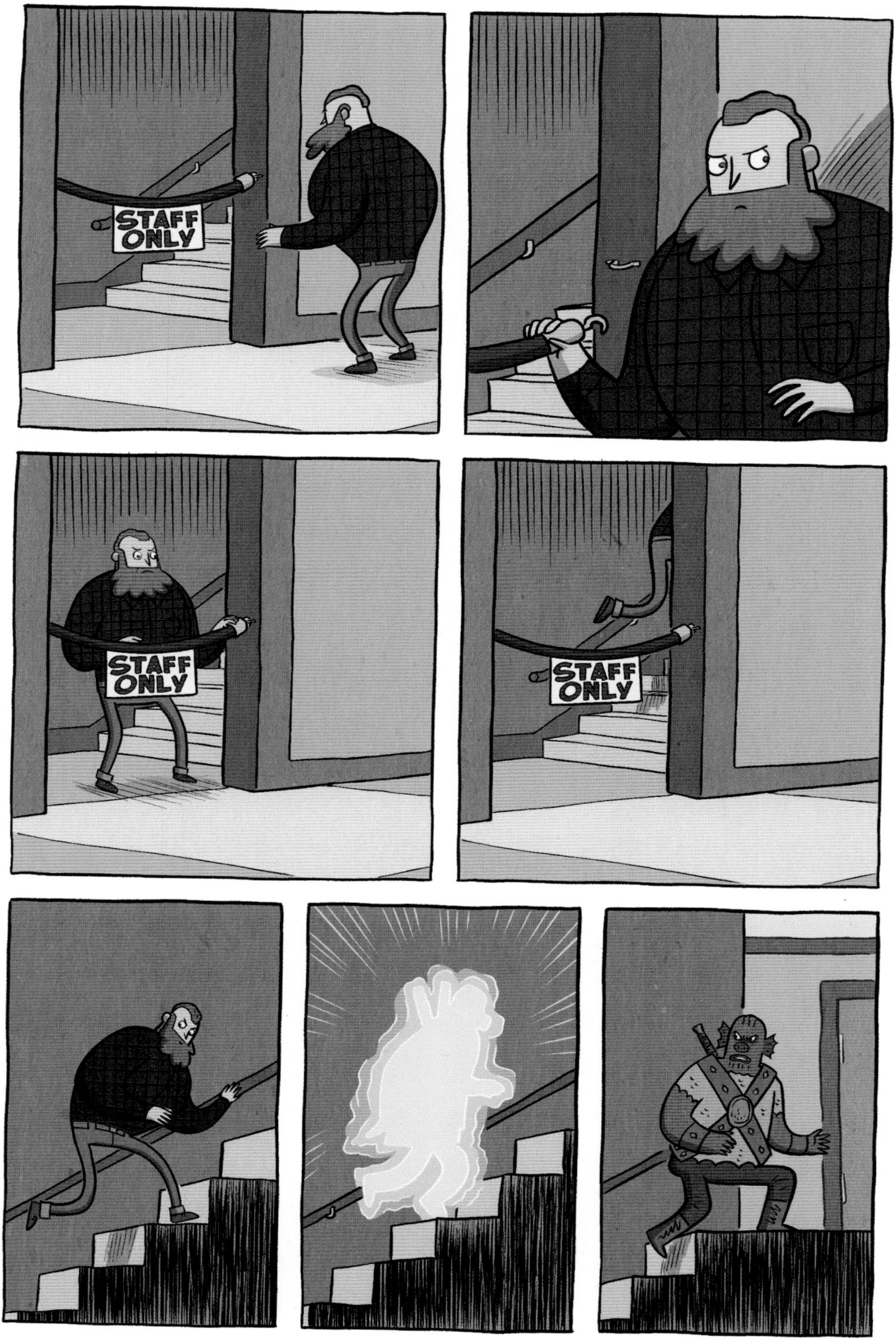
STAFF ONLY
STAFF ONLY
STAFF ONLY

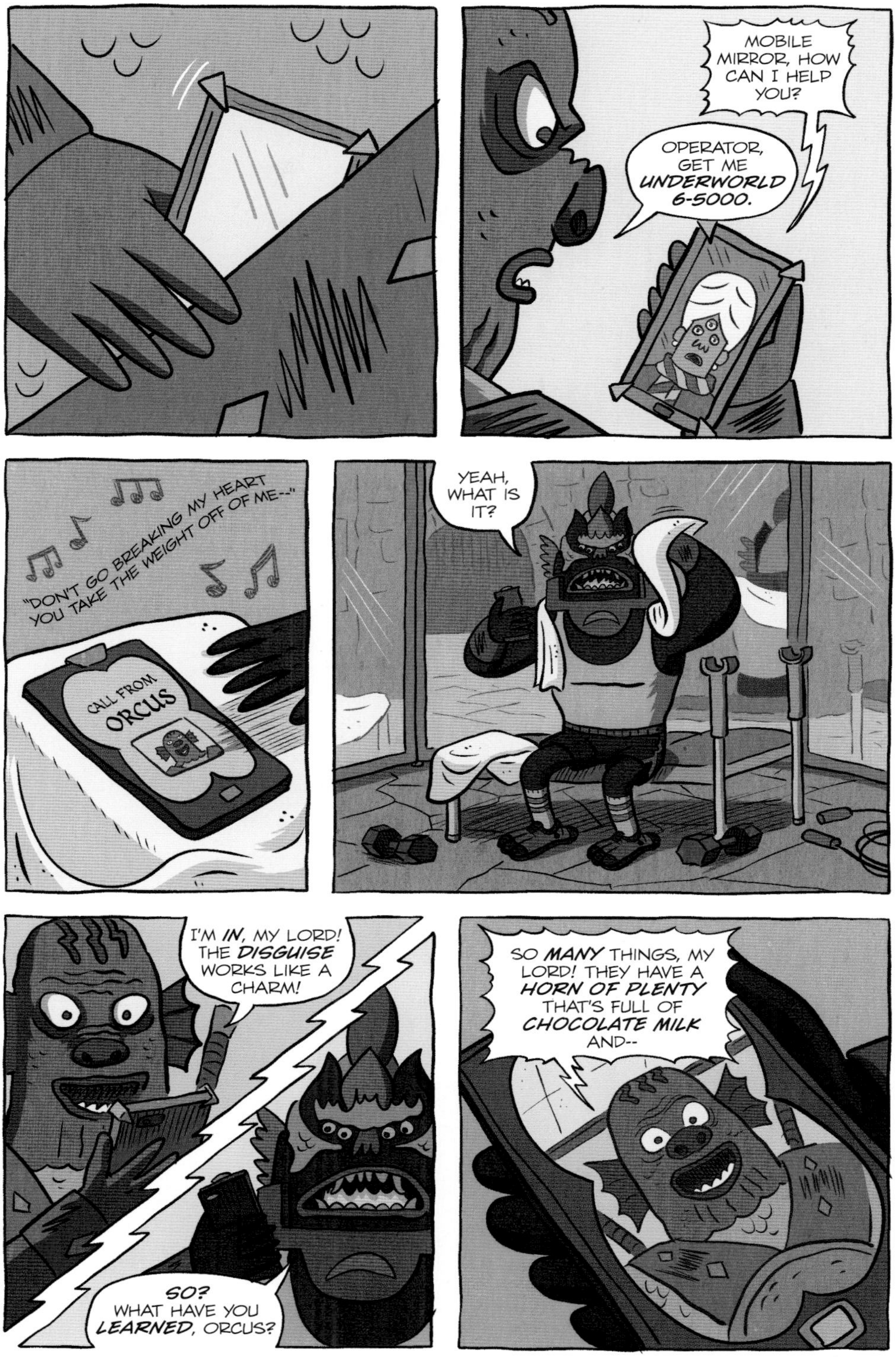

MOBILE MIRROR, HOW CAN I HELP YOU?
OPERATOR, GET ME UNDERWORLD 6-5000.
"DON'T GO BREAKING MY HEART YOU TAKE THE WEIGHT OFF OF ME--"
CALL FROM ORCUS
YEAH, WHAT IS IT?
I'M IN, MY LORD! THE DISGUISE WORKS LIKE A CHARM!
SO? WHAT HAVE YOU LEARNED, ORCUS?
SO MANY THINGS, MY LORD! THEY HAVE A HORN OF PLENTY THAT'S FULL OF CHOCOLATE MILK AND--

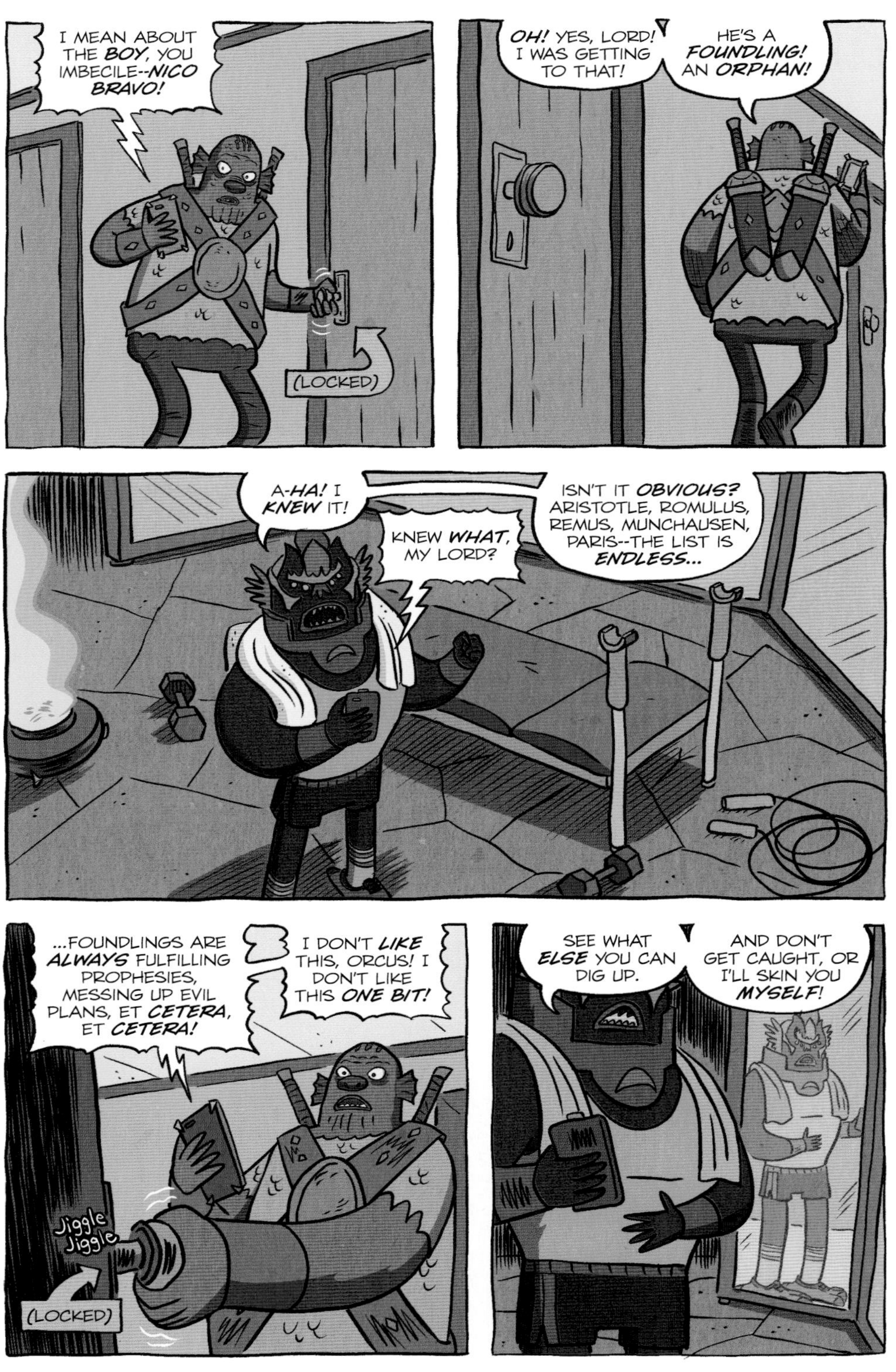

I MEAN ABOUT THE BOY, YOU IMBECILE--NICO BRAVO!
(LOCKED)
OH! YES, LORD! I WAS GETTING TO THAT!
HE'S A FOUNDLING! AN ORPHAN!
A-HA! I KNEW IT!
KNEW WHAT, MY LORD?
ISN'T IT OBVIOUS? ARISTOTLE, ROMULUS, REMUS, MUNCHAUSEN, PARIS--THE LIST IS ENDLESS...
...FOUNDLINGS ARE ALWAYS FULFILLING PROPHESIES, MESSING UP EVIL PLANS, ET CETERA, ET CETERA!
I DON'T LIKE THIS, ORCUS! I DON'T LIKE THIS ONE BIT!
Jiggle Jiggle
(LOCKED)
SEE WHAT ELSE YOU CAN DIG UP.
AND DON'T GET CAUGHT, OR I'LL SKIN YOU MYSELF!

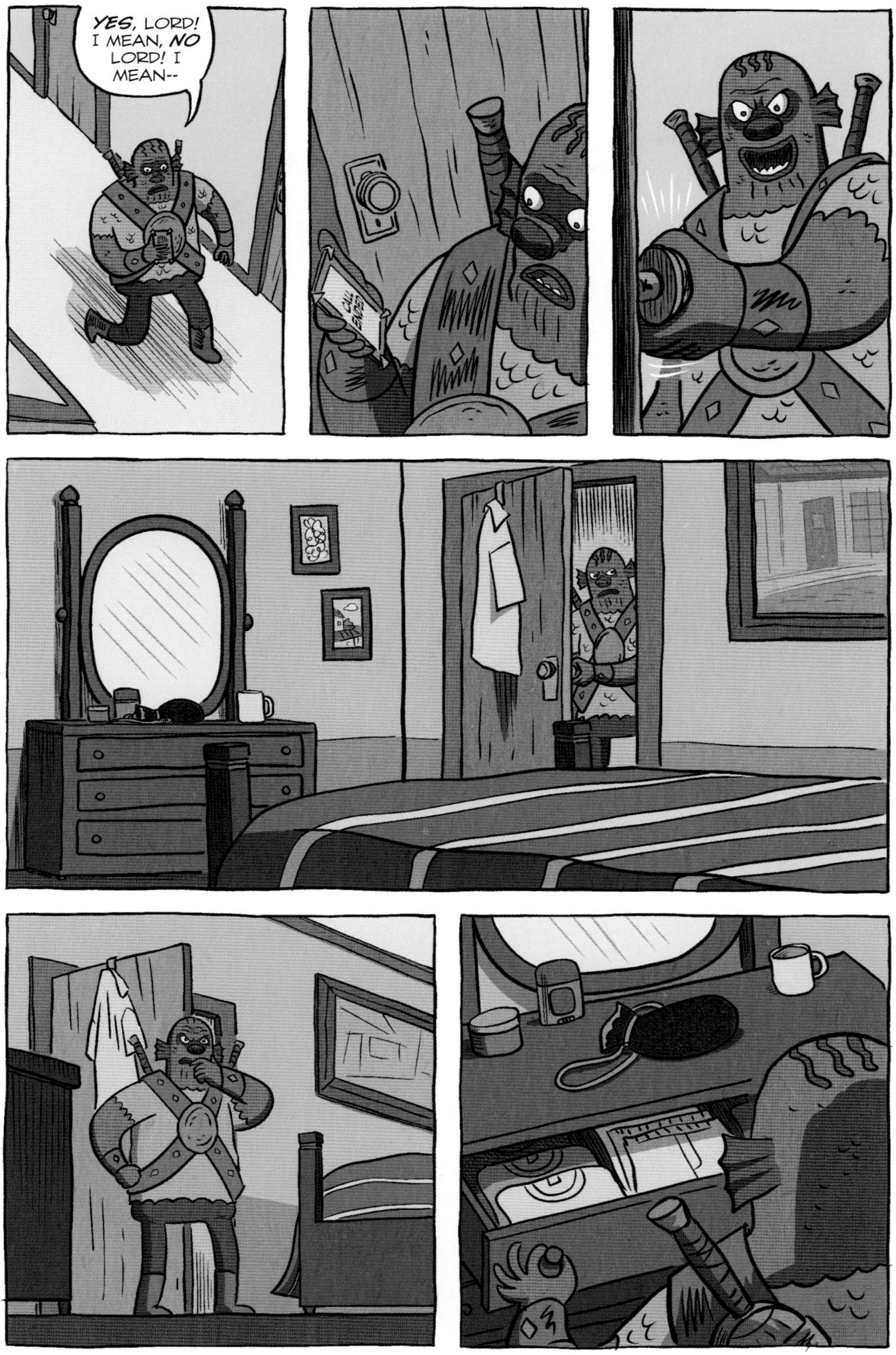
YES, LORD! I MEAN, NO LORD! I MEAN--
CALL ENDED

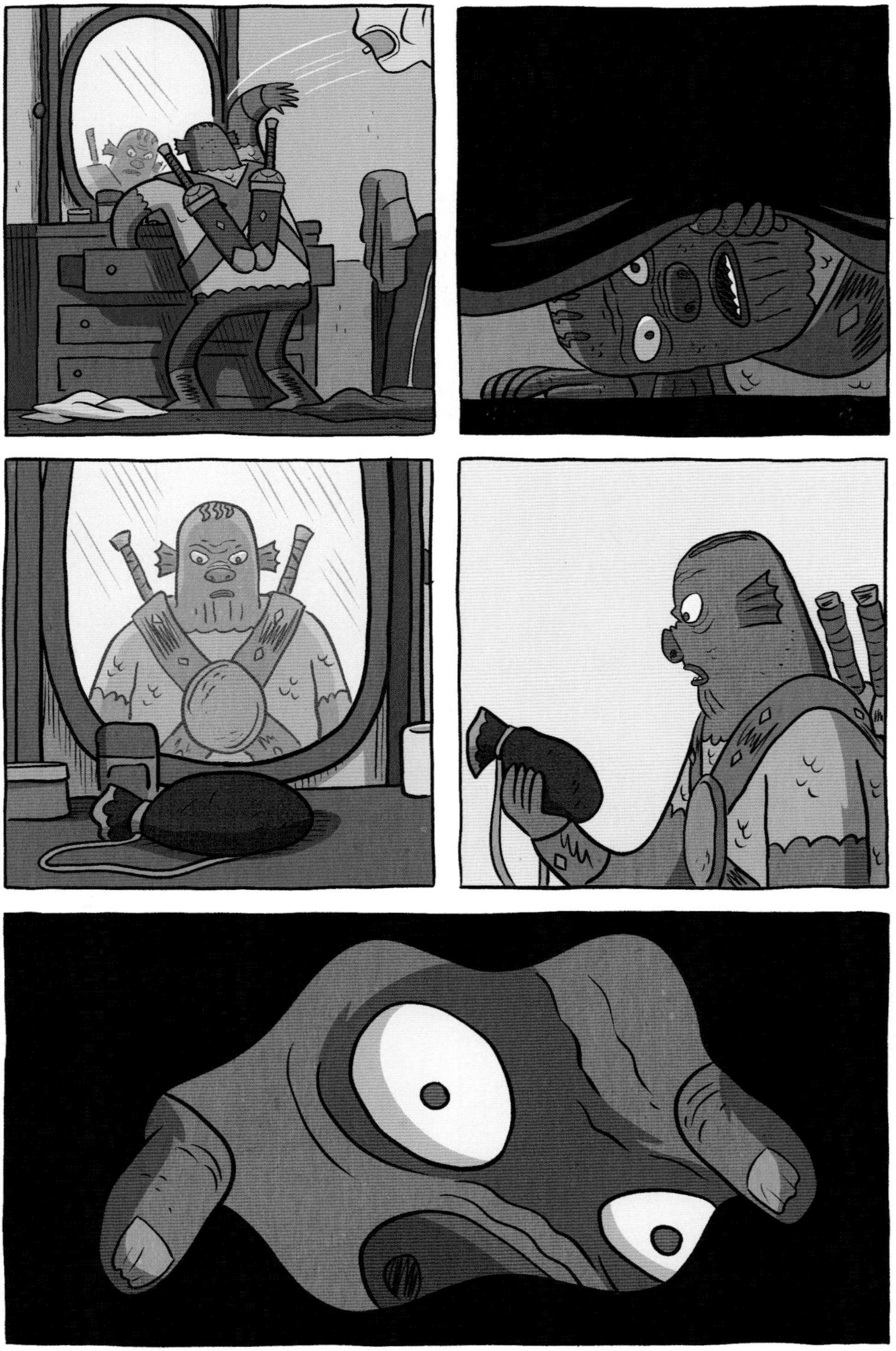

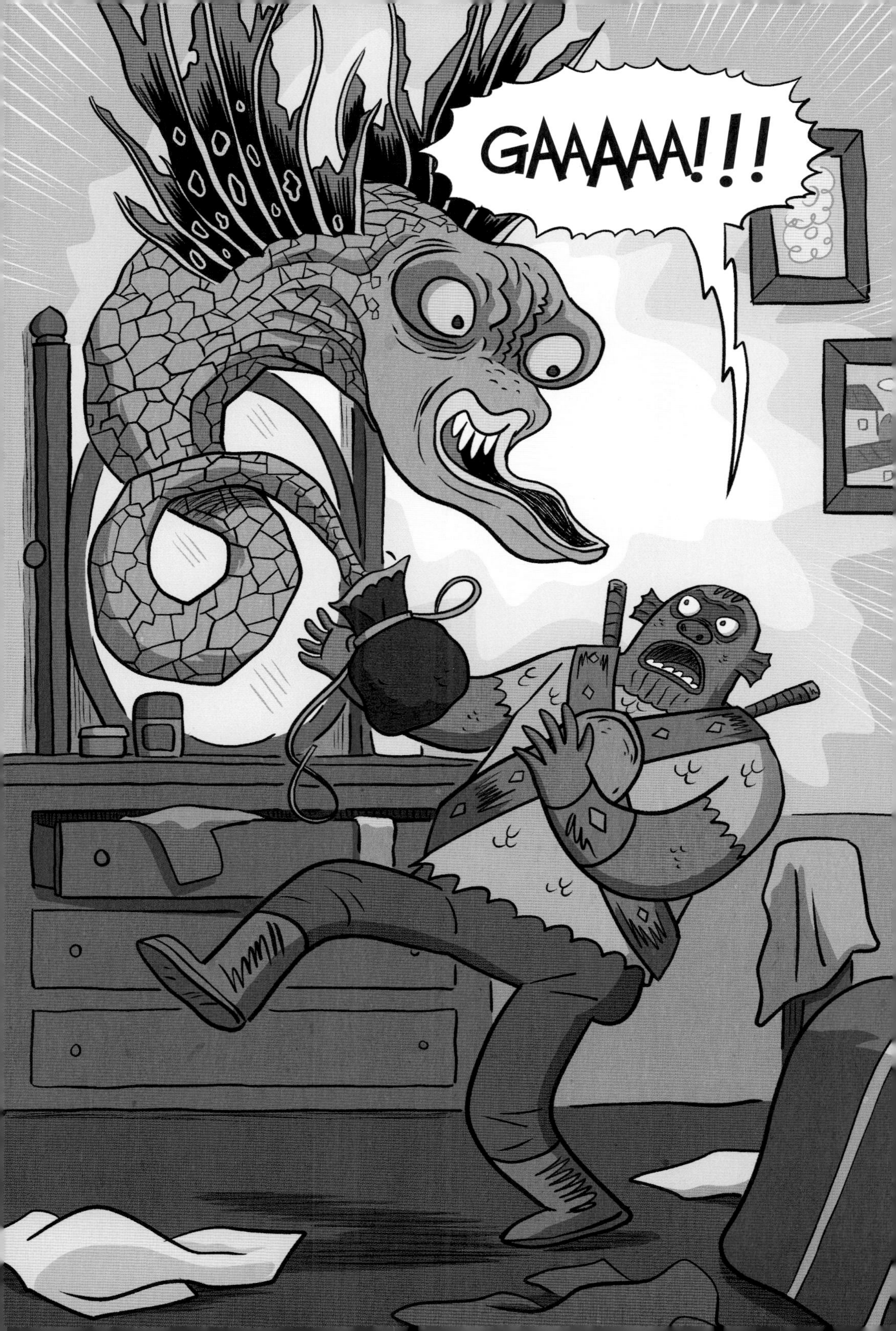
GAAAAA!!!

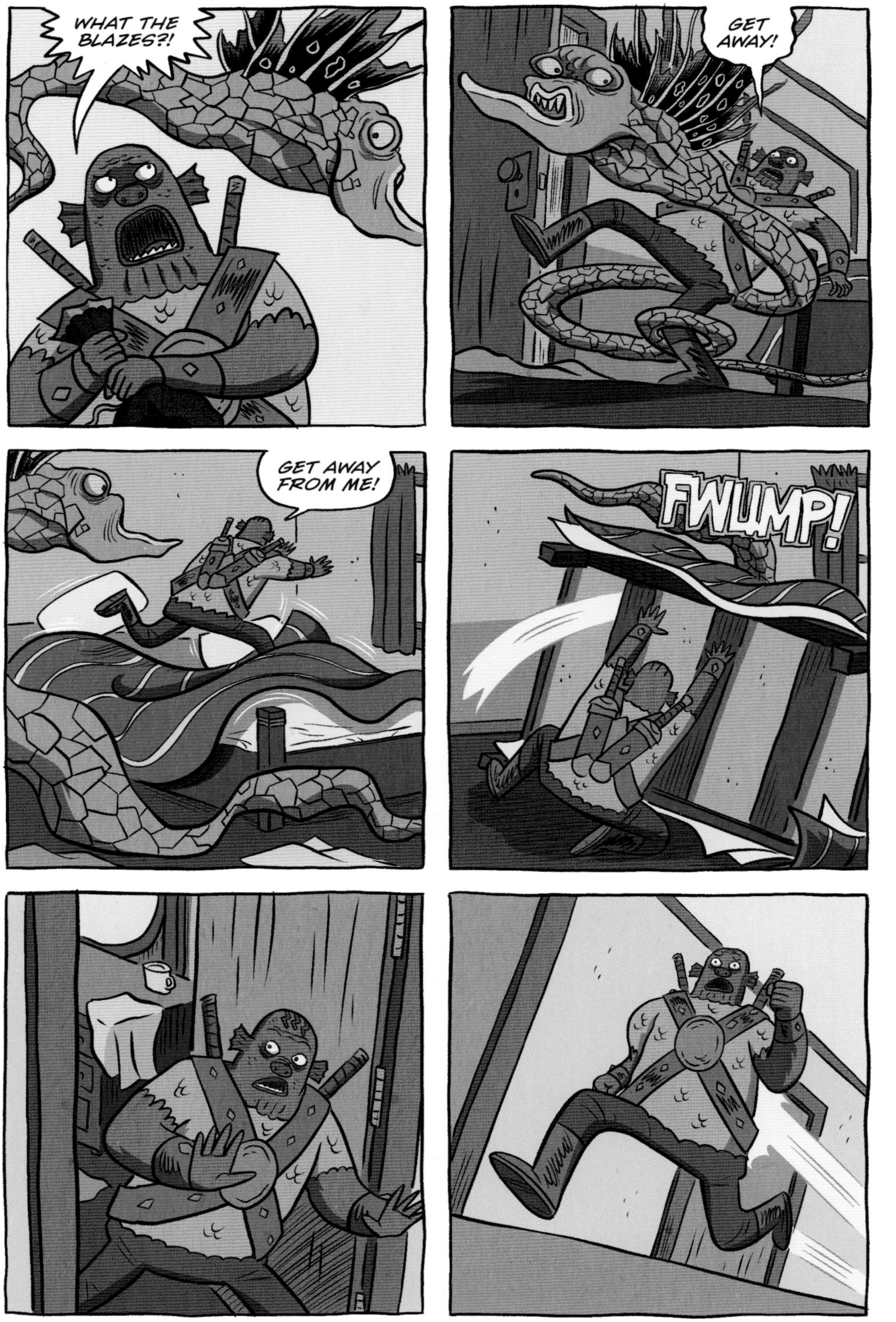
WHAT THE BLAZES?!
GET AWAY!
GET AWAY FROM ME!
FWUMP!

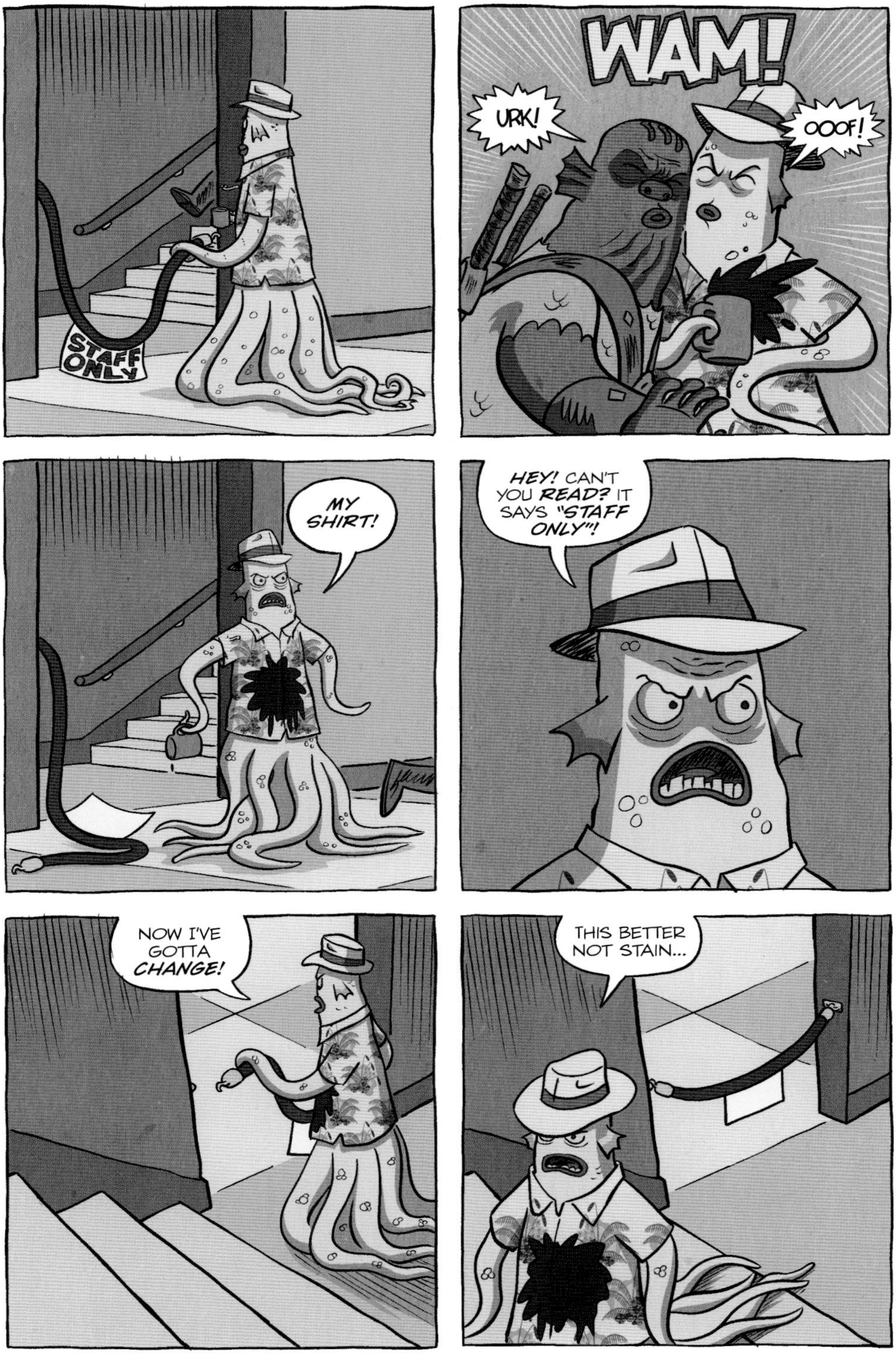

WAM!
URK!
OOOF!
MY SHIRT!
HEY! CAN'T YOU READ? IT SAYS "STAFF ONLY"!
STAFF ONLY
NOW I'VE GOTTA CHANGE!
THIS BETTER NOT STAIN...

THAT'S FUNNY...WHY'S MY *DOOR* OPEN?

SORES AND PUSTULES!

WHAT *HAPPENED* IN HERE?

MY ROOM'S BEEN *RANSACKED!*

MY *POUCH OF MISERY!*

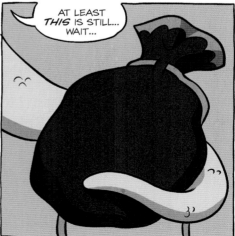

AT LEAST *THIS* IS STILL... WAIT...

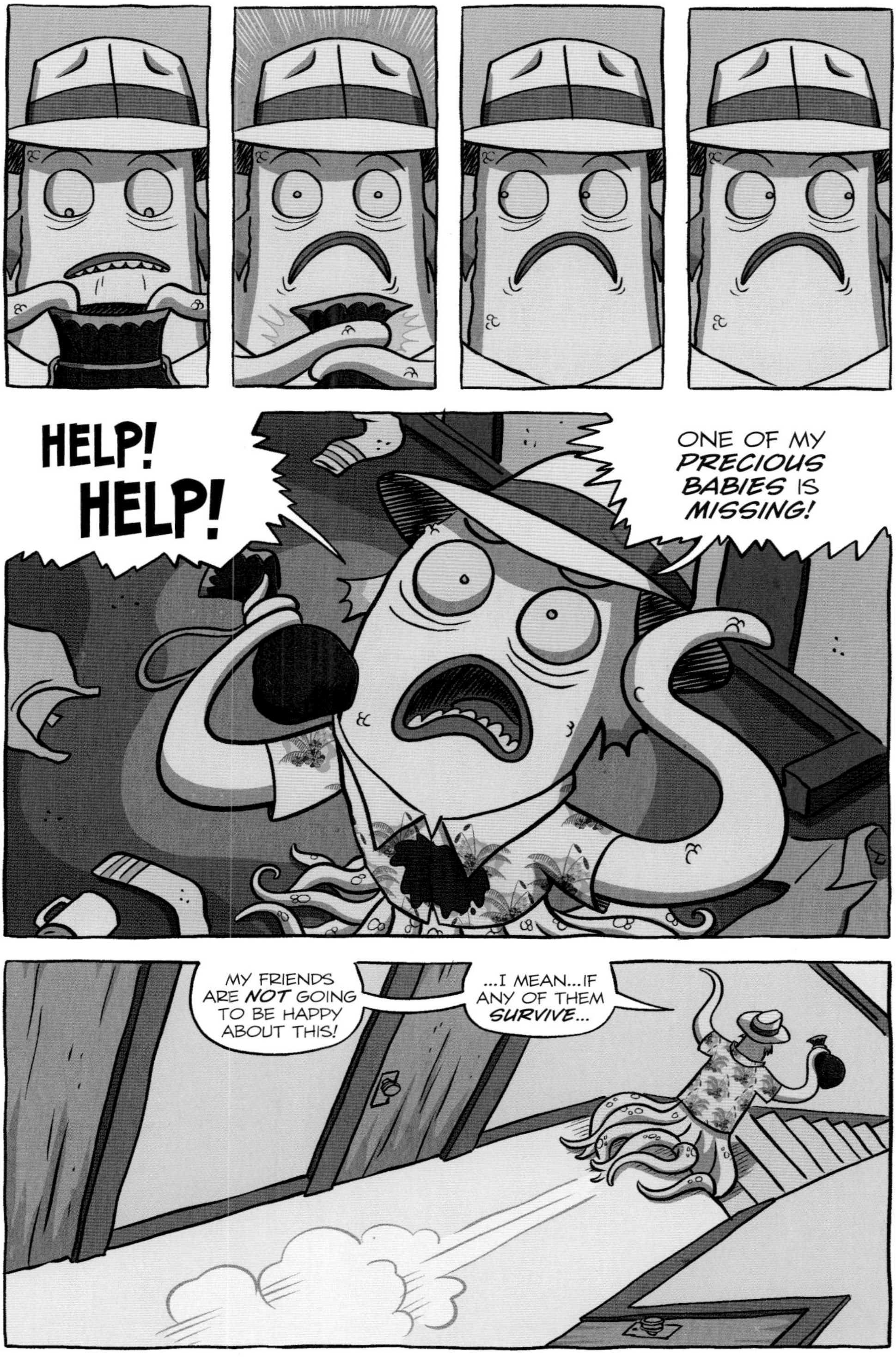
HELP! HELP!
ONE OF MY PRECIOUS BABIES IS MISSING!
MY FRIENDS ARE NOT GOING TO BE HAPPY ABOUT THIS!
...I MEAN...IF ANY OF THEM SURVIVE...

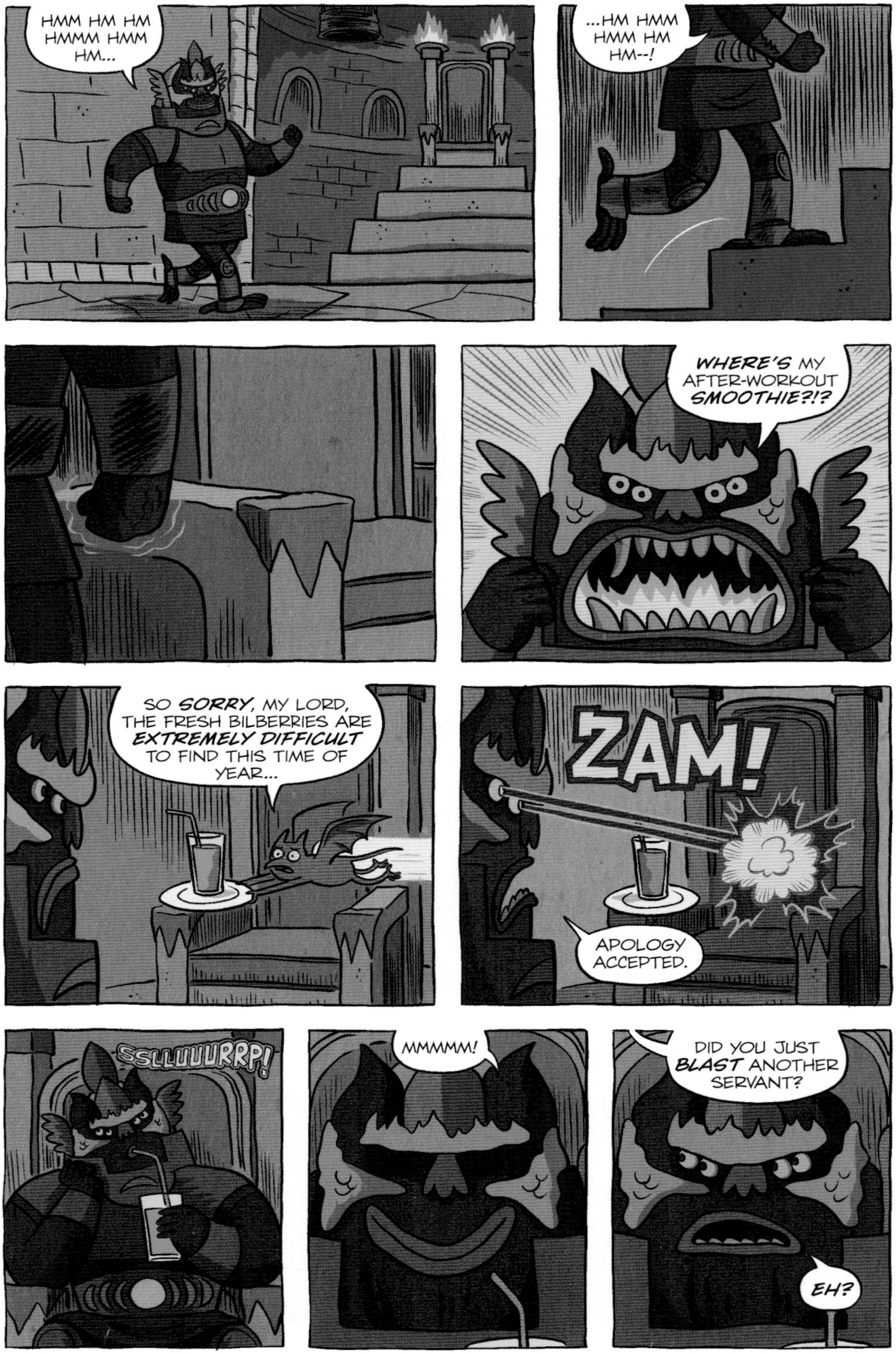
HMM HM HM HMMM HMM HM...
...HM HMM HMM HM HM--!
WHERE'S MY AFTER-WORKOUT SMOOTHIE?!?
SO SORRY, MY LORD, THE FRESH BILBERRIES ARE EXTREMELY DIFFICULT TO FIND THIS TIME OF YEAR...
ZAM!
APOLOGY ACCEPTED.
SSLLUUURRP!
MMMMM!
DID YOU JUST BLAST ANOTHER SERVANT?
EH?

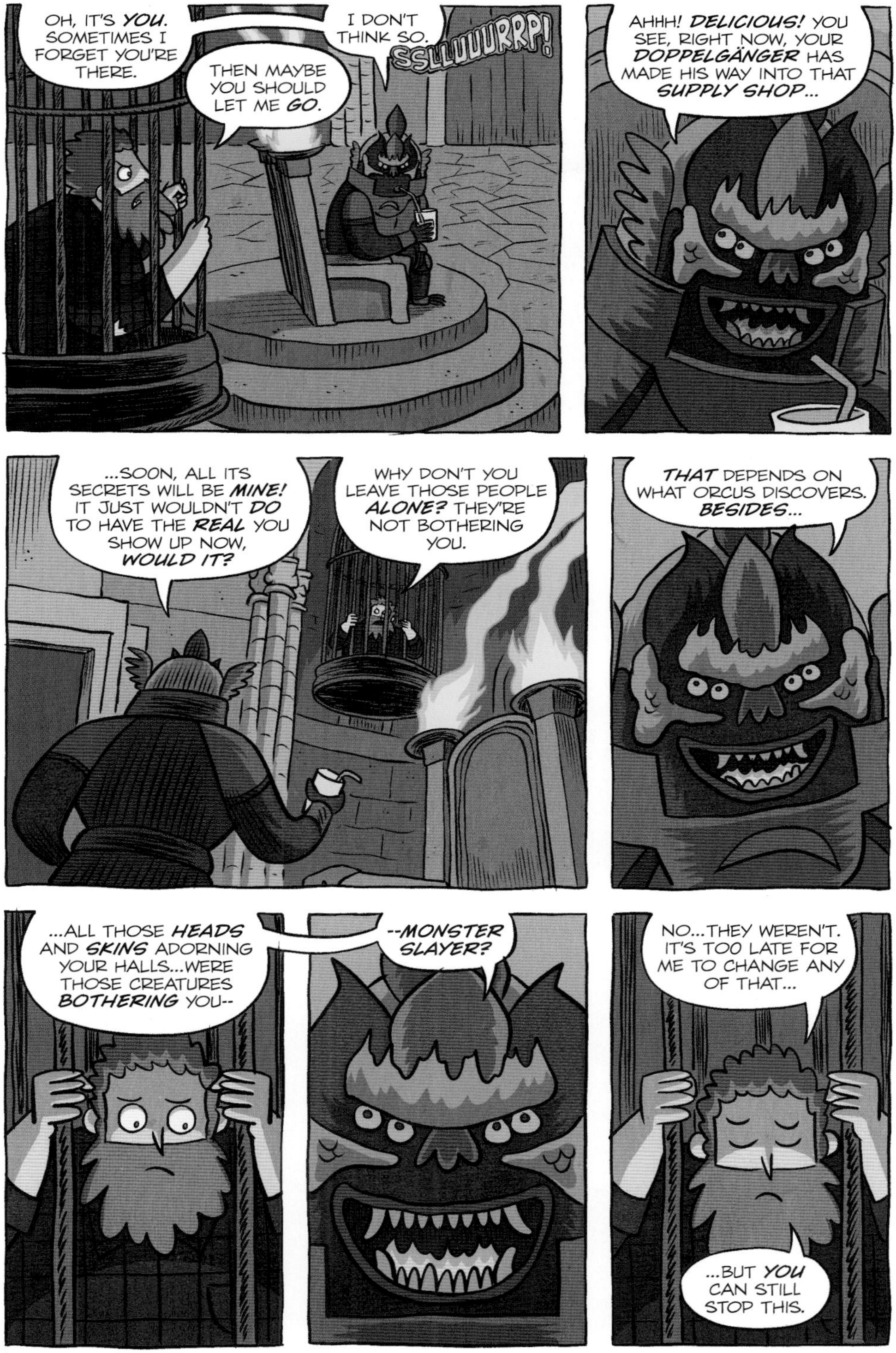
OH, IT'S YOU. SOMETIMES I FORGET YOU'RE THERE.
THEN MAYBE YOU SHOULD LET ME GO.
I DON'T THINK SO.
SSLLUUURRP!
AHHH! DELICIOUS! YOU SEE, RIGHT NOW, YOUR DOPPELGÄNGER HAS MADE HIS WAY INTO THAT SUPPLY SHOP...
...SOON, ALL ITS SECRETS WILL BE MINE! IT JUST WOULDN'T DO TO HAVE THE REAL YOU SHOW UP NOW, WOULD IT?
WHY DON'T YOU LEAVE THOSE PEOPLE ALONE? THEY'RE NOT BOTHERING YOU.
THAT DEPENDS ON WHAT ORCUS DISCOVERS. BESIDES...
...ALL THOSE HEADS AND SKINS ADORNING YOUR HALLS...WERE THOSE CREATURES BOTHERING YOU--
--MONSTER SLAYER?
NO...THEY WEREN'T. IT'S TOO LATE FOR ME TO CHANGE ANY OF THAT...
...BUT YOU CAN STILL STOP THIS.

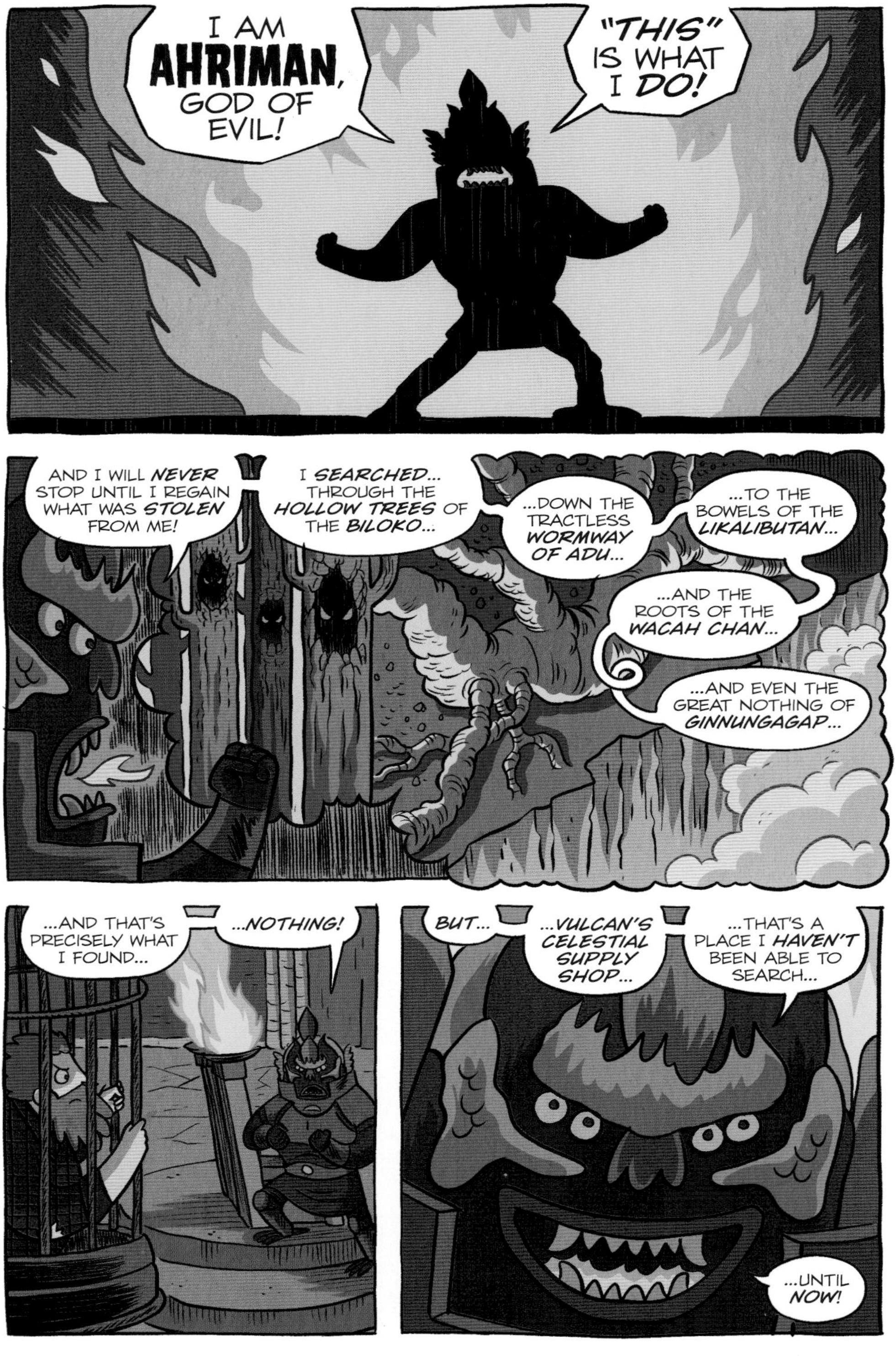
I AM AHRIMAN, GOD OF EVIL!
"THIS" IS WHAT I DO!
AND I WILL NEVER STOP UNTIL I REGAIN WHAT WAS STOLEN FROM ME!
I SEARCHED... THROUGH THE HOLLOW TREES OF THE BILOKO...
...DOWN THE TRACTLESS WORMWAY OF ADU...
...TO THE BOWELS OF THE LIKALIBUTAN...
...AND THE ROOTS OF THE WACAH CHAN...
...AND EVEN THE GREAT NOTHING OF GINNUNGAGAP...
...AND THAT'S PRECISELY WHAT I FOUND...
...NOTHING!
BUT...
...VULCAN'S CELESTIAL SUPPLY SHOP...
...THAT'S A PLACE I HAVEN'T BEEN ABLE TO SEARCH...
...UNTIL NOW!

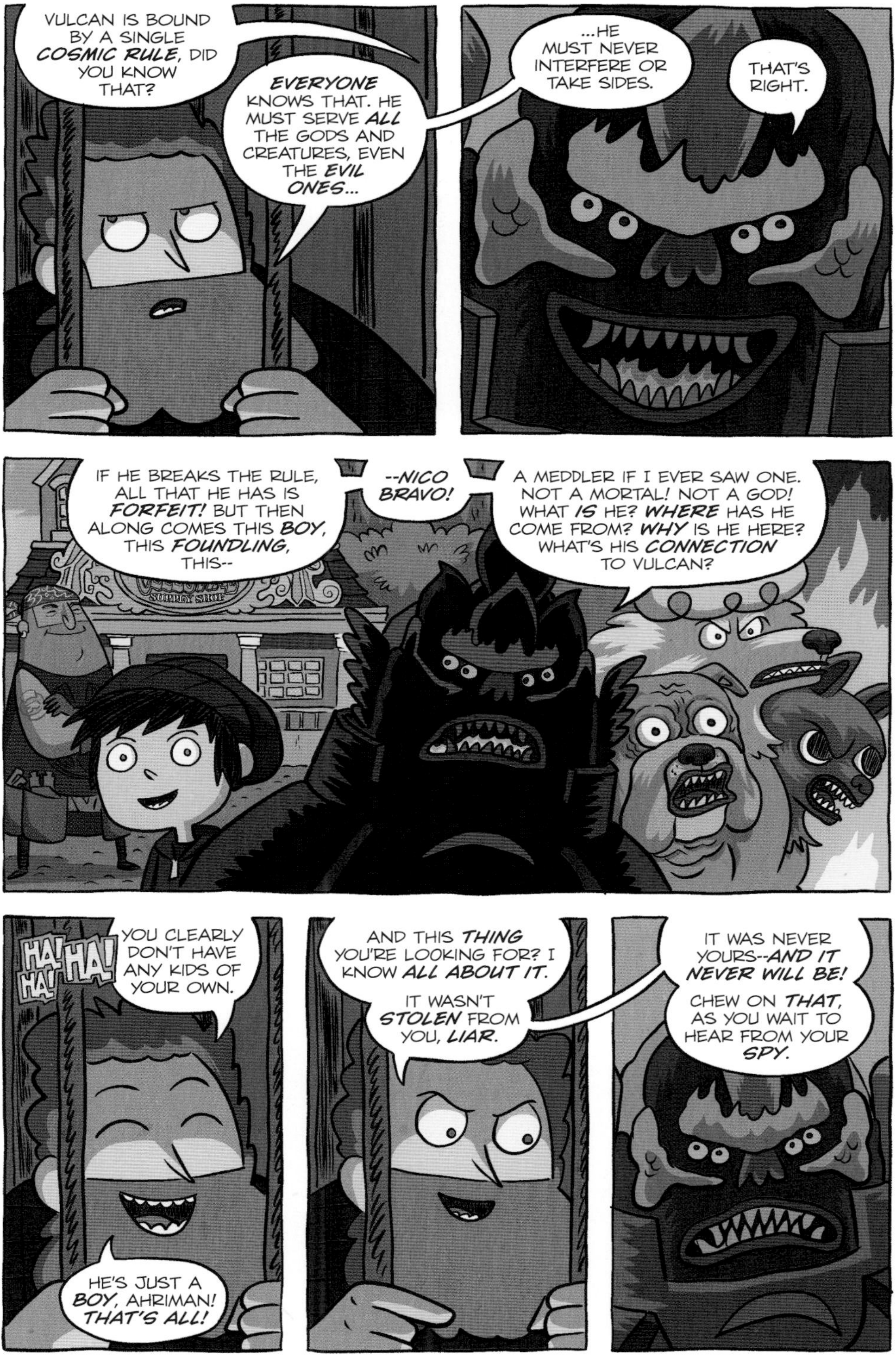
VULCAN IS BOUND BY A SINGLE COSMIC RULE, DID YOU KNOW THAT?
EVERYONE KNOWS THAT. HE MUST SERVE ALL THE GODS AND CREATURES, EVEN THE EVIL ONES...
...HE MUST NEVER INTERFERE OR TAKE SIDES.
THAT'S RIGHT.
IF HE BREAKS THE RULE, ALL THAT HE HAS IS FORFEIT! BUT THEN ALONG COMES THIS BOY, THIS FOUNDLING, THIS--
--NICO BRAVO!
A MEDDLER IF I EVER SAW ONE. NOT A MORTAL! NOT A GOD! WHAT IS HE? WHERE HAS HE COME FROM? WHY IS HE HERE? WHAT'S HIS CONNECTION TO VULCAN?
SUPPLY SHOP
HA! HA! HA!
YOU CLEARLY DON'T HAVE ANY KIDS OF YOUR OWN.
HE'S JUST A BOY, AHRIMAN! THAT'S ALL!
AND THIS THING YOU'RE LOOKING FOR? I KNOW ALL ABOUT IT.
IT WASN'T STOLEN FROM YOU, LIAR.
IT WAS NEVER YOURS--AND IT NEVER WILL BE!
CHEW ON THAT, AS YOU WAIT TO HEAR FROM YOUR SPY.

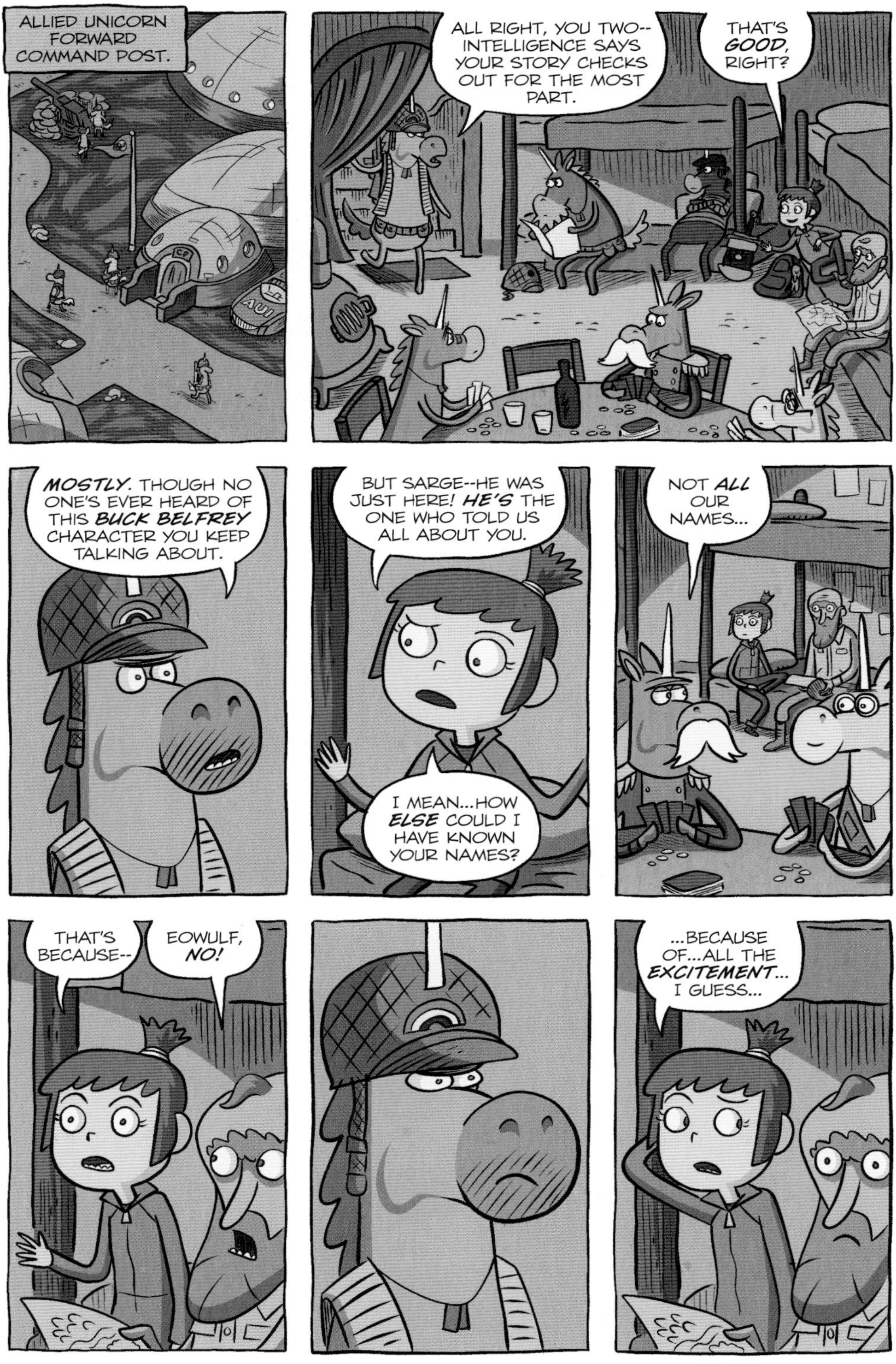
ALLIED UNICORN FORWARD COMMAND POST.
AUI
ALL RIGHT, YOU TWO-- INTELLIGENCE SAYS YOUR STORY CHECKS OUT FOR THE MOST PART.
THAT'S GOOD, RIGHT?
MOSTLY. THOUGH NO ONE'S EVER HEARD OF THIS BUCK BELFREY CHARACTER YOU KEEP TALKING ABOUT.
BUT SARGE--HE WAS JUST HERE! HE'S THE ONE WHO TOLD US ALL ABOUT YOU.
I MEAN...HOW ELSE COULD I HAVE KNOWN YOUR NAMES?
NOT ALL OUR NAMES...
THAT'S BECAUSE--
EOWULF, NO!
...BECAUSE OF...ALL THE EXCITEMENT... I GUESS...

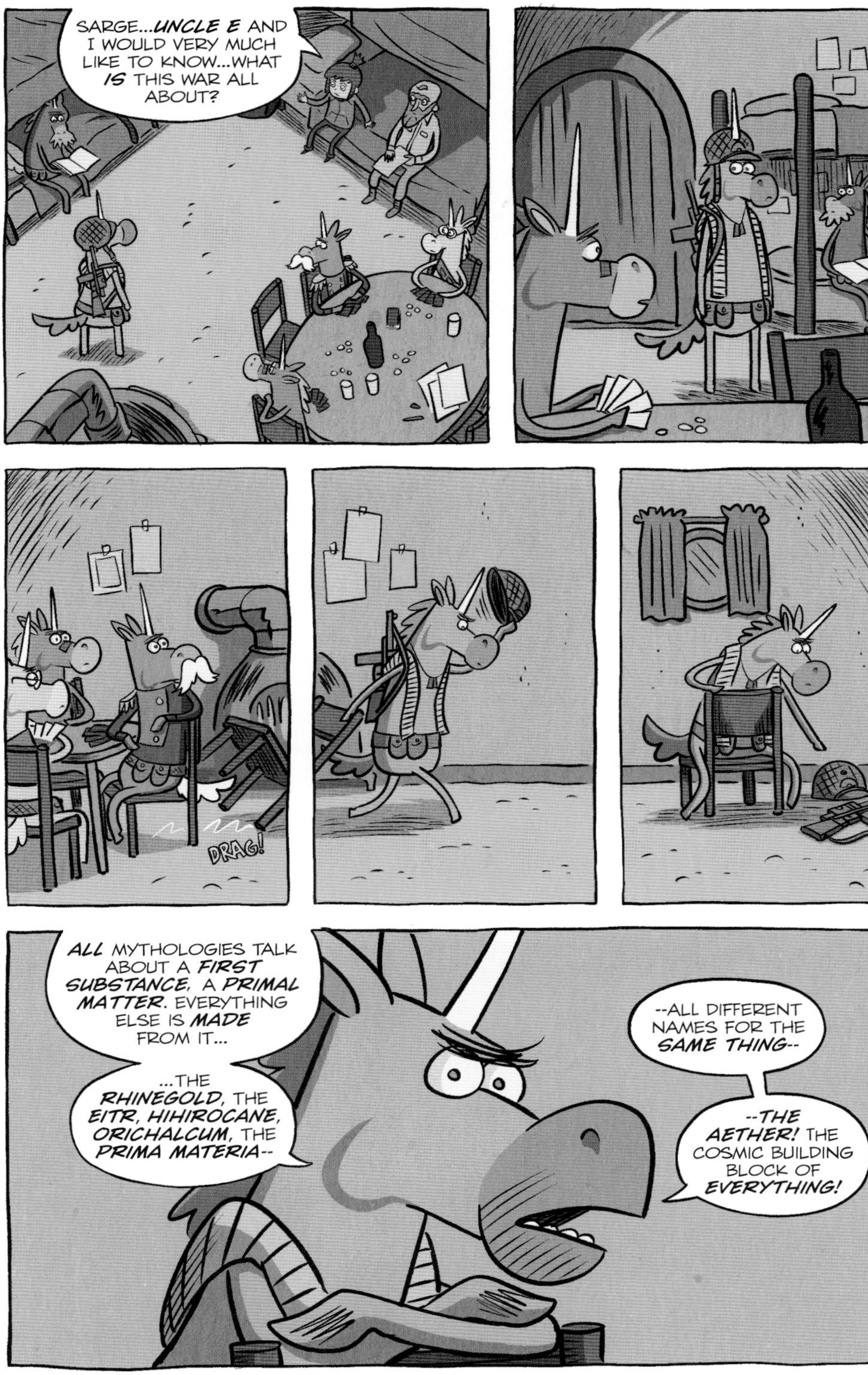
SARGE...UNCLE E AND I WOULD VERY MUCH LIKE TO KNOW...WHAT IS THIS WAR ALL ABOUT?
DRAG!
ALL MYTHOLOGIES TALK ABOUT A FIRST SUBSTANCE, A PRIMAL MATTER. EVERYTHING ELSE IS MADE FROM IT...
...THE RHINEGOLD, THE EITR, HIHIROCANE, ORICHALCUM, THE PRIMA MATERIA--
--ALL DIFFERENT NAMES FOR THE SAME THING--
--THE AETHER! THE COSMIC BUILDING BLOCK OF EVERYTHING!

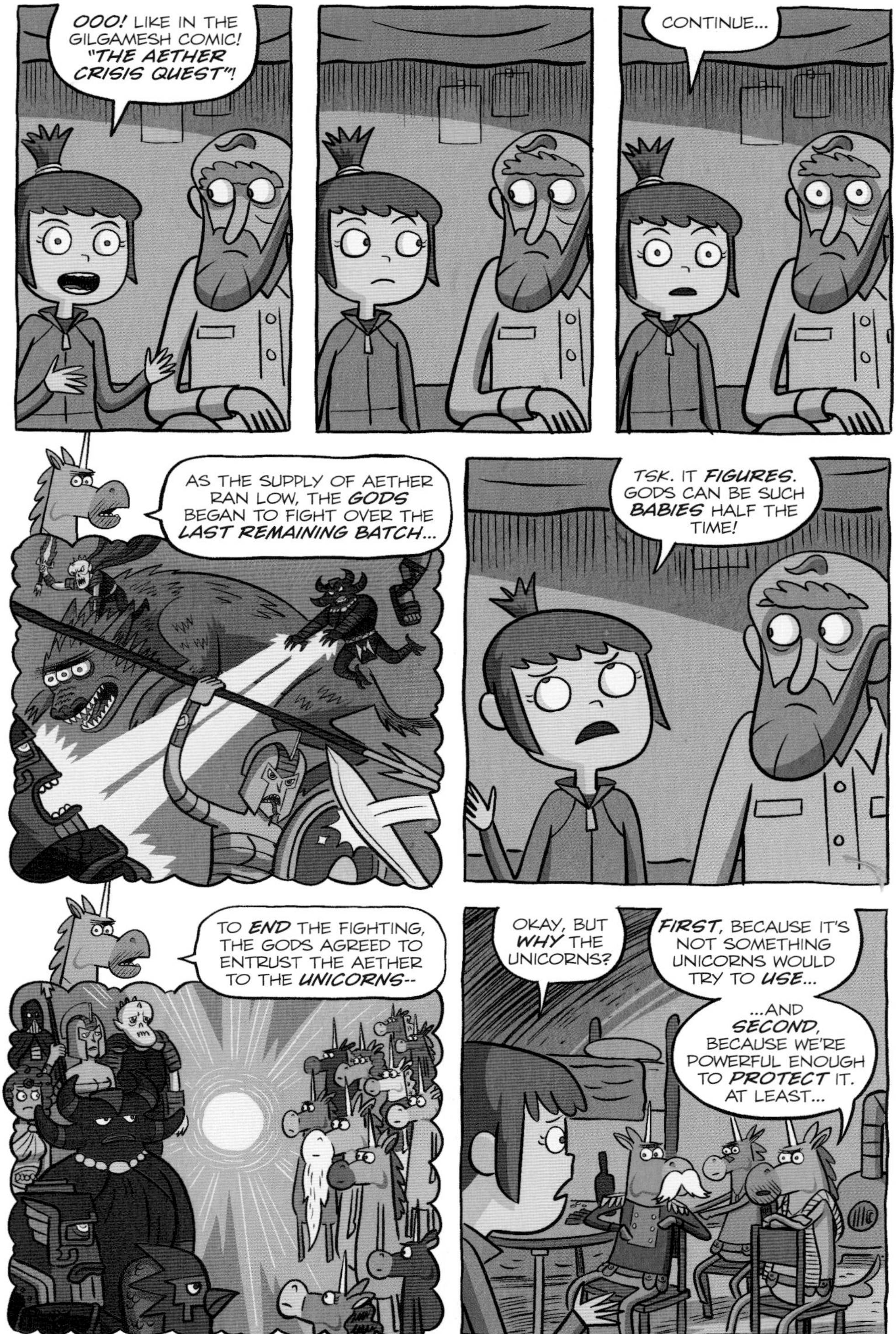
OOO! LIKE IN THE GILGAMESH COMIC! "THE AETHER CRISIS QUEST"!
CONTINUE...
AS THE SUPPLY OF AETHER RAN LOW, THE GODS BEGAN TO FIGHT OVER THE LAST REMAINING BATCH...
TSK. IT FIGURES. GODS CAN BE SUCH BABIES HALF THE TIME!
TO END THE FIGHTING, THE GODS AGREED TO ENTRUST THE AETHER TO THE UNICORNS--
OKAY, BUT WHY THE UNICORNS?
FIRST, BECAUSE IT'S NOT SOMETHING UNICORNS WOULD TRY TO USE...
...AND SECOND, BECAUSE WE'RE POWERFUL ENOUGH TO PROTECT IT. AT LEAST...

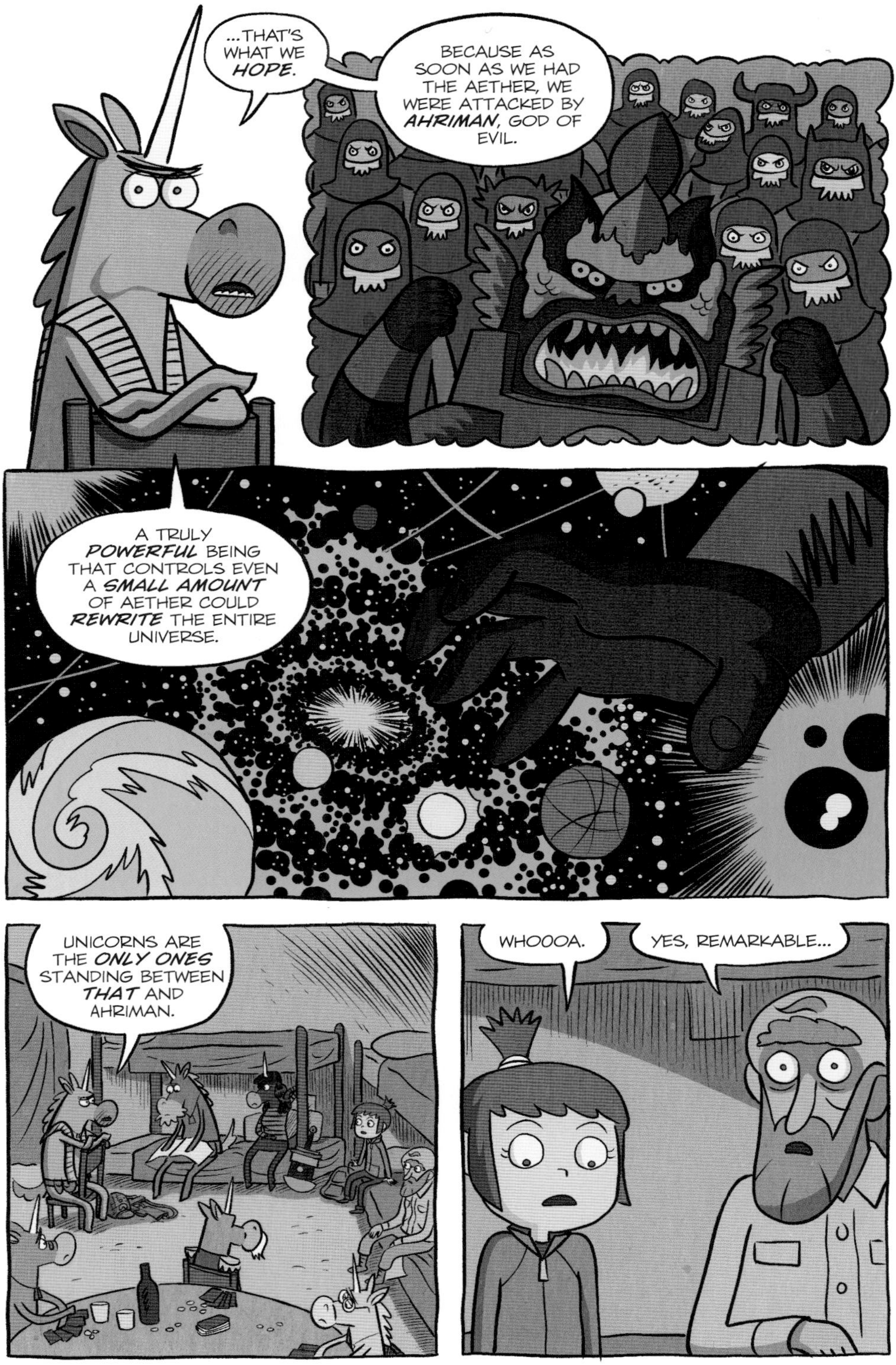
...THAT'S WHAT WE HOPE.
BECAUSE AS SOON AS WE HAD THE AETHER, WE WERE ATTACKED BY AHRIMAN, GOD OF EVIL.
A TRULY POWERFUL BEING THAT CONTROLS EVEN A SMALL AMOUNT OF AETHER COULD REWRITE THE ENTIRE UNIVERSE.
UNICORNS ARE THE ONLY ONES STANDING BETWEEN THAT AND AHRIMAN.
WHOOOA.
YES, REMARKABLE...

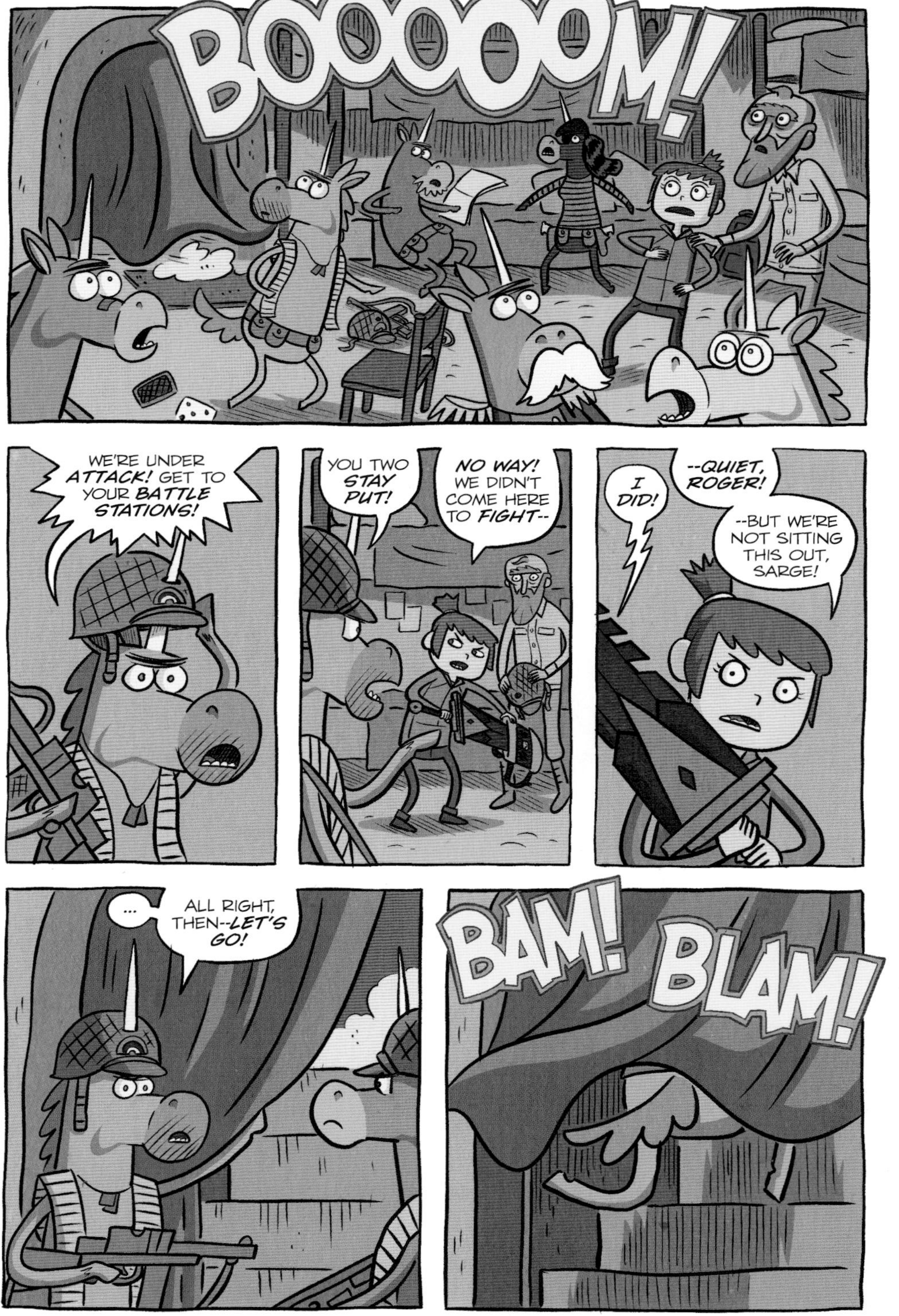
BOOOOOM!
WE'RE UNDER ATTACK! GET TO YOUR BATTLE STATIONS!
YOU TWO STAY PUT!
NO WAY! WE DIDN'T COME HERE TO FIGHT--
I DID!
--QUIET, ROGER!
--BUT WE'RE NOT SITTING THIS OUT, SARGE!
...
ALL RIGHT, THEN--LET'S GO!
BAM!
BLAM!

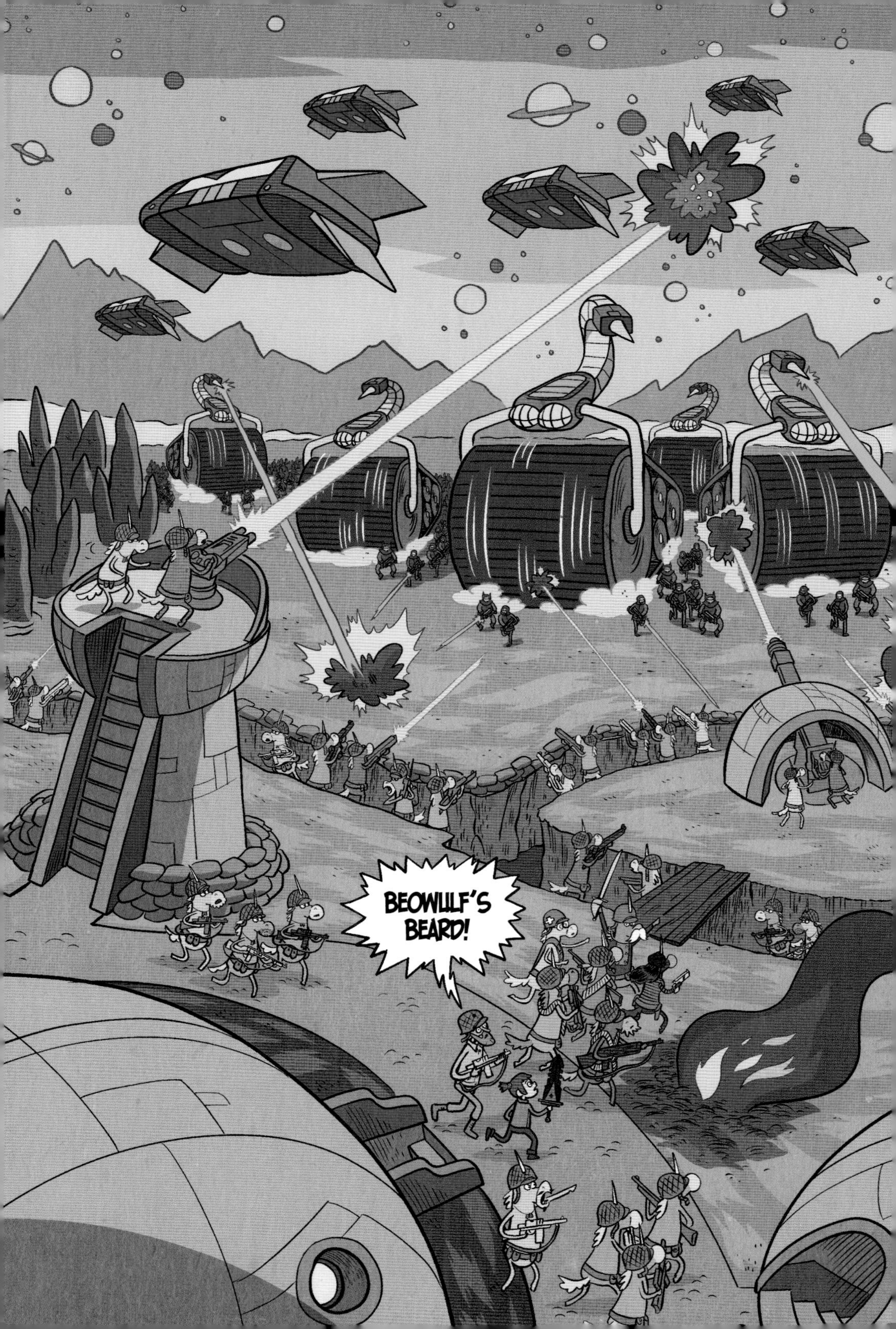
BEOWULF'S BEARD!

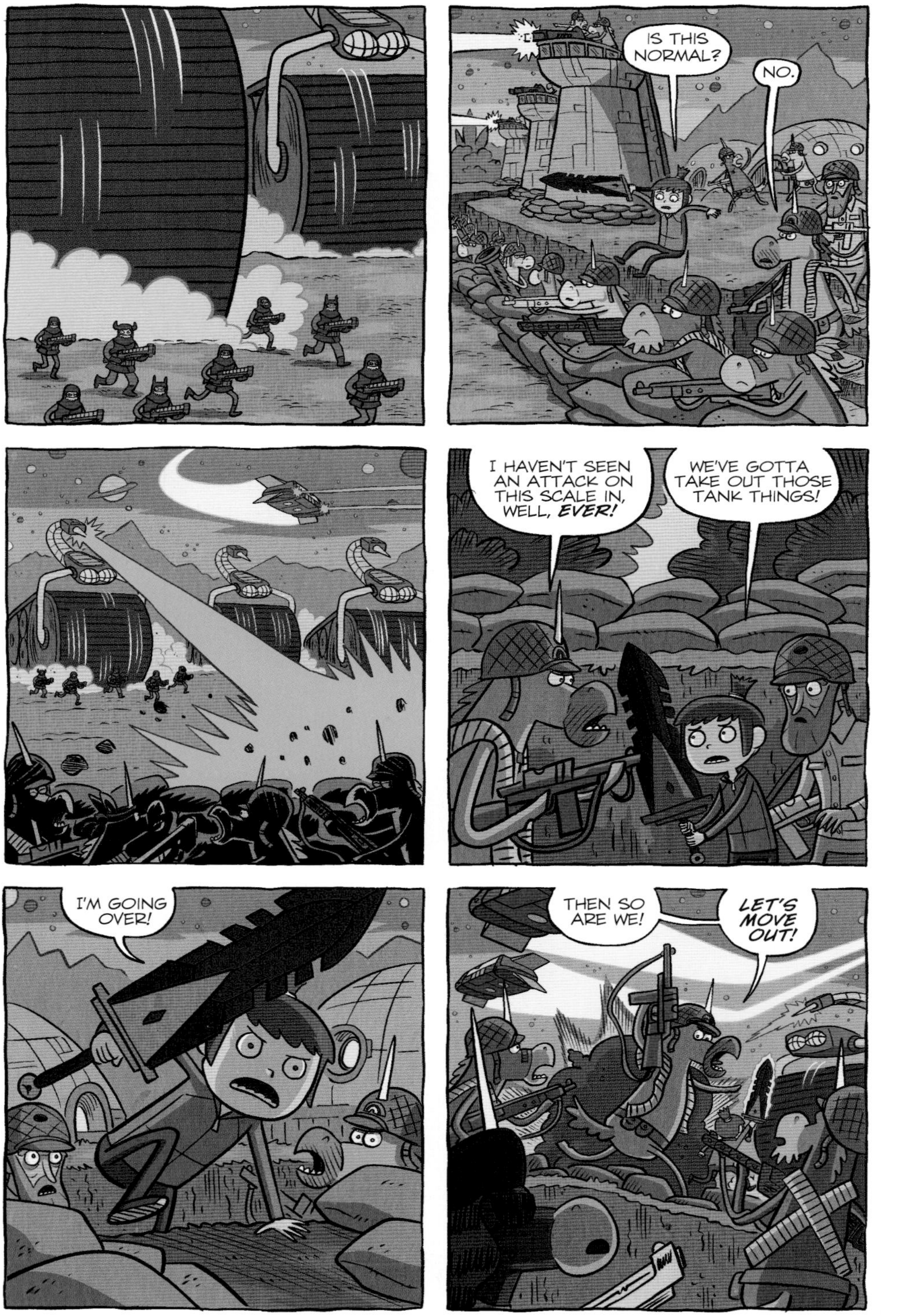
IS THIS NORMAL?
NO.
I HAVEN'T SEEN AN ATTACK ON THIS SCALE IN, WELL, *EVER!*
WE'VE GOTTA TAKE OUT THOSE TANK THINGS!
I'M GOING OVER!
THEN SO ARE WE!
LET'S MOVE OUT!

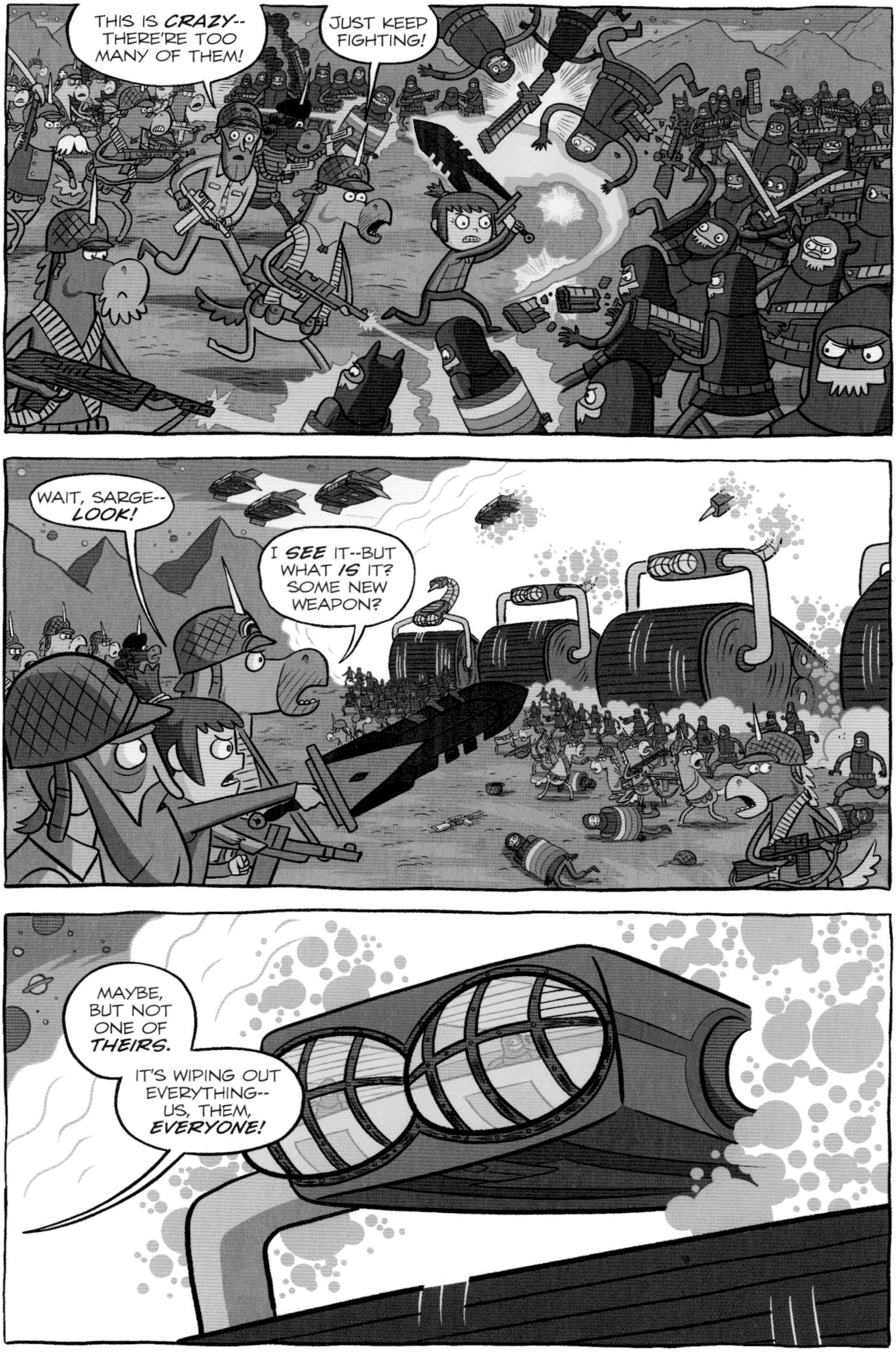

THIS IS CRAZY-- THERE'RE TOO MANY OF THEM!
JUST KEEP FIGHTING!
WAIT, SARGE-- LOOK!
I SEE IT--BUT WHAT IS IT? SOME NEW WEAPON?
MAYBE, BUT NOT ONE OF THEIRS.
IT'S WIPING OUT EVERYTHING-- US, THEM, EVERYONE!

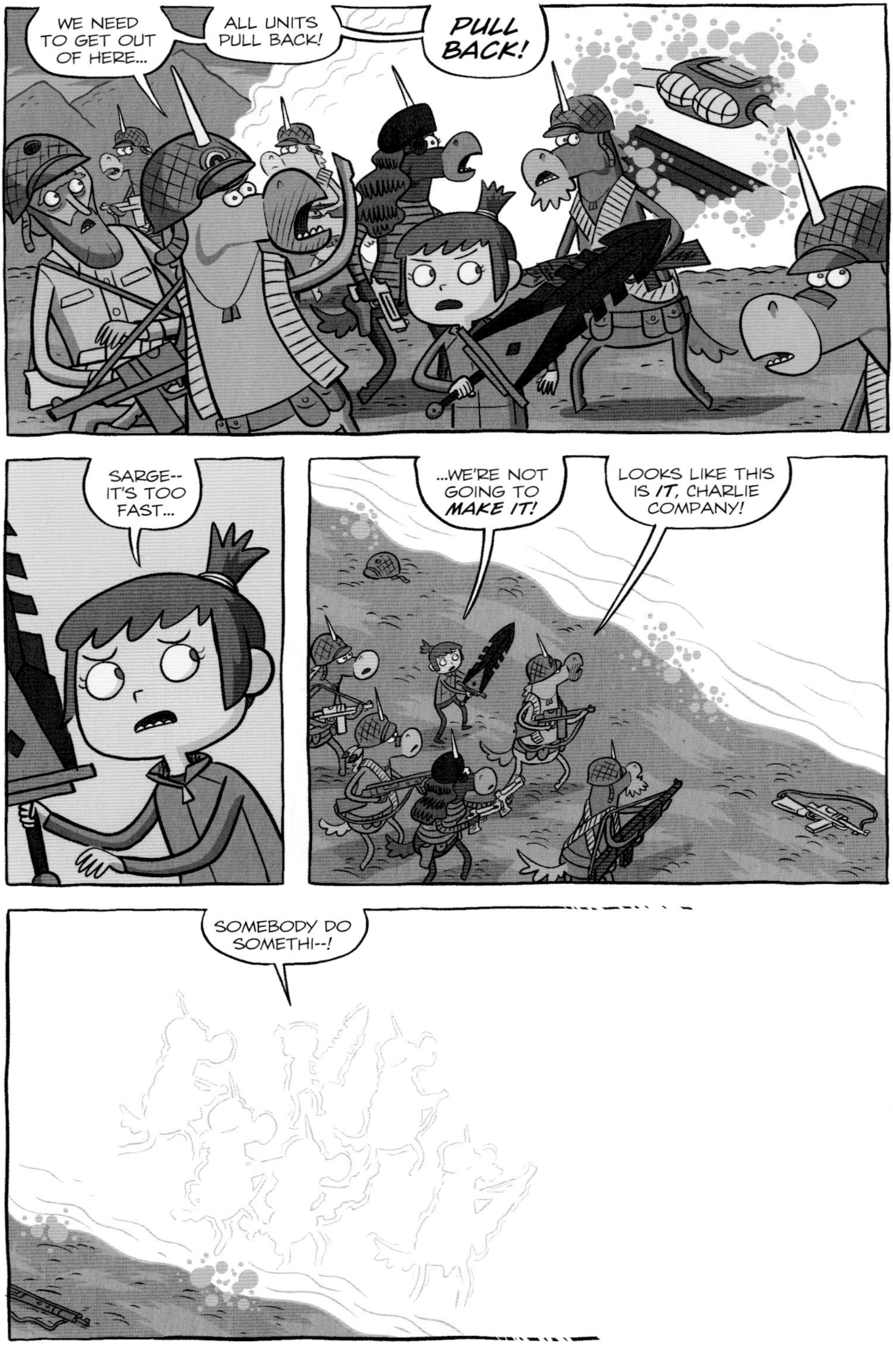
WE NEED TO GET OUT OF HERE...
ALL UNITS PULL BACK!
PULL BACK!
SARGE-- IT'S TOO FAST...
...WE'RE NOT GOING TO MAKE IT!
LOOKS LIKE THIS IS IT, CHARLIE COMPANY!
SOMEBODY DO SOMETHI--!

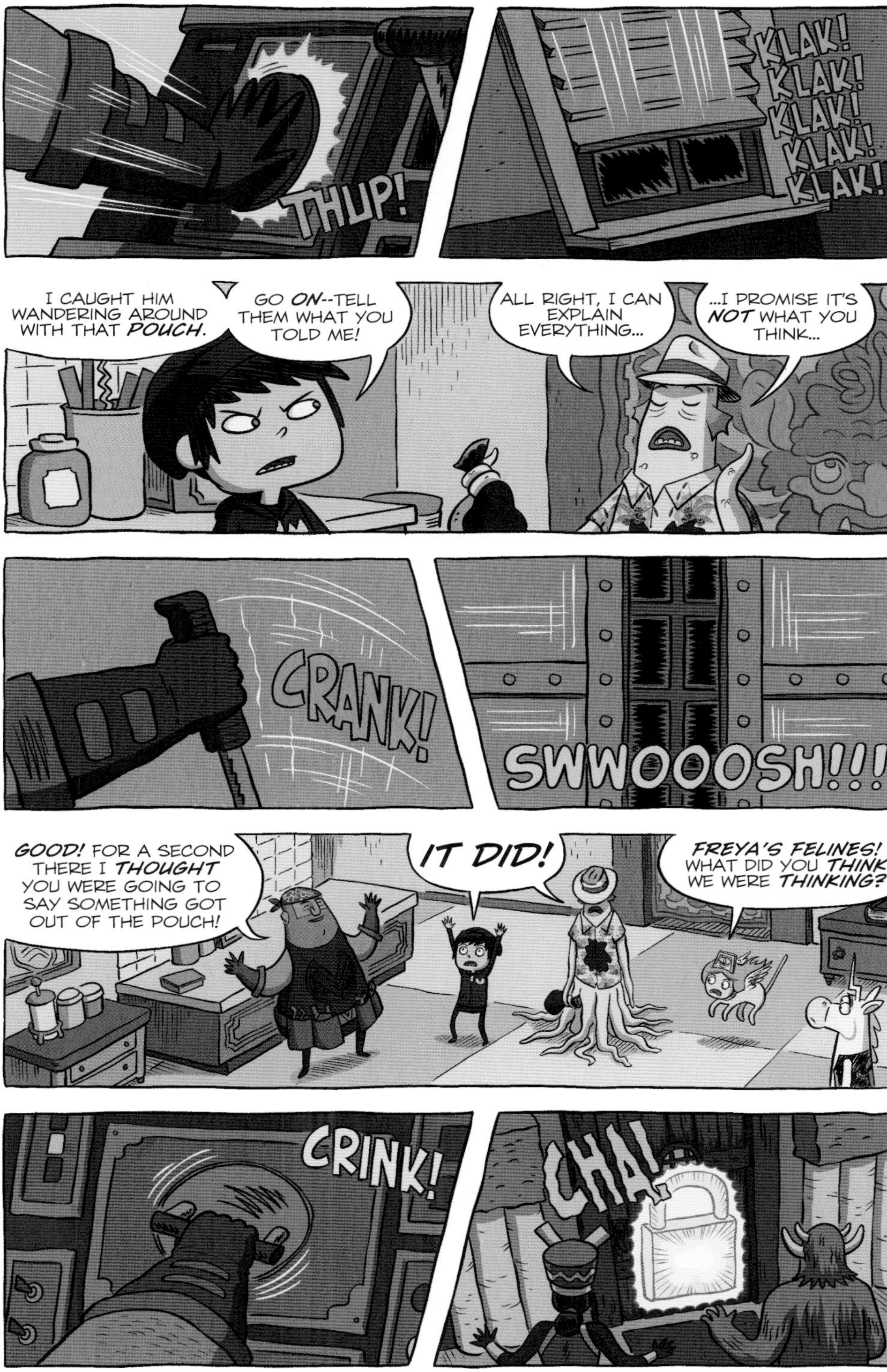
THUP!
KLAK! KLAK! KLAK! KLAK! KLAK!
I CAUGHT HIM WANDERING AROUND WITH THAT *POUCH*.
GO *ON*--TELL THEM WHAT YOU TOLD ME!
ALL RIGHT, I CAN EXPLAIN EVERYTHING...
...I PROMISE IT'S *NOT* WHAT YOU THINK...
CRANK!
SWWOOOSH!!!
GOOD! FOR A SECOND THERE I *THOUGHT* YOU WERE GOING TO SAY SOMETHING GOT OUT OF THE POUCH!
IT DID!
FREYA'S FELINES! WHAT DID YOU *THINK* WE WERE *THINKING?*
CRINK!
CHA!

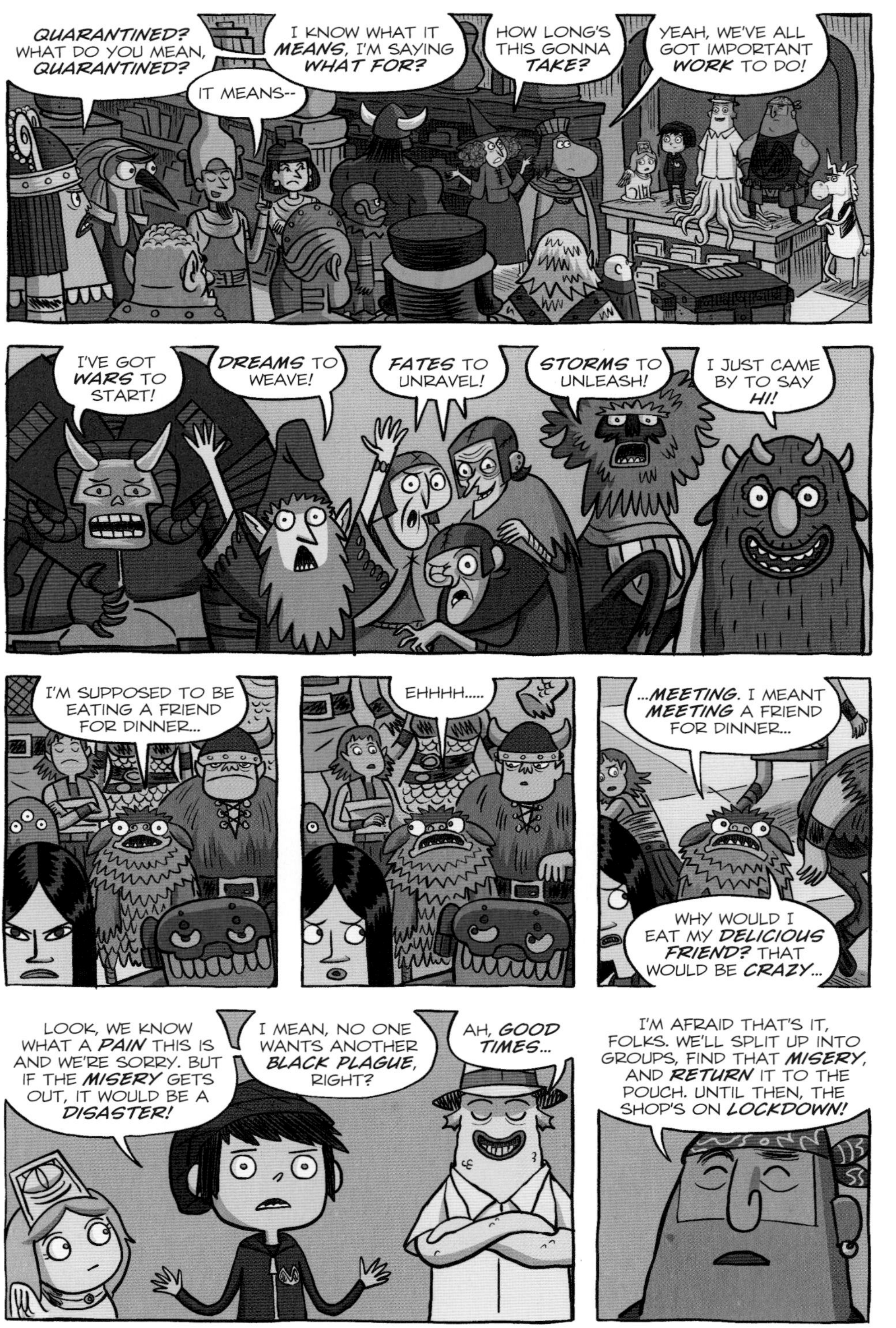

QUARANTINED? WHAT DO YOU MEAN, QUARANTINED?
IT MEANS--
I KNOW WHAT IT MEANS, I'M SAYING WHAT FOR?
HOW LONG'S THIS GONNA TAKE?
YEAH, WE'VE ALL GOT IMPORTANT WORK TO DO!
I'VE GOT WARS TO START!
DREAMS TO WEAVE!
FATES TO UNRAVEL!
STORMS TO UNLEASH!
I JUST CAME BY TO SAY HI!
I'M SUPPOSED TO BE EATING A FRIEND FOR DINNER...
EHHHH.....
...MEETING. I MEANT MEETING A FRIEND FOR DINNER...
WHY WOULD I EAT MY DELICIOUS FRIEND? THAT WOULD BE CRAZY...
LOOK, WE KNOW WHAT A PAIN THIS IS AND WE'RE SORRY. BUT IF THE MISERY GETS OUT, IT WOULD BE A DISASTER!
I MEAN, NO ONE WANTS ANOTHER BLACK PLAGUE, RIGHT?
AH, GOOD TIMES...
I'M AFRAID THAT'S IT, FOLKS. WE'LL SPLIT UP INTO GROUPS, FIND THAT MISERY, AND RETURN IT TO THE POUCH. UNTIL THEN, THE SHOP'S ON LOCKDOWN!

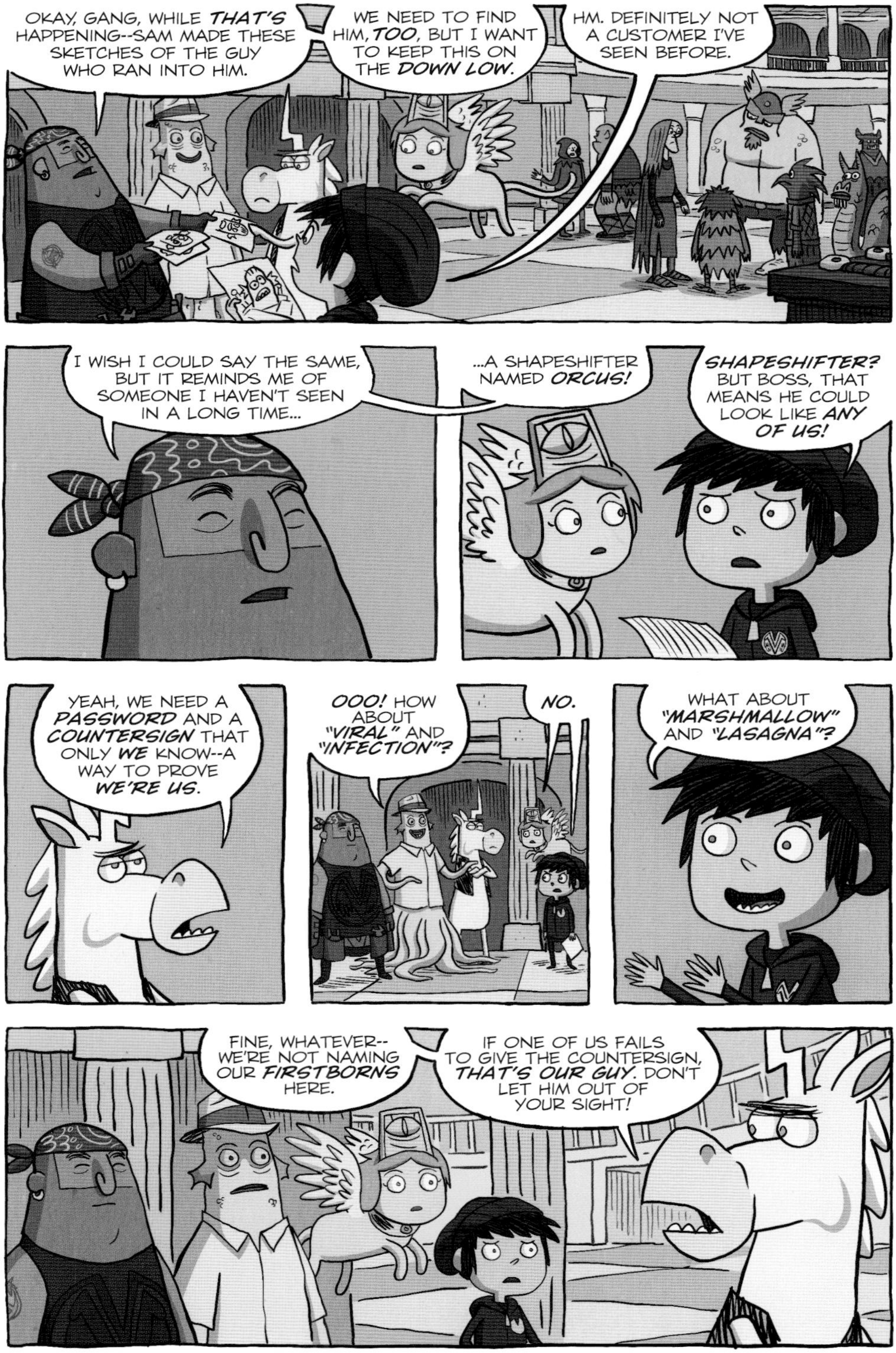
OKAY, GANG, WHILE THAT'S HAPPENING--SAM MADE THESE SKETCHES OF THE GUY WHO RAN INTO HIM.
WE NEED TO FIND HIM, TOO, BUT I WANT TO KEEP THIS ON THE DOWN LOW.
HM. DEFINITELY NOT A CUSTOMER I'VE SEEN BEFORE.
I WISH I COULD SAY THE SAME, BUT IT REMINDS ME OF SOMEONE I HAVEN'T SEEN IN A LONG TIME...
...A SHAPESHIFTER NAMED ORCUS!
SHAPESHIFTER? BUT BOSS, THAT MEANS HE COULD LOOK LIKE ANY OF US!
YEAH, WE NEED A PASSWORD AND A COUNTERSIGN THAT ONLY WE KNOW--A WAY TO PROVE WE'RE US.
OOO! HOW ABOUT "VIRAL" AND "INFECTION"?
NO.
WHAT ABOUT "MARSHMALLOW" AND "LASAGNA"?
FINE, WHATEVER-- WE'RE NOT NAMING OUR FIRSTBORNS HERE.
IF ONE OF US FAILS TO GIVE THE COUNTERSIGN, THAT'S OUR GUY. DON'T LET HIM OUT OF YOUR SIGHT!

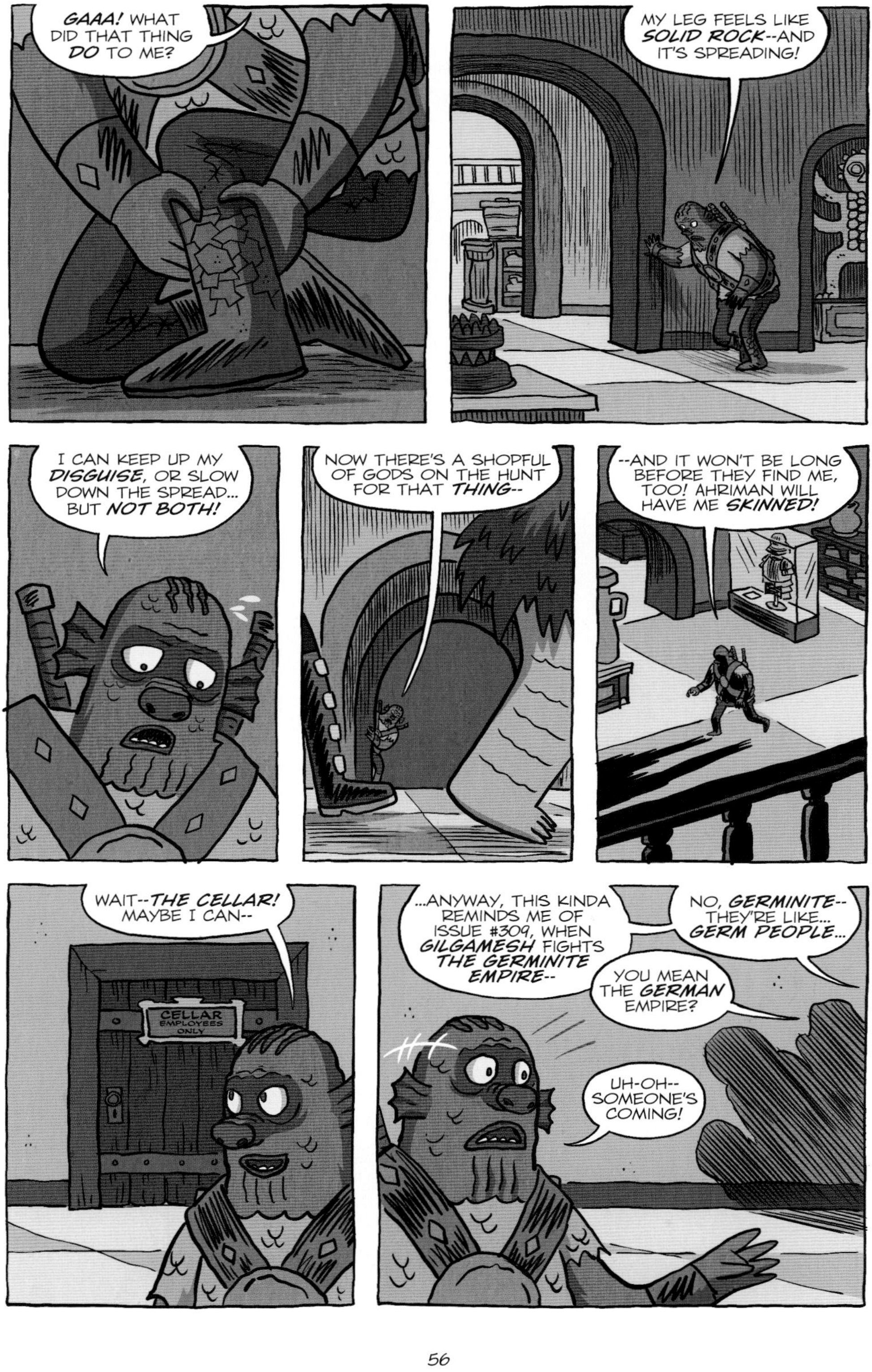
GAAA! WHAT DID THAT THING DO TO ME?
MY LEG FEELS LIKE SOLID ROCK--AND IT'S SPREADING!
I CAN KEEP UP MY DISGUISE, OR SLOW DOWN THE SPREAD... BUT NOT BOTH!
NOW THERE'S A SHOPFUL OF GODS ON THE HUNT FOR THAT THING--
--AND IT WON'T BE LONG BEFORE THEY FIND ME, TOO! AHRIMAN WILL HAVE ME SKINNED!
WAIT--THE CELLAR! MAYBE I CAN--
CELLAR EMPLOYEES ONLY
...ANYWAY, THIS KINDA REMINDS ME OF ISSUE #309, WHEN GILGAMESH FIGHTS THE GERMINITE EMPIRE--
YOU MEAN THE GERMAN EMPIRE?
NO, GERMINITE-- THEY'RE LIKE... GERM PEOPLE...
UH-OH-- SOMEONE'S COMING!

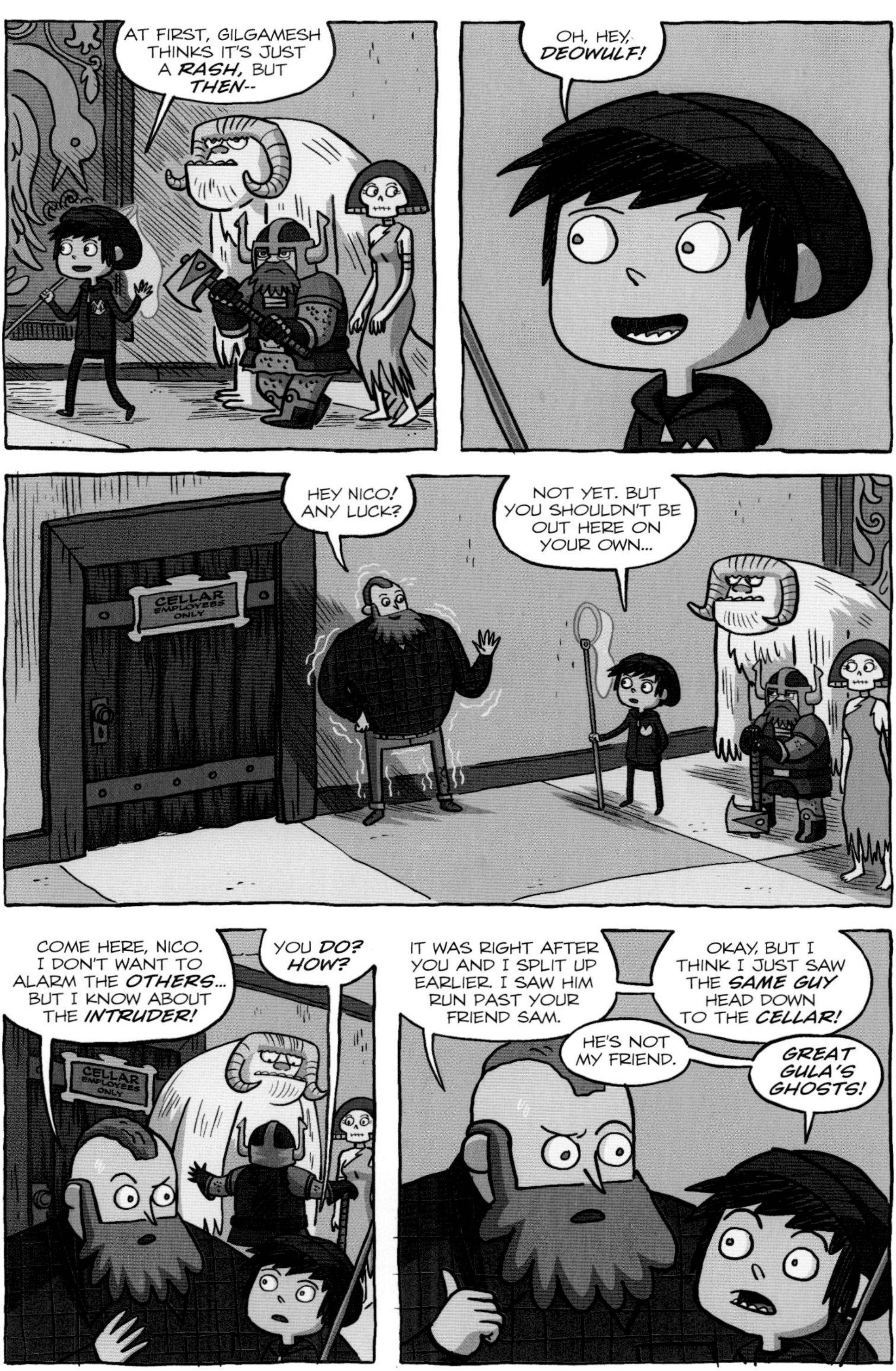

AT FIRST, GILGAMESH THINKS IT'S JUST A RASH, BUT THEN--
OH, HEY, DEOWULF!
HEY NICO! ANY LUCK?
NOT YET. BUT YOU SHOULDN'T BE OUT HERE ON YOUR OWN...
CELLAR EMPLOYEES ONLY
COME HERE, NICO. I DON'T WANT TO ALARM THE OTHERS... BUT I KNOW ABOUT THE INTRUDER!
YOU DO? HOW?
CELLAR EMPLOYEES ONLY
IT WAS RIGHT AFTER YOU AND I SPLIT UP EARLIER. I SAW HIM RUN PAST YOUR FRIEND SAM.
HE'S NOT MY FRIEND.
OKAY, BUT I THINK I JUST SAW THE SAME GUY HEAD DOWN TO THE CELLAR!
GREAT GULA'S GHOSTS!

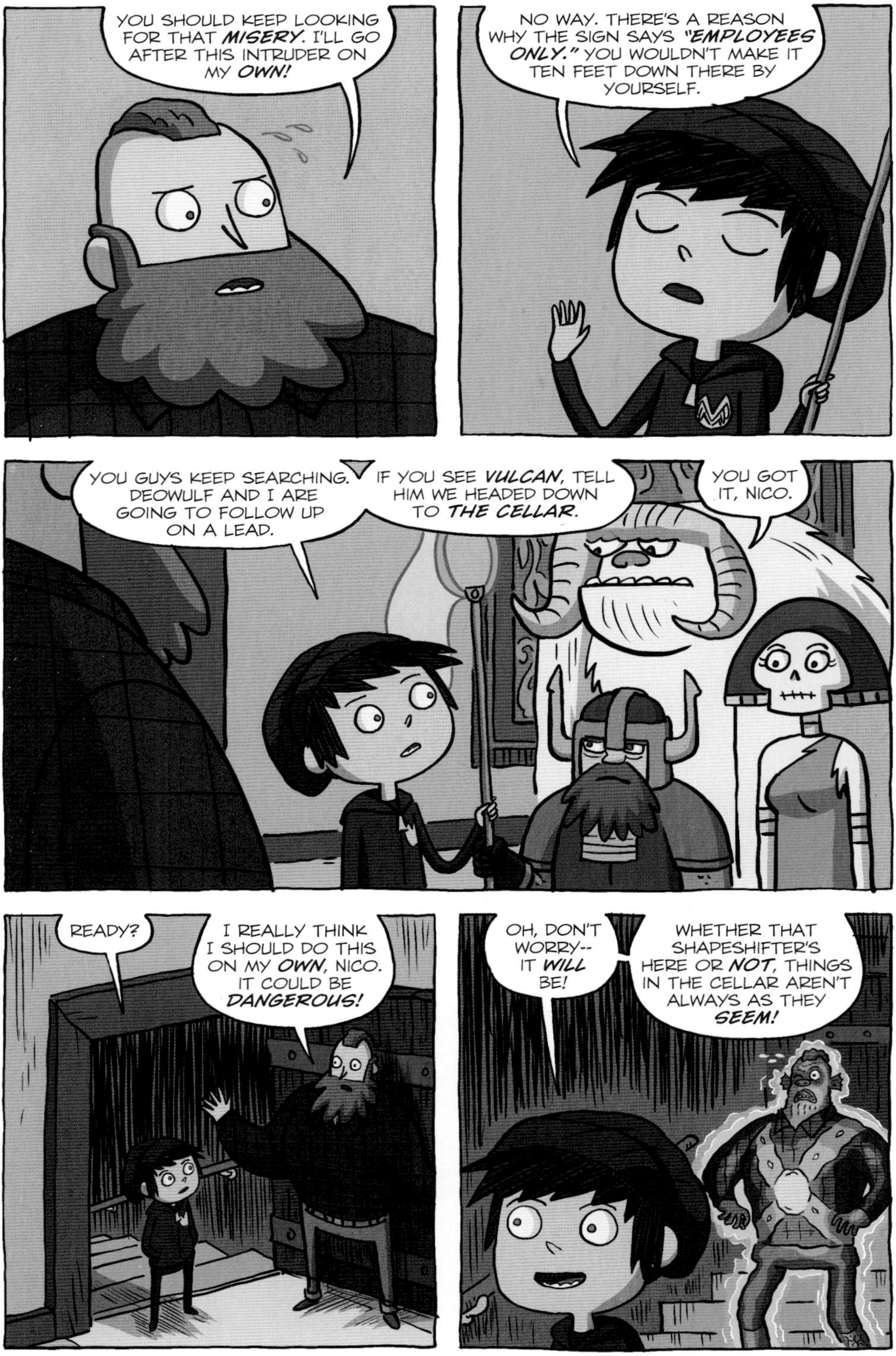
YOU SHOULD KEEP LOOKING FOR THAT MISERY. I'LL GO AFTER THIS INTRUDER ON MY OWN!
NO WAY. THERE'S A REASON WHY THE SIGN SAYS "EMPLOYEES ONLY." YOU WOULDN'T MAKE IT TEN FEET DOWN THERE BY YOURSELF.
YOU GUYS KEEP SEARCHING. DEOWULF AND I ARE GOING TO FOLLOW UP ON A LEAD.
IF YOU SEE VULCAN, TELL HIM WE HEADED DOWN TO THE CELLAR.
YOU GOT IT, NICO.
READY?
I REALLY THINK I SHOULD DO THIS ON MY OWN, NICO. IT COULD BE DANGEROUS!
OH, DON'T WORRY-- IT WILL BE!
WHETHER THAT SHAPESHIFTER'S HERE OR NOT, THINGS IN THE CELLAR AREN'T ALWAYS AS THEY SEEM!

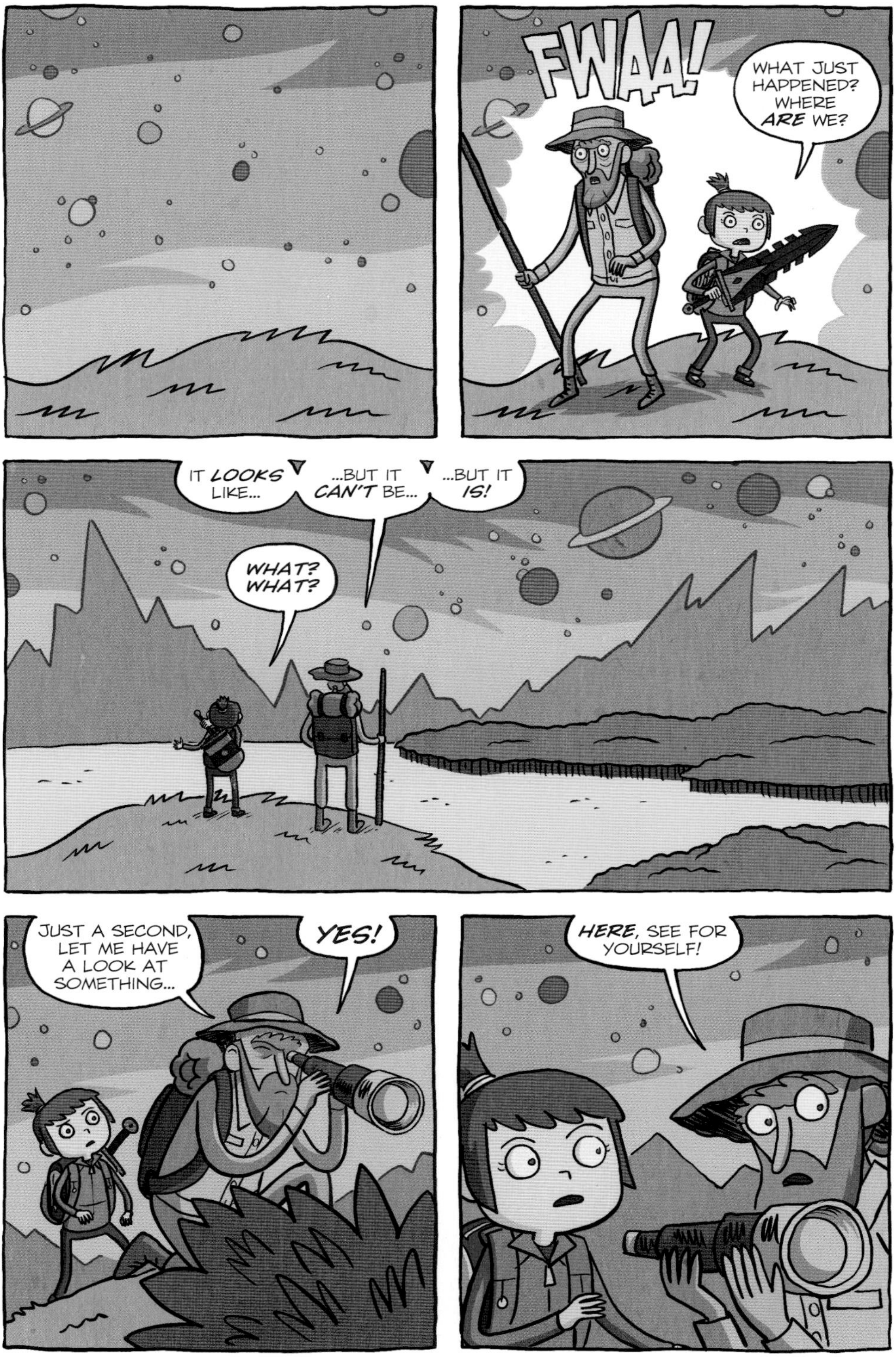
FWAA!
WHAT JUST HAPPENED? WHERE ARE WE?
IT LOOKS LIKE...
...BUT IT CAN'T BE...
...BUT IT IS!
WHAT? WHAT?
JUST A SECOND, LET ME HAVE A LOOK AT SOMETHING...
YES!
HERE, SEE FOR YOURSELF!

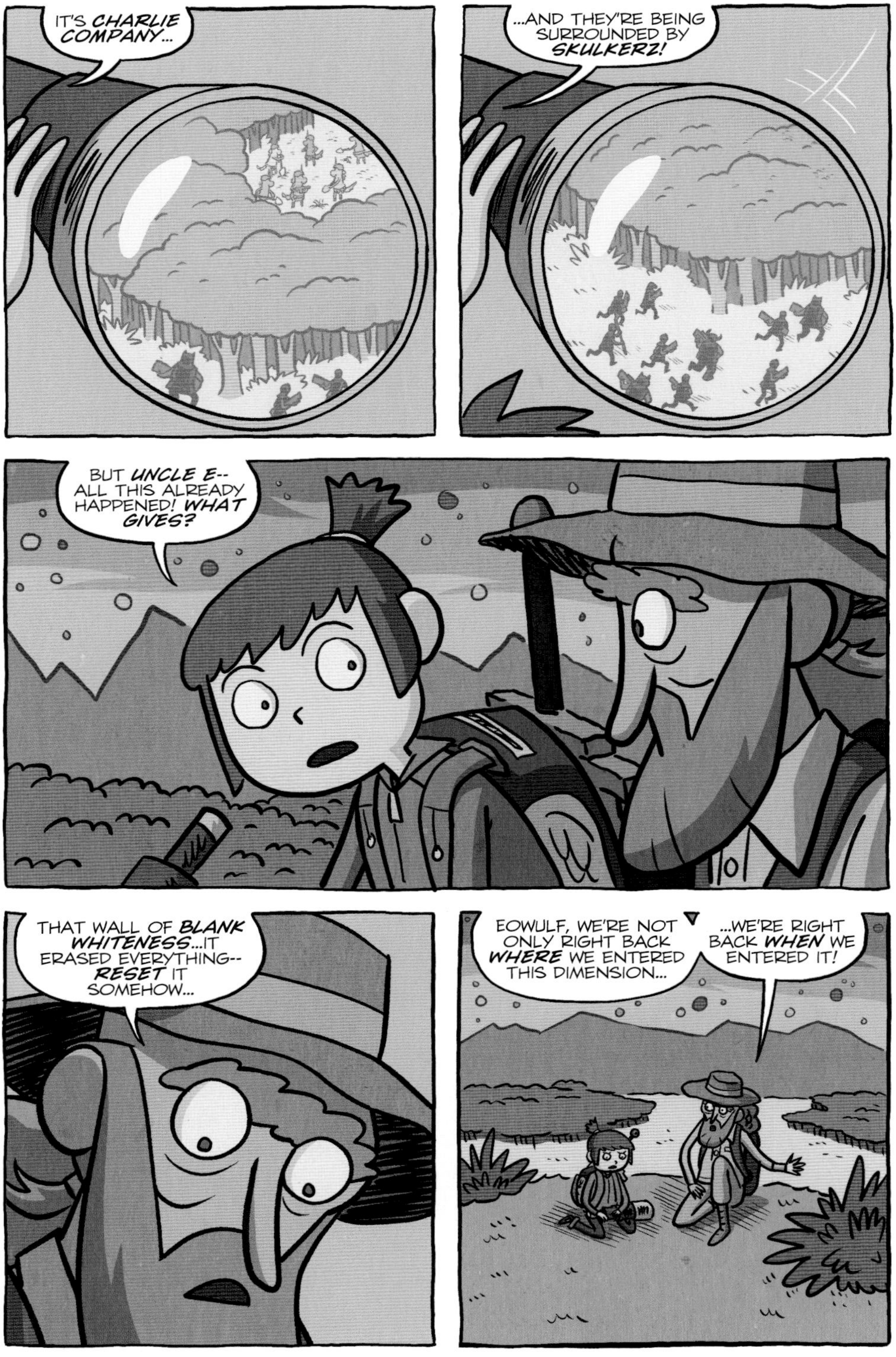
IT'S CHARLIE COMPANY...
...AND THEY'RE BEING SURROUNDED BY SKULKERZ!
BUT UNCLE E-- ALL THIS ALREADY HAPPENED! WHAT GIVES?
THAT WALL OF BLANK WHITENESS...IT ERASED EVERYTHING-- RESET IT SOMEHOW...
EOWULF, WE'RE NOT ONLY RIGHT BACK WHERE WE ENTERED THIS DIMENSION...
...WE'RE RIGHT BACK WHEN WE ENTERED IT!

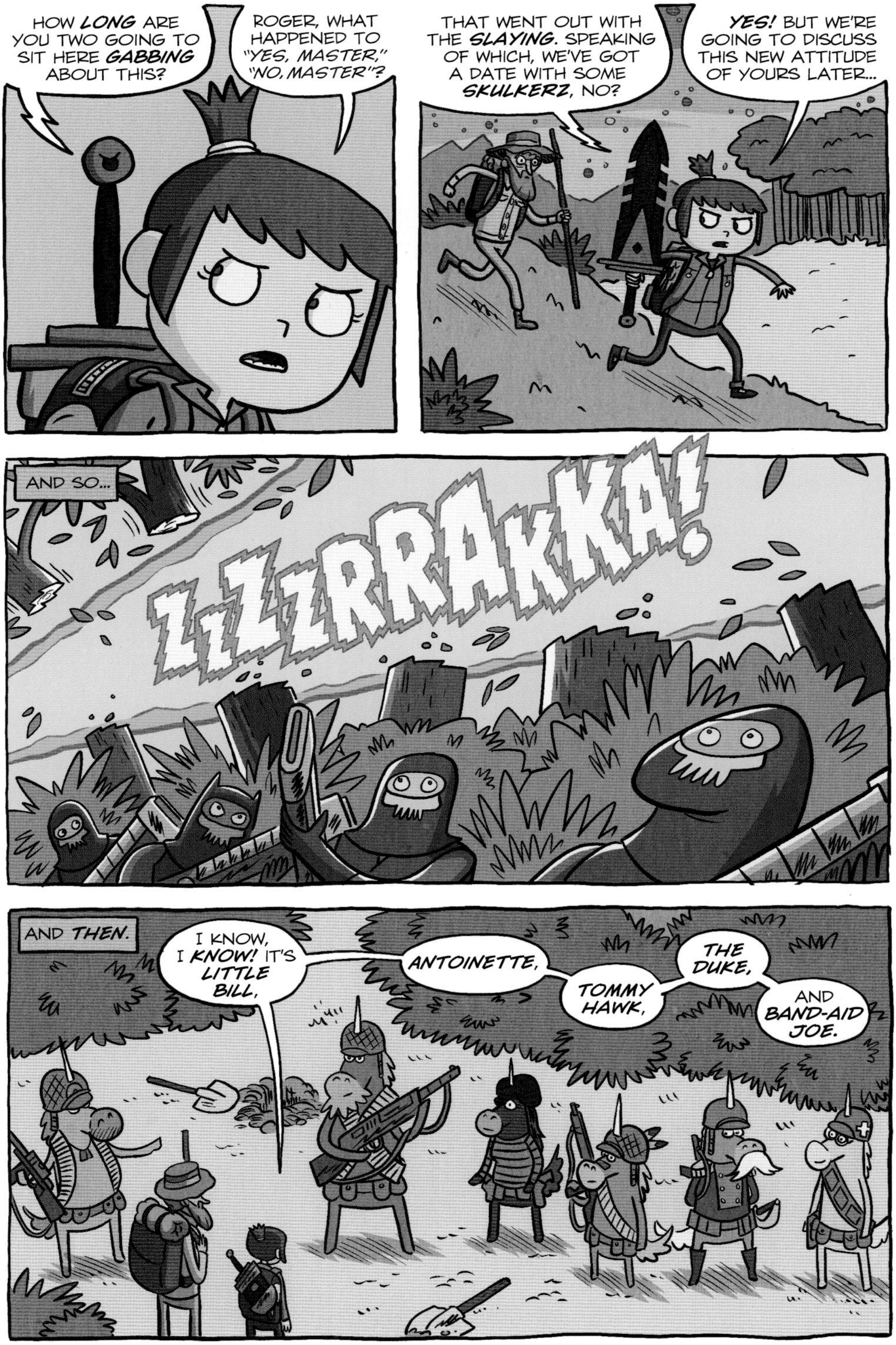

HOW LONG ARE YOU TWO GOING TO SIT HERE GABBING ABOUT THIS?
ROGER, WHAT HAPPENED TO "YES, MASTER," "NO, MASTER"?
THAT WENT OUT WITH THE SLAYING. SPEAKING OF WHICH, WE'VE GOT A DATE WITH SOME SKULKERZ, NO?
YES! BUT WE'RE GOING TO DISCUSS THIS NEW ATTITUDE OF YOURS LATER...
AND SO...
ZzZZRRAKKA!
AND THEN.
I KNOW, I KNOW! IT'S LITTLE BILL,
ANTOINETTE,
TOMMY HAWK,
THE DUKE,
AND BAND-AID JOE.

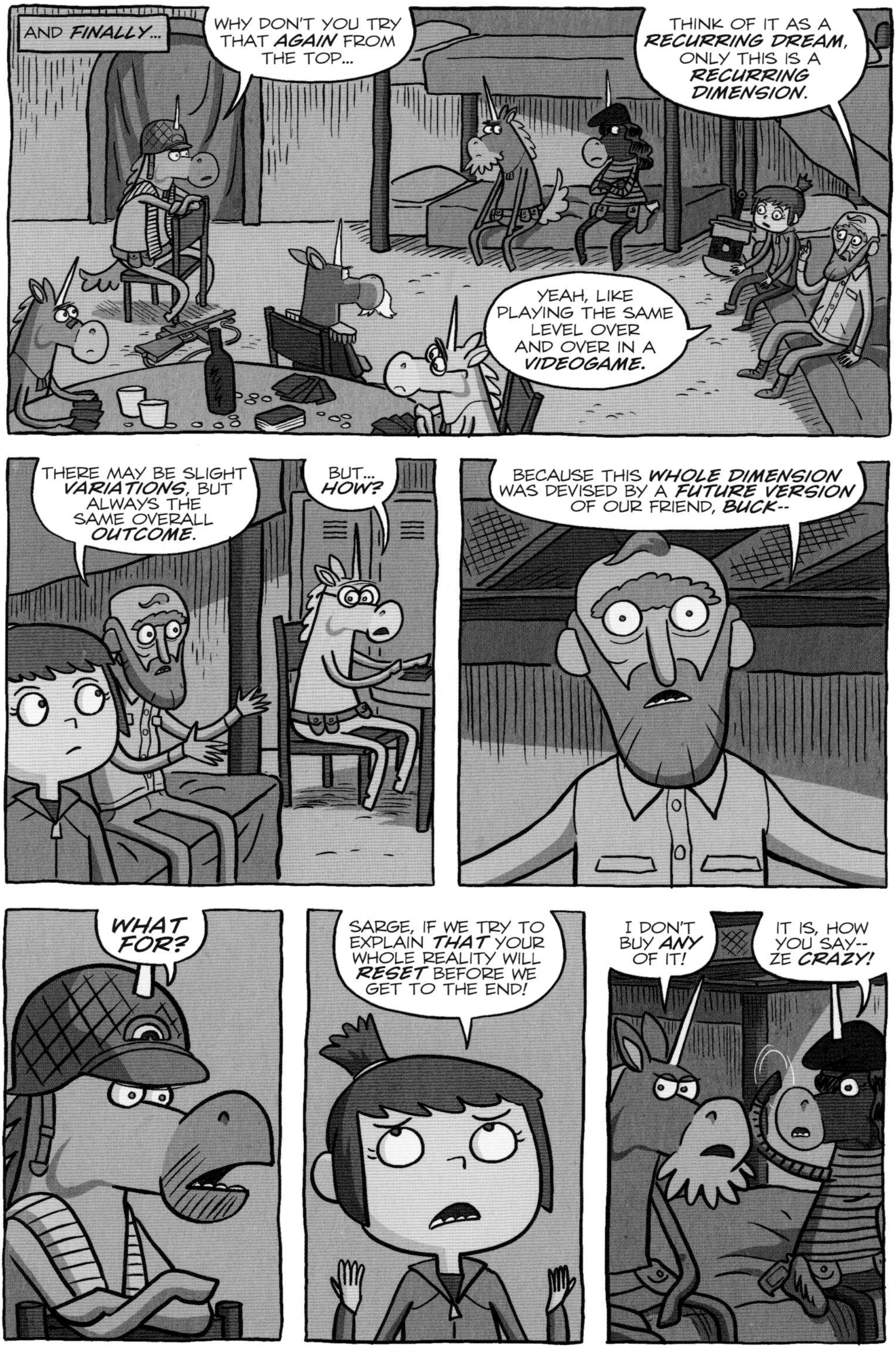
AND *FINALLY*...
WHY DON'T YOU TRY THAT *AGAIN* FROM THE TOP...
THINK OF IT AS A *RECURRING DREAM*, ONLY THIS IS A *RECURRING DIMENSION*.
YEAH, LIKE PLAYING THE SAME LEVEL OVER AND OVER IN A *VIDEOGAME*.
THERE MAY BE SLIGHT *VARIATIONS*, BUT ALWAYS THE SAME OVERALL *OUTCOME*.
BUT... *HOW?*
BECAUSE THIS *WHOLE DIMENSION* WAS DEVISED BY A *FUTURE VERSION* OF OUR FRIEND, *BUCK*--
WHAT FOR?
SARGE, IF WE TRY TO EXPLAIN *THAT* YOUR WHOLE REALITY WILL *RESET* BEFORE WE GET TO THE END!
I DON'T BUY *ANY* OF IT!
IT IS, HOW YOU SAY-- ZE *CRAZY!*

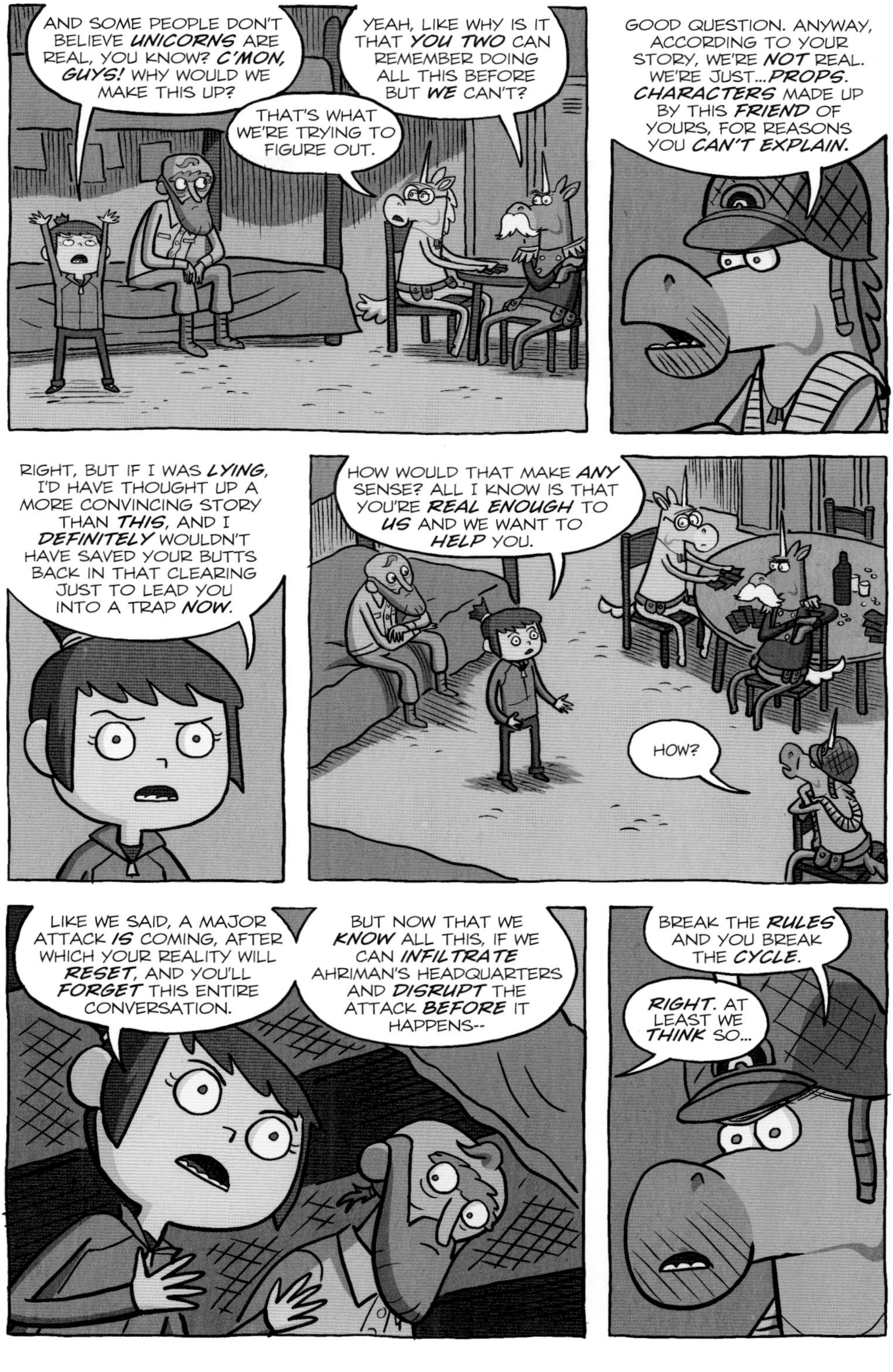
AND SOME PEOPLE DON'T BELIEVE UNICORNS ARE REAL, YOU KNOW? C'MON, GUYS! WHY WOULD WE MAKE THIS UP?
YEAH, LIKE WHY IS IT THAT YOU TWO CAN REMEMBER DOING ALL THIS BEFORE BUT WE CAN'T?
THAT'S WHAT WE'RE TRYING TO FIGURE OUT.
GOOD QUESTION. ANYWAY, ACCORDING TO YOUR STORY, WE'RE NOT REAL. WE'RE JUST...PROPS. CHARACTERS MADE UP BY THIS FRIEND OF YOURS, FOR REASONS YOU CAN'T EXPLAIN.
RIGHT, BUT IF I WAS LYING, I'D HAVE THOUGHT UP A MORE CONVINCING STORY THAN THIS, AND I DEFINITELY WOULDN'T HAVE SAVED YOUR BUTTS BACK IN THAT CLEARING JUST TO LEAD YOU INTO A TRAP NOW.
HOW WOULD THAT MAKE ANY SENSE? ALL I KNOW IS THAT YOU'RE REAL ENOUGH TO US AND WE WANT TO HELP YOU.
HOW?
LIKE WE SAID, A MAJOR ATTACK IS COMING, AFTER WHICH YOUR REALITY WILL RESET, AND YOU'LL FORGET THIS ENTIRE CONVERSATION.
BUT NOW THAT WE KNOW ALL THIS, IF WE CAN INFILTRATE AHRIMAN'S HEADQUARTERS AND DISRUPT THE ATTACK BEFORE IT HAPPENS--
BREAK THE RULES AND YOU BREAK THE CYCLE.
RIGHT. AT LEAST WE THINK SO...

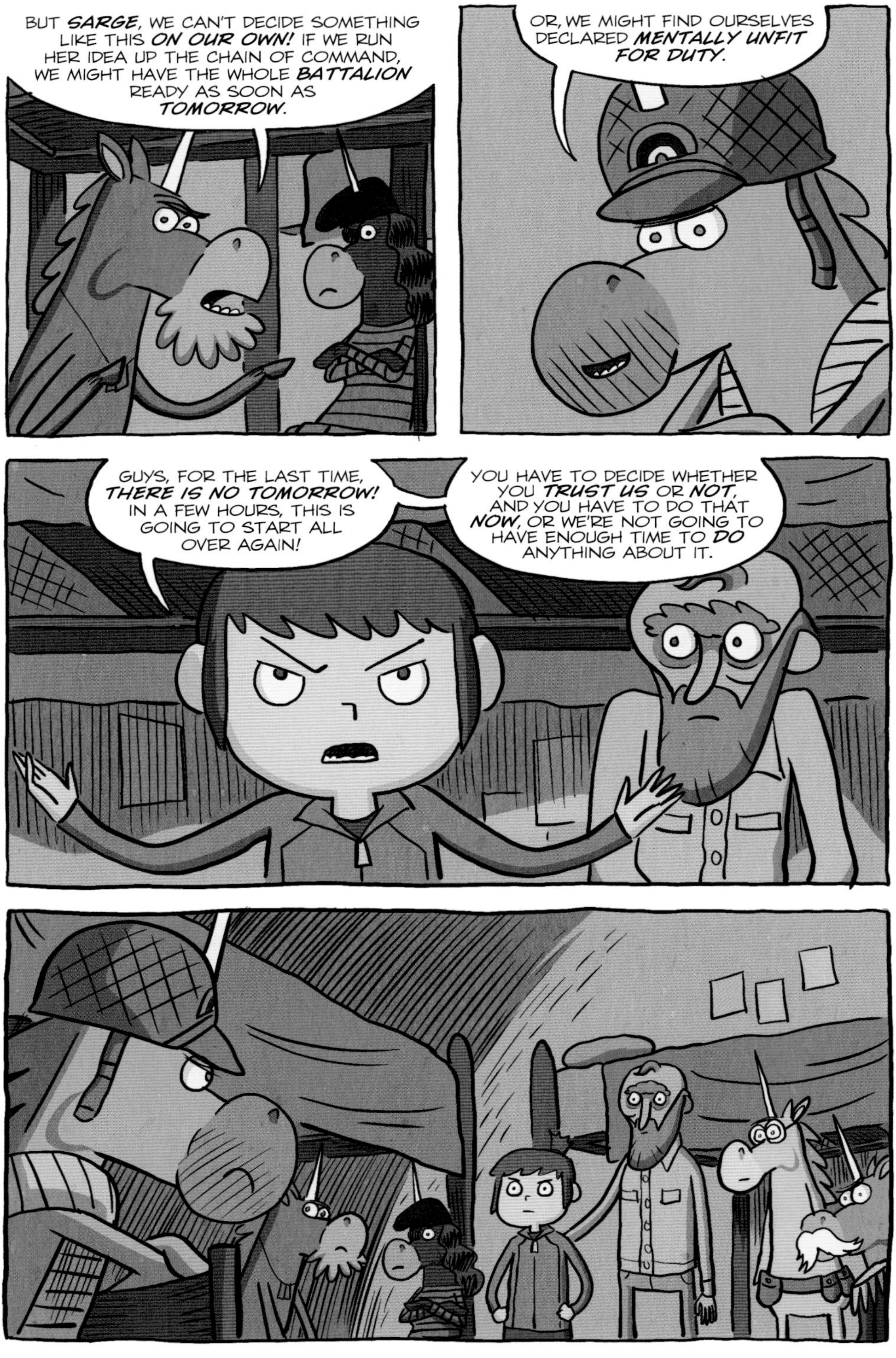
BUT SARGE, WE CAN'T DECIDE SOMETHING LIKE THIS ON OUR OWN! IF WE RUN HER IDEA UP THE CHAIN OF COMMAND, WE MIGHT HAVE THE WHOLE BATTALION READY AS SOON AS TOMORROW.
OR, WE MIGHT FIND OURSELVES DECLARED MENTALLY UNFIT FOR DUTY.
GUYS, FOR THE LAST TIME, THERE IS NO TOMORROW! IN A FEW HOURS, THIS IS GOING TO START ALL OVER AGAIN!
YOU HAVE TO DECIDE WHETHER YOU TRUST US OR NOT, AND YOU HAVE TO DO THAT NOW, OR WE'RE NOT GOING TO HAVE ENOUGH TIME TO DO ANYTHING ABOUT IT.

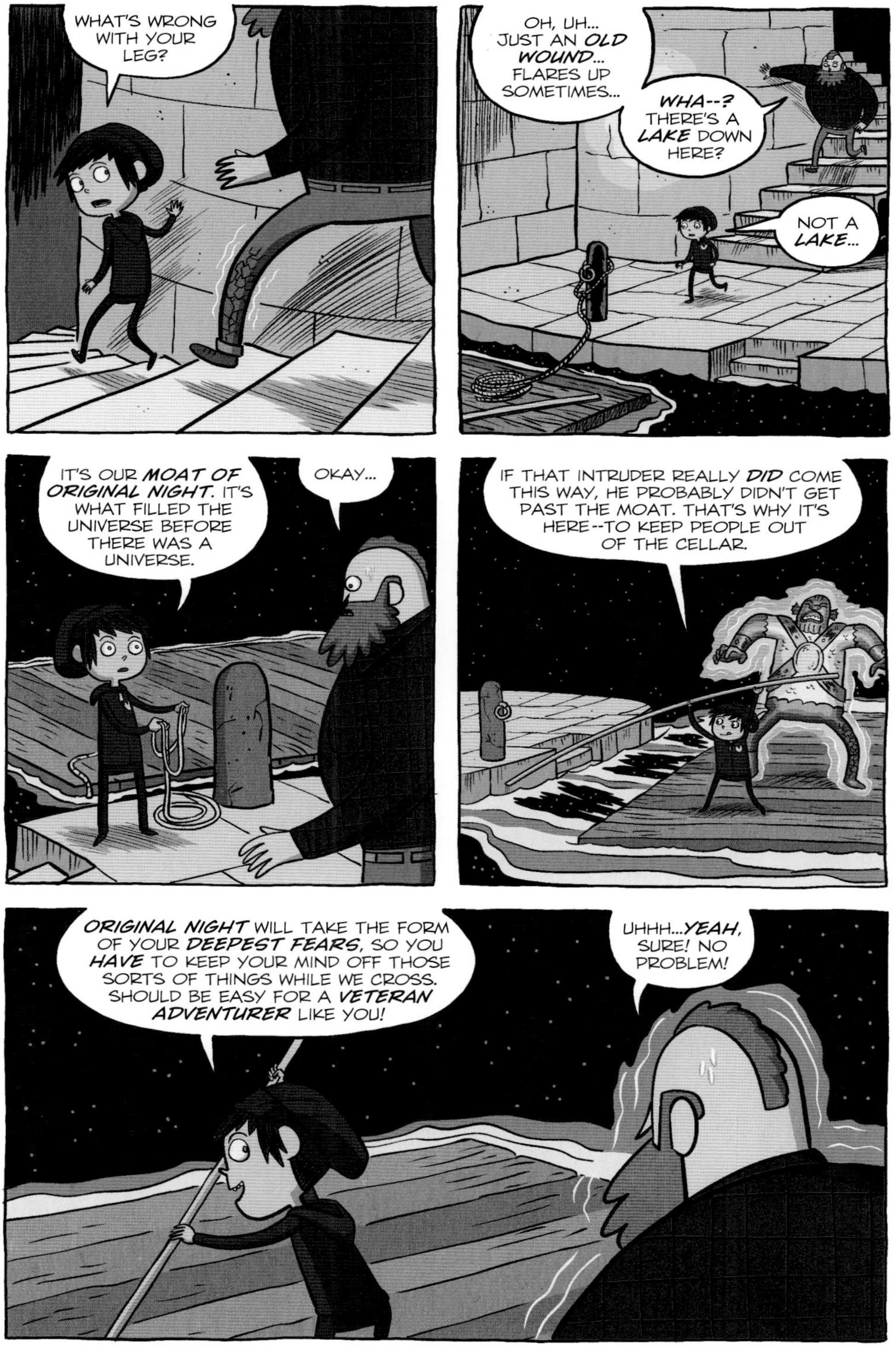
WHAT'S WRONG WITH YOUR LEG?
OH, UH... JUST AN **OLD WOUND**... FLARES UP SOMETIMES...
WHA--? THERE'S A **LAKE** DOWN HERE?
NOT A **LAKE**...
IT'S OUR **MOAT OF ORIGINAL NIGHT**. IT'S WHAT FILLED THE UNIVERSE BEFORE THERE WAS A UNIVERSE.
OKAY...
IF THAT INTRUDER REALLY **DID** COME THIS WAY, HE PROBABLY DIDN'T GET PAST THE MOAT. THAT'S WHY IT'S HERE--TO KEEP PEOPLE OUT OF THE CELLAR.
ORIGINAL NIGHT WILL TAKE THE FORM OF YOUR **DEEPEST FEARS**, SO YOU **HAVE** TO KEEP YOUR MIND OFF THOSE SORTS OF THINGS WHILE WE CROSS. SHOULD BE EASY FOR A **VETERAN ADVENTURER** LIKE YOU!
UHHH...**YEAH**, SURE! NO PROBLEM!

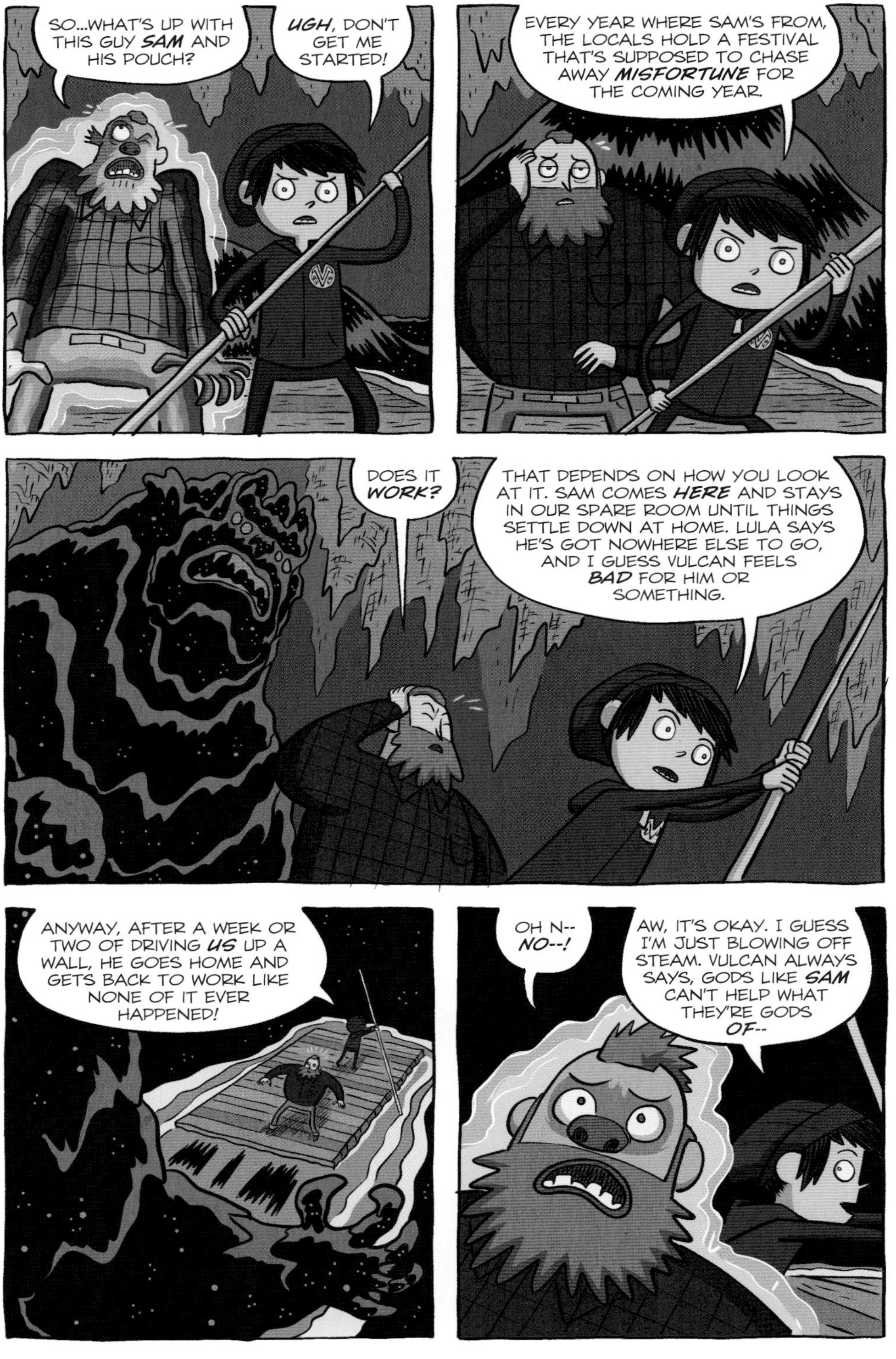
SO...WHAT'S UP WITH THIS GUY SAM AND HIS POUCH?
UGH, DON'T GET ME STARTED!
EVERY YEAR WHERE SAM'S FROM, THE LOCALS HOLD A FESTIVAL THAT'S SUPPOSED TO CHASE AWAY MISFORTUNE FOR THE COMING YEAR.
DOES IT WORK?
THAT DEPENDS ON HOW YOU LOOK AT IT. SAM COMES HERE AND STAYS IN OUR SPARE ROOM UNTIL THINGS SETTLE DOWN AT HOME. LULA SAYS HE'S GOT NOWHERE ELSE TO GO, AND I GUESS VULCAN FEELS BAD FOR HIM OR SOMETHING.
ANYWAY, AFTER A WEEK OR TWO OF DRIVING US UP A WALL, HE GOES HOME AND GETS BACK TO WORK LIKE NONE OF IT EVER HAPPENED!
OH N-- NO--!
AW, IT'S OKAY. I GUESS I'M JUST BLOWING OFF STEAM. VULCAN ALWAYS SAYS, GODS LIKE SAM CAN'T HELP WHAT THEY'RE GODS OF--

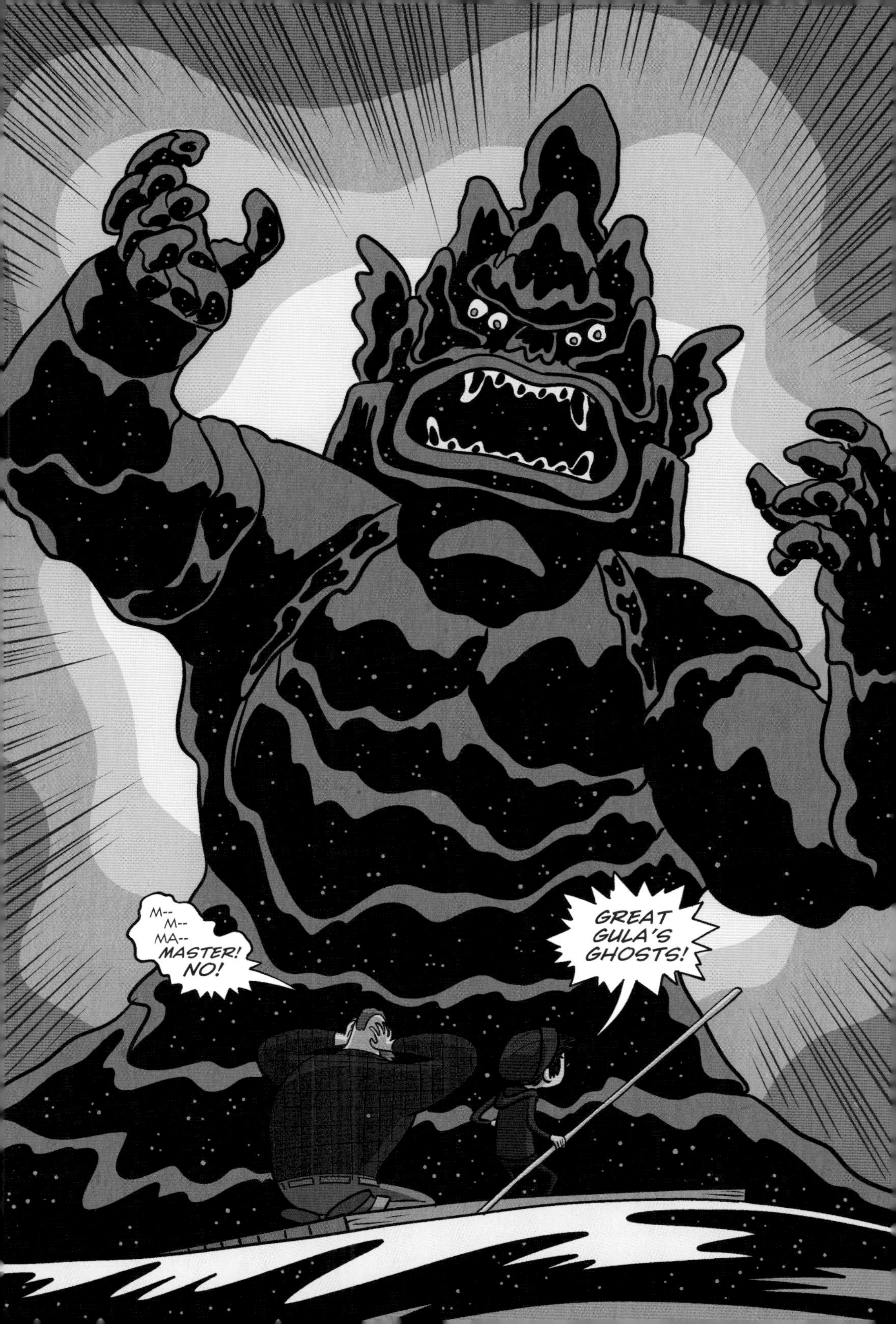
M-- M-- MA-- MASTER! NO!
GREAT GULA'S GHOSTS!

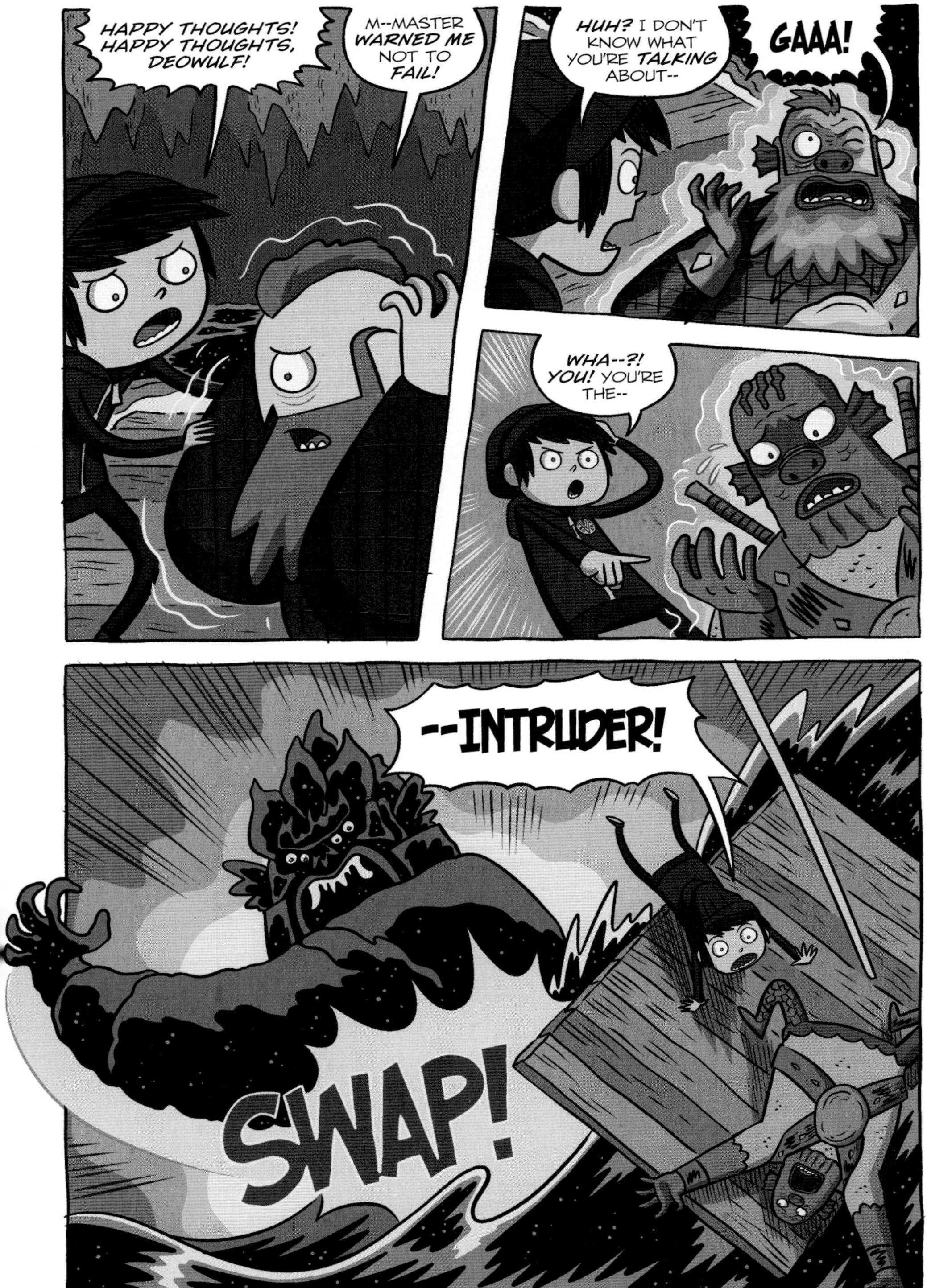
HAPPY THOUGHTS! HAPPY THOUGHTS, DEOWULF!
M--MASTER WARNED ME NOT TO FAIL!
HUH? I DON'T KNOW WHAT YOU'RE TALKING ABOUT--
GAAA!
WHA--?! YOU! YOU'RE THE--
--INTRUDER!
SWAP!

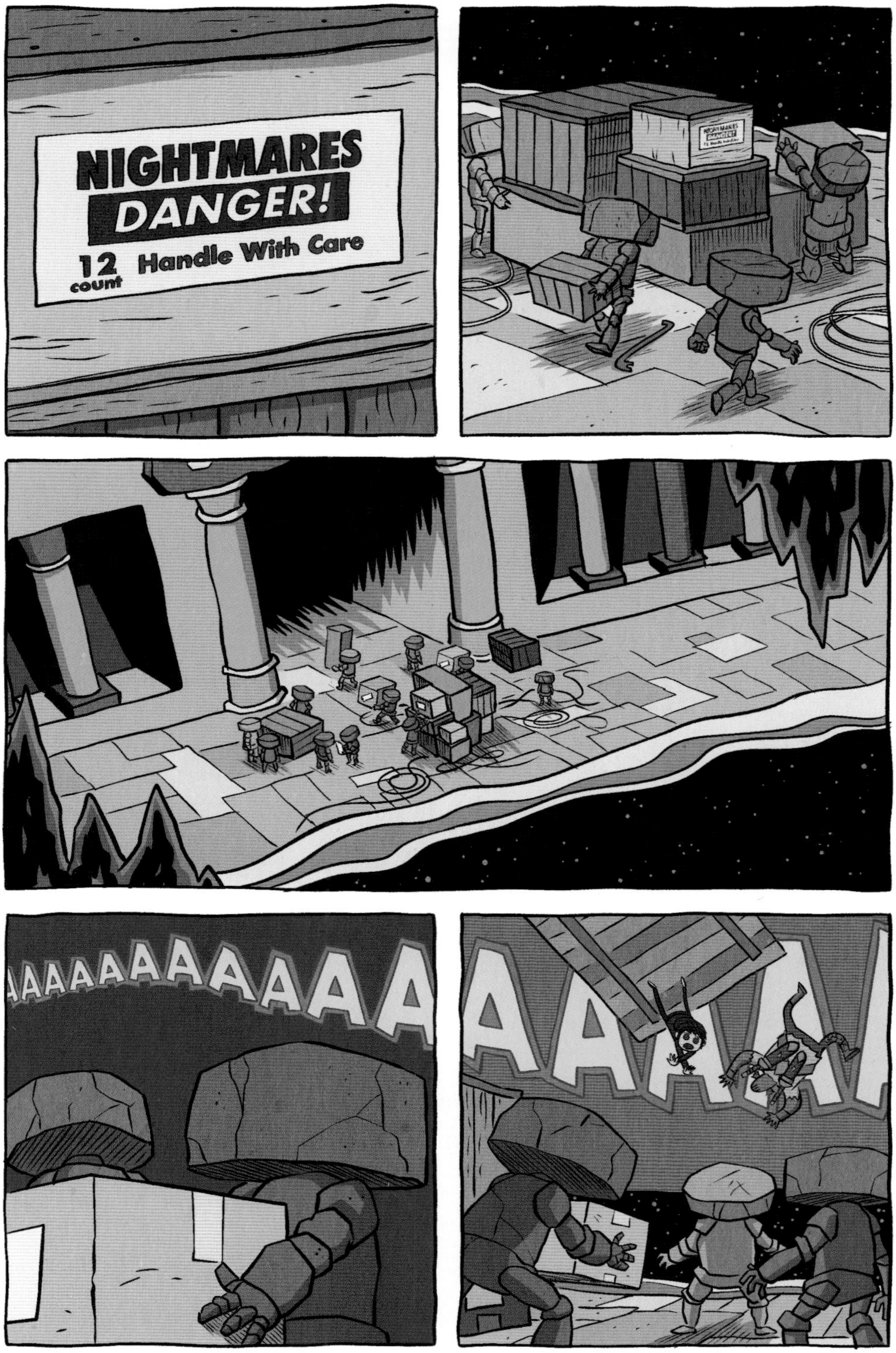
NIGHTMARES
DANGER!
12 count Handle With Care
AAAAAAAAAAAA
AAAAA

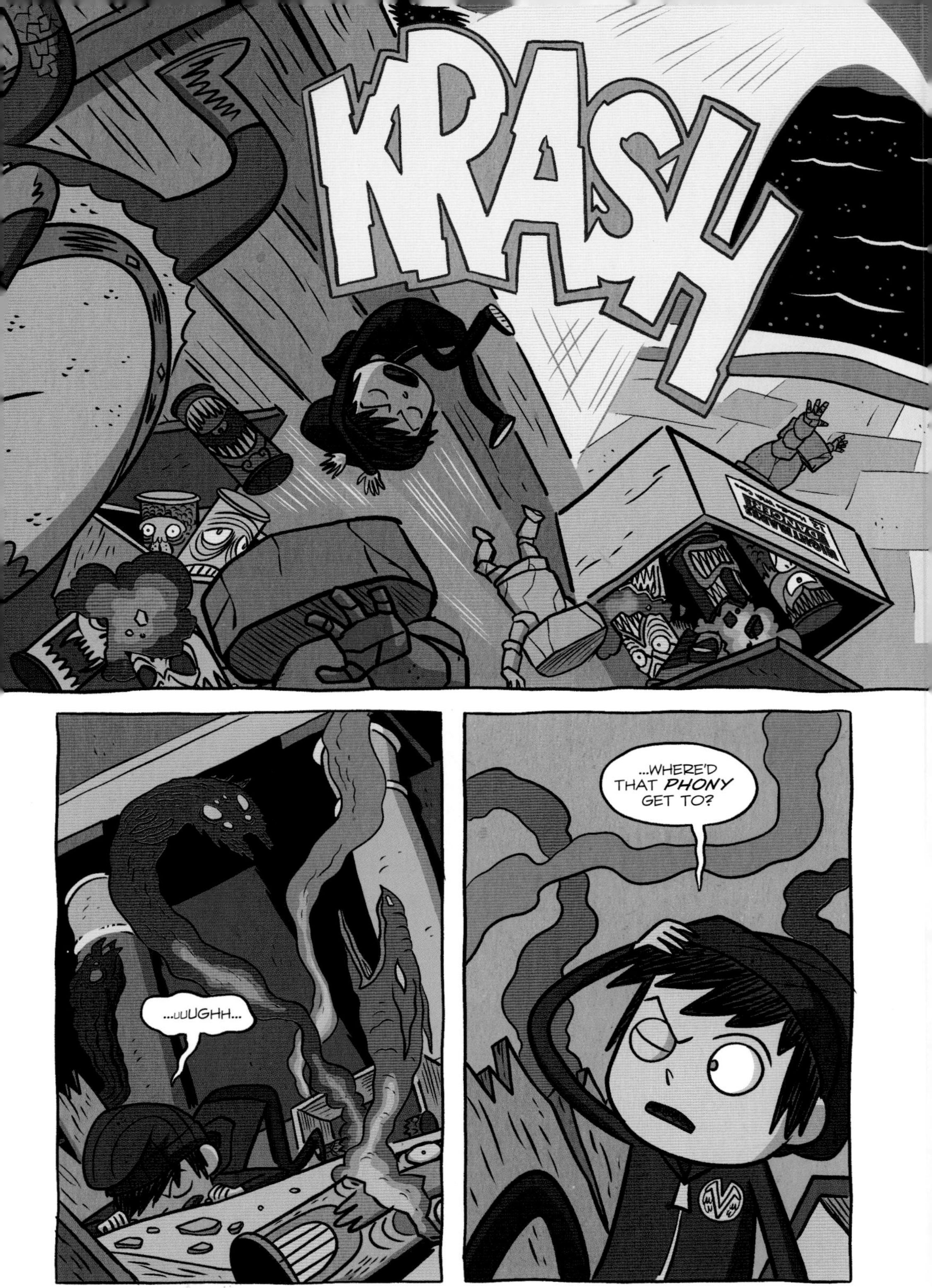
KRASH
...uuUGHH...
...WHERE'D THAT PHONY GET TO?

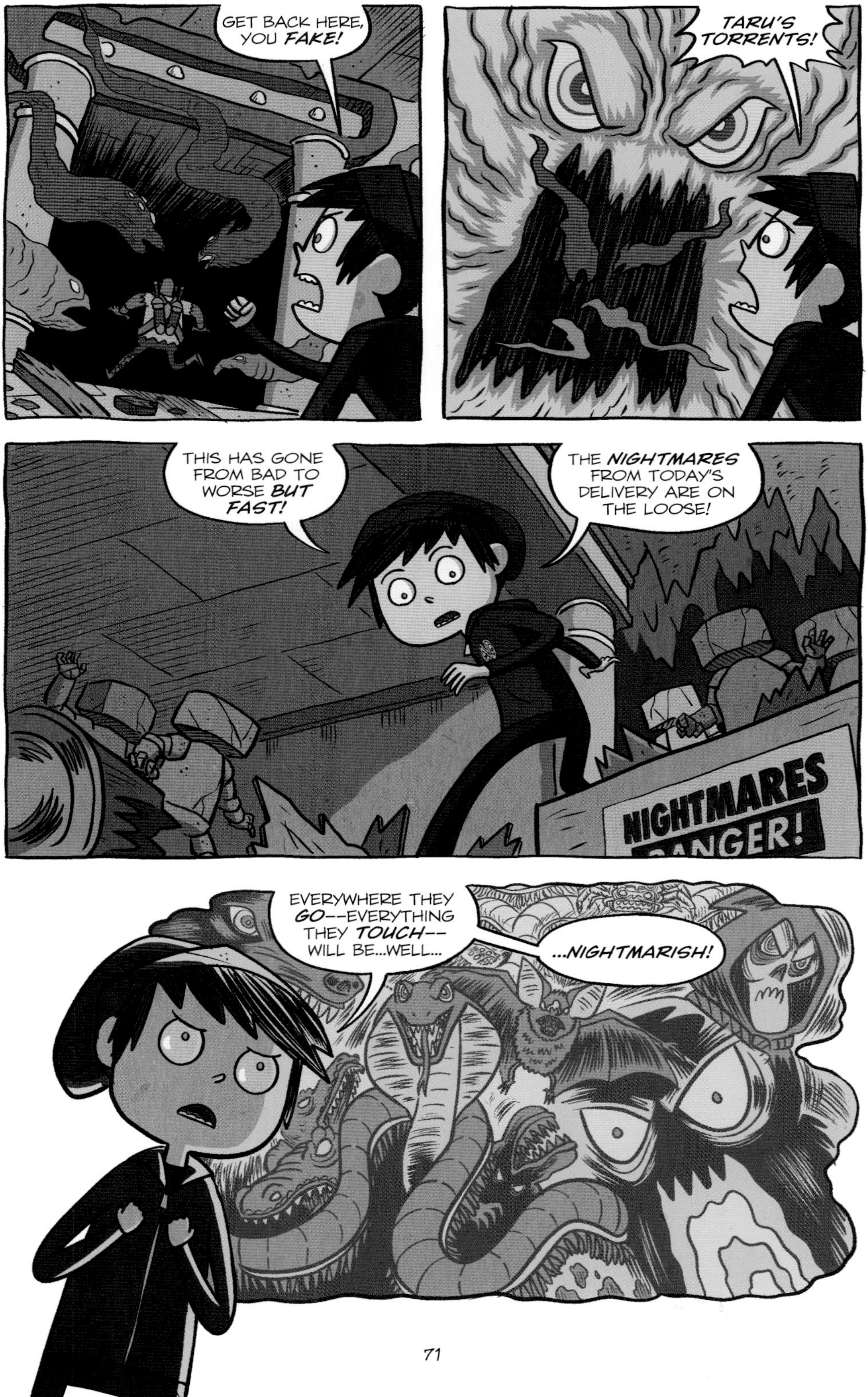
GET BACK HERE, YOU FAKE!
TARU'S TORRENTS!
THIS HAS GONE FROM BAD TO WORSE BUT FAST!
THE NIGHTMARES FROM TODAY'S DELIVERY ARE ON THE LOOSE!
NIGHTMARES
DANGER!
EVERYWHERE THEY GO--EVERYTHING THEY TOUCH--WILL BE...WELL...
...NIGHTMARISH!

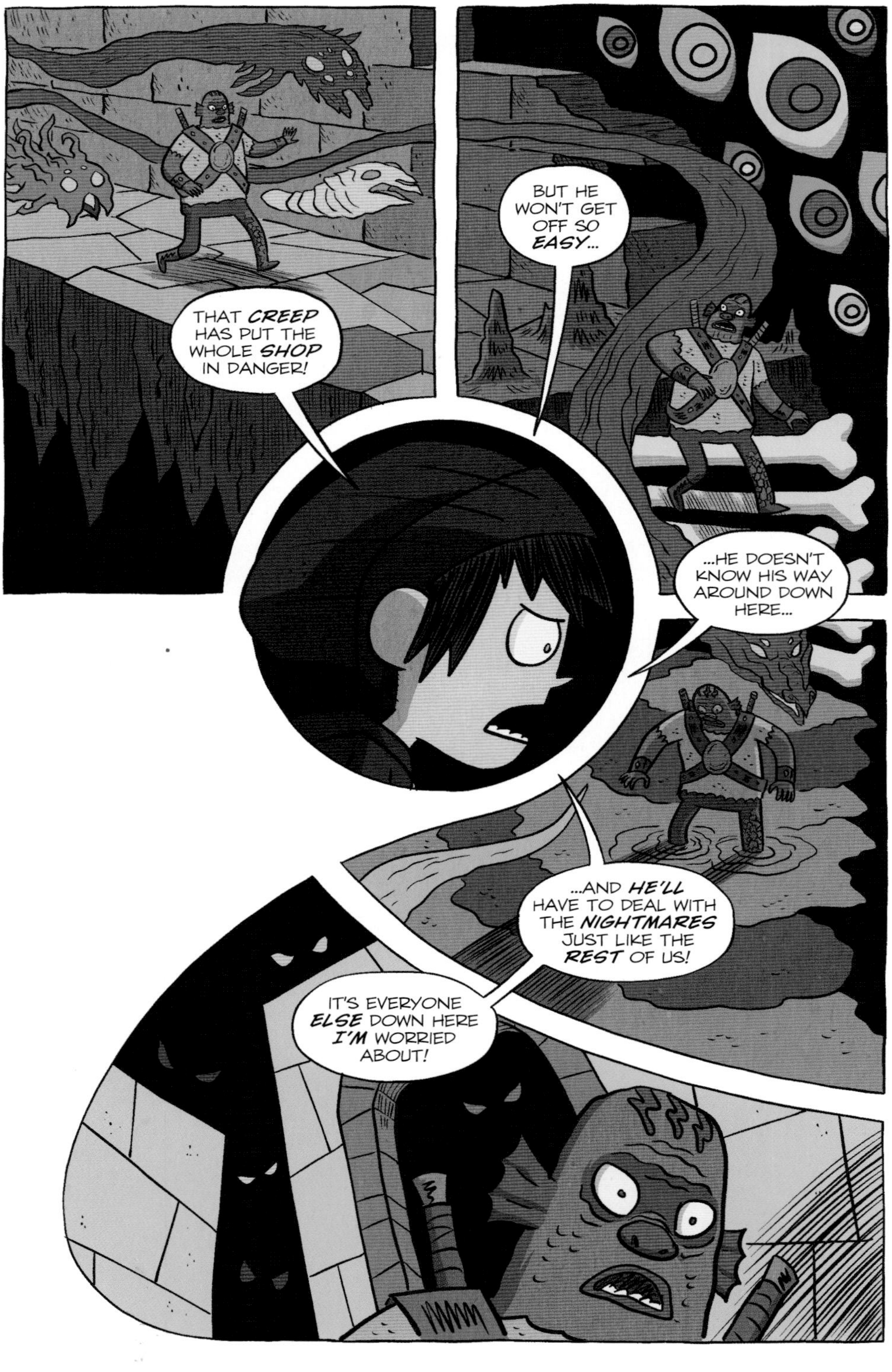
THAT CREEP HAS PUT THE WHOLE SHOP IN DANGER!
BUT HE WON'T GET OFF SO EASY...
...HE DOESN'T KNOW HIS WAY AROUND DOWN HERE...
...AND HE'LL HAVE TO DEAL WITH THE NIGHTMARES JUST LIKE THE REST OF US!
IT'S EVERYONE ELSE DOWN HERE I'M WORRIED ABOUT!

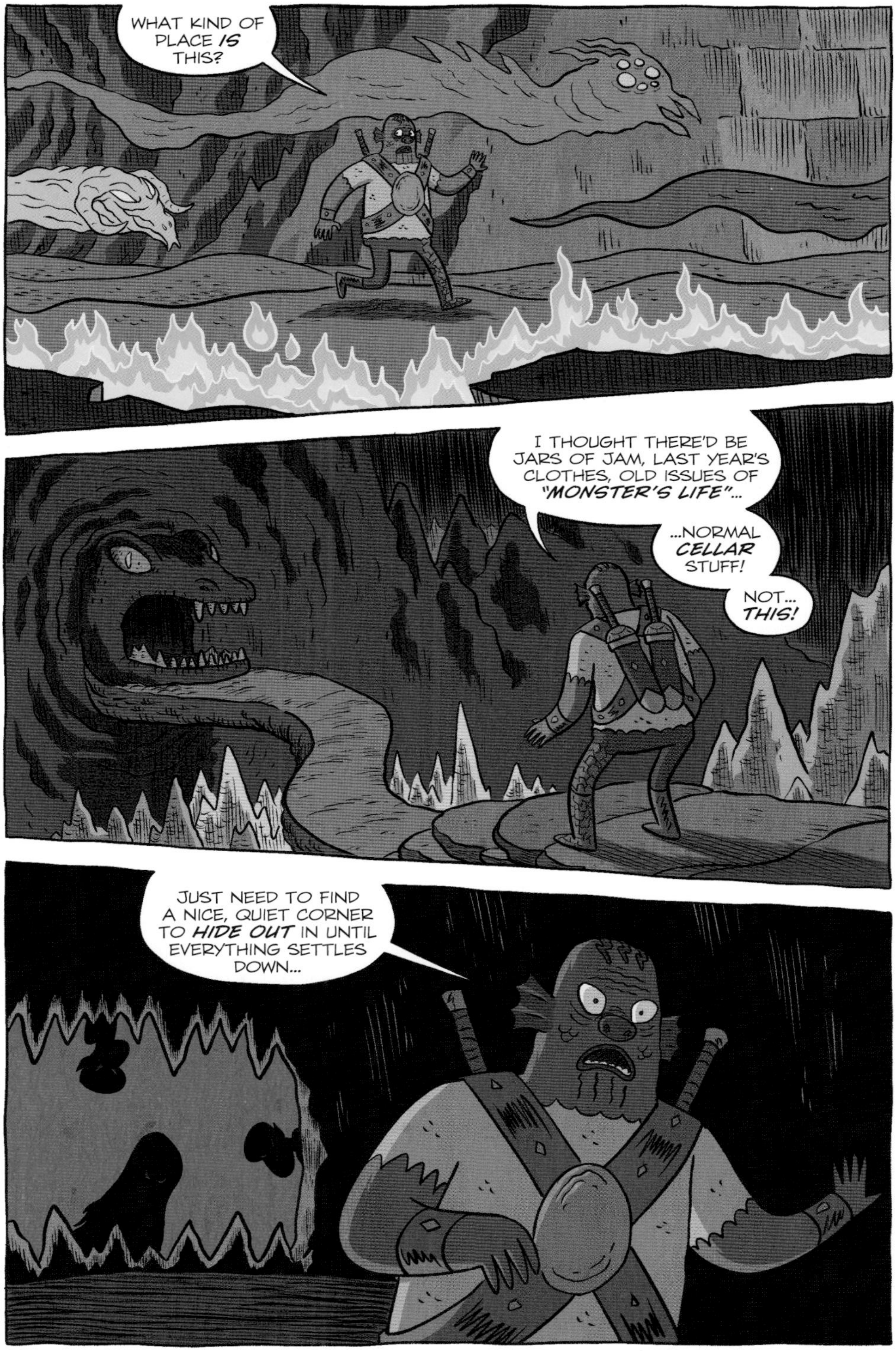
WHAT KIND OF PLACE IS THIS?
I THOUGHT THERE'D BE JARS OF JAM, LAST YEAR'S CLOTHES, OLD ISSUES OF "MONSTER'S LIFE"...
...NORMAL CELLAR STUFF!
NOT... THIS!
JUST NEED TO FIND A NICE, QUIET CORNER TO HIDE OUT IN UNTIL EVERYTHING SETTLES DOWN...

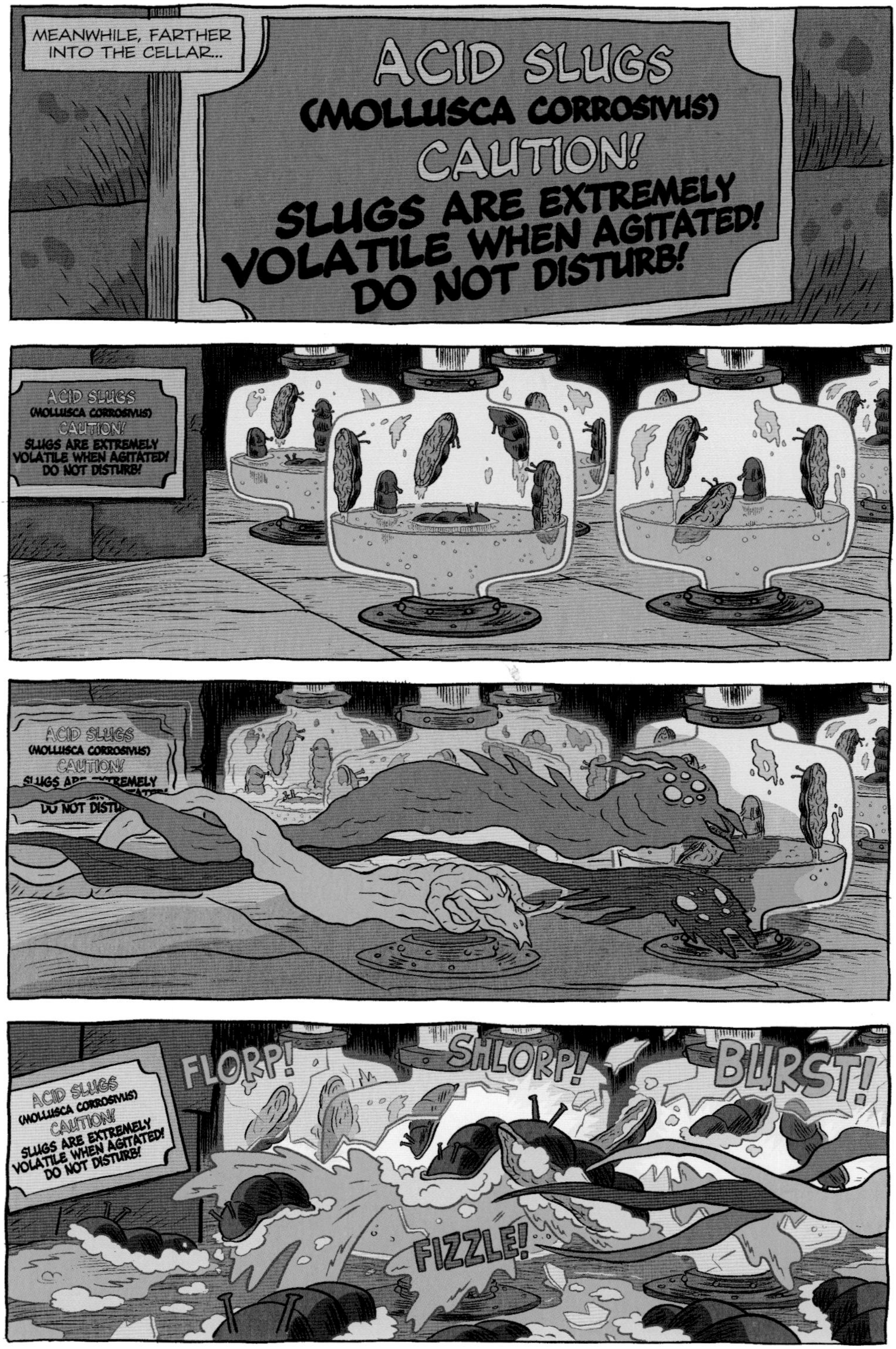
MEANWHILE, FARTHER INTO THE CELLAR...
ACID SLUGS
(MOLLUSCA CORROSIVUS)
CAUTION!
SLUGS ARE EXTREMELY VOLATILE WHEN AGITATED! DO NOT DISTURB!
ACID SLUGS
(MOLLUSCA CORROSIVUS)
CAUTION!
SLUGS ARE EXTREMELY VOLATILE WHEN AGITATED! DO NOT DISTURB!
ACID SLUGS
(MOLLUSCA CORROSIVUS)
CAUTION!
SLUGS ARE EXTREMELY
DO NOT DISTU
ACID SLUGS
(MOLLUSCA CORROSIVUS)
CAUTION!
SLUGS ARE EXTREMELY VOLATILE WHEN AGITATED! DO NOT DISTURB!
FLORP!
SHLORP!
BURST!
FIZZLE!

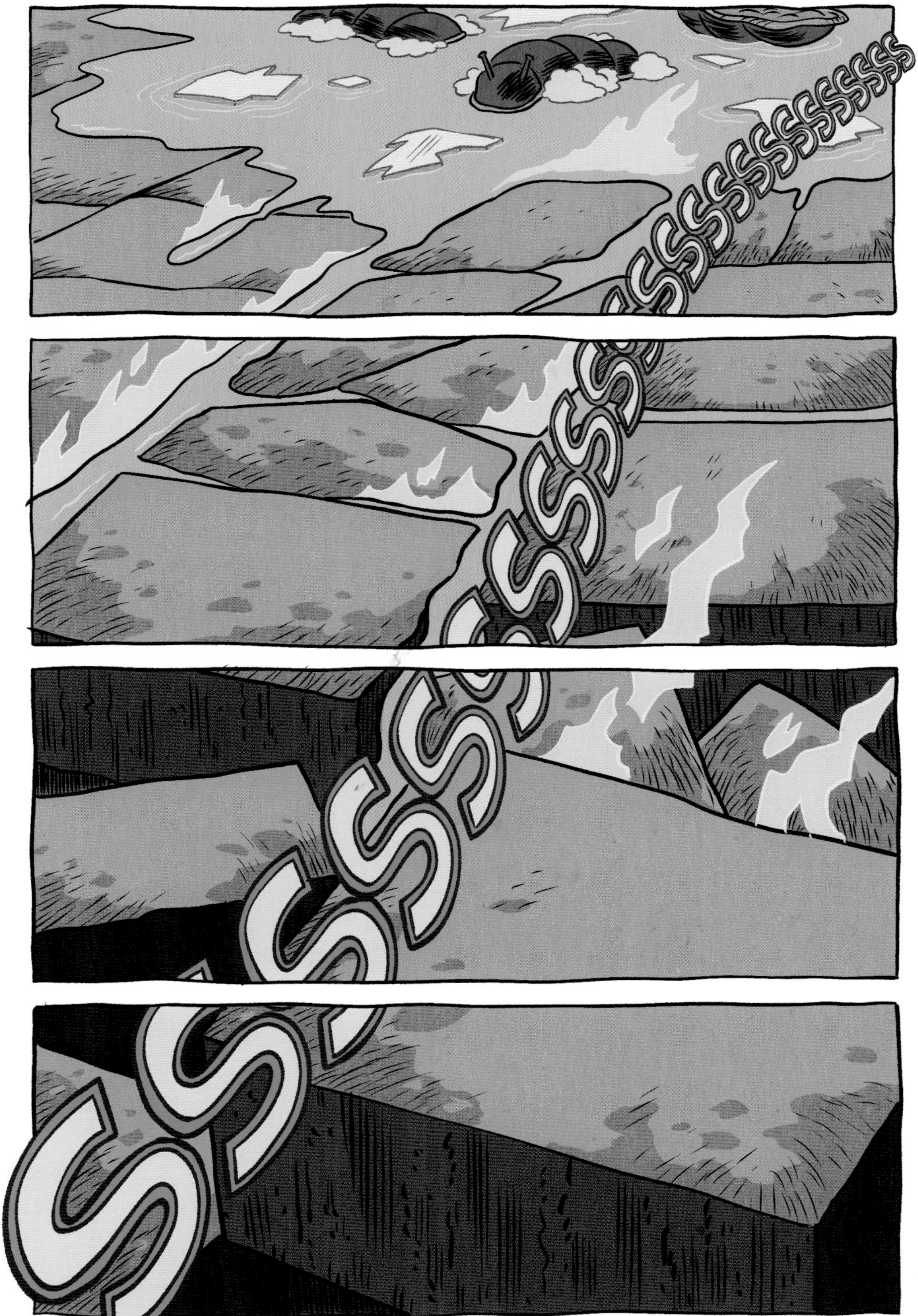
SSSSSSSSSSSSSSSSSSSSSSSSSSSSSSSSSS

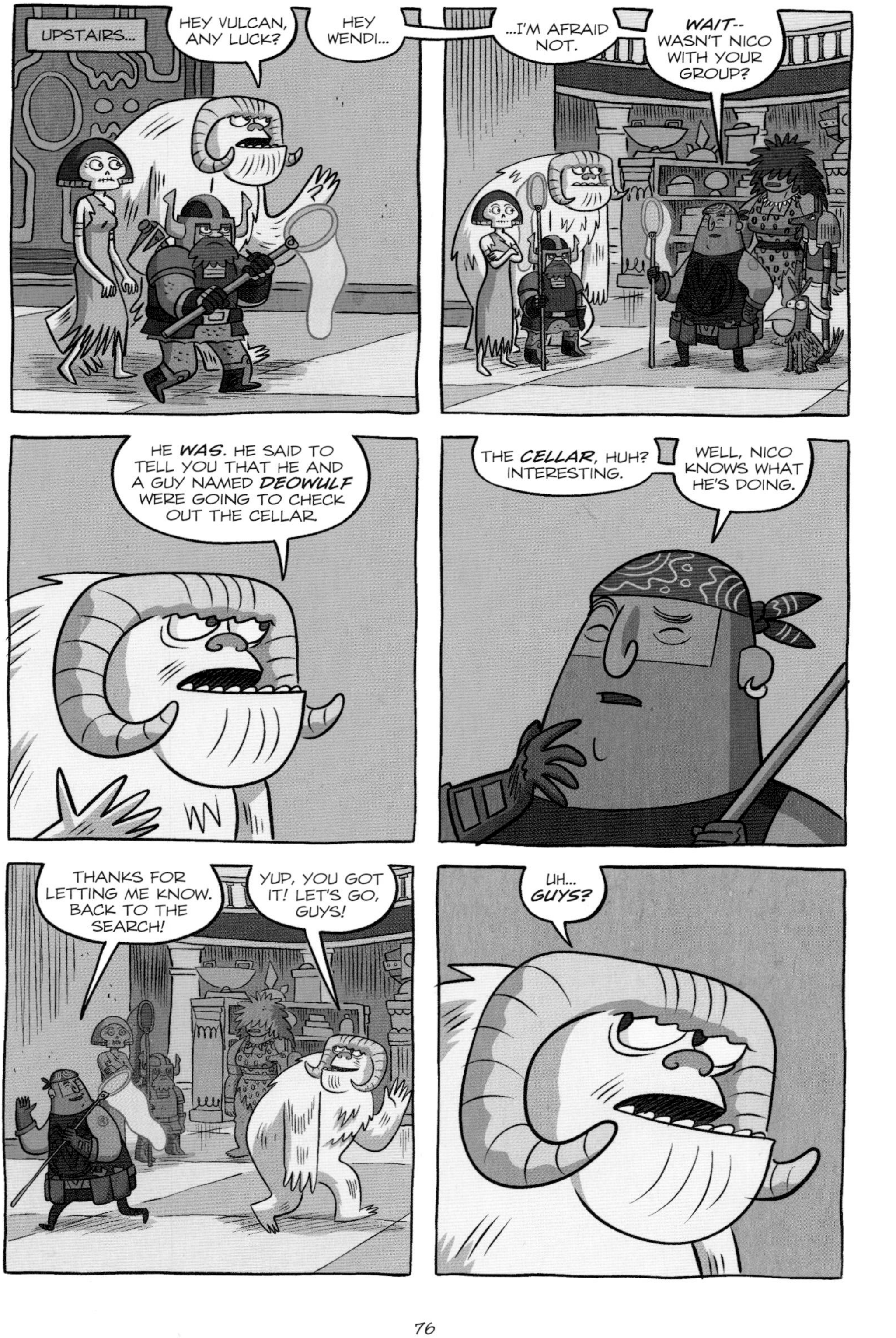
UPSTAIRS...
HEY VULCAN, ANY LUCK?
HEY WENDI...
...I'M AFRAID NOT.
WAIT-- WASN'T NICO WITH YOUR GROUP?
HE WAS. HE SAID TO TELL YOU THAT HE AND A GUY NAMED DEOWULF WERE GOING TO CHECK OUT THE CELLAR.
THE CELLAR, HUH? INTERESTING.
WELL, NICO KNOWS WHAT HE'S DOING.
THANKS FOR LETTING ME KNOW. BACK TO THE SEARCH!
YUP, YOU GOT IT! LET'S GO, GUYS!
UH... GUYS?

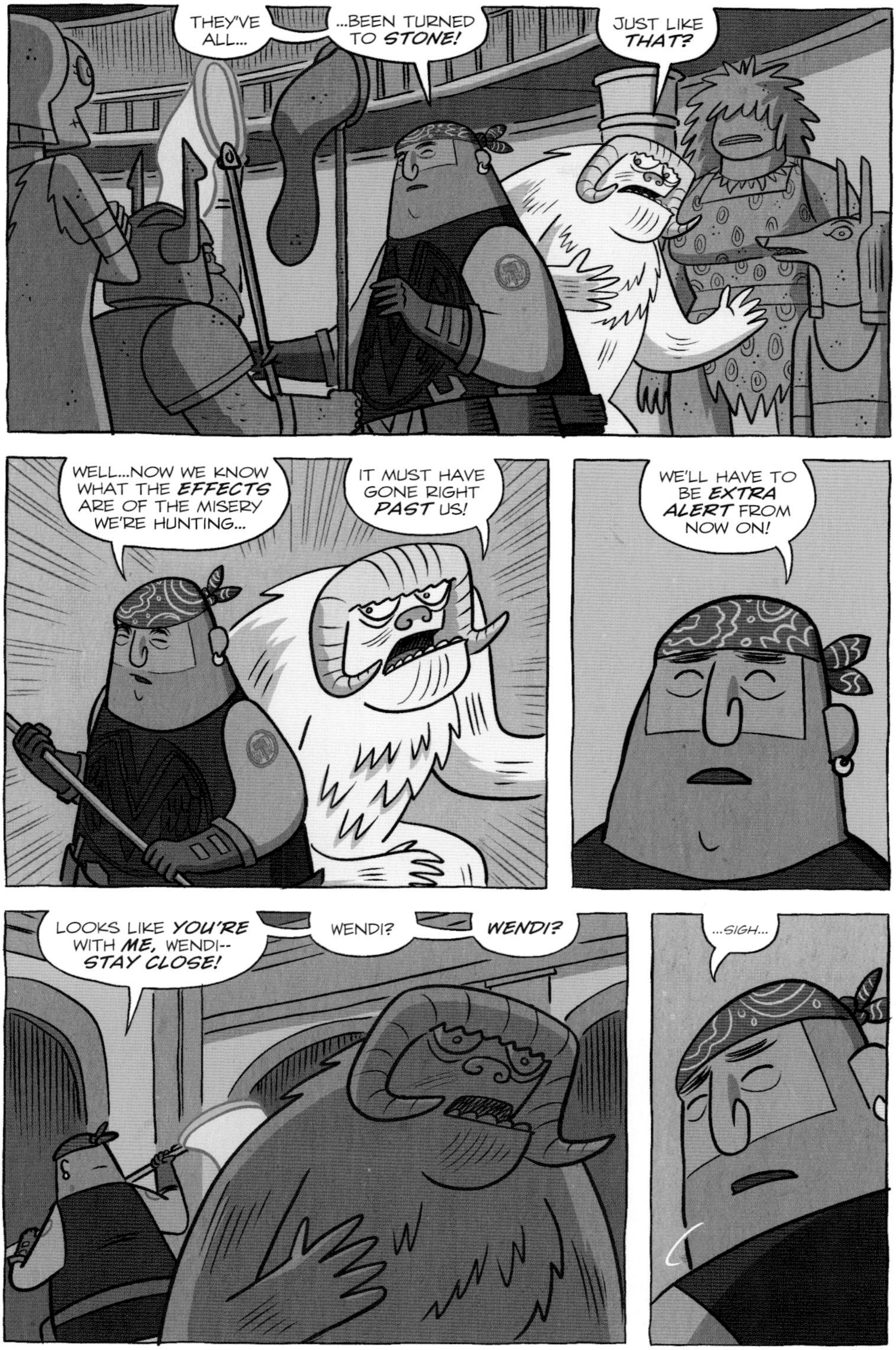
THEY'VE ALL...
...BEEN TURNED TO **STONE!**
JUST LIKE **THAT?**
WELL...NOW WE KNOW WHAT THE **EFFECTS** ARE OF THE MISERY WE'RE HUNTING...
IT MUST HAVE GONE RIGHT **PAST** US!
WE'LL HAVE TO BE **EXTRA ALERT** FROM NOW ON!
LOOKS LIKE **YOU'RE** WITH **ME,** WENDI-- **STAY CLOSE!**
WENDI?
WENDI?
...SIGH...

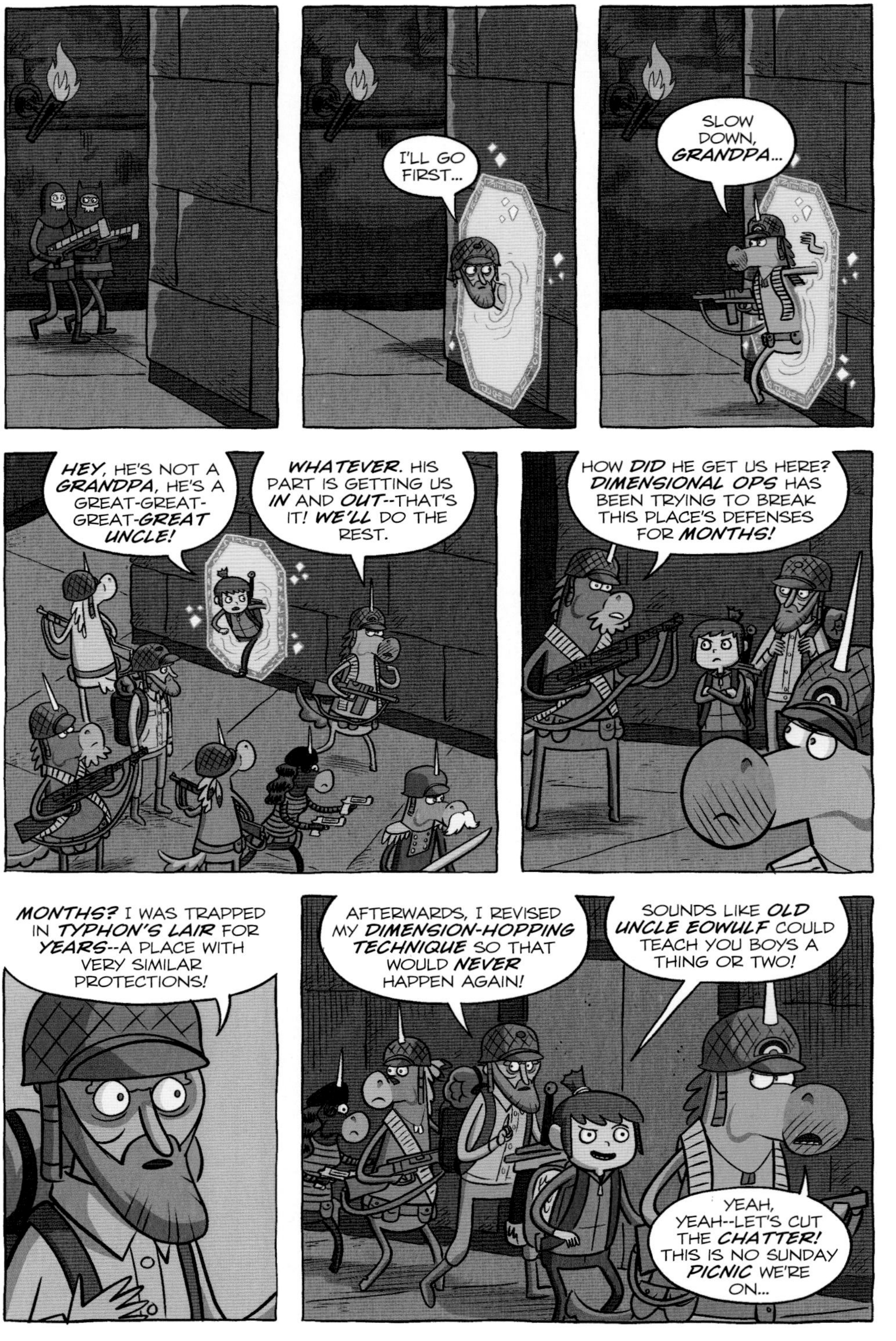
I'LL GO FIRST...
SLOW DOWN, GRANDPA...
HEY, HE'S NOT A GRANDPA, HE'S A GREAT-GREAT-GREAT-GREAT UNCLE!
WHATEVER. HIS PART IS GETTING US IN AND OUT--THAT'S IT! WE'LL DO THE REST.
HOW DID HE GET US HERE? DIMENSIONAL OPS HAS BEEN TRYING TO BREAK THIS PLACE'S DEFENSES FOR MONTHS!
MONTHS? I WAS TRAPPED IN TYPHON'S LAIR FOR YEARS--A PLACE WITH VERY SIMILAR PROTECTIONS!
AFTERWARDS, I REVISED MY DIMENSION-HOPPING TECHNIQUE SO THAT WOULD NEVER HAPPEN AGAIN!
SOUNDS LIKE OLD UNCLE EOWULF COULD TEACH YOU BOYS A THING OR TWO!
YEAH, YEAH--LET'S CUT THE CHATTER! THIS IS NO SUNDAY PICNIC WE'RE ON...

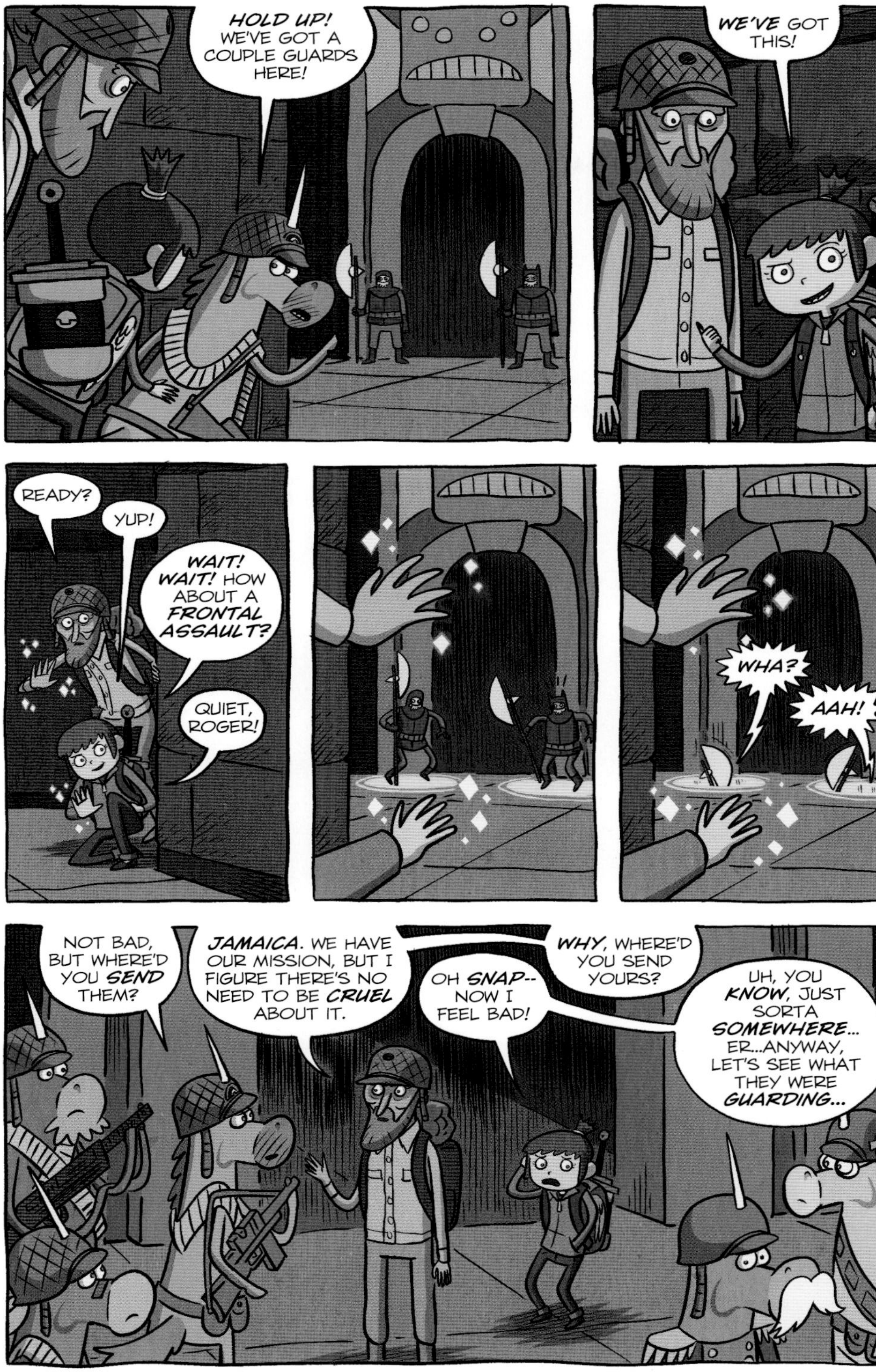

HOLD UP! WE'VE GOT A COUPLE GUARDS HERE!
WE'VE GOT THIS!
READY?
YUP!
WAIT! WAIT! HOW ABOUT A FRONTAL ASSAULT?
QUIET, ROGER!
WHA?
AAH!
NOT BAD, BUT WHERE'D YOU SEND THEM?
JAMAICA. WE HAVE OUR MISSION, BUT I FIGURE THERE'S NO NEED TO BE CRUEL ABOUT IT.
OH SNAP-- NOW I FEEL BAD!
WHY, WHERE'D YOU SEND YOURS?
UH, YOU KNOW, JUST SORTA SOMEWHERE... ER...ANYWAY, LET'S SEE WHAT THEY WERE GUARDING...

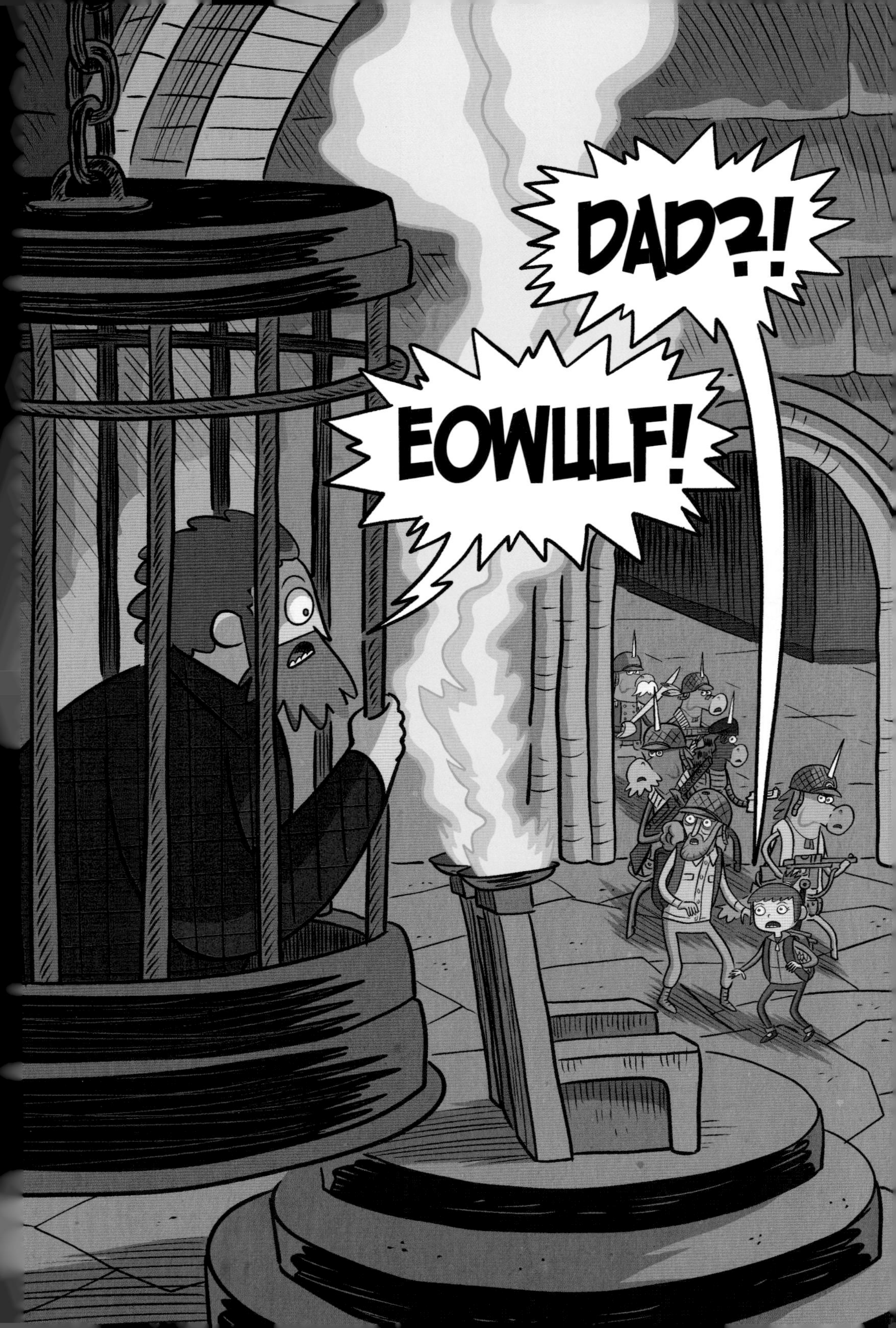
DAD?!
EOWULF!

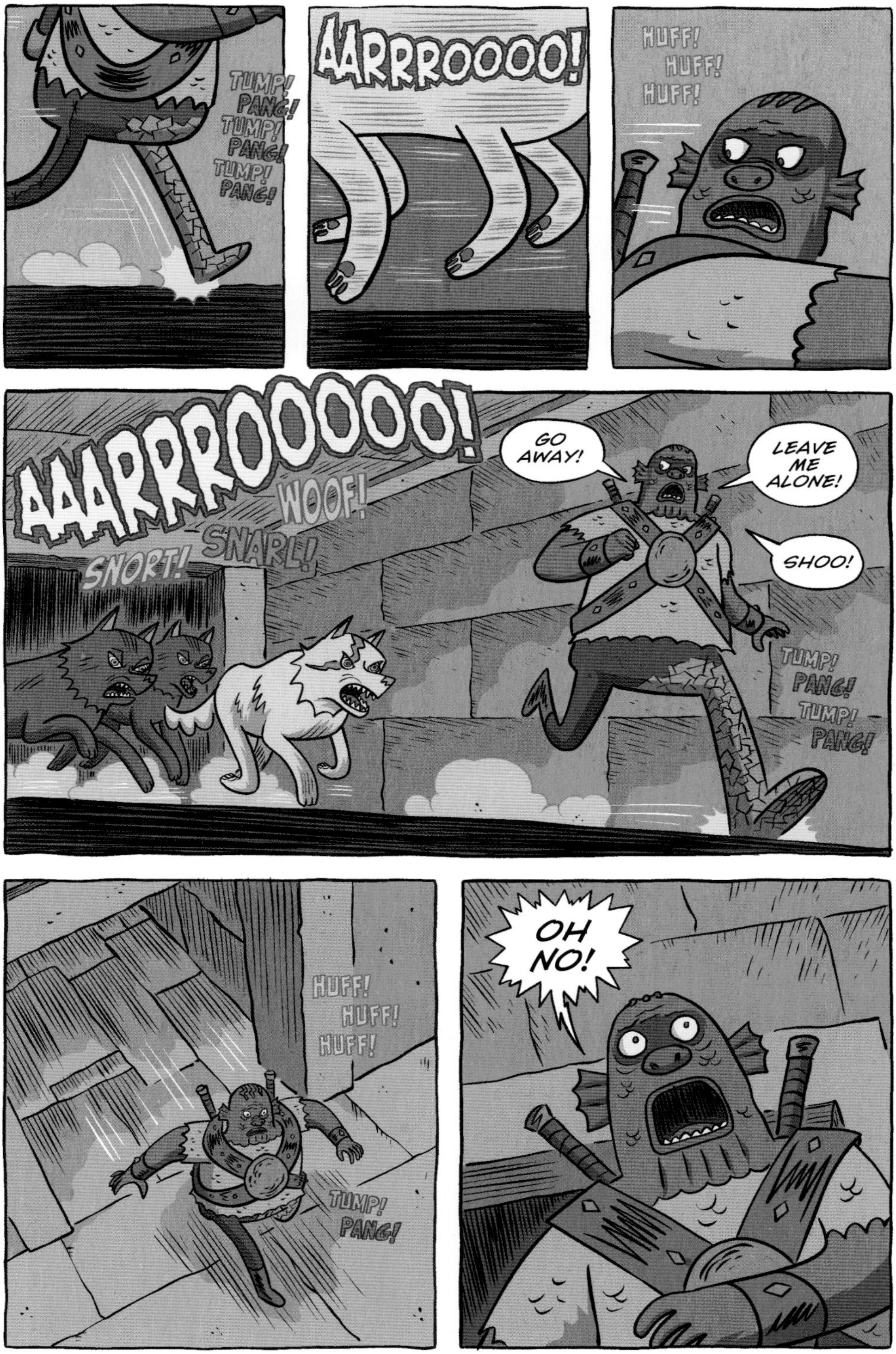
TUMP!
PANG!
TUMP!
PANG!
TUMP!
PANG!
AARRROOOO!
HUFF!
HUFF!
HUFF!
AAARRROOOOO!
WOOF!
SNARL!
SNORT!
GO AWAY!
LEAVE ME ALONE!
SHOO!
TUMP!
PANG!
TUMP!
PANG!
HUFF!
HUFF!
HUFF!
TUMP!
PANG!
OH NO!

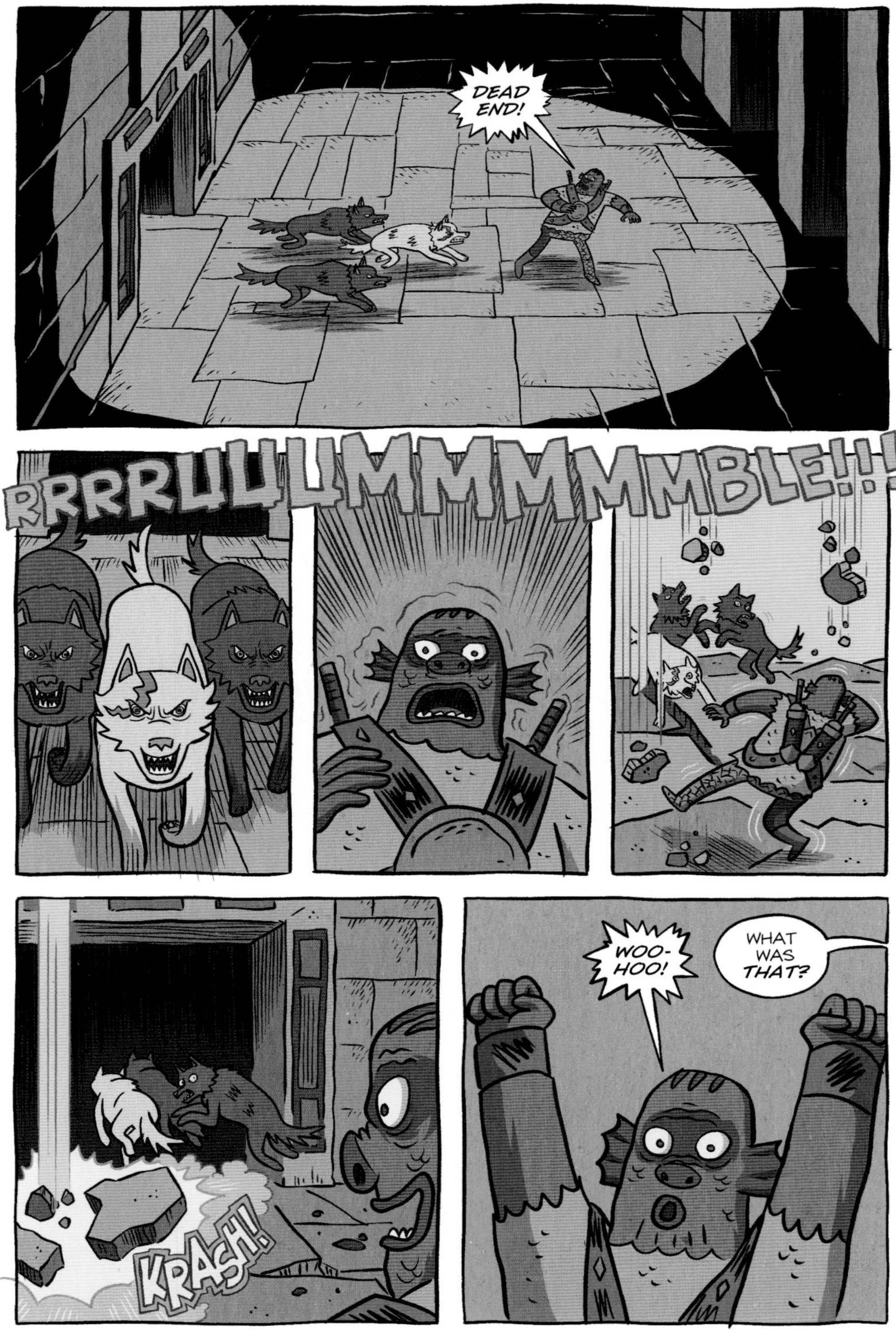
DEAD END!
RRRRUUUMMMMMMBLE!!!
KRASH!
WOO-HOO!
WHAT WAS THAT?

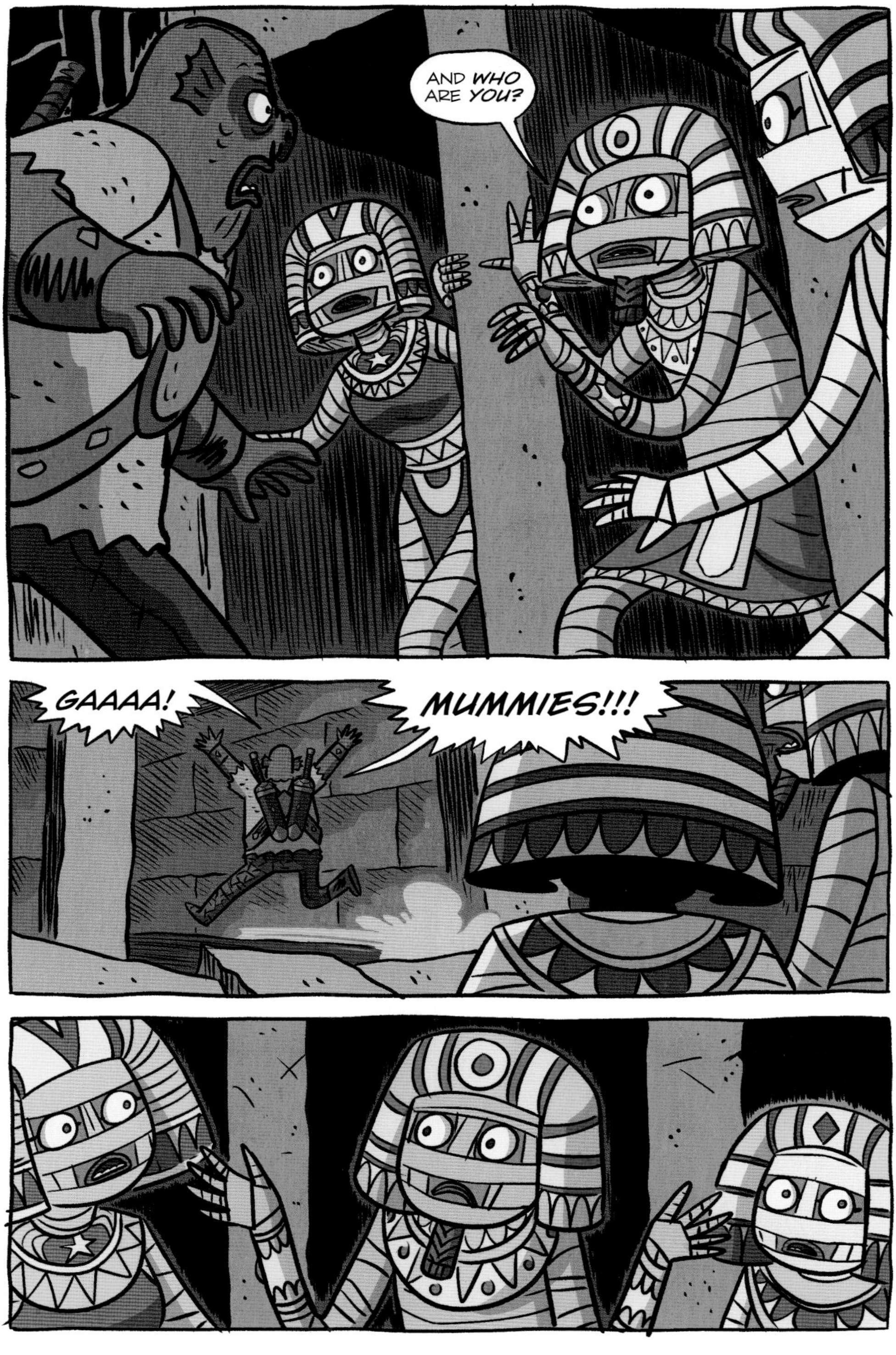
AND *WHO* ARE *YOU?*
GAAAA!
MUMMIES!!!

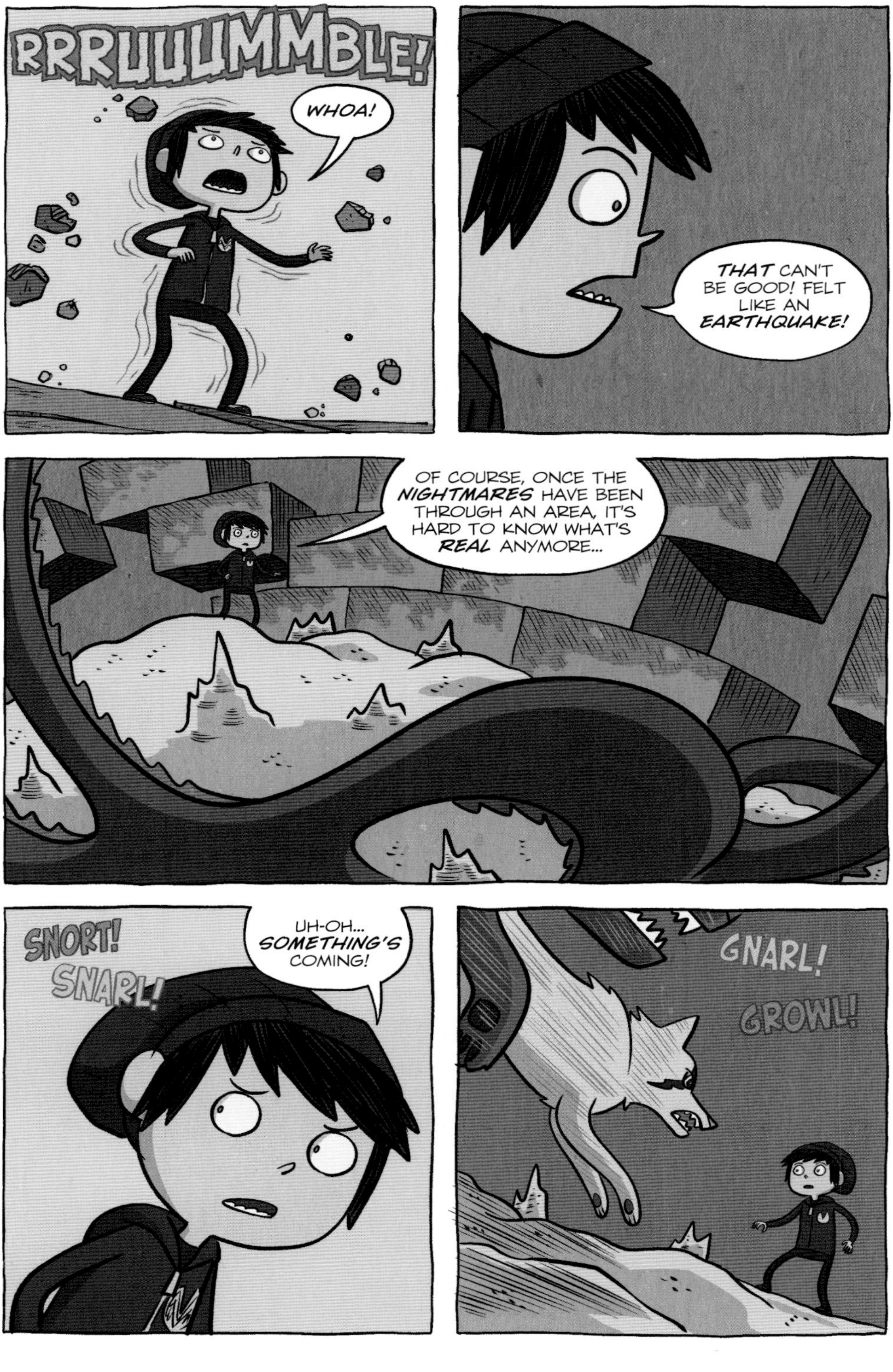
RRRUUUMMBLE!
WHOA!
THAT CAN'T BE GOOD! FELT LIKE AN EARTHQUAKE!
OF COURSE, ONCE THE NIGHTMARES HAVE BEEN THROUGH AN AREA, IT'S HARD TO KNOW WHAT'S REAL ANYMORE...
SNORT!
SNARL!
UH-OH... SOMETHING'S COMING!
GNARL!
GROWL!

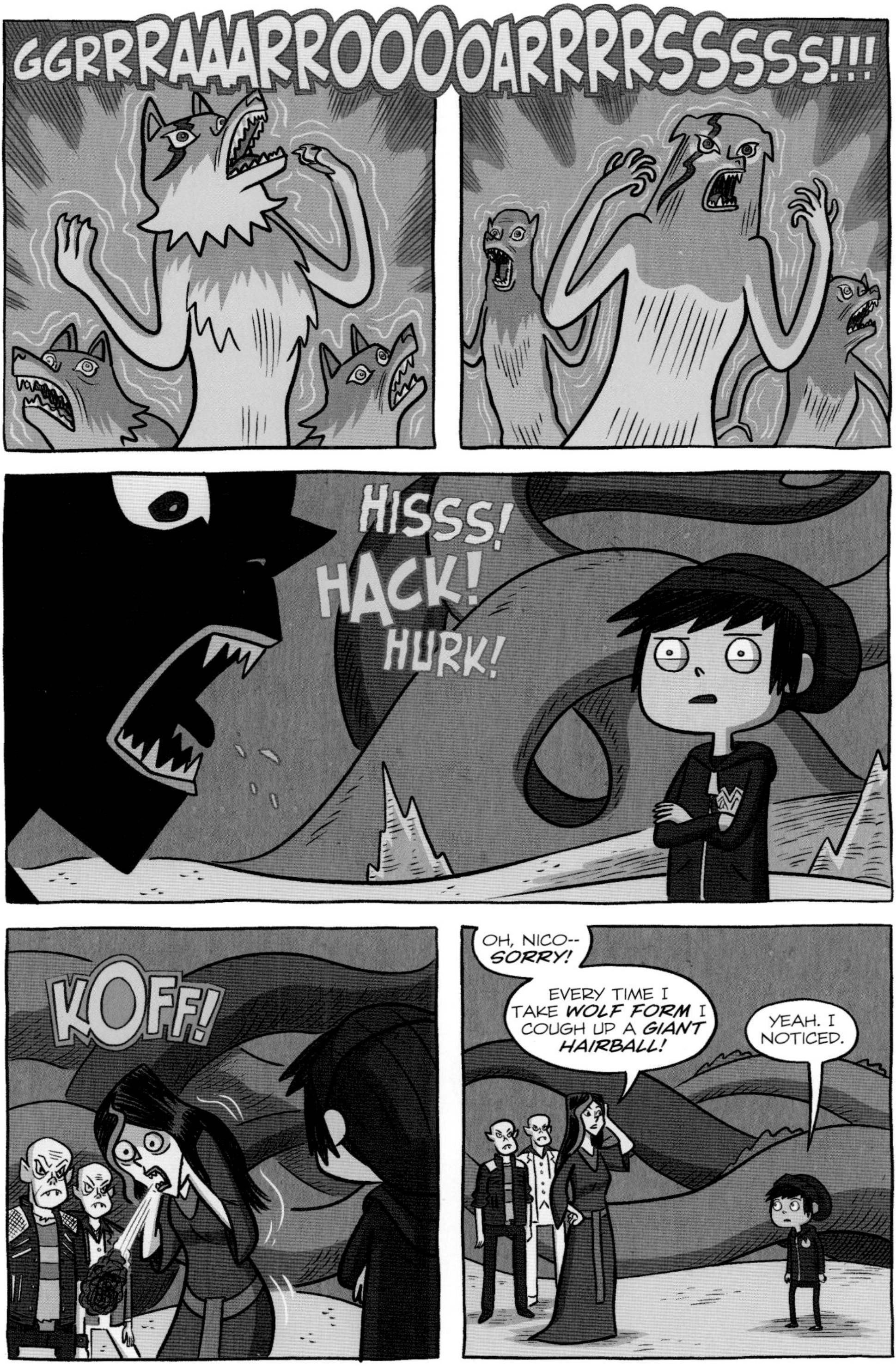
GGRRRAAARROOOOARRRRSSSSS!!!
HISSS!
HACK!
HURK!
KOFF!
OH, NICO-- SORRY!
EVERY TIME I TAKE WOLF FORM I COUGH UP A GIANT HAIRBALL!
YEAH. I NOTICED.

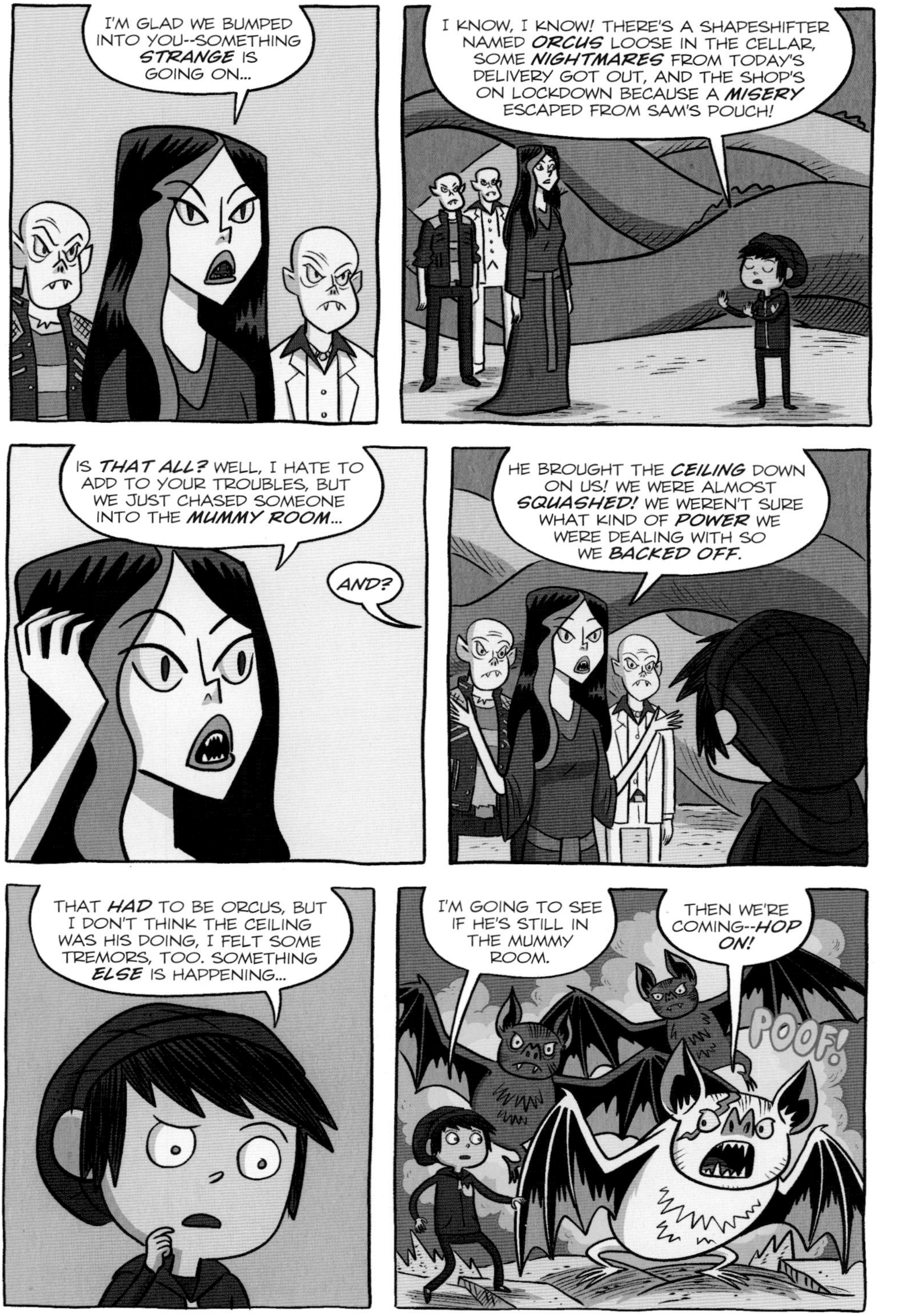

I'M GLAD WE BUMPED INTO YOU--SOMETHING STRANGE IS GOING ON...
I KNOW, I KNOW! THERE'S A SHAPESHIFTER NAMED ORCUS LOOSE IN THE CELLAR, SOME NIGHTMARES FROM TODAY'S DELIVERY GOT OUT, AND THE SHOP'S ON LOCKDOWN BECAUSE A MISERY ESCAPED FROM SAM'S POUCH!
IS THAT ALL? WELL, I HATE TO ADD TO YOUR TROUBLES, BUT WE JUST CHASED SOMEONE INTO THE MUMMY ROOM...
AND?
HE BROUGHT THE CEILING DOWN ON US! WE WERE ALMOST SQUASHED! WE WEREN'T SURE WHAT KIND OF POWER WE WERE DEALING WITH SO WE BACKED OFF.
THAT HAD TO BE ORCUS, BUT I DON'T THINK THE CEILING WAS HIS DOING, I FELT SOME TREMORS, TOO. SOMETHING ELSE IS HAPPENING...
I'M GOING TO SEE IF HE'S STILL IN THE MUMMY ROOM.
THEN WE'RE COMING--HOP ON!
POOF!

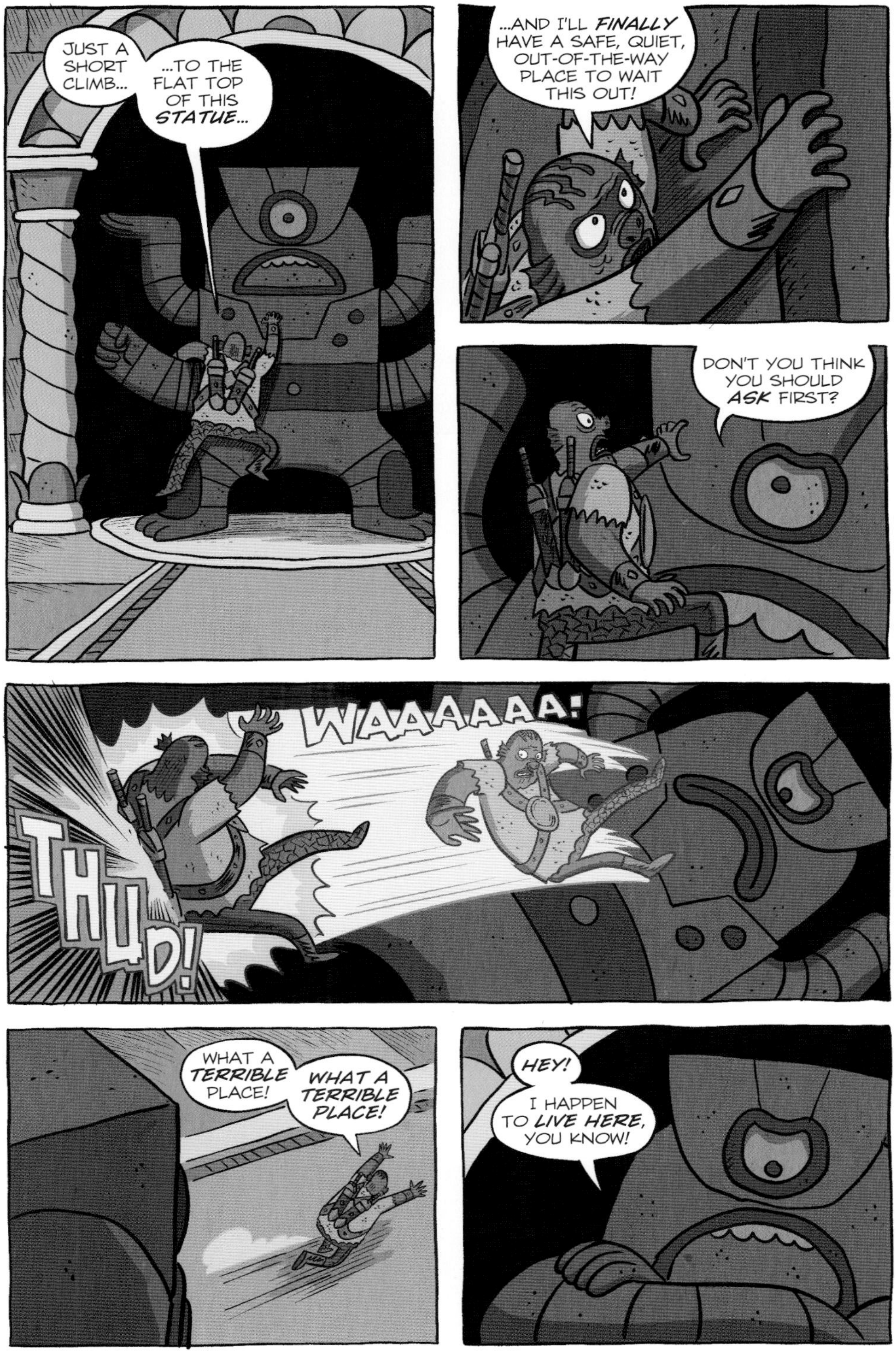
JUST A SHORT CLIMB...
...TO THE FLAT TOP OF THIS STATUE...
...AND I'LL FINALLY HAVE A SAFE, QUIET, OUT-OF-THE-WAY PLACE TO WAIT THIS OUT!
DON'T YOU THINK YOU SHOULD ASK FIRST?
WAAAAAAA!
THUD!
WHAT A TERRIBLE PLACE!
WHAT A TERRIBLE PLACE!
HEY!
I HAPPEN TO LIVE HERE, YOU KNOW!

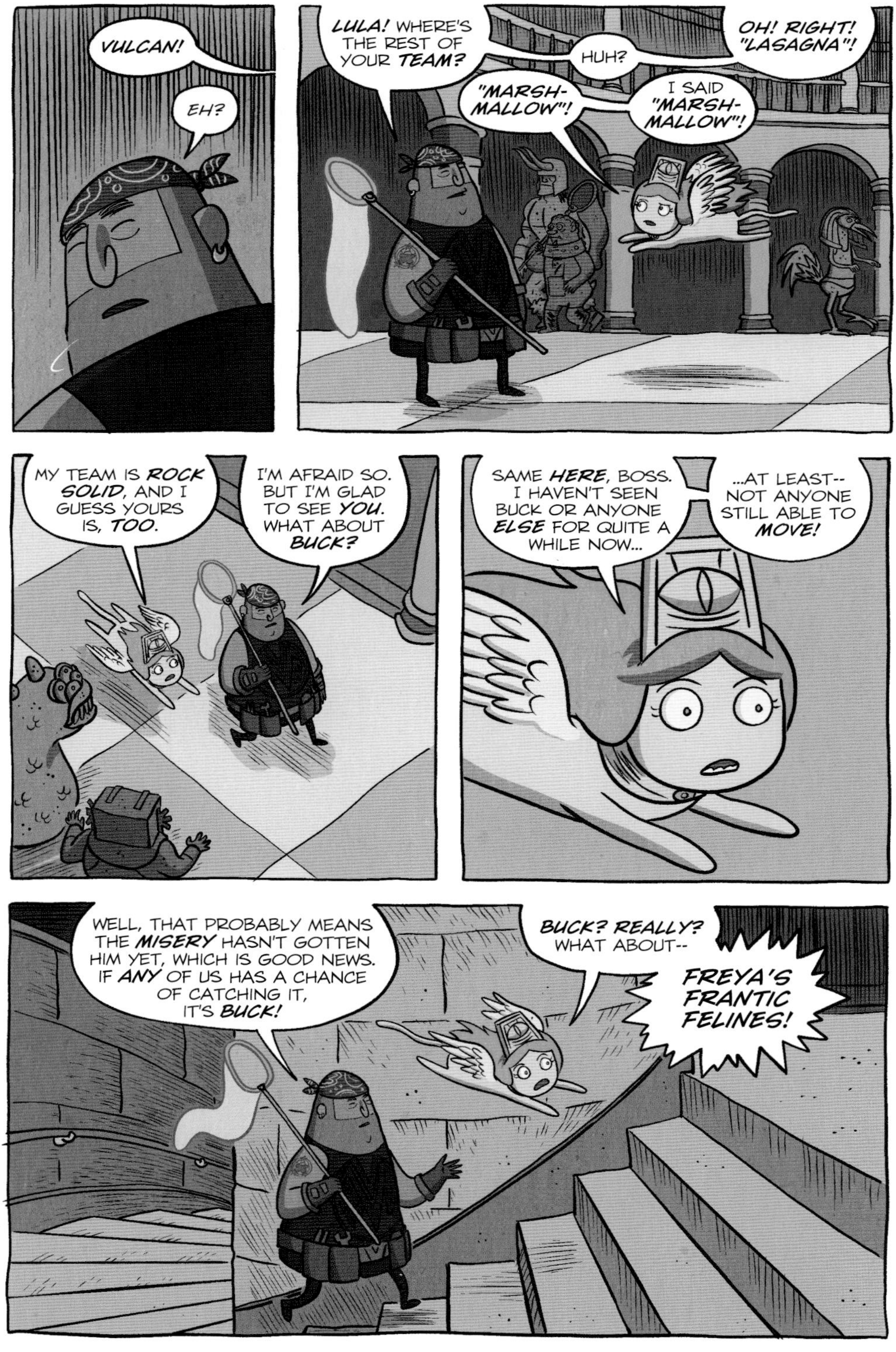
VULCAN!
EH?
LULA! WHERE'S THE REST OF YOUR TEAM?
HUH?
"MARSH-MALLOW"!
I SAID "MARSH-MALLOW"!
OH! RIGHT! "LASAGNA"!
MY TEAM IS ROCK SOLID, AND I GUESS YOURS IS, TOO.
I'M AFRAID SO. BUT I'M GLAD TO SEE YOU. WHAT ABOUT BUCK?
SAME HERE, BOSS. I HAVEN'T SEEN BUCK OR ANYONE ELSE FOR QUITE A WHILE NOW...
...AT LEAST-- NOT ANYONE STILL ABLE TO MOVE!
WELL, THAT PROBABLY MEANS THE MISERY HASN'T GOTTEN HIM YET, WHICH IS GOOD NEWS. IF ANY OF US HAS A CHANCE OF CATCHING IT, IT'S BUCK!
BUCK? REALLY? WHAT ABOUT--
FREYA'S FRANTIC FELINES!

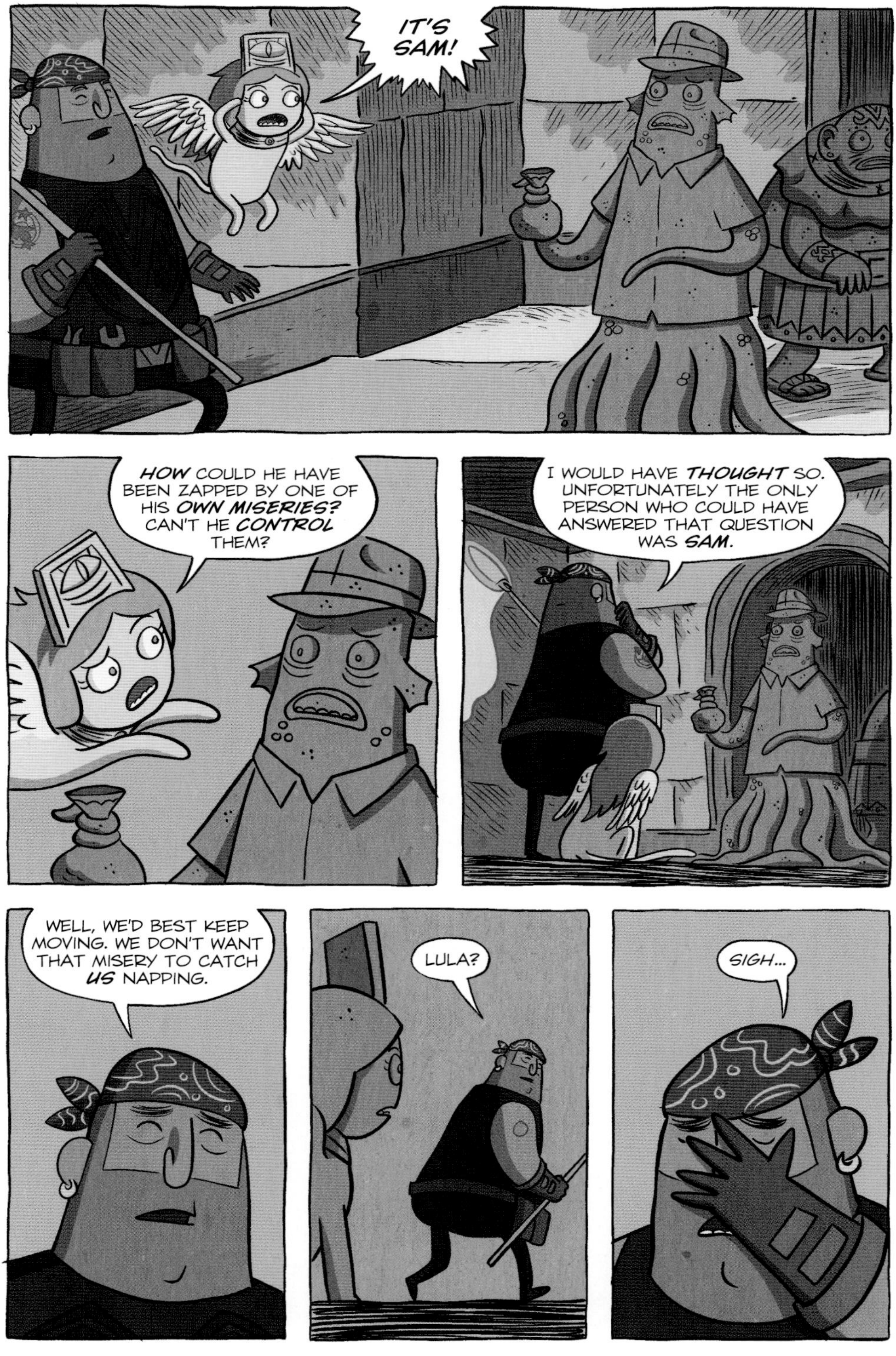
IT'S SAM!
HOW COULD HE HAVE BEEN ZAPPED BY ONE OF HIS OWN MISERIES? CAN'T HE CONTROL THEM?
I WOULD HAVE THOUGHT SO. UNFORTUNATELY THE ONLY PERSON WHO COULD HAVE ANSWERED THAT QUESTION WAS SAM.
WELL, WE'D BEST KEEP MOVING. WE DON'T WANT THAT MISERY TO CATCH US NAPPING.
LULA?
SIGH...

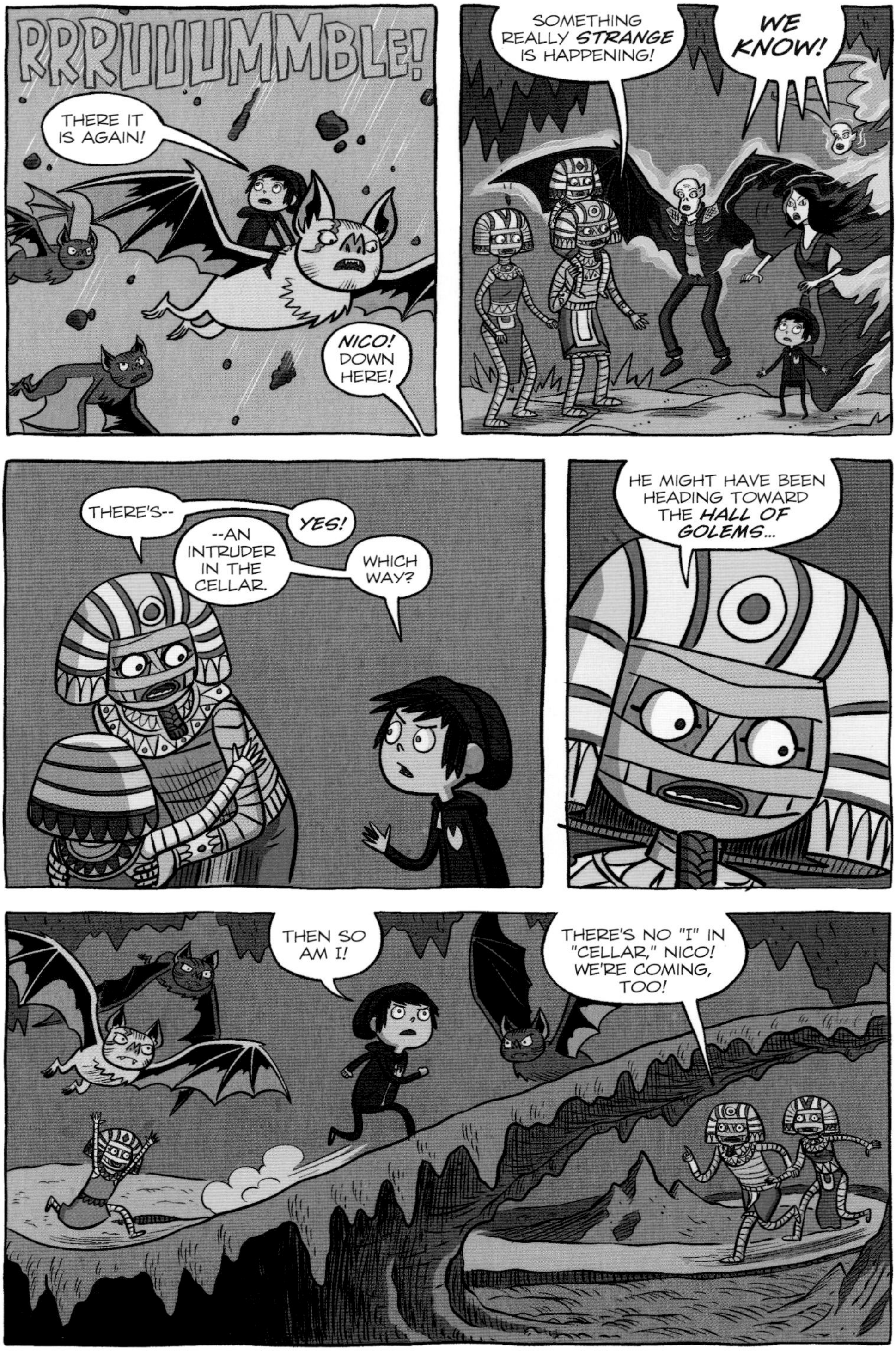
RRRUUUMMBLE!
THERE IT IS AGAIN!
NICO! DOWN HERE!
SOMETHING REALLY STRANGE IS HAPPENING!
WE KNOW!
THERE'S--
--AN INTRUDER IN THE CELLAR.
YES!
WHICH WAY?
HE MIGHT HAVE BEEN HEADING TOWARD THE HALL OF GOLEMS...
THEN SO AM I!
THERE'S NO "I" IN "CELLAR," NICO! WE'RE COMING, TOO!

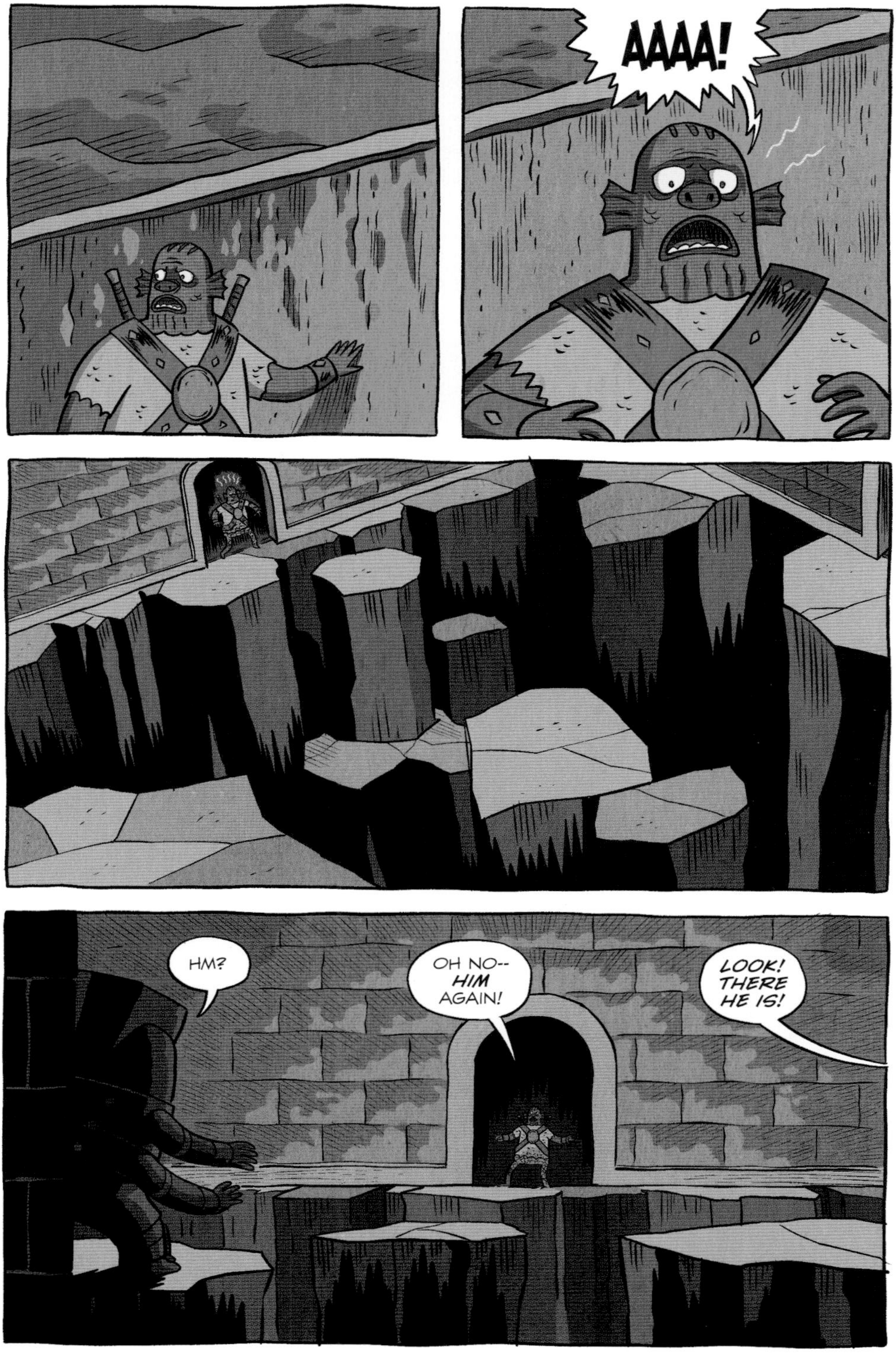
AAAA!
HM?
OH NO-- HIM AGAIN!
LOOK! THERE HE IS!

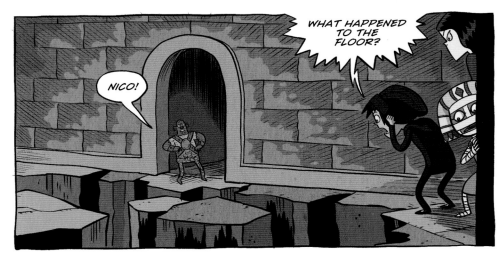

NICO!

WHAT HAPPENED TO THE FLOOR?

THE CELLAR'S *COLLAPSING!* WHAT COULD HAVE CAUSED THIS?

HOLD ON-- THIS COULD BE *VERY BAD!*

YA *THINK?*

I *DO,* LISTEN--

WHEN *VULCAN* FIRST BUILT THE SUPPLY SHOP, *MUMMIES* WERE THERE TO ADVISE ON THE CONSTRUCTION.

THE CELLAR IS FOUNDED ON A SERIES OF *BULWARKS* DESIGNED TO HOLD THE MOAT OF ORIGINAL NIGHT *IN PLACE.*

IF THOSE STRUCTURES ARE *COLLAPSING...*

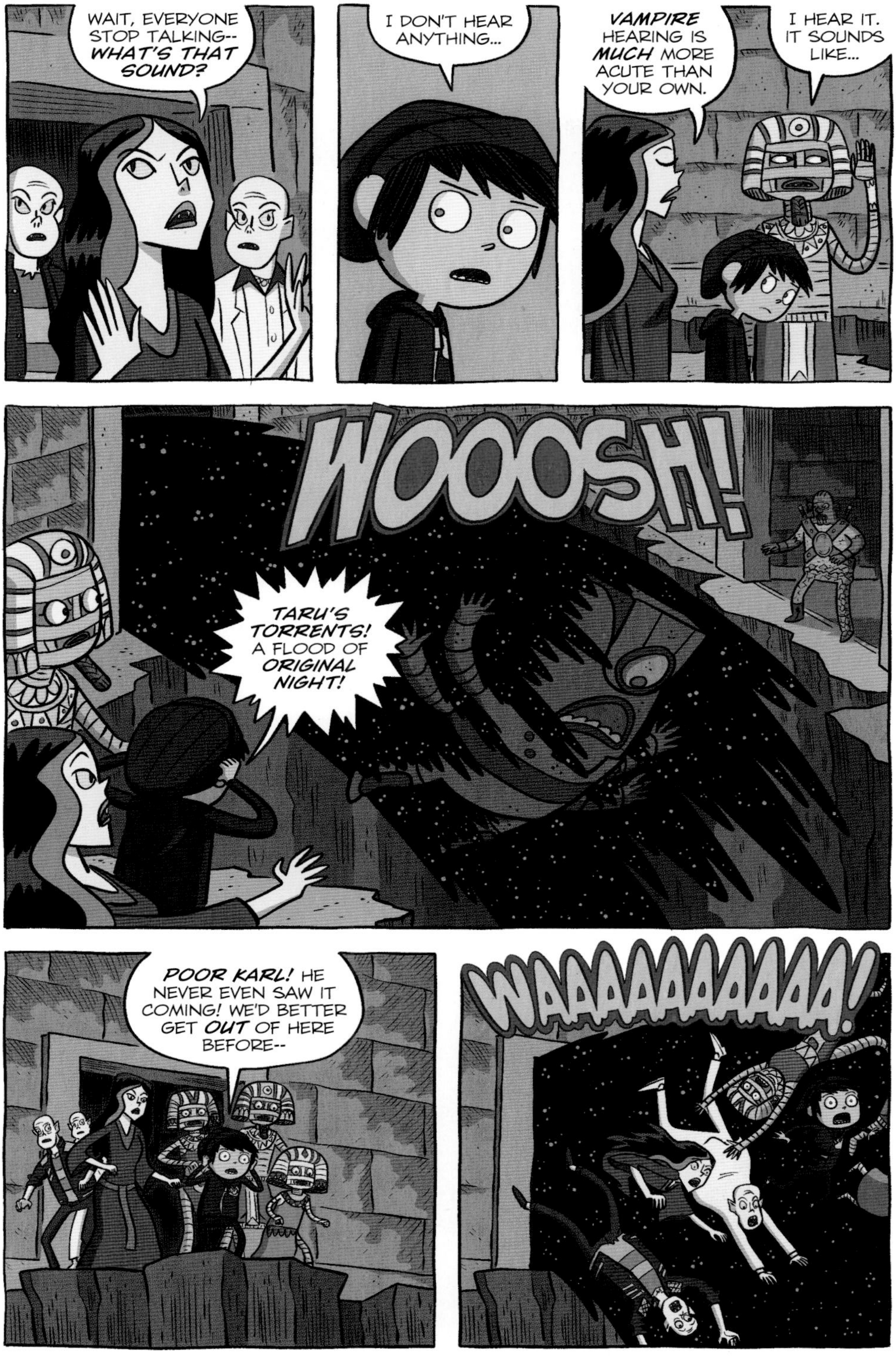
WAIT, EVERYONE STOP TALKING-- WHAT'S THAT SOUND?
I DON'T HEAR ANYTHING...
VAMPIRE HEARING IS MUCH MORE ACUTE THAN YOUR OWN.
I HEAR IT. IT SOUNDS LIKE...
WOOOSH!
TARU'S TORRENTS! A FLOOD OF ORIGINAL NIGHT!
POOR KARL! HE NEVER EVEN SAW IT COMING! WE'D BETTER GET OUT OF HERE BEFORE--
WAAAAAAAAAA!

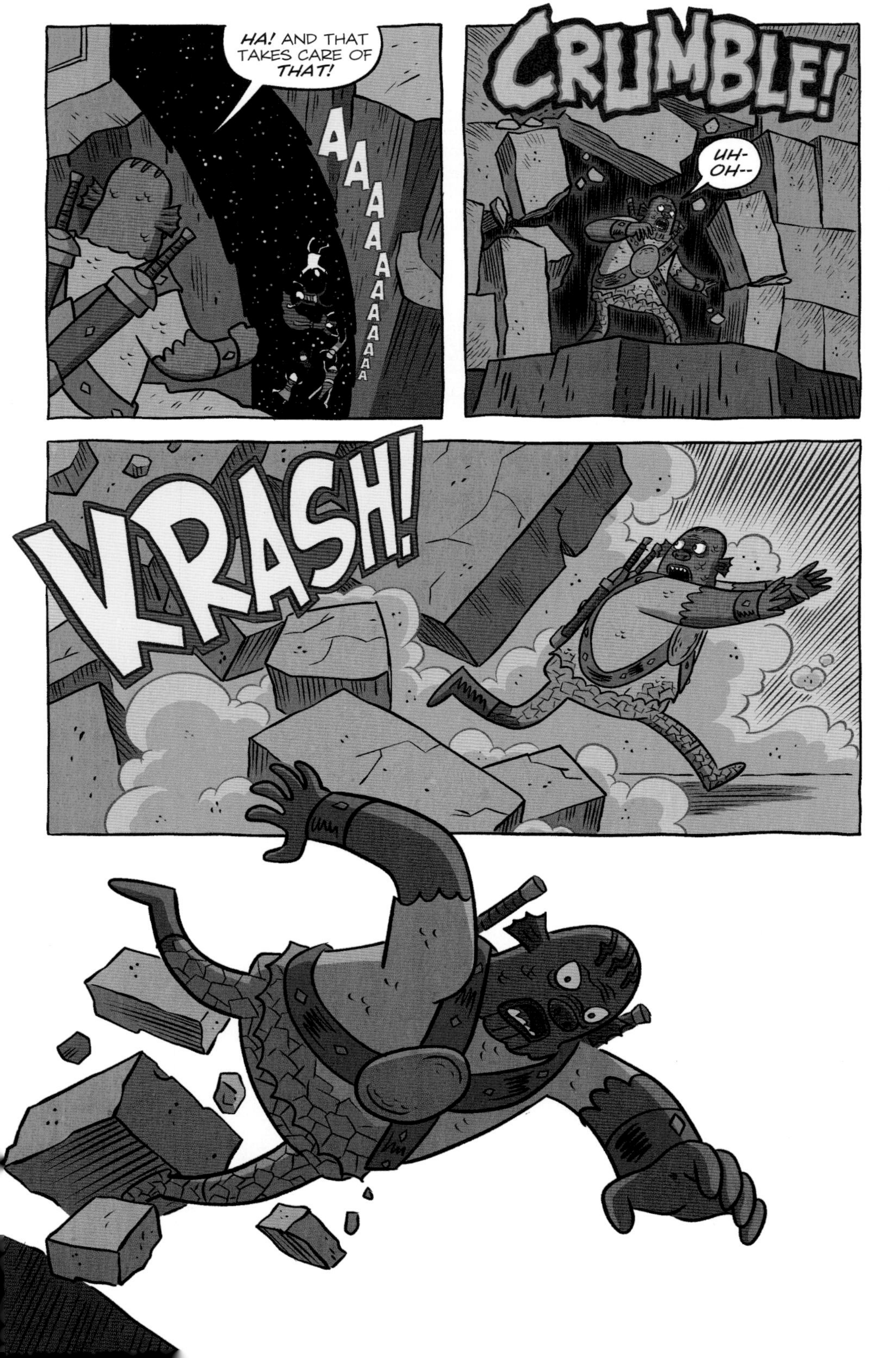
HA! AND THAT TAKES CARE OF THAT!
AAAAAAAAAAA
CRUMBLE!
UH-OH--
KRASH!

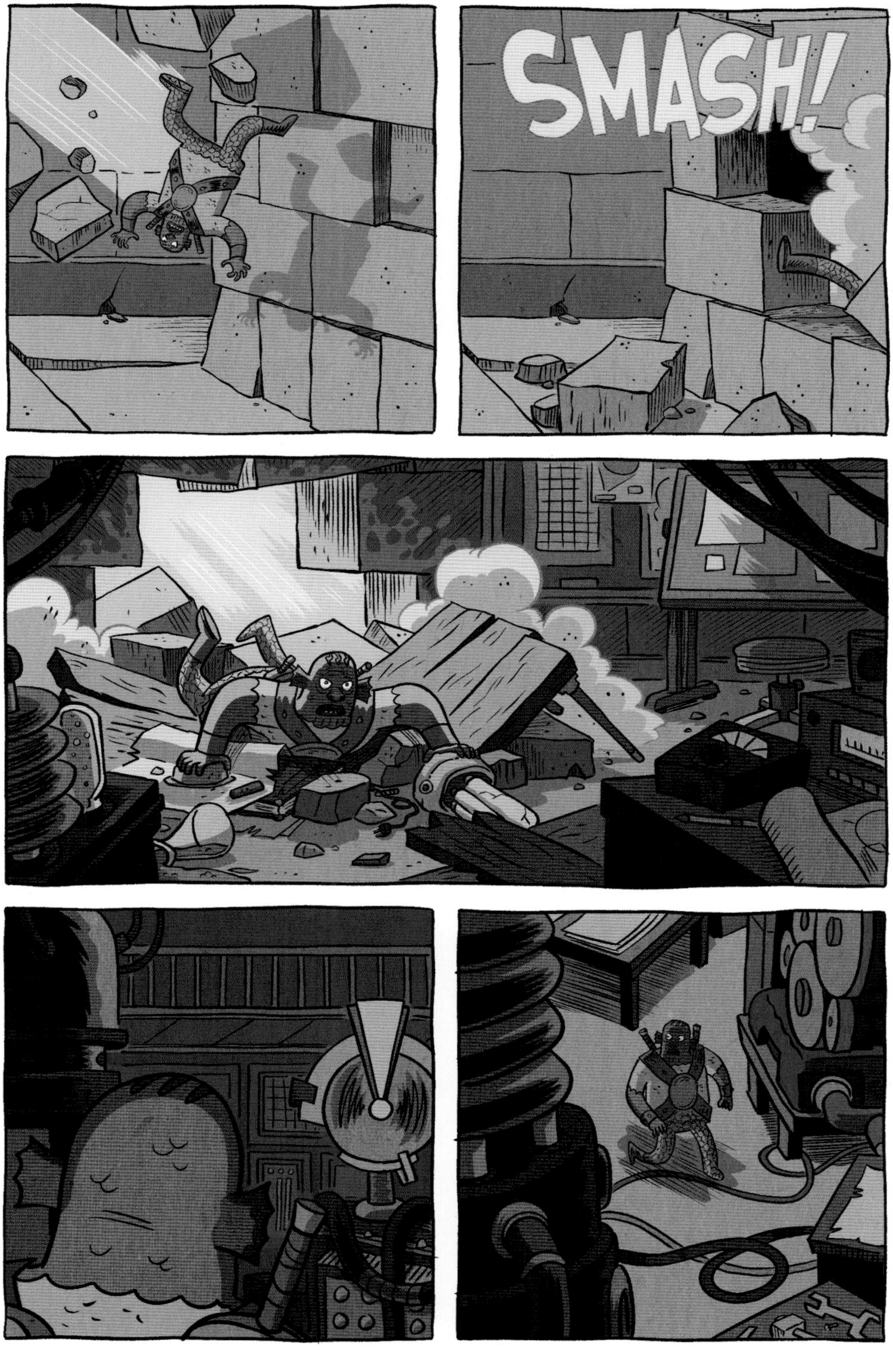
SMASH!

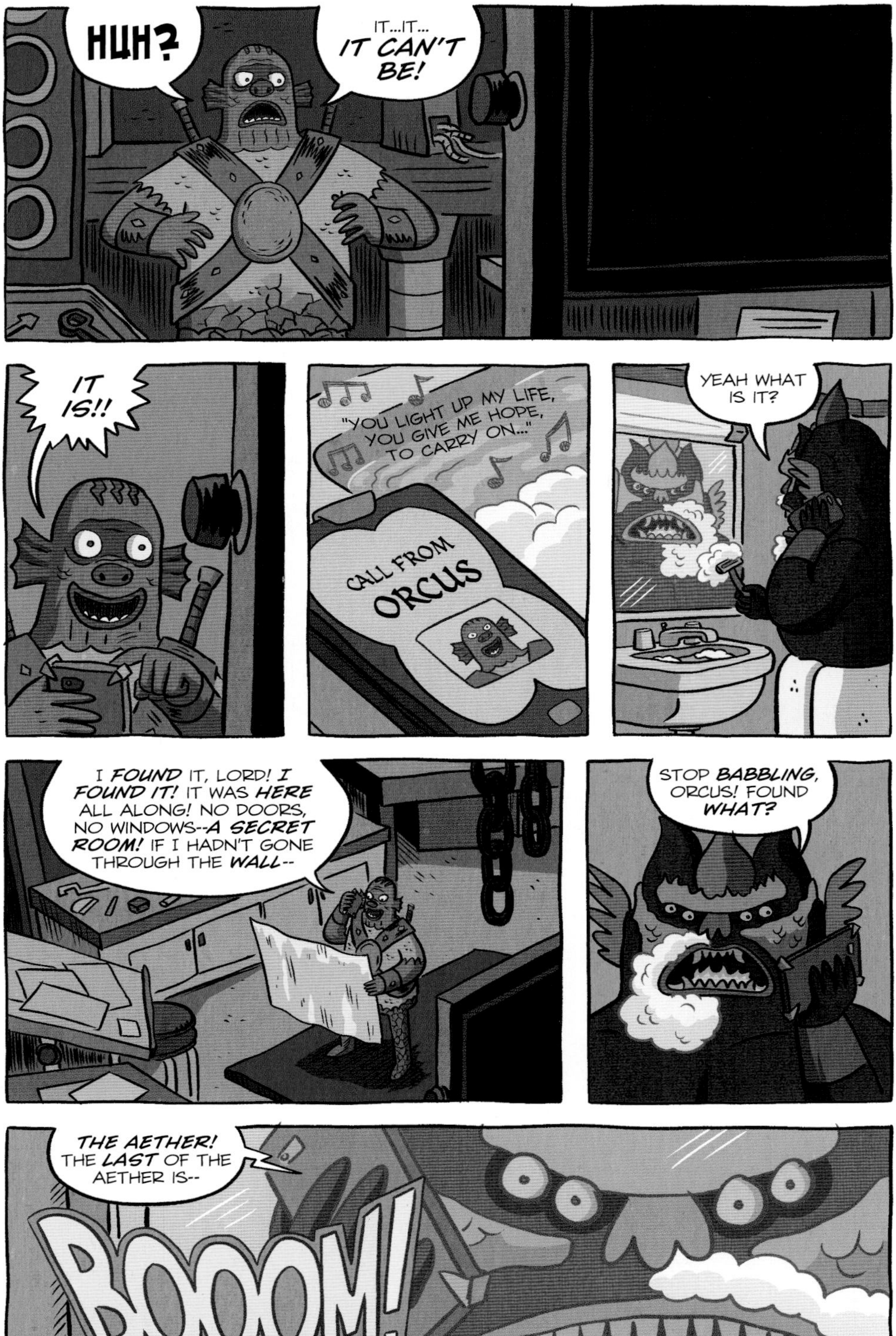
HUH?
IT...IT... IT CAN'T BE!
IT IS!!
"YOU LIGHT UP MY LIFE, YOU GIVE ME HOPE, TO CARRY ON..."
CALL FROM ORCUS
YEAH WHAT IS IT?
I FOUND IT, LORD! I FOUND IT! IT WAS HERE ALL ALONG! NO DOORS, NO WINDOWS--A SECRET ROOM! IF I HADN'T GONE THROUGH THE WALL--
STOP BABBLING, ORCUS! FOUND WHAT?
THE AETHER! THE LAST OF THE AETHER IS--
BOOOM!

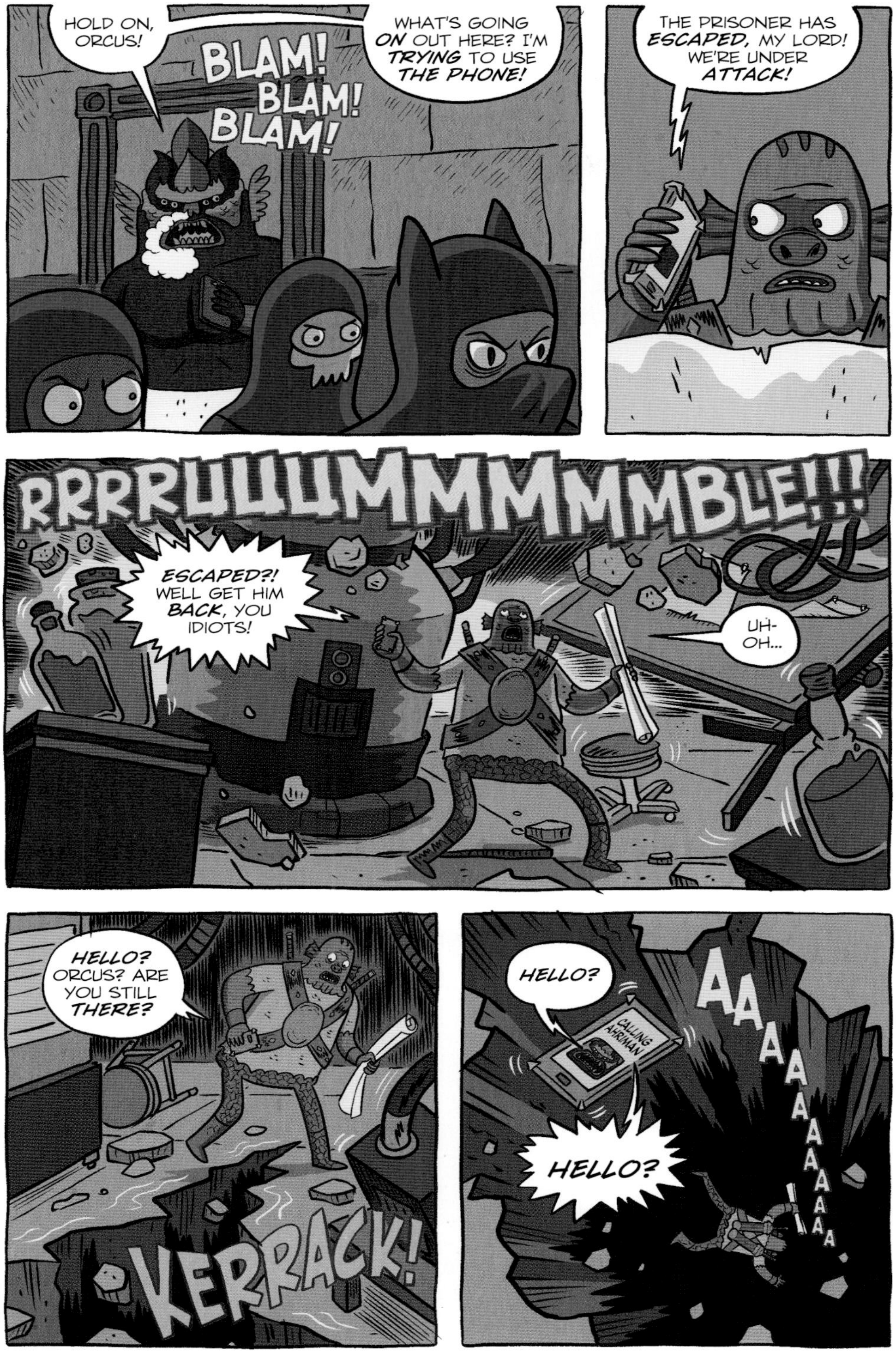
HOLD ON, ORCUS!
BLAM! BLAM! BLAM!
WHAT'S GOING ON OUT HERE? I'M TRYING TO USE THE PHONE!
THE PRISONER HAS ESCAPED, MY LORD! WE'RE UNDER ATTACK!
RRRRUUUMMMMMMBLE!!!
ESCAPED?! WELL GET HIM BACK, YOU IDIOTS!
UH-OH...
HELLO? ORCUS? ARE YOU STILL THERE?
KERRACK!
HELLO?
CALLING AHRIMAN
AAAAAAAAAAAA
HELLO?

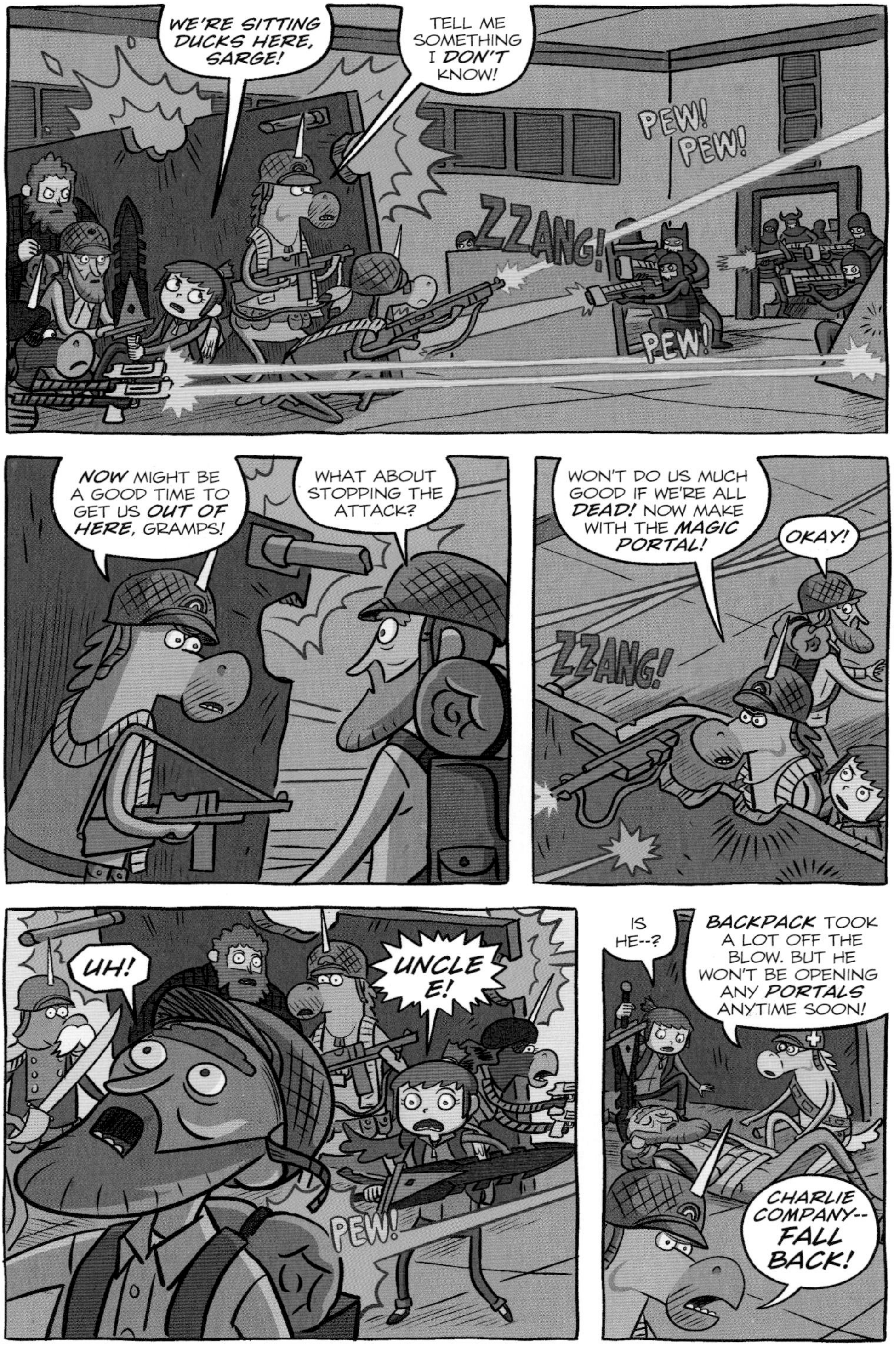

WE'RE SITTING DUCKS HERE, SARGE!
TELL ME SOMETHING I DON'T KNOW!
PEW! PEW!
ZZANG!
PEW!
NOW MIGHT BE A GOOD TIME TO GET US OUT OF HERE, GRAMPS!
WHAT ABOUT STOPPING THE ATTACK?
WON'T DO US MUCH GOOD IF WE'RE ALL DEAD! NOW MAKE WITH THE MAGIC PORTAL!
OKAY!
ZZANG!
UH!
UNCLE E!
PEW!
IS HE--?
BACKPACK TOOK A LOT OFF THE BLOW. BUT HE WON'T BE OPENING ANY PORTALS ANYTIME SOON!
CHARLIE COMPANY-- FALL BACK!

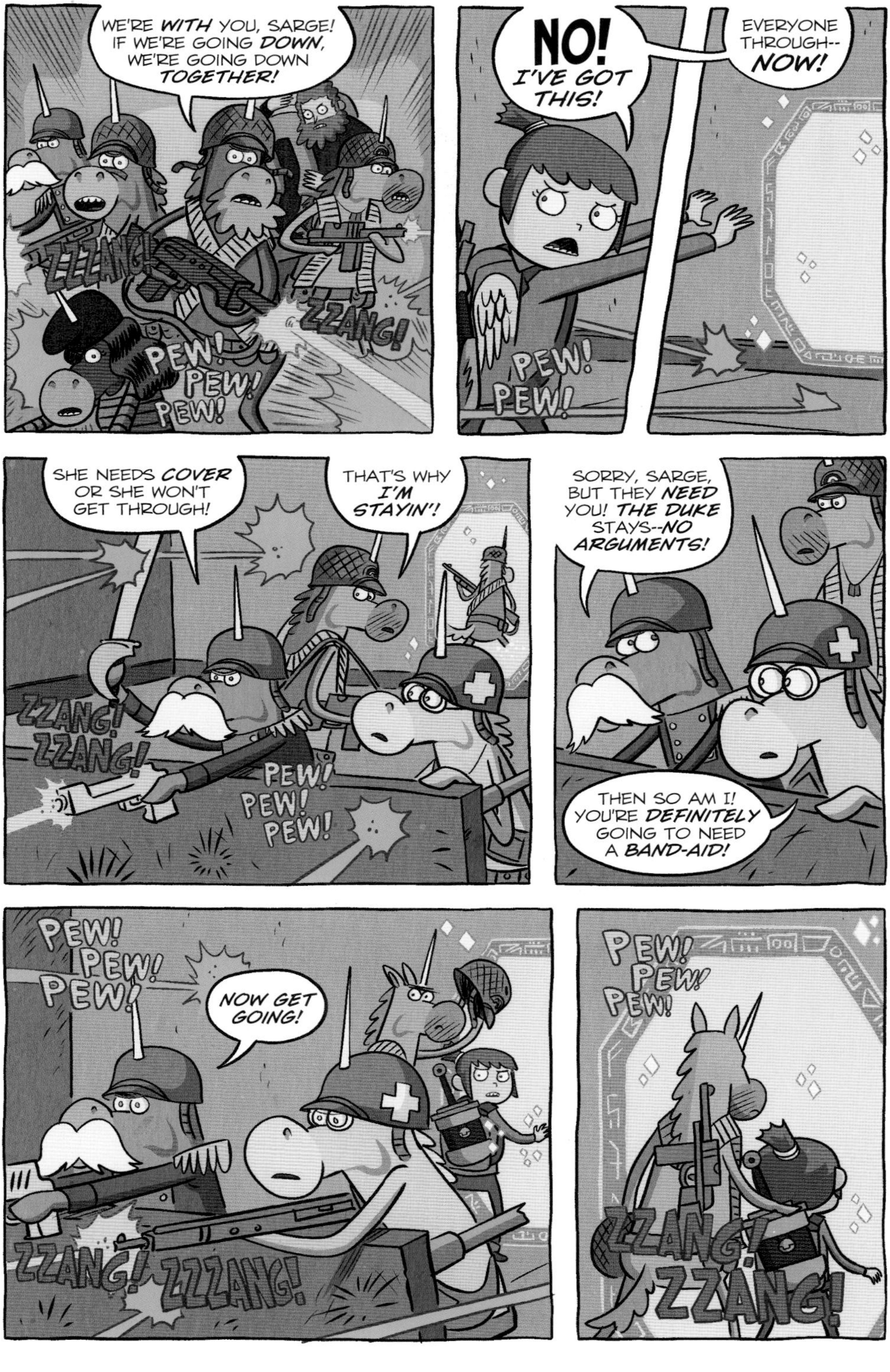
WE'RE WITH YOU, SARGE! IF WE'RE GOING DOWN, WE'RE GOING DOWN TOGETHER!
ZZZANG!
ZZANG!
PEW! PEW! PEW!
NO! I'VE GOT THIS!
EVERYONE THROUGH-- NOW!
PEW! PEW!
SHE NEEDS COVER OR SHE WON'T GET THROUGH!
THAT'S WHY I'M STAYIN'!
ZZANG! ZZANG!
PEW! PEW! PEW!
SORRY, SARGE, BUT THEY NEED YOU! THE DUKE STAYS--NO ARGUMENTS!
THEN SO AM I! YOU'RE DEFINITELY GOING TO NEED A BAND-AID!
PEW! PEW! PEW!
NOW GET GOING!
ZZANG! ZZZANG!
PEW! PEW! PEW!
ZZANG! ZZANG!

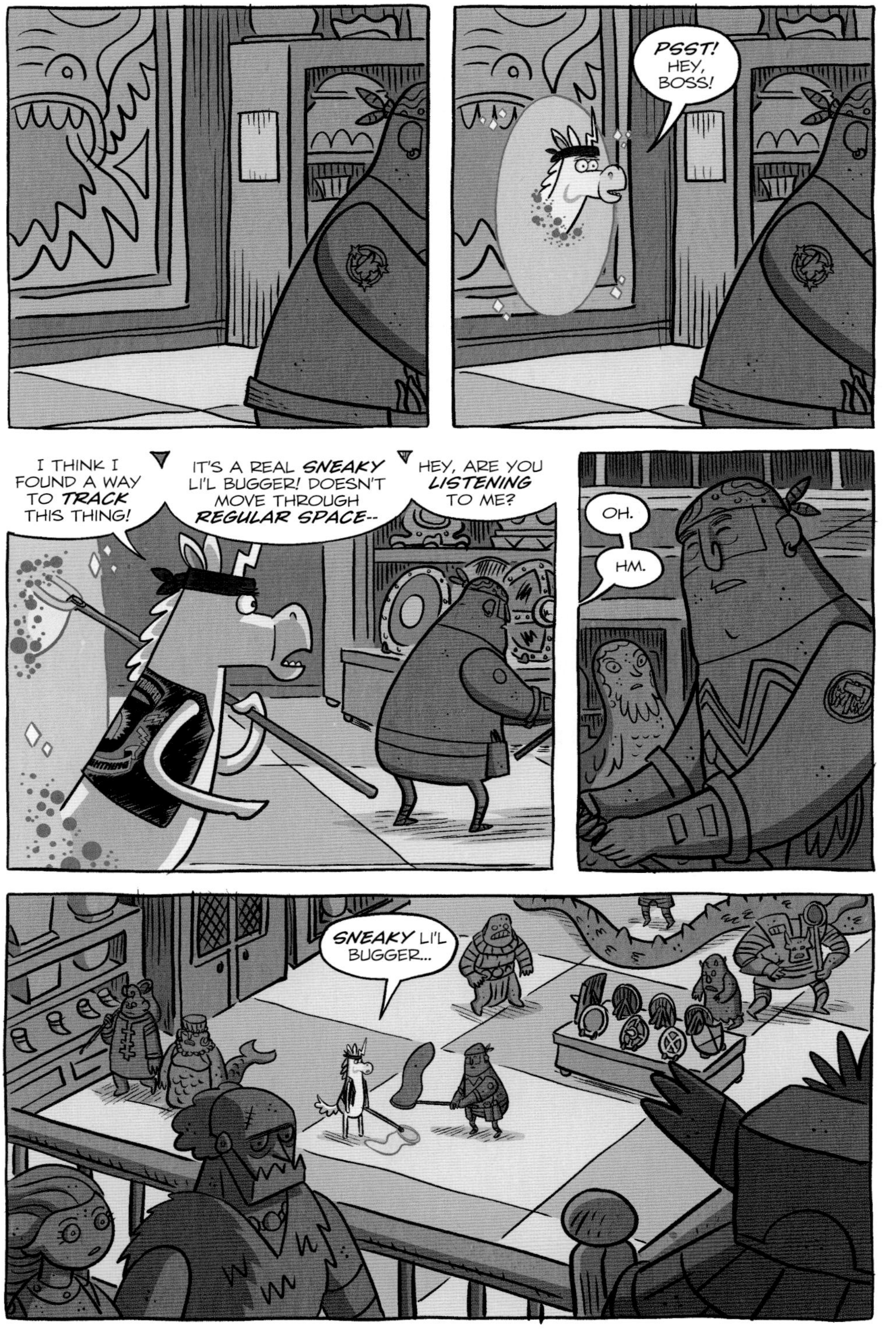
PSST! HEY, BOSS!
I THINK I FOUND A WAY TO TRACK THIS THING!
IT'S A REAL SNEAKY LI'L BUGGER! DOESN'T MOVE THROUGH REGULAR SPACE--
HEY, ARE YOU LISTENING TO ME?
OH.
HM.
SNEAKY LI'L BUGGER...

PART 2:
THE HEART
OF THE MATTER.

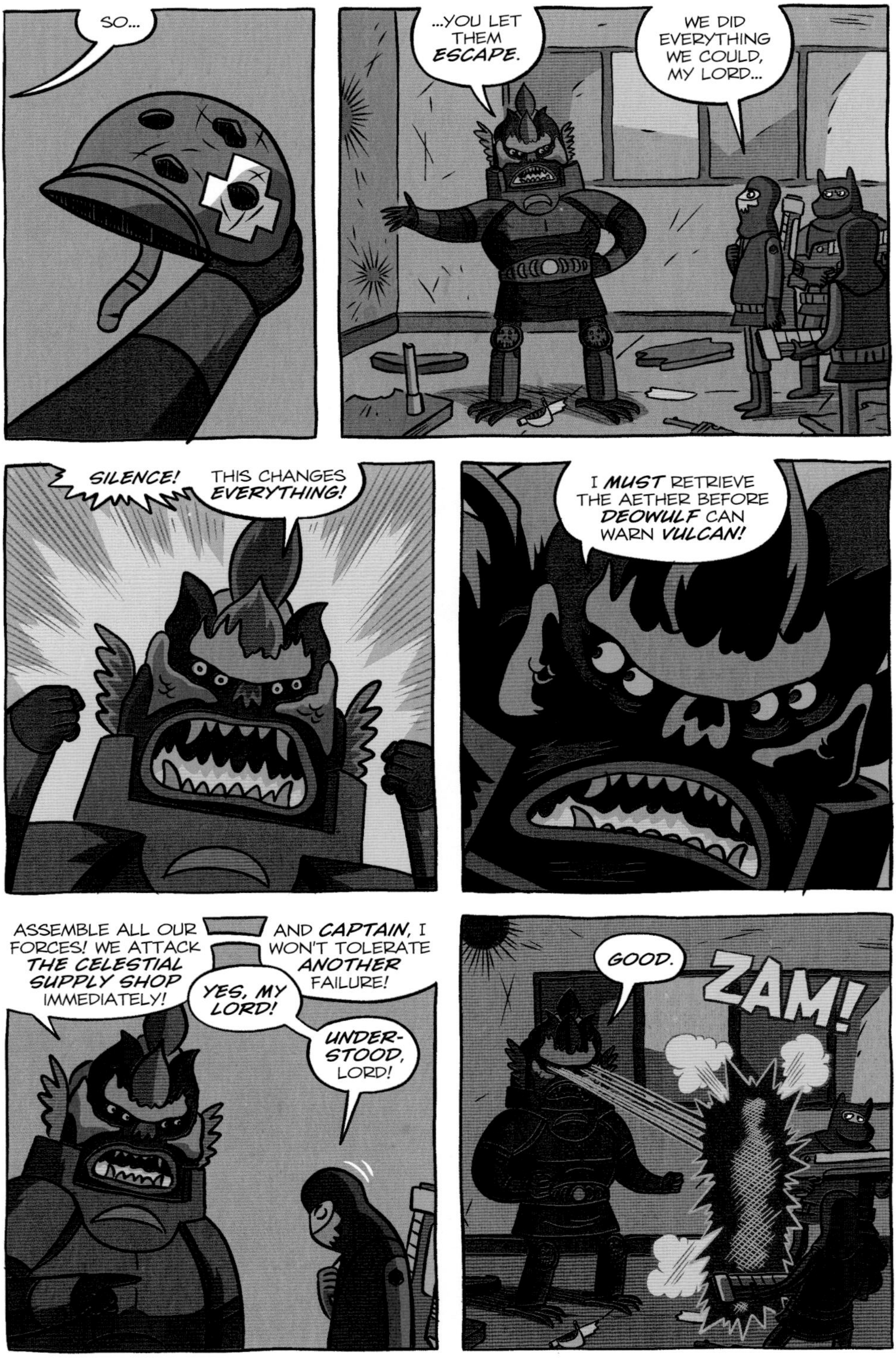
SO...
...YOU LET THEM ESCAPE.
WE DID EVERYTHING WE COULD, MY LORD...
SILENCE!
THIS CHANGES EVERYTHING!
I MUST RETRIEVE THE AETHER BEFORE DEOWULF CAN WARN VULCAN!
ASSEMBLE ALL OUR FORCES! WE ATTACK THE CELESTIAL SUPPLY SHOP IMMEDIATELY!
YES, MY LORD!
AND CAPTAIN, I WON'T TOLERATE ANOTHER FAILURE!
UNDER-STOOD, LORD!
GOOD.
ZAM!

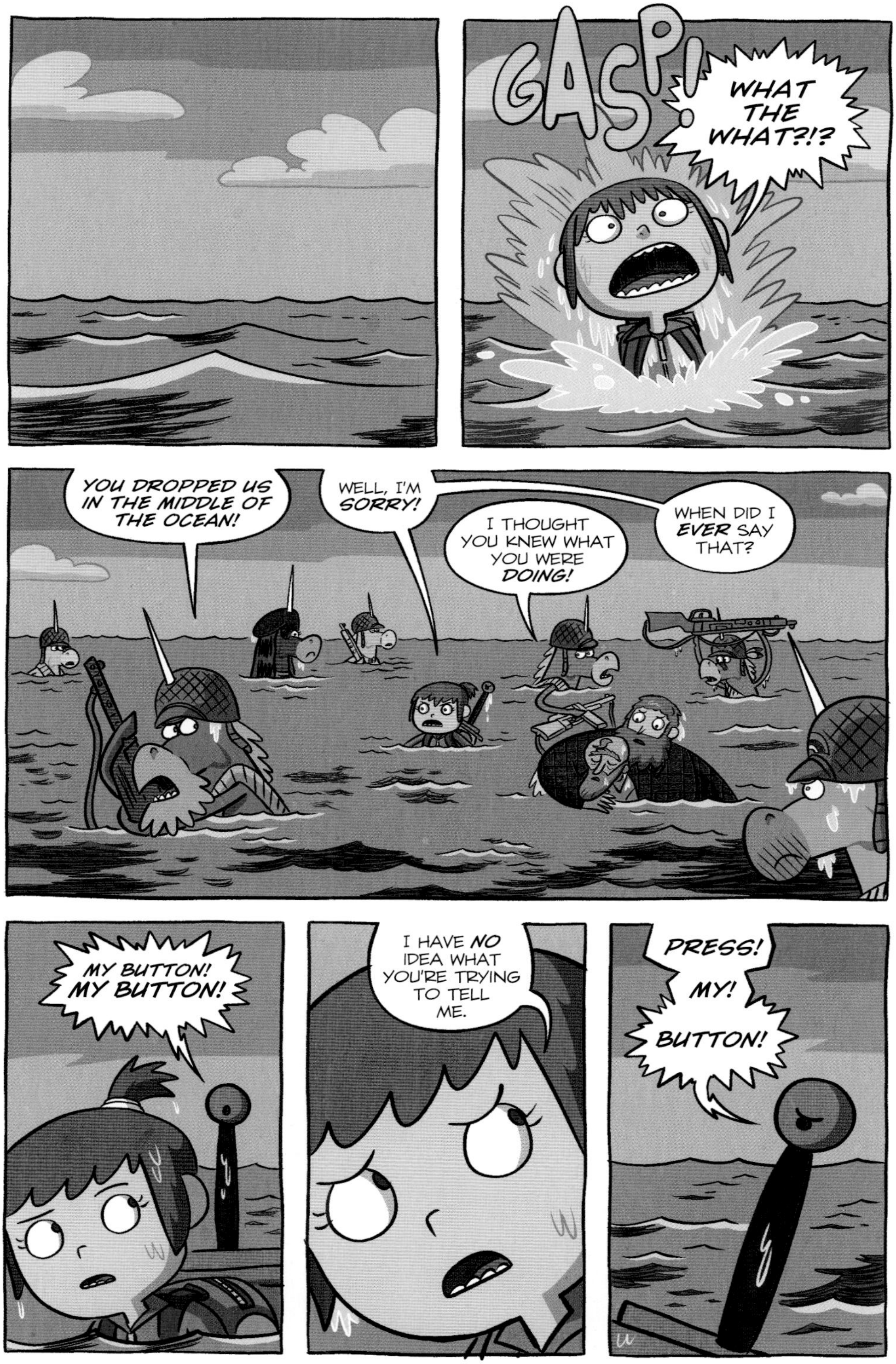
GASP!
WHAT THE WHAT?!?
YOU DROPPED US IN THE MIDDLE OF THE OCEAN!
WELL, I'M SORRY!
I THOUGHT YOU KNEW WHAT YOU WERE DOING!
WHEN DID I EVER SAY THAT?
MY BUTTON! MY BUTTON!
I HAVE NO IDEA WHAT YOU'RE TRYING TO TELL ME.
PRESS!
MY!
BUTTON!

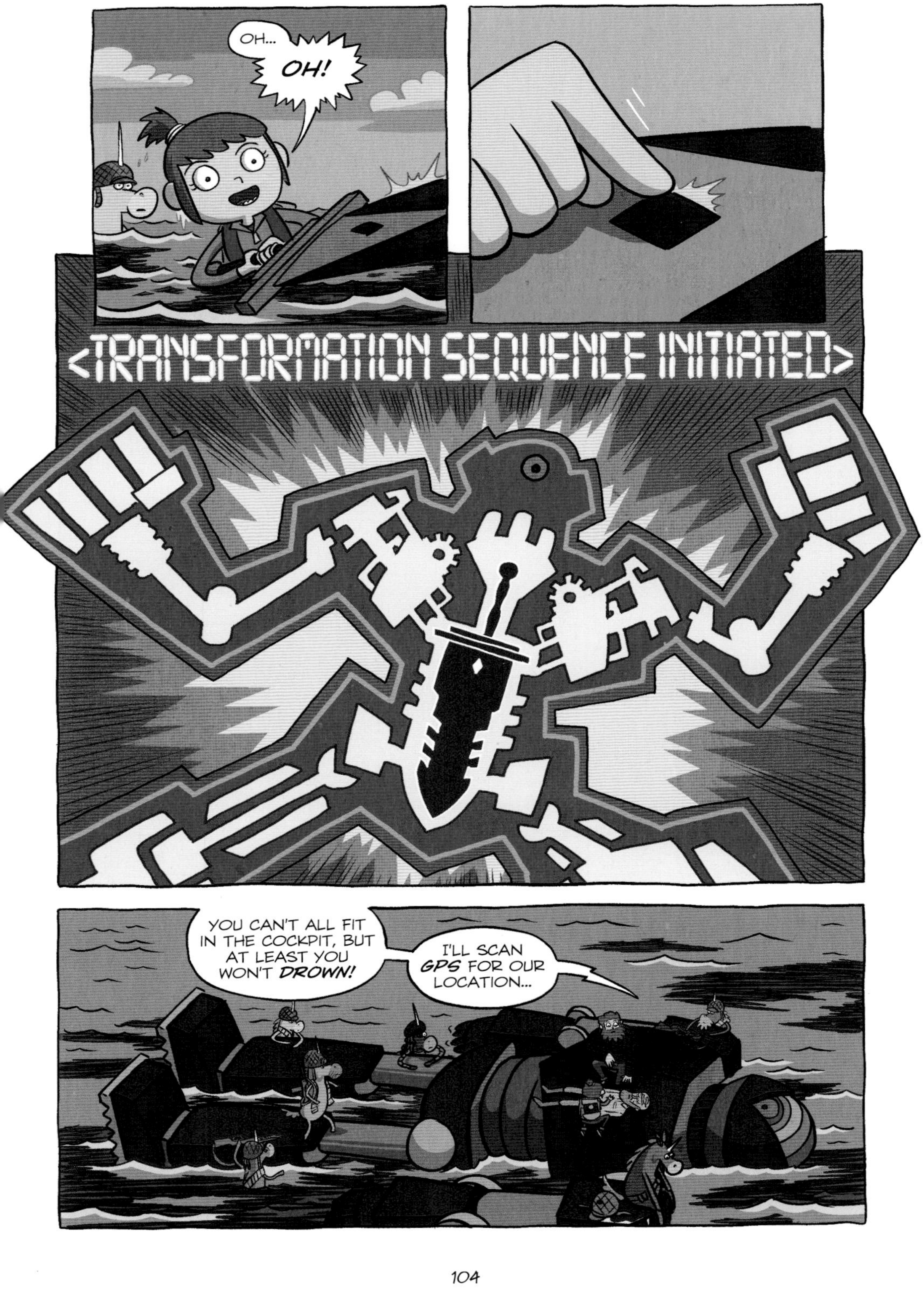

OH...
OH!
<TRANSFORMATION SEQUENCE INITIATED>
YOU CAN'T ALL FIT IN THE COCKPIT, BUT AT LEAST YOU WON'T DROWN!
I'LL SCAN GPS FOR OUR LOCATION...

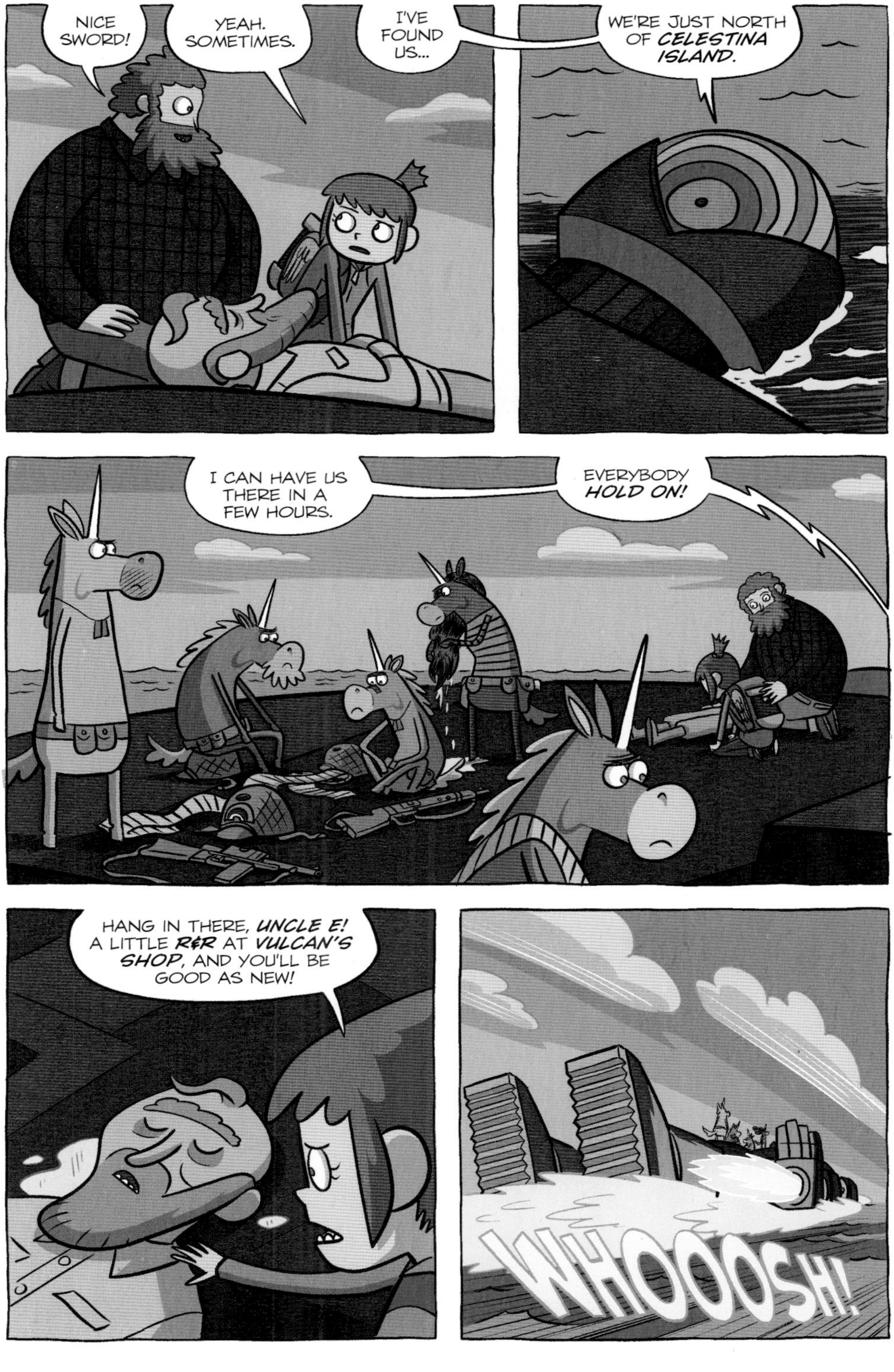
NICE SWORD!
YEAH. SOMETIMES.
I'VE FOUND US...
WE'RE JUST NORTH OF CELESTINA ISLAND.
I CAN HAVE US THERE IN A FEW HOURS.
EVERYBODY HOLD ON!
HANG IN THERE, UNCLE E! A LITTLE R&R AT VULCAN'S SHOP, AND YOU'LL BE GOOD AS NEW!
WHOOOSH!

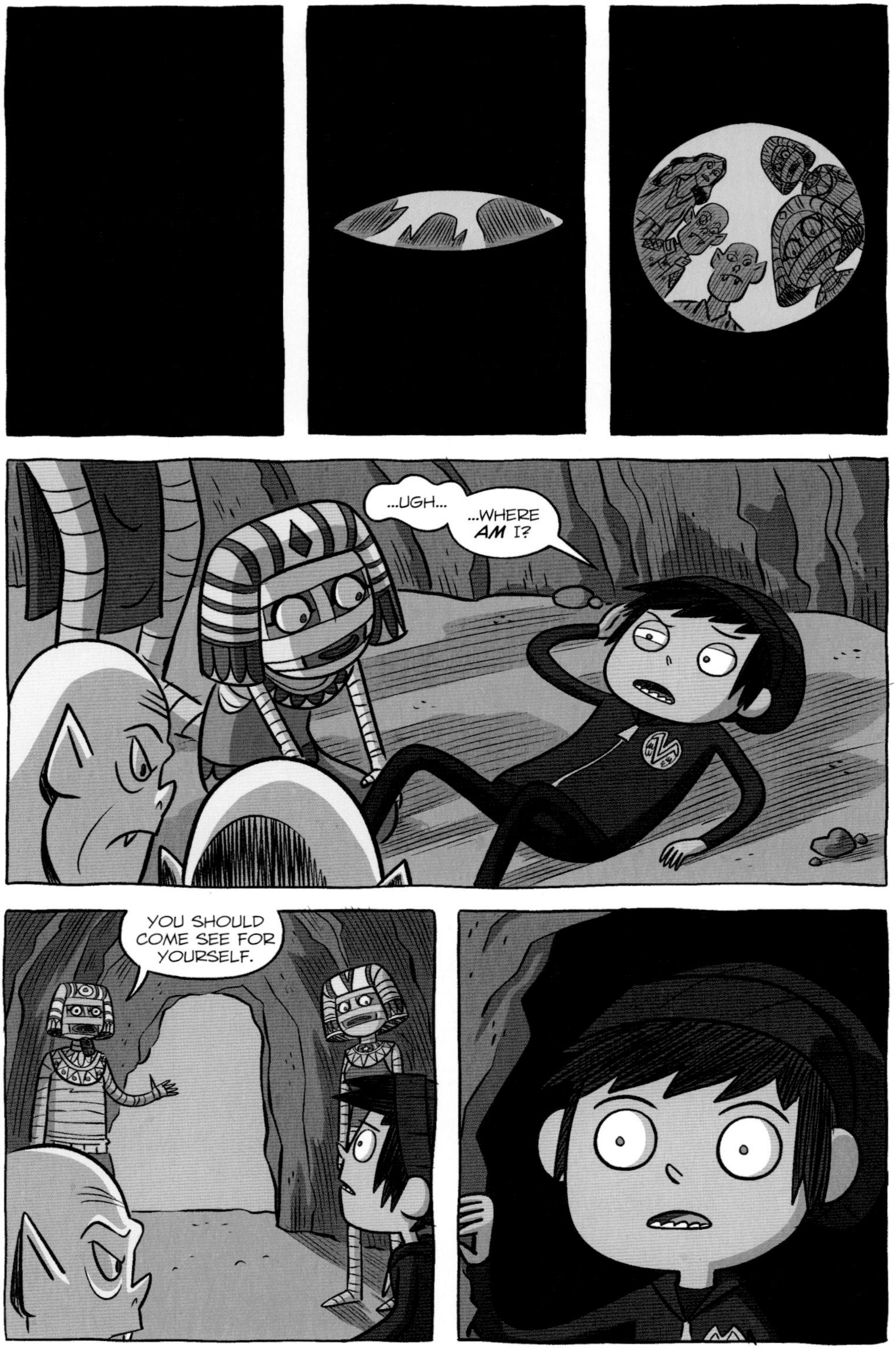
...UGH...
...WHERE AM I?
YOU SHOULD COME SEE FOR YOURSELF.

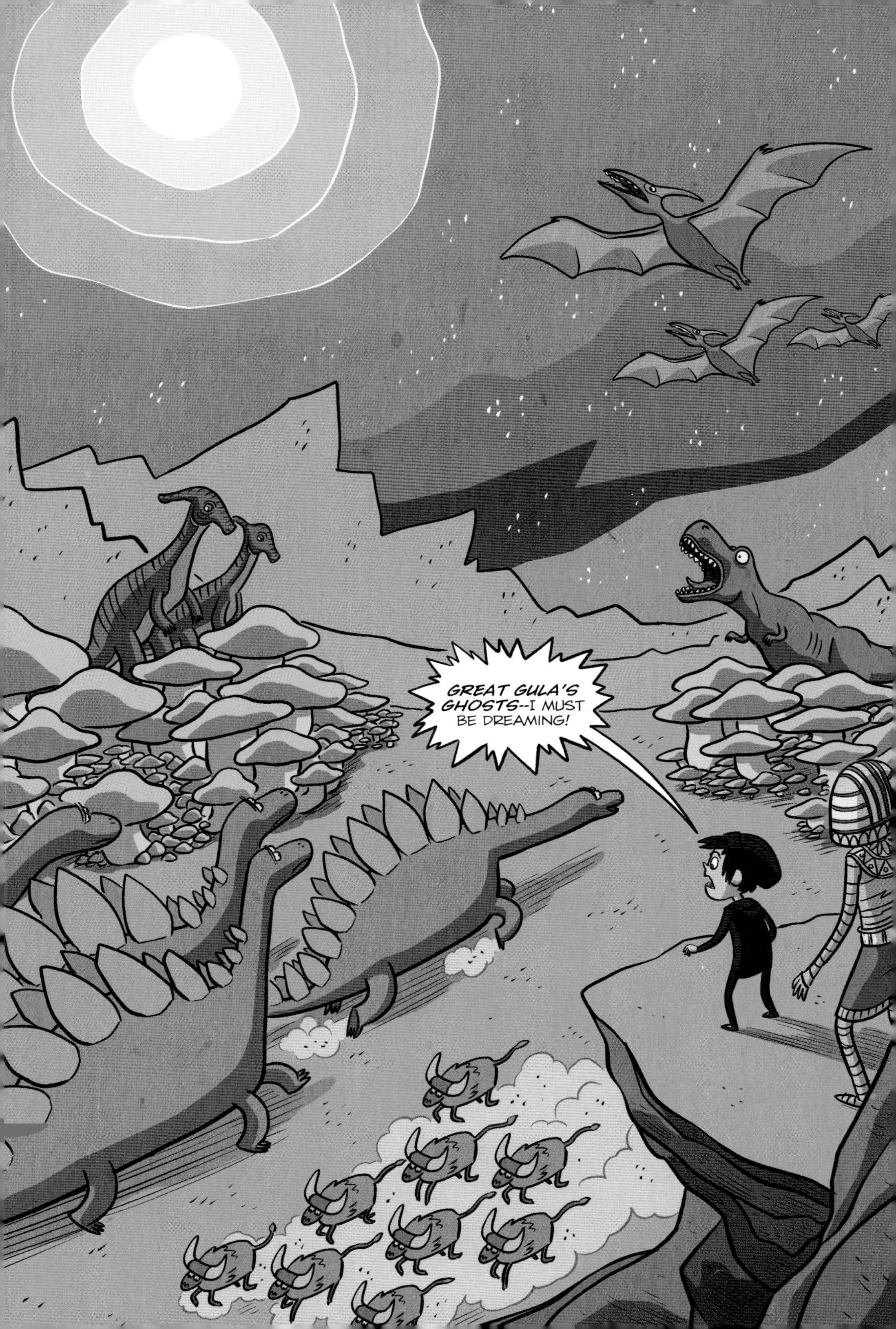
GREAT GULA'S GHOSTS--I MUST BE DREAMING!

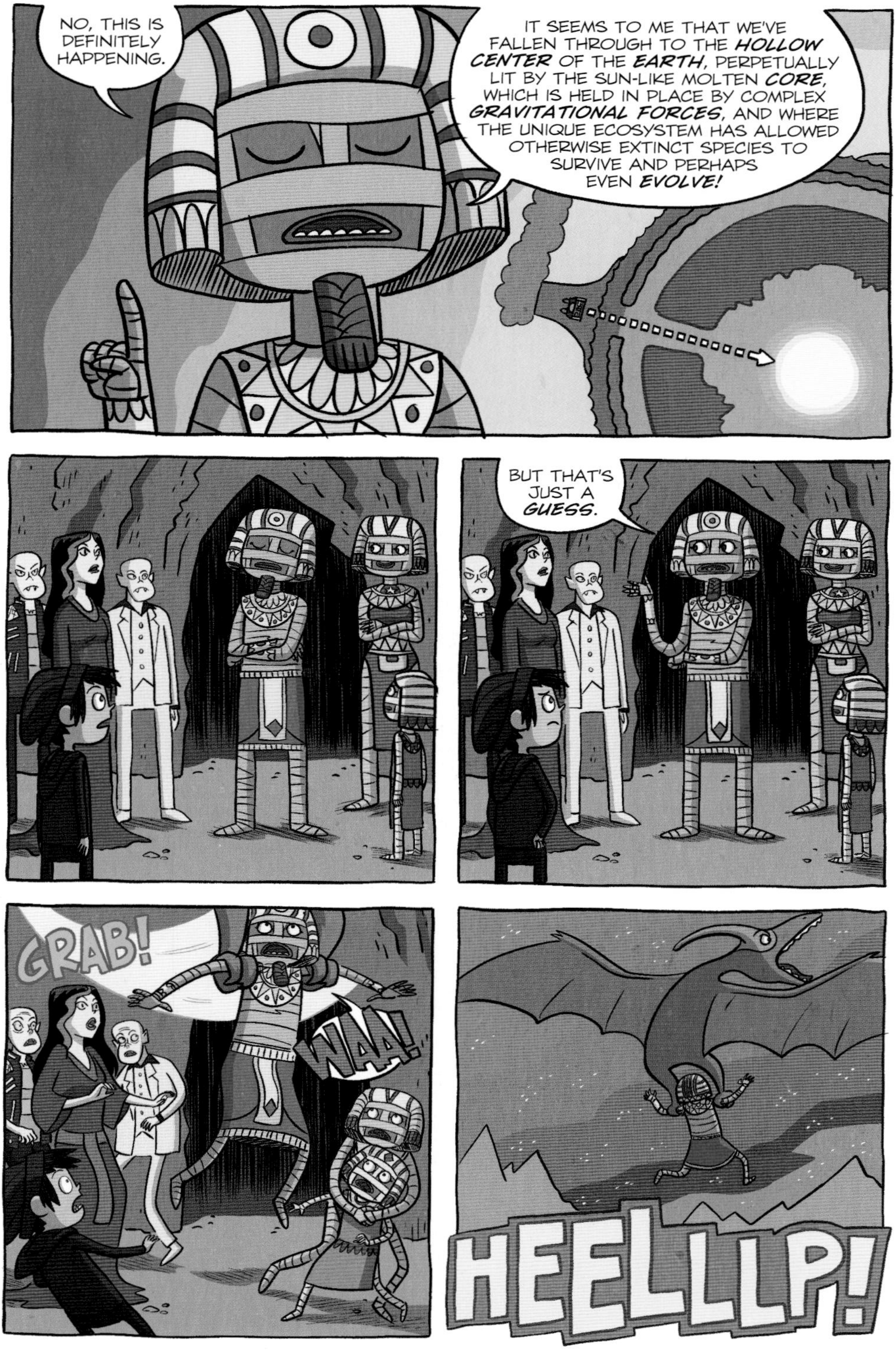
NO, THIS IS DEFINITELY HAPPENING.
IT SEEMS TO ME THAT WE'VE FALLEN THROUGH TO THE HOLLOW CENTER OF THE EARTH, PERPETUALLY LIT BY THE SUN-LIKE MOLTEN CORE, WHICH IS HELD IN PLACE BY COMPLEX GRAVITATIONAL FORCES, AND WHERE THE UNIQUE ECOSYSTEM HAS ALLOWED OTHERWISE EXTINCT SPECIES TO SURVIVE AND PERHAPS EVEN EVOLVE!
CORE
BUT THAT'S JUST A GUESS.
GRAB!
WAA!
HEELLLP!

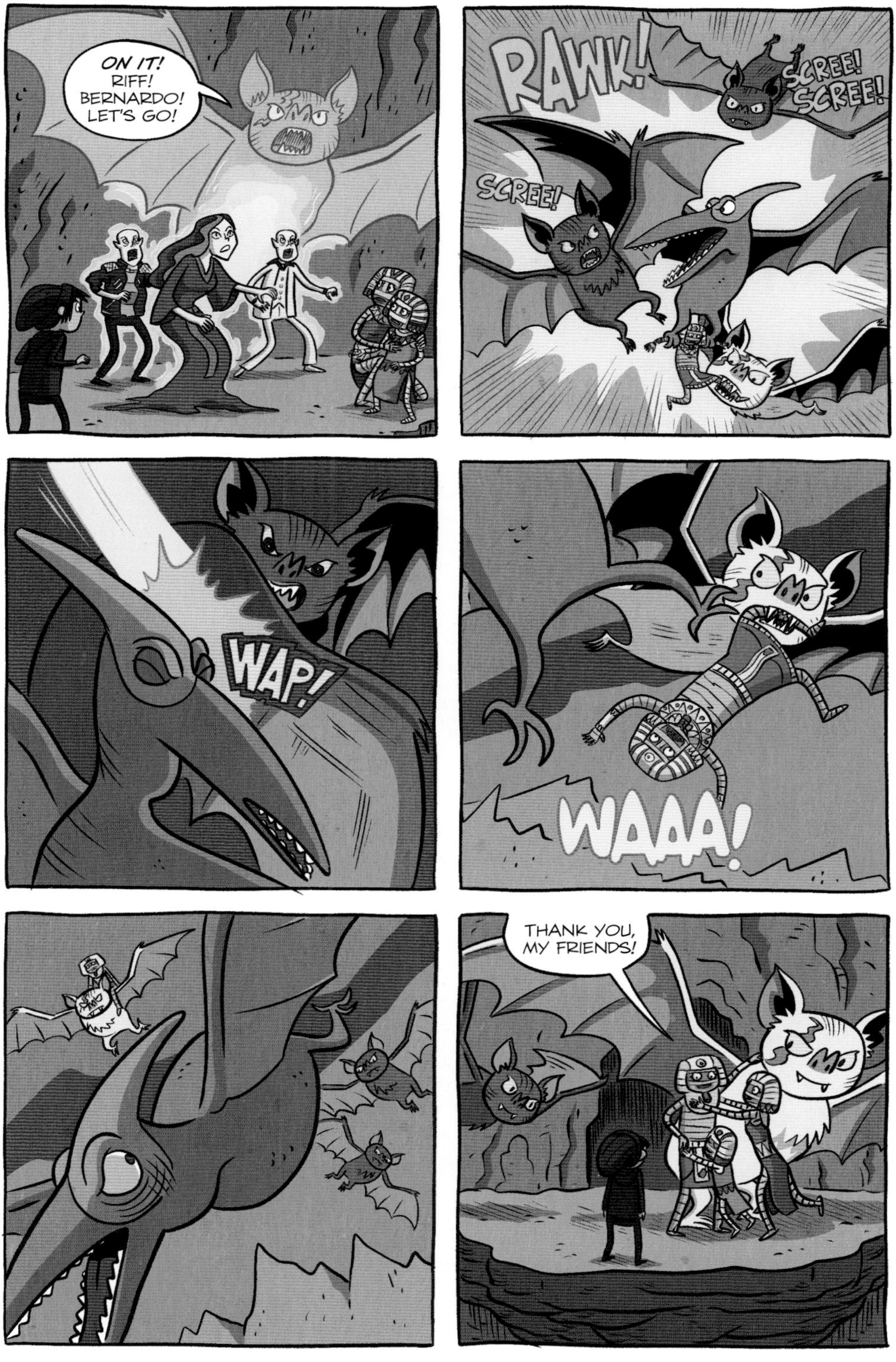
ON IT!
RIFF!
BERNARDO!
LET'S GO!
RAWK!
SCREE! SCREE!
SCREE!
WAP!
WAAA!
THANK YOU, MY FRIENDS!

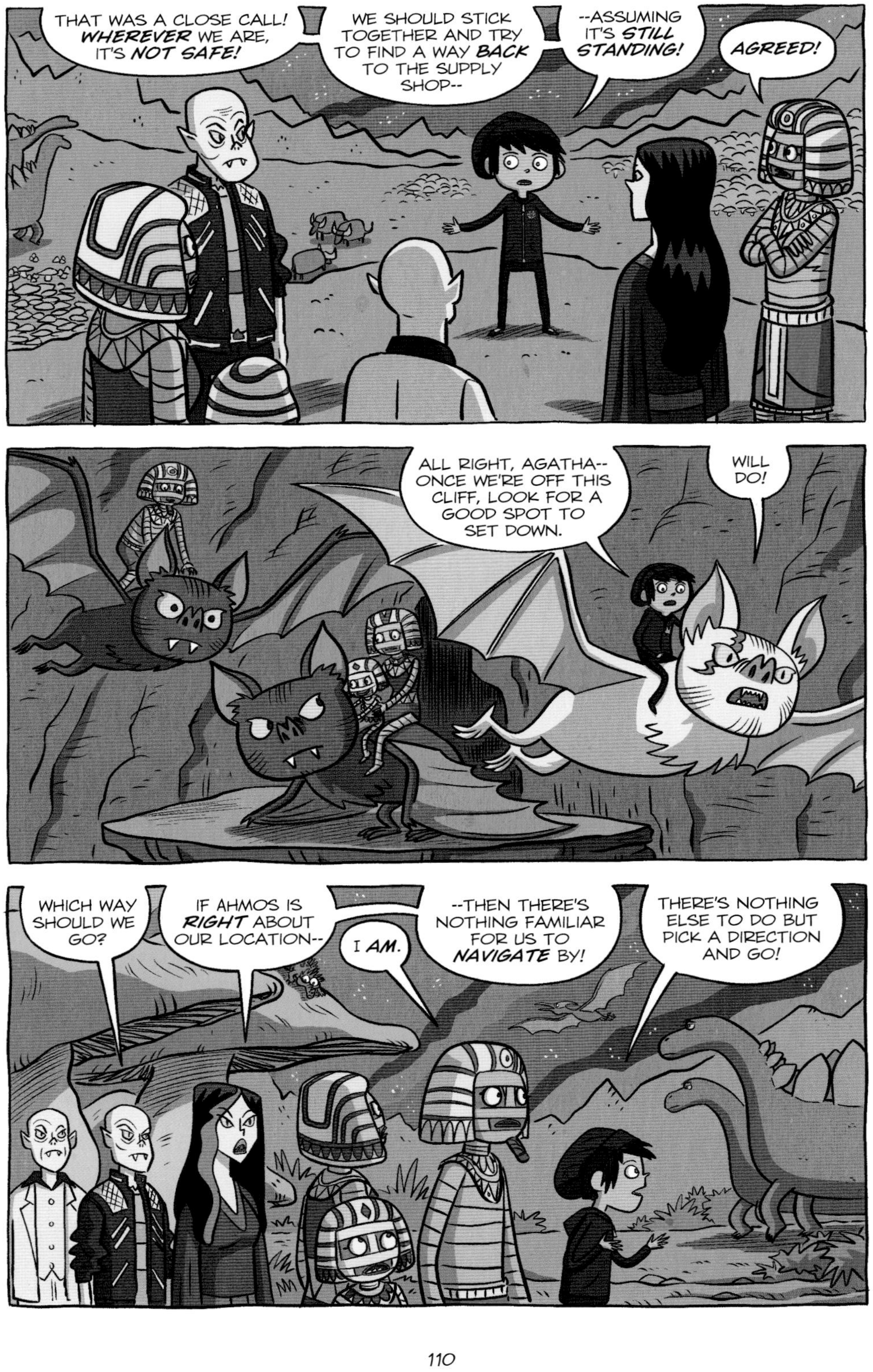
THAT WAS A CLOSE CALL! WHEREVER WE ARE, IT'S NOT SAFE!
WE SHOULD STICK TOGETHER AND TRY TO FIND A WAY BACK TO THE SUPPLY SHOP--
--ASSUMING IT'S STILL STANDING!
AGREED!
ALL RIGHT, AGATHA-- ONCE WE'RE OFF THIS CLIFF, LOOK FOR A GOOD SPOT TO SET DOWN.
WILL DO!
WHICH WAY SHOULD WE GO?
IF AHMOS IS RIGHT ABOUT OUR LOCATION--
I AM.
--THEN THERE'S NOTHING FAMILIAR FOR US TO NAVIGATE BY!
THERE'S NOTHING ELSE TO DO BUT PICK A DIRECTION AND GO!

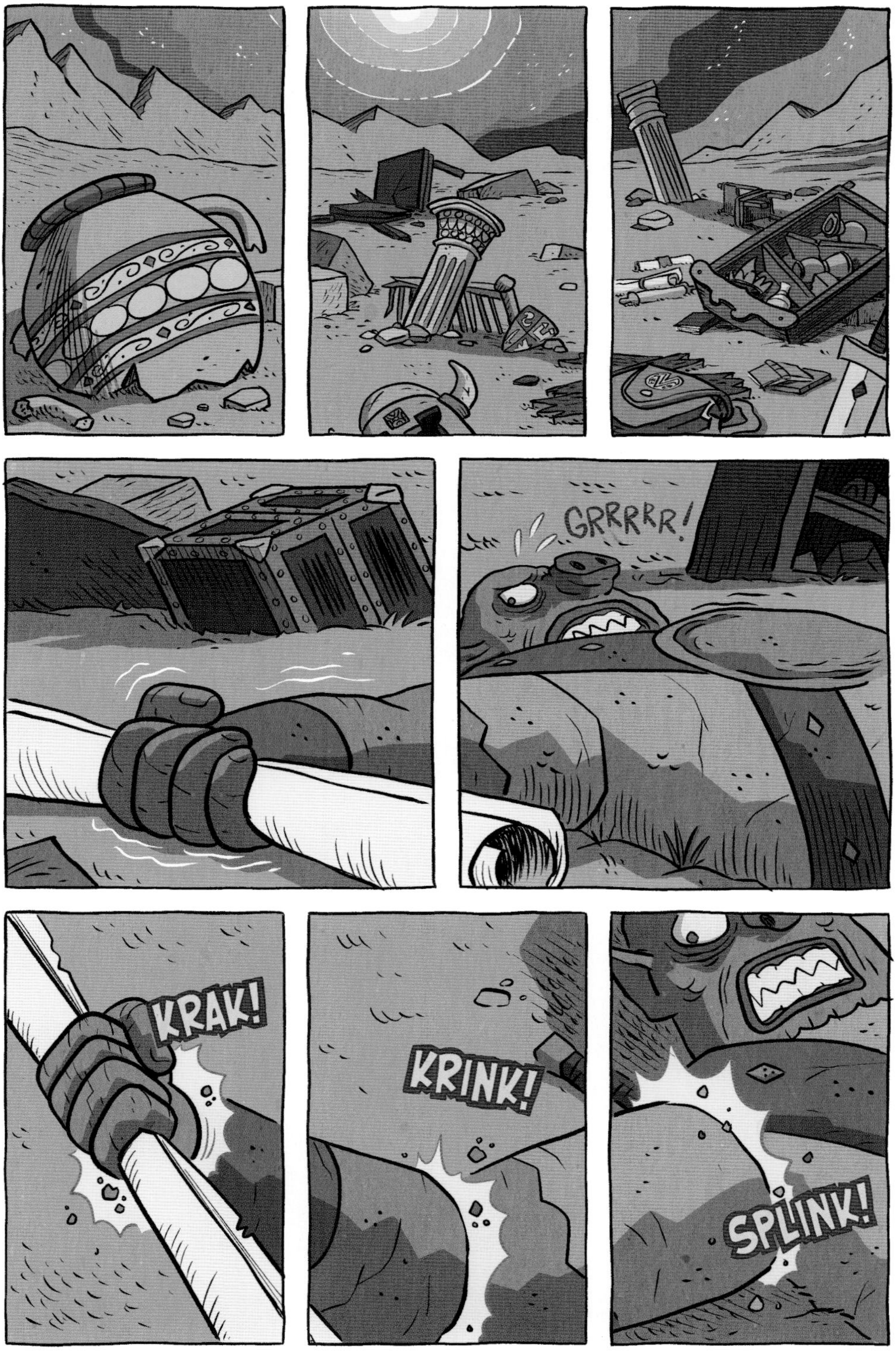
GRRRRR!
KRAK!
KRINK!
SPLINK!

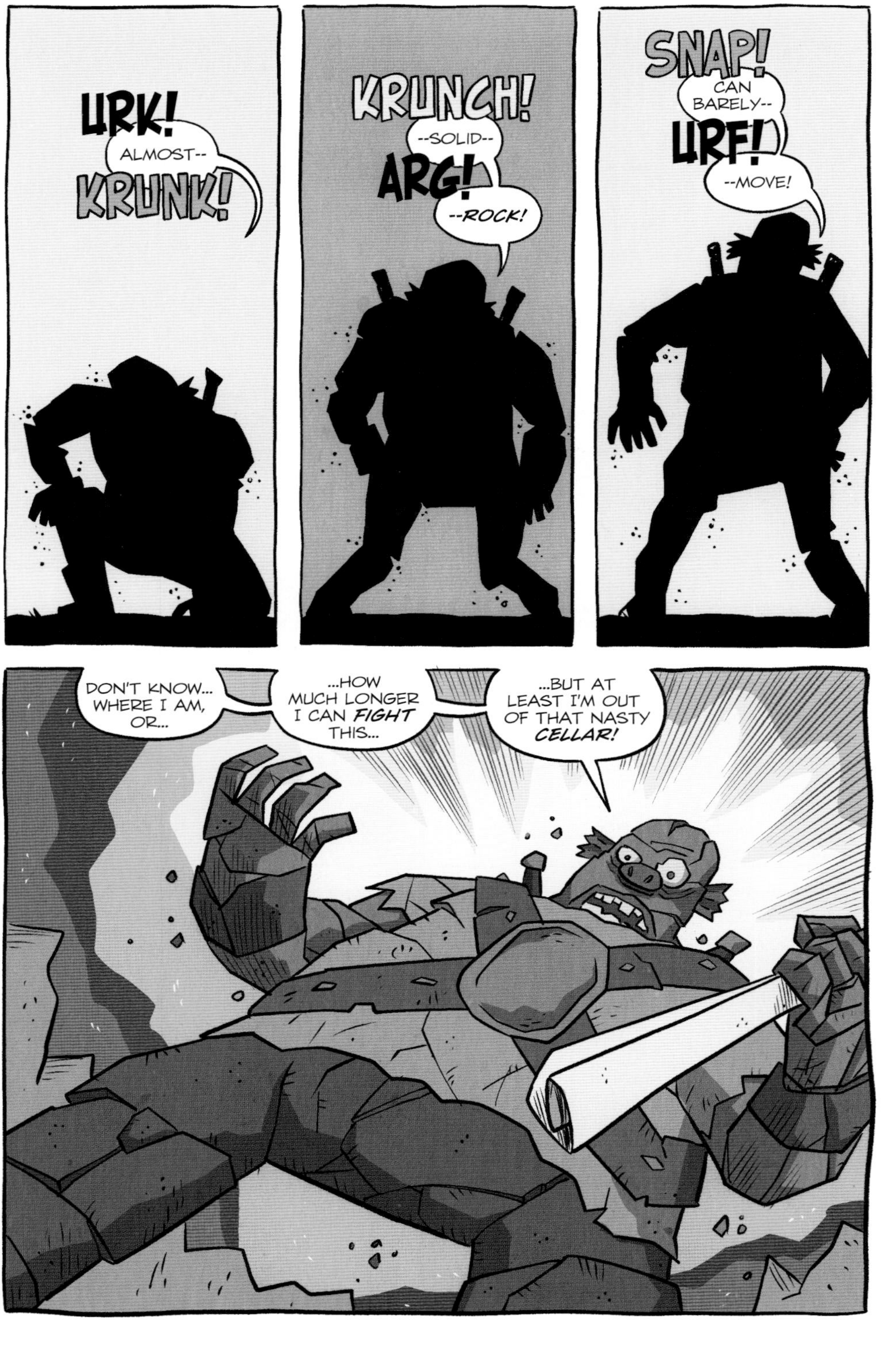
URK!
ALMOST--
KRUNK!
KRUNCH!
--SOLID--
ARG!
--ROCK!
SNAP!
CAN BARELY--
URF!
--MOVE!
DON'T KNOW... WHERE I AM, OR...
...HOW MUCH LONGER I CAN *FIGHT* THIS...
...BUT AT LEAST I'M OUT OF THAT NASTY *CELLAR!*

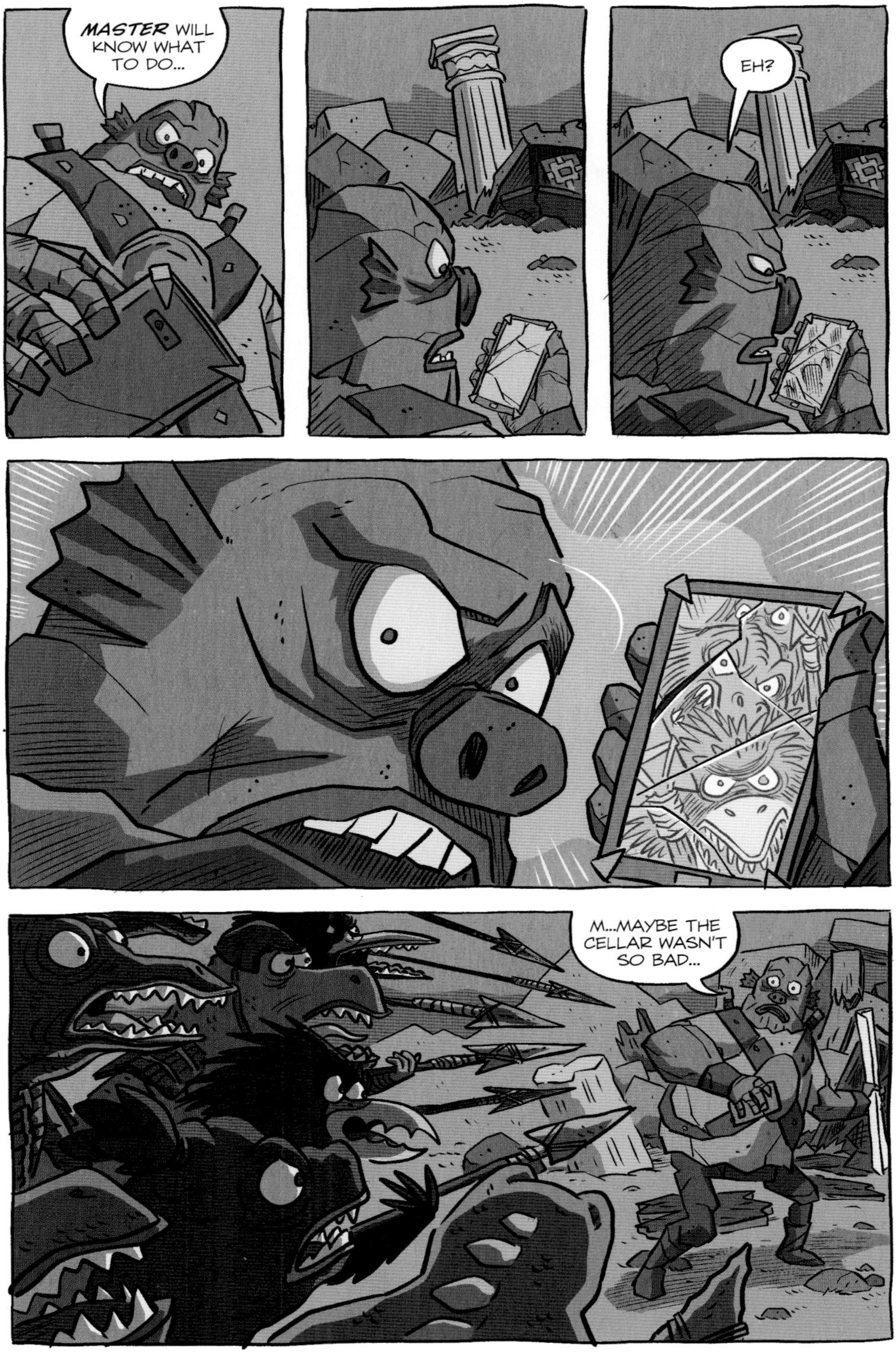
MASTER WILL KNOW WHAT TO DO...
EH?
M...MAYBE THE CELLAR WASN'T SO BAD...

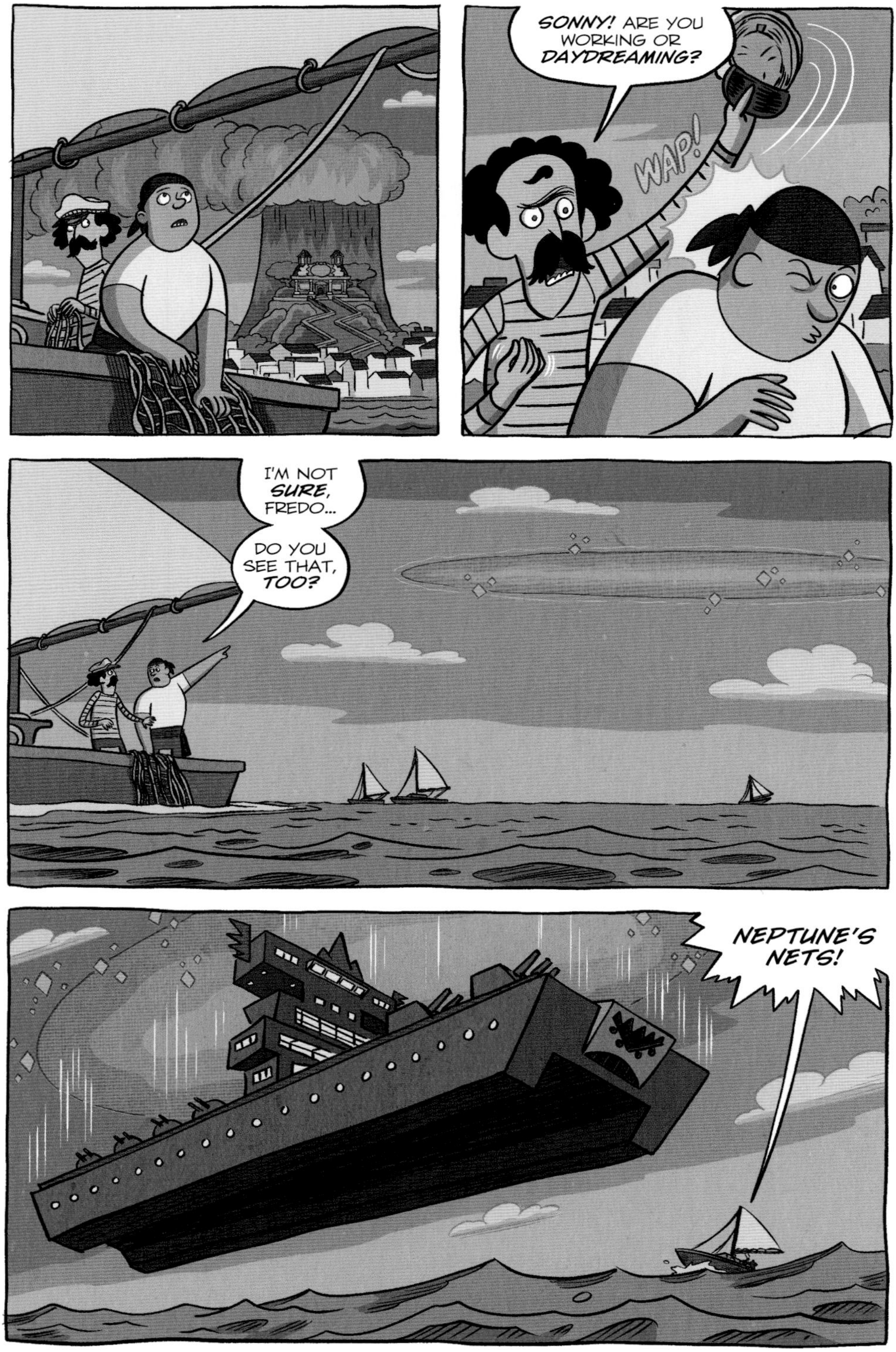
SONNY! ARE YOU WORKING OR DAYDREAMING?
WAP!
I'M NOT SURE, FREDO...
DO YOU SEE THAT, TOO?
NEPTUNE'S NETS!

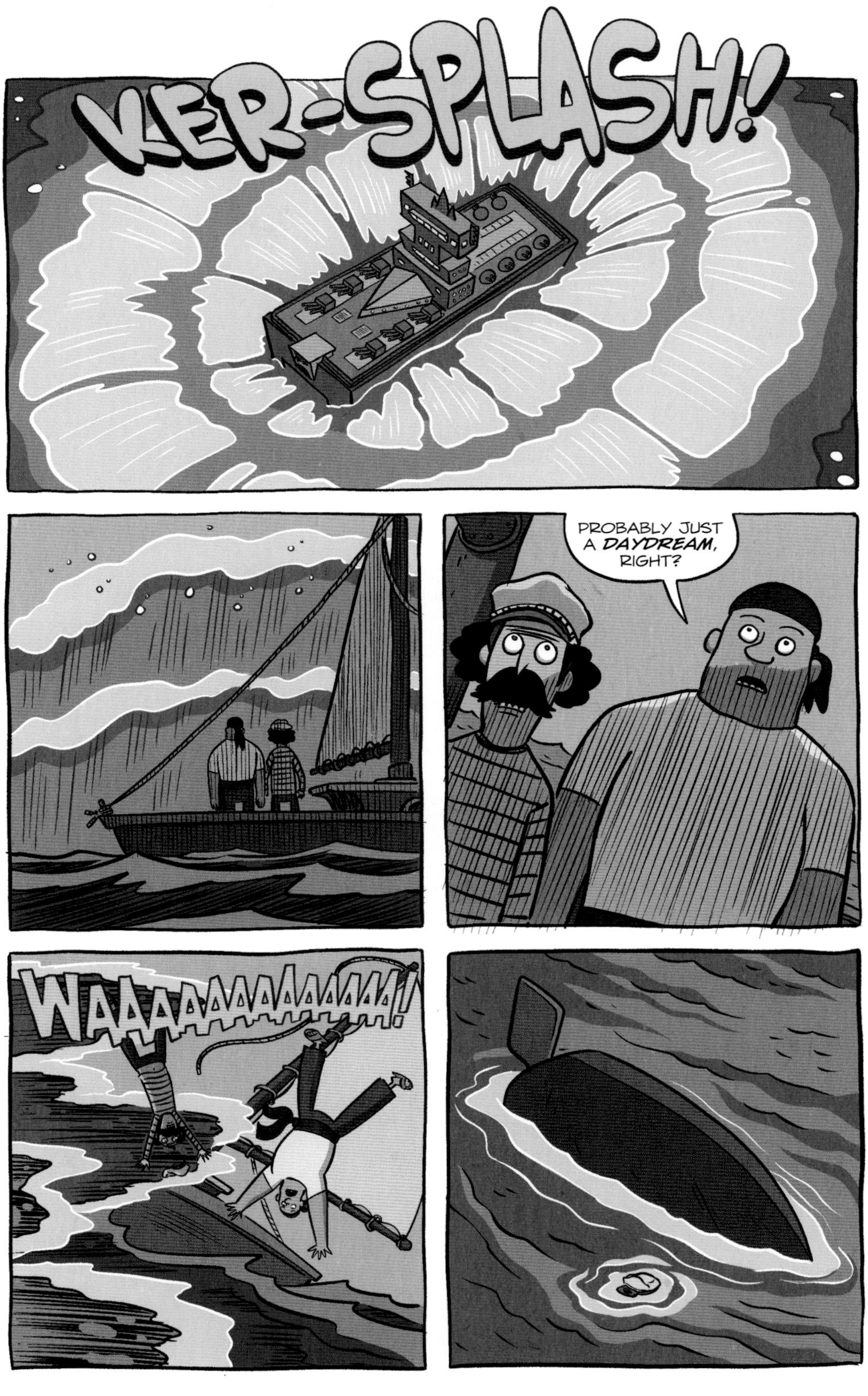
KER-SPLASH!
PROBABLY JUST A DAYDREAM, RIGHT?
WAAAAAAAAAAAAA!

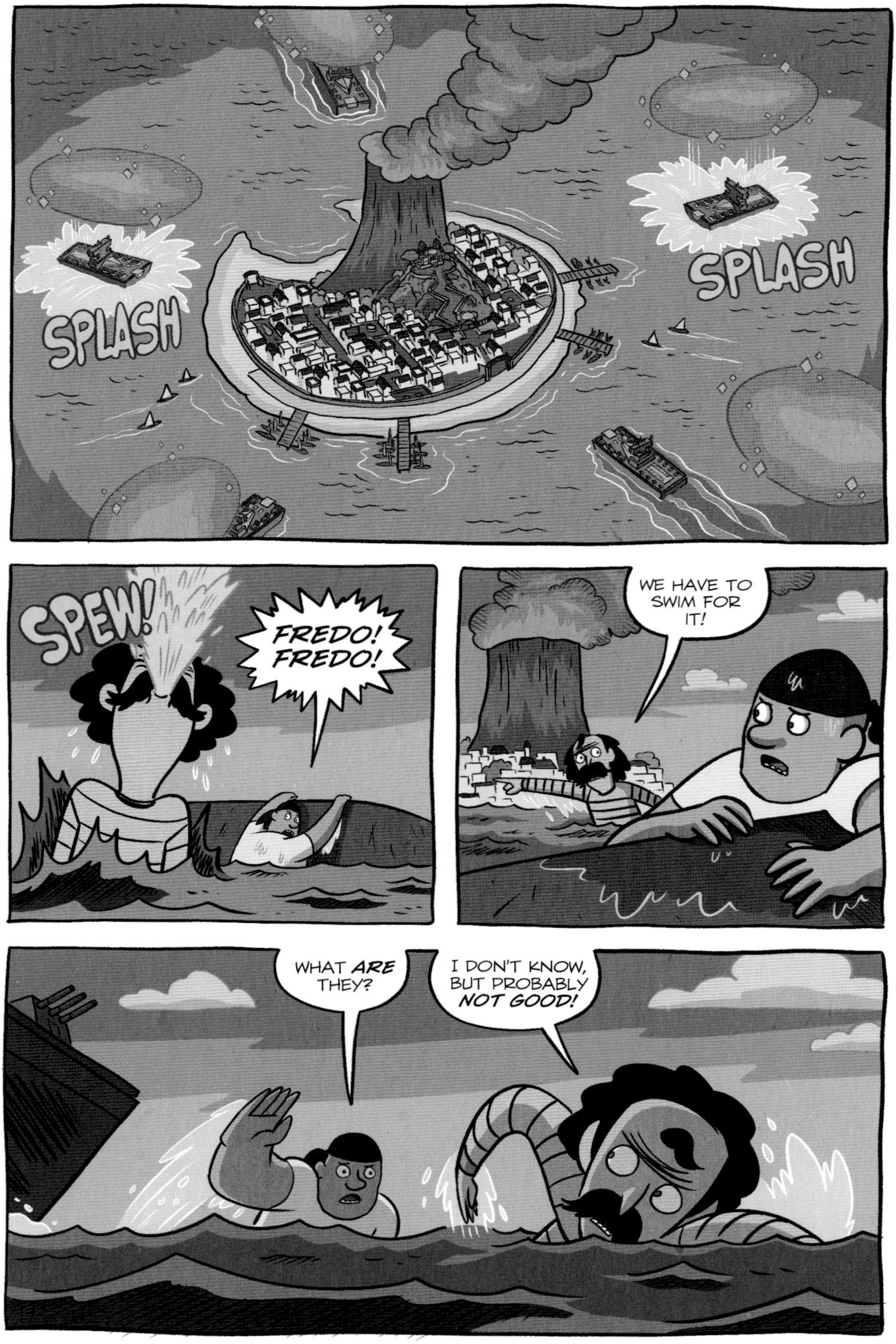
SPLASH
SPLASH
SPEW!
FREDO! FREDO!
WE HAVE TO SWIM FOR IT!
WHAT ARE THEY?
I DON'T KNOW, BUT PROBABLY NOT GOOD!

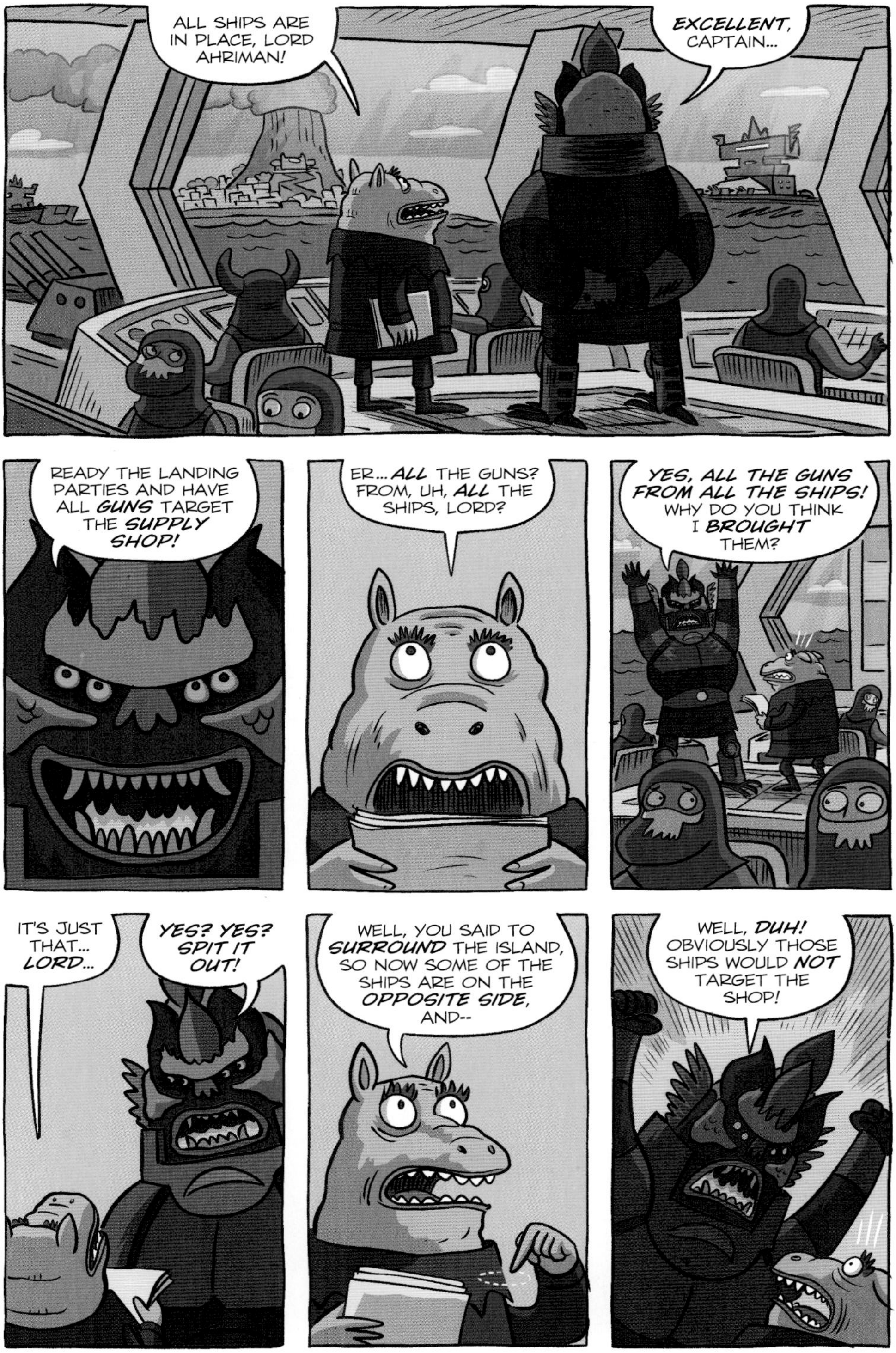
ALL SHIPS ARE IN PLACE, LORD AHRIMAN!
EXCELLENT, CAPTAIN...
READY THE LANDING PARTIES AND HAVE ALL GUNS TARGET THE SUPPLY SHOP!
ER... ALL THE GUNS? FROM, UH, ALL THE SHIPS, LORD?
YES, ALL THE GUNS FROM ALL THE SHIPS! WHY DO YOU THINK I BROUGHT THEM?
IT'S JUST THAT... LORD...
YES? YES? SPIT IT OUT!
WELL, YOU SAID TO SURROUND THE ISLAND, SO NOW SOME OF THE SHIPS ARE ON THE OPPOSITE SIDE, AND--
WELL, DUH! OBVIOUSLY THOSE SHIPS WOULD NOT TARGET THE SHOP!

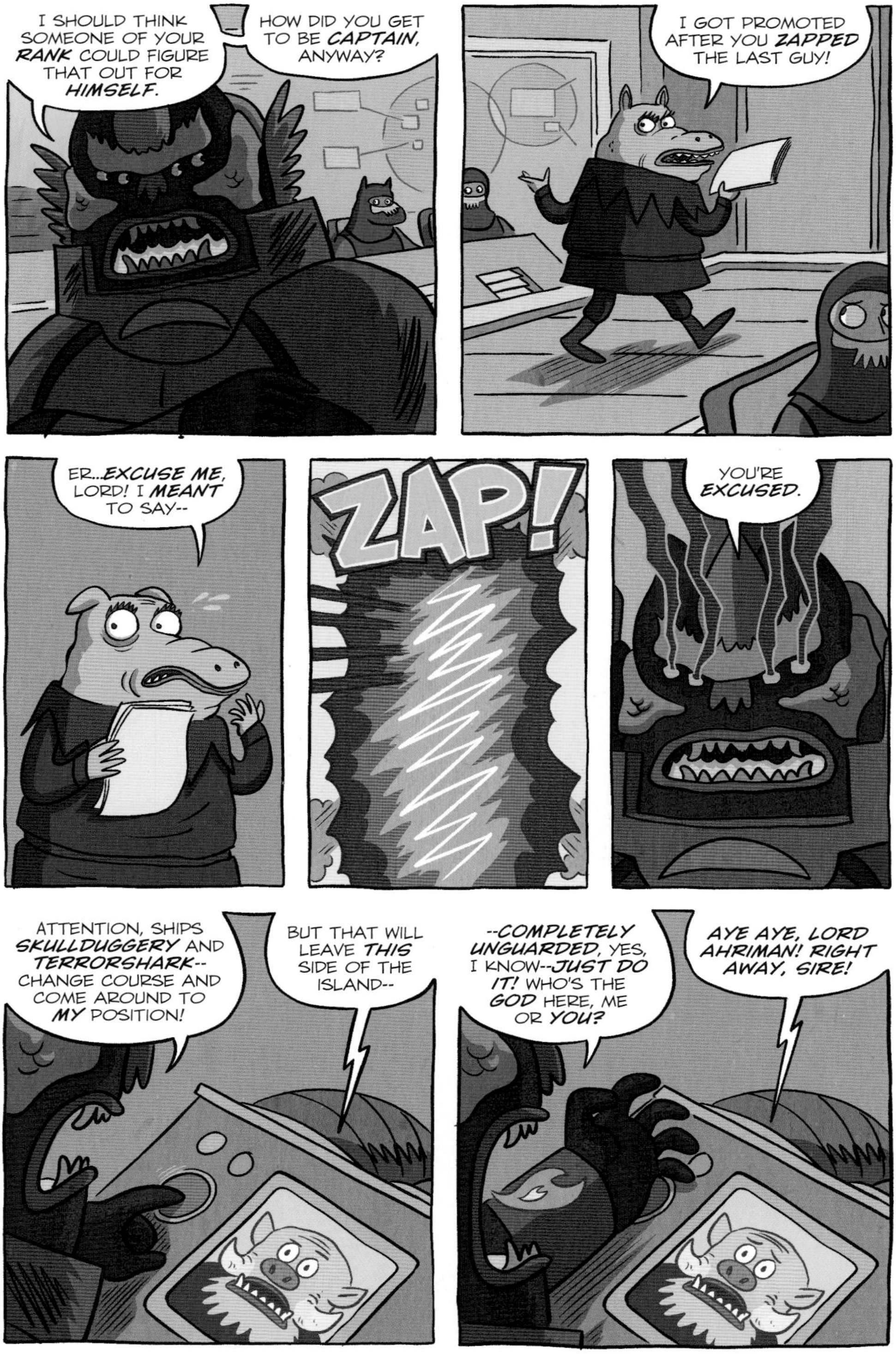
I SHOULD THINK SOMEONE OF YOUR RANK COULD FIGURE THAT OUT FOR HIMSELF.
HOW DID YOU GET TO BE CAPTAIN, ANYWAY?
I GOT PROMOTED AFTER YOU ZAPPED THE LAST GUY!
ER...EXCUSE ME, LORD! I MEANT TO SAY--
ZAP!
YOU'RE EXCUSED.
ATTENTION, SHIPS SKULLDUGGERY AND TERRORSHARK--CHANGE COURSE AND COME AROUND TO MY POSITION!
BUT THAT WILL LEAVE THIS SIDE OF THE ISLAND--
--COMPLETELY UNGUARDED, YES, I KNOW--JUST DO IT! WHO'S THE GOD HERE, ME OR YOU?
AYE AYE, LORD AHRIMAN! RIGHT AWAY, SIRE!

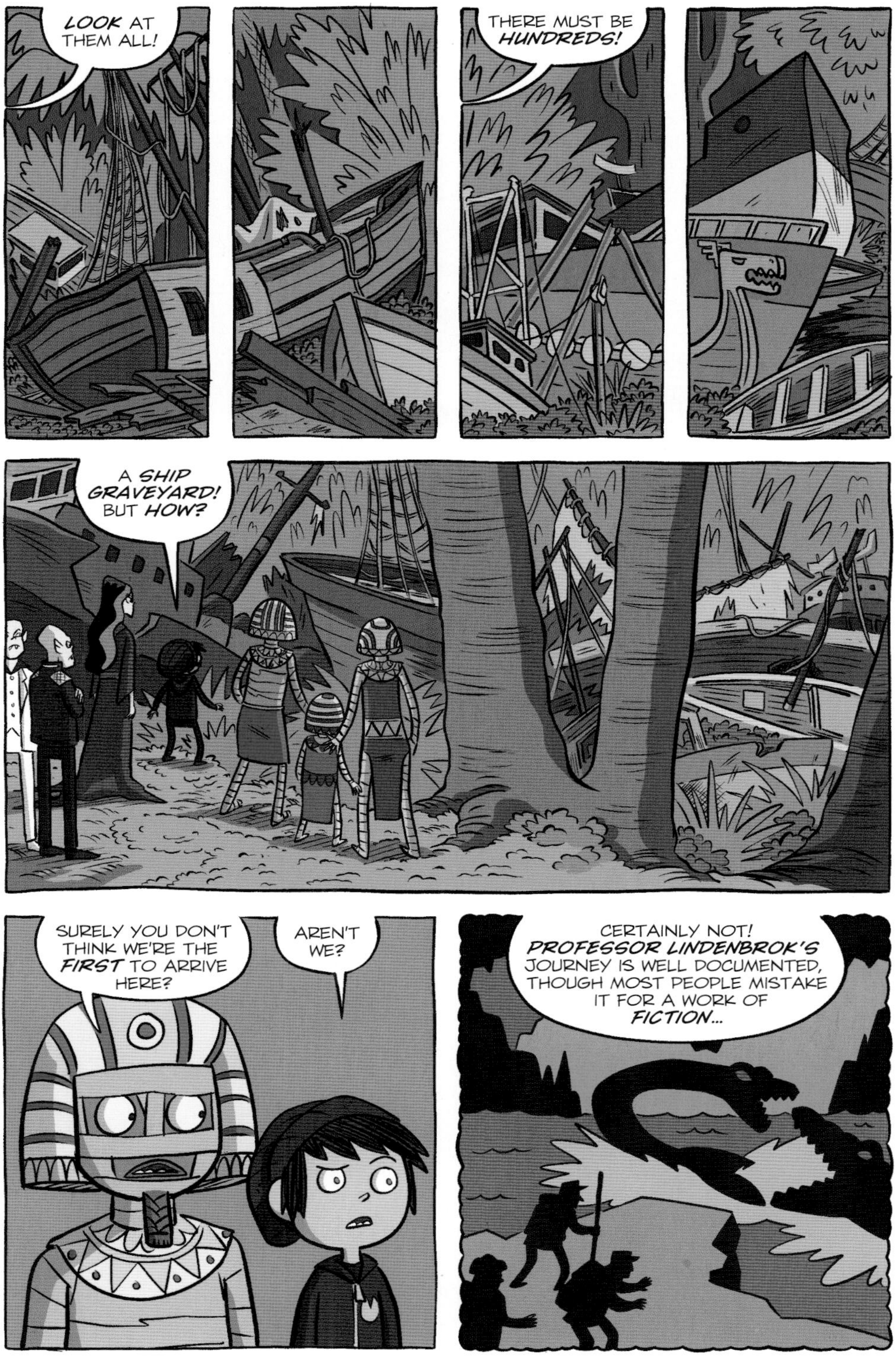
LOOK AT THEM ALL!
THERE MUST BE HUNDREDS!
A SHIP GRAVEYARD! BUT HOW?
SURELY YOU DON'T THINK WE'RE THE FIRST TO ARRIVE HERE?
AREN'T WE?
CERTAINLY NOT! PROFESSOR LINDENBROK'S JOURNEY IS WELL DOCUMENTED, THOUGH MOST PEOPLE MISTAKE IT FOR A WORK OF FICTION...

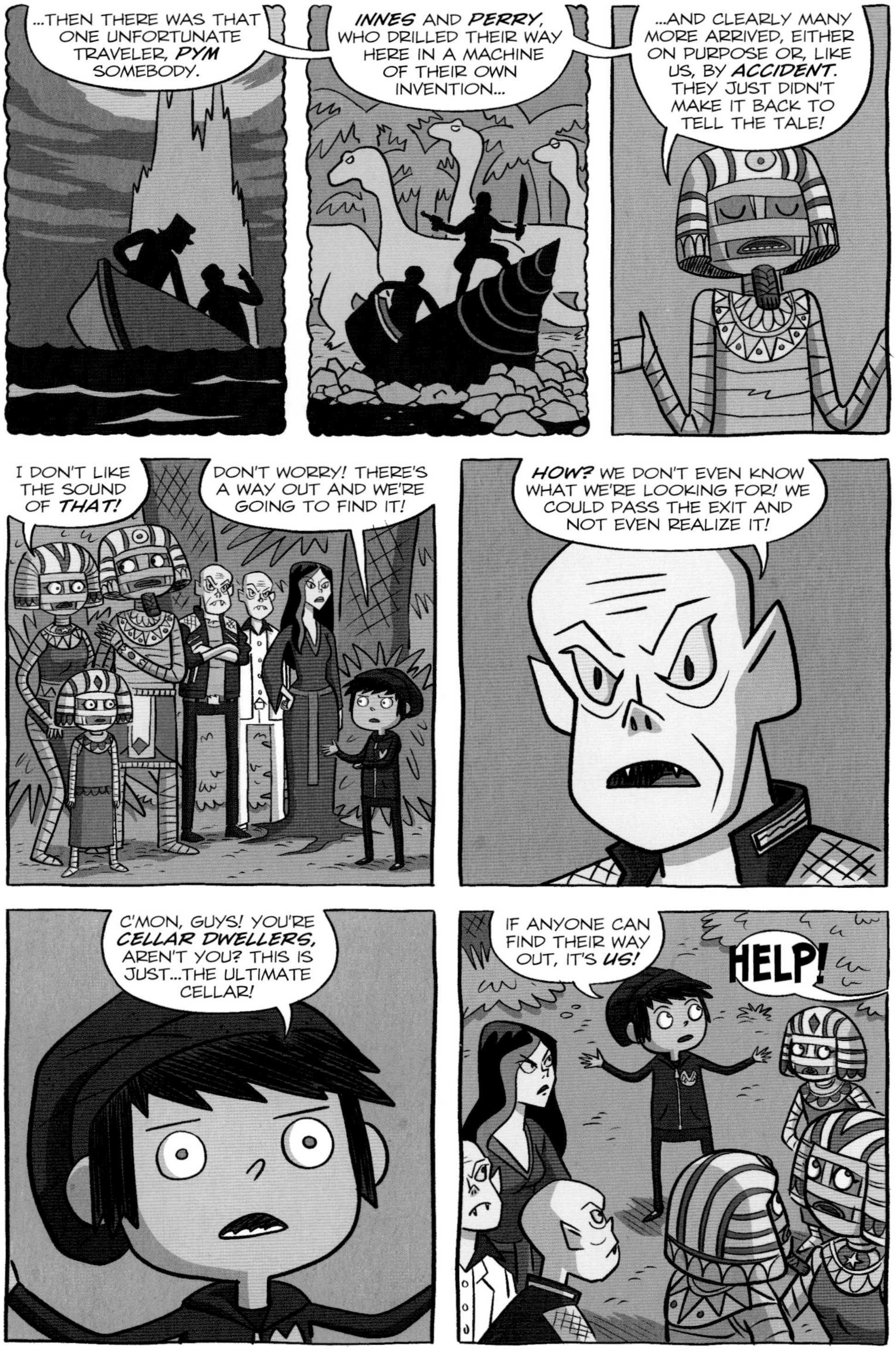
...THEN THERE WAS THAT ONE UNFORTUNATE TRAVELER, PYM SOMEBODY.
INNES AND PERRY, WHO DRILLED THEIR WAY HERE IN A MACHINE OF THEIR OWN INVENTION...
...AND CLEARLY MANY MORE ARRIVED, EITHER ON PURPOSE OR, LIKE US, BY ACCIDENT. THEY JUST DIDN'T MAKE IT BACK TO TELL THE TALE!
I DON'T LIKE THE SOUND OF THAT!
DON'T WORRY! THERE'S A WAY OUT AND WE'RE GOING TO FIND IT!
HOW? WE DON'T EVEN KNOW WHAT WE'RE LOOKING FOR! WE COULD PASS THE EXIT AND NOT EVEN REALIZE IT!
C'MON, GUYS! YOU'RE CELLAR DWELLERS, AREN'T YOU? THIS IS JUST...THE ULTIMATE CELLAR!
IF ANYONE CAN FIND THEIR WAY OUT, IT'S US!
HELP!

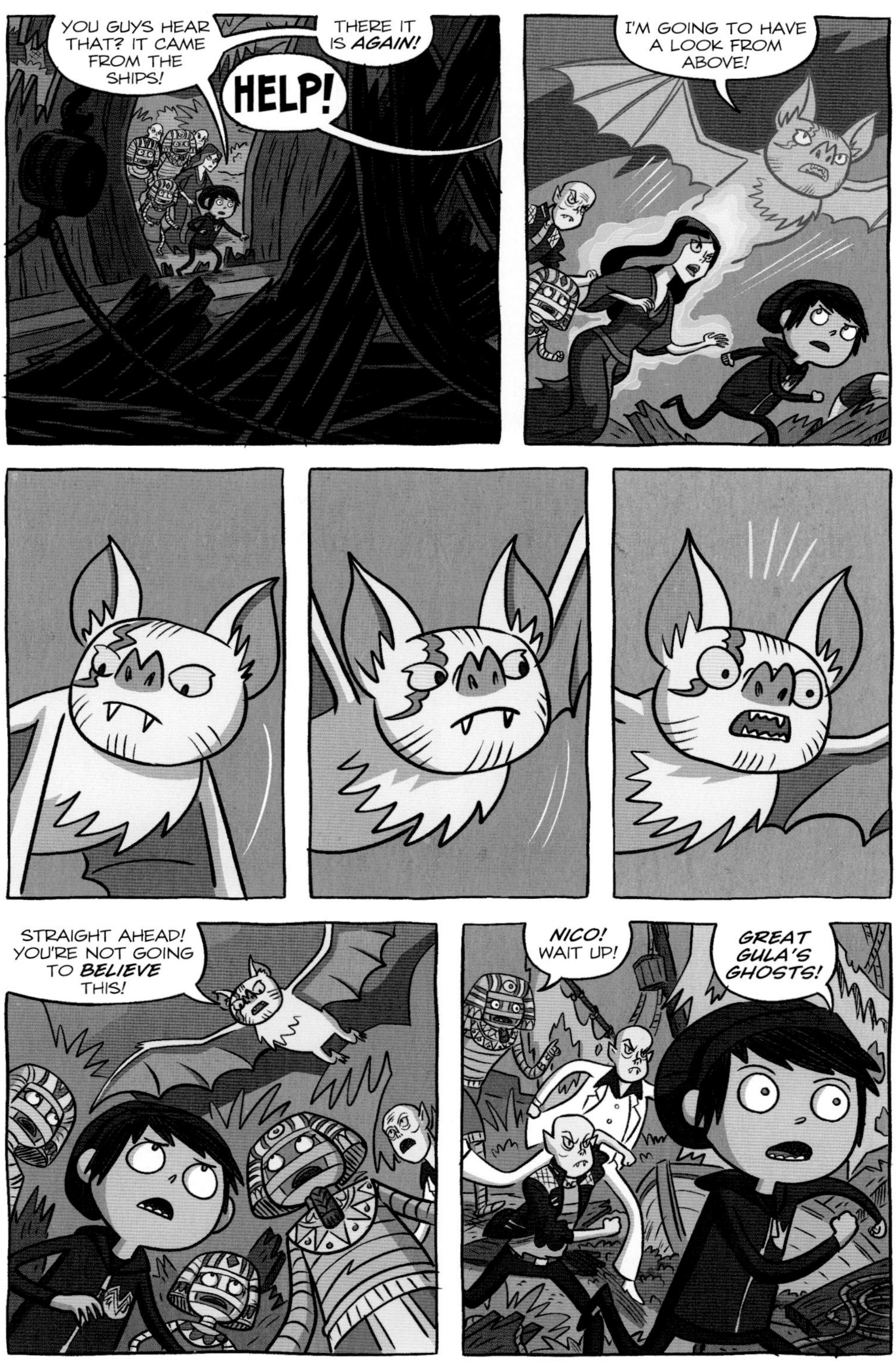

YOU GUYS HEAR THAT? IT CAME FROM THE SHIPS!
THERE IT IS *AGAIN!*
HELP!
I'M GOING TO HAVE A LOOK FROM ABOVE!
STRAIGHT AHEAD! YOU'RE NOT GOING TO *BELIEVE* THIS!
NICO! WAIT UP!
GREAT GULA'S GHOSTS!

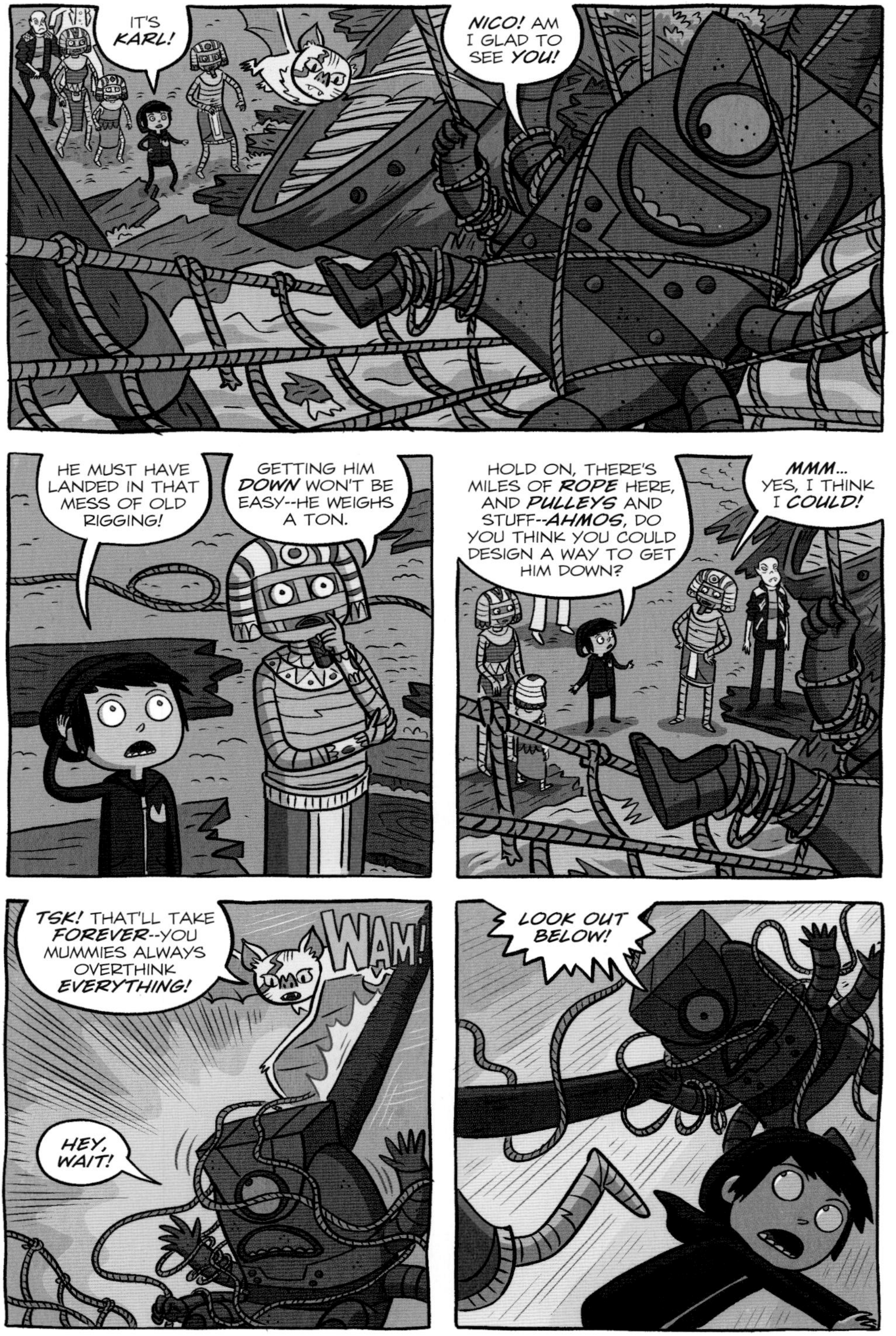
IT'S KARL!
NICO! AM I GLAD TO SEE YOU!
HE MUST HAVE LANDED IN THAT MESS OF OLD RIGGING!
GETTING HIM DOWN WON'T BE EASY--HE WEIGHS A TON.
HOLD ON, THERE'S MILES OF ROPE HERE, AND PULLEYS AND STUFF--AHMOS, DO YOU THINK YOU COULD DESIGN A WAY TO GET HIM DOWN?
MMM... YES, I THINK I COULD!
TSK! THAT'LL TAKE FOREVER--YOU MUMMIES ALWAYS OVERTHINK EVERYTHING!
WAM!
HEY, WAIT!
LOOK OUT BELOW!

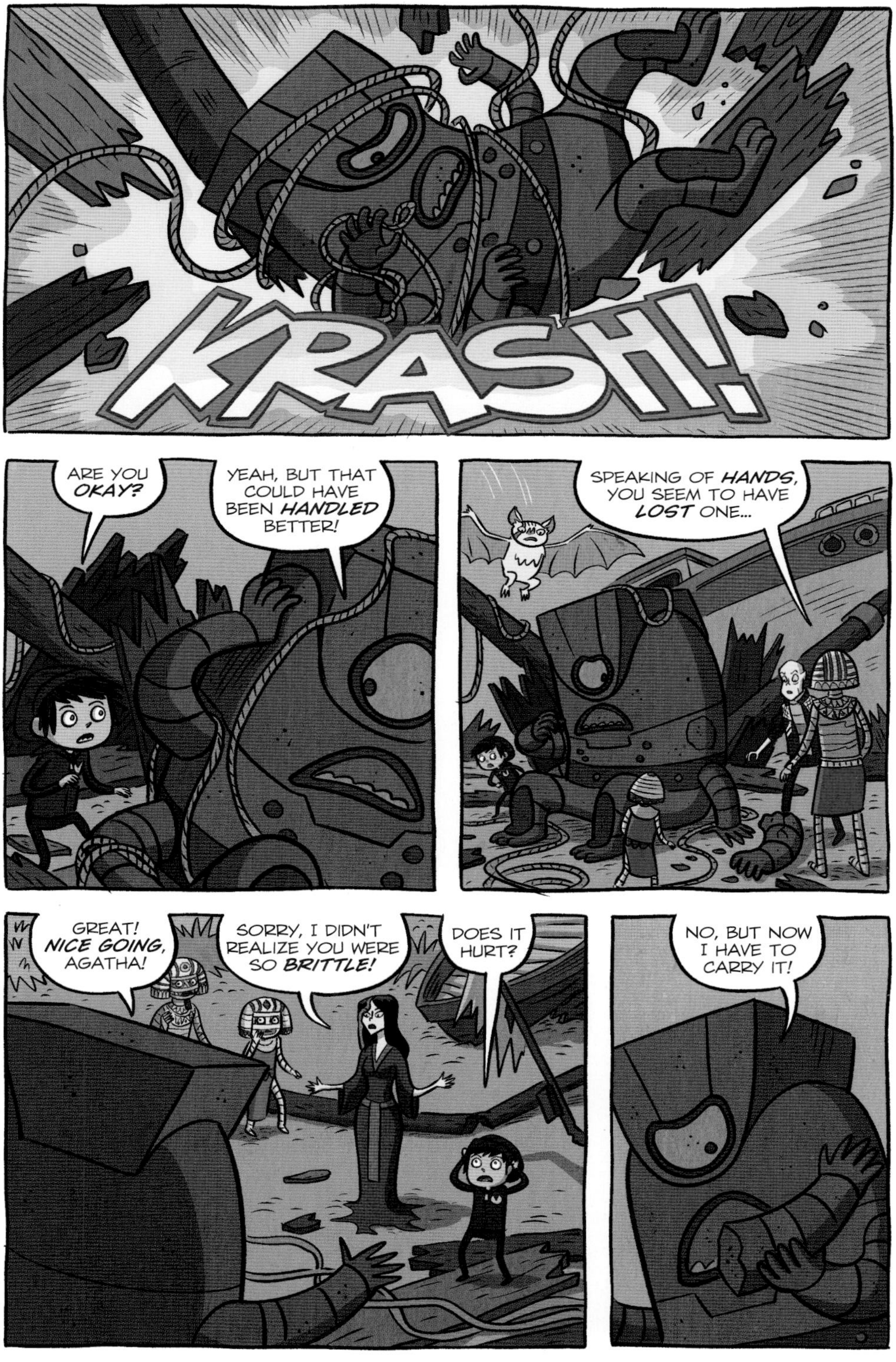
KRASH!!
ARE YOU OKAY?
YEAH, BUT THAT COULD HAVE BEEN HANDLED BETTER!
SPEAKING OF HANDS, YOU SEEM TO HAVE LOST ONE...
GREAT! NICE GOING, AGATHA!
SORRY, I DIDN'T REALIZE YOU WERE SO BRITTLE!
DOES IT HURT?
NO, BUT NOW I HAVE TO CARRY IT!

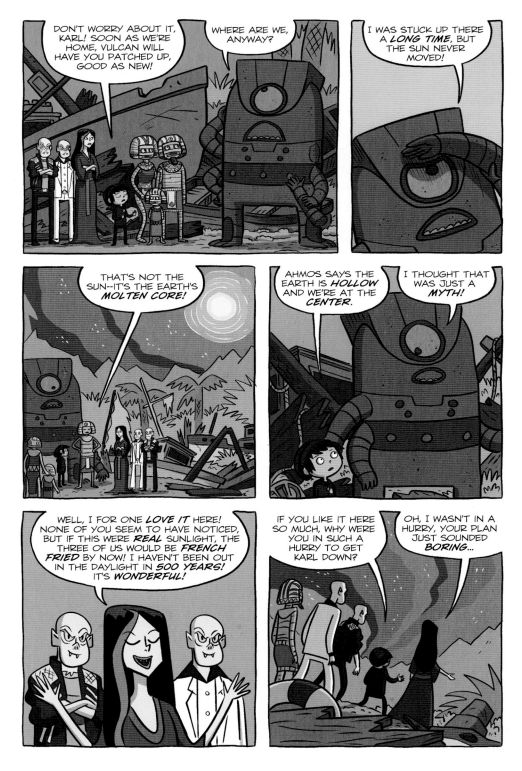

DON'T WORRY ABOUT IT, KARL! SOON AS WE'RE HOME, VULCAN WILL HAVE YOU PATCHED UP, GOOD AS NEW!

WHERE ARE WE, ANYWAY?

I WAS STUCK UP THERE A *LONG TIME*, BUT THE SUN NEVER MOVED!

THAT'S NOT THE SUN--IT'S THE EARTH'S *MOLTEN CORE*!

AHMOS SAYS THE EARTH IS *HOLLOW* AND WE'RE AT THE *CENTER*.

I THOUGHT THAT WAS JUST A *MYTH*!

WELL, I FOR ONE *LOVE IT* HERE! NONE OF YOU SEEM TO HAVE NOTICED, BUT IF THIS WERE *REAL* SUNLIGHT, THE THREE OF US WOULD BE *FRENCH FRIED* BY NOW! I HAVEN'T BEEN OUT IN THE DAYLIGHT IN *500 YEARS!* IT'S *WONDERFUL!*

IF YOU LIKE IT HERE SO MUCH, WHY WERE YOU IN SUCH A HURRY TO GET KARL DOWN?

OH, I WASN'T IN A HURRY, YOUR PLAN JUST SOUNDED *BORING...*

124

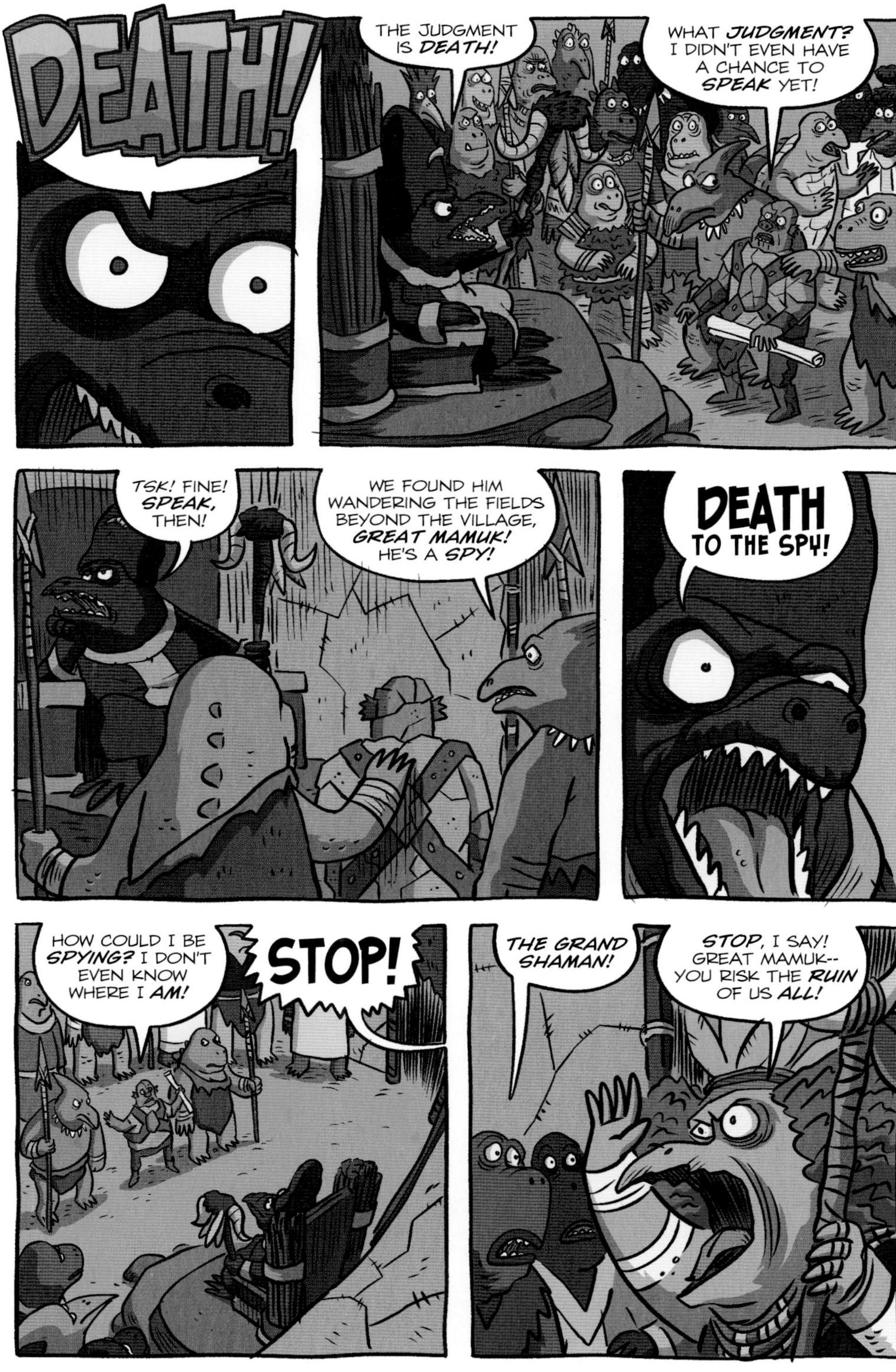
DEATH!
THE JUDGMENT IS DEATH!
WHAT JUDGMENT? I DIDN'T EVEN HAVE A CHANCE TO SPEAK YET!
TSK! FINE! SPEAK, THEN!
WE FOUND HIM WANDERING THE FIELDS BEYOND THE VILLAGE, GREAT MAMUK! HE'S A SPY!
DEATH TO THE SPY!
HOW COULD I BE SPYING? I DON'T EVEN KNOW WHERE I AM!
STOP!
THE GRAND SHAMAN!
STOP, I SAY! GREAT MAMUK-- YOU RISK THE RUIN OF US ALL!

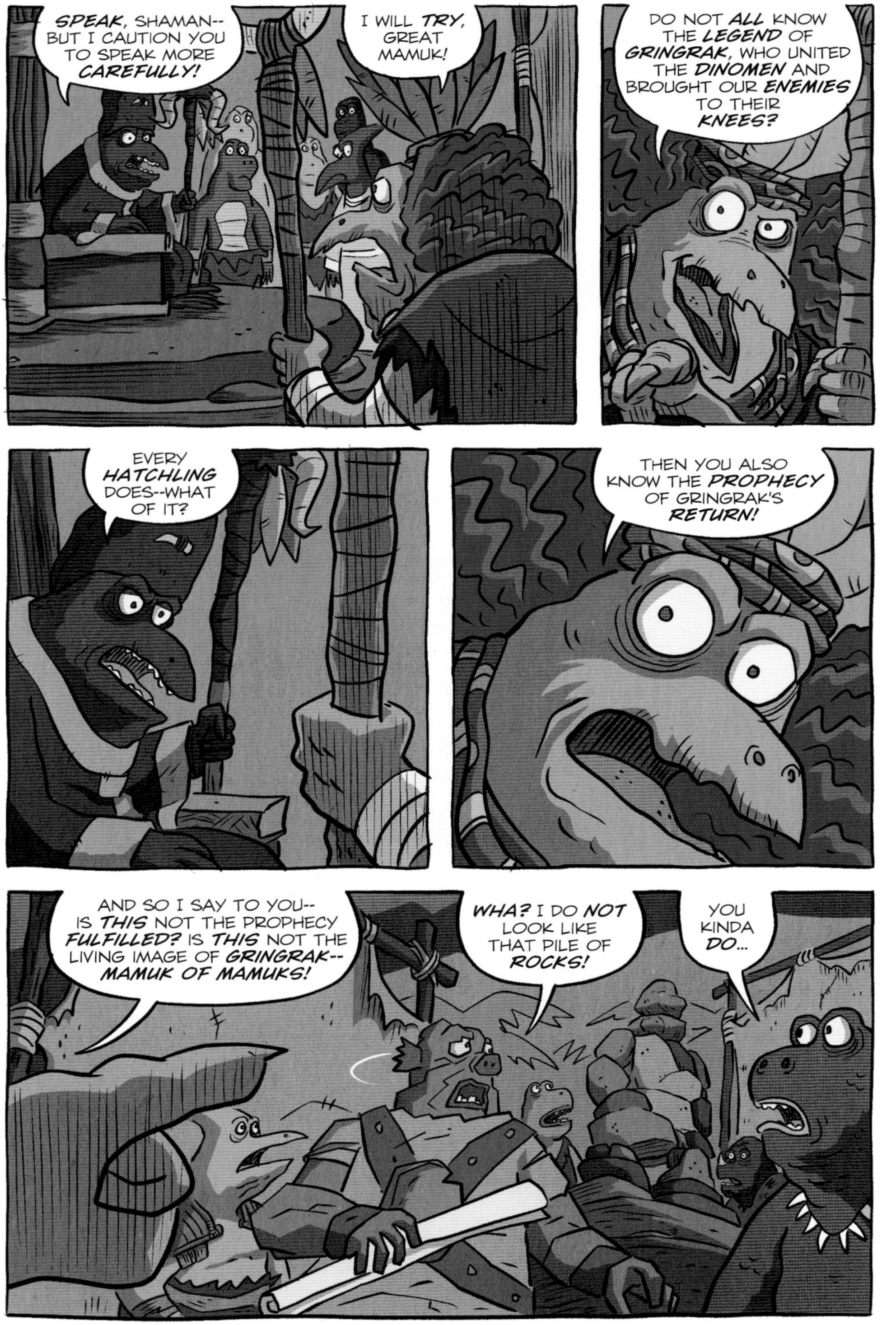
SPEAK, SHAMAN-- BUT I CAUTION YOU TO SPEAK MORE CAREFULLY!
I WILL TRY, GREAT MAMUK!
DO NOT ALL KNOW THE LEGEND OF GRINGRAK, WHO UNITED THE DINOMEN AND BROUGHT OUR ENEMIES TO THEIR KNEES?
EVERY HATCHLING DOES--WHAT OF IT?
THEN YOU ALSO KNOW THE PROPHECY OF GRINGRAK'S RETURN!
AND SO I SAY TO YOU-- IS THIS NOT THE PROPHECY FULFILLED? IS THIS NOT THE LIVING IMAGE OF GRINGRAK-- MAMUK OF MAMUKS!
WHA? I DO NOT LOOK LIKE THAT PILE OF ROCKS!
YOU KINDA DO...

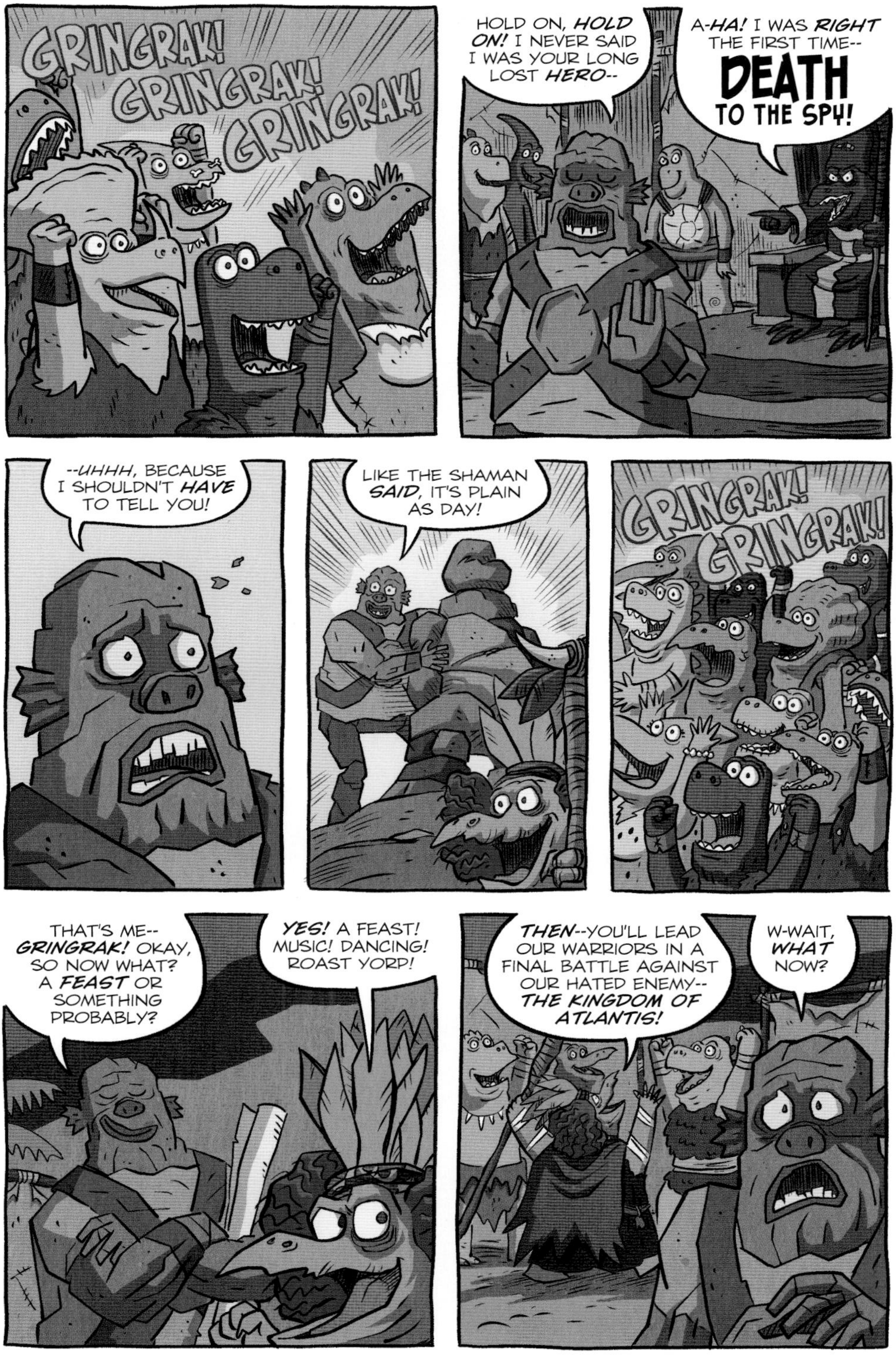
GRINGRAK!
GRINGRAK!
GRINGRAK!
HOLD ON, HOLD ON! I NEVER SAID I WAS YOUR LONG LOST HERO--
A-HA! I WAS RIGHT THE FIRST TIME--
DEATH TO THE SPY!
--UHHH, BECAUSE I SHOULDN'T HAVE TO TELL YOU!
LIKE THE SHAMAN SAID, IT'S PLAIN AS DAY!
GRINGRAK!
GRINGRAK!
THAT'S ME--GRINGRAK! OKAY, SO NOW WHAT? A FEAST OR SOMETHING PROBABLY?
YES! A FEAST! MUSIC! DANCING! ROAST YORP!
THEN--YOU'LL LEAD OUR WARRIORS IN A FINAL BATTLE AGAINST OUR HATED ENEMY--THE KINGDOM OF ATLANTIS!
W-WAIT, WHAT NOW?

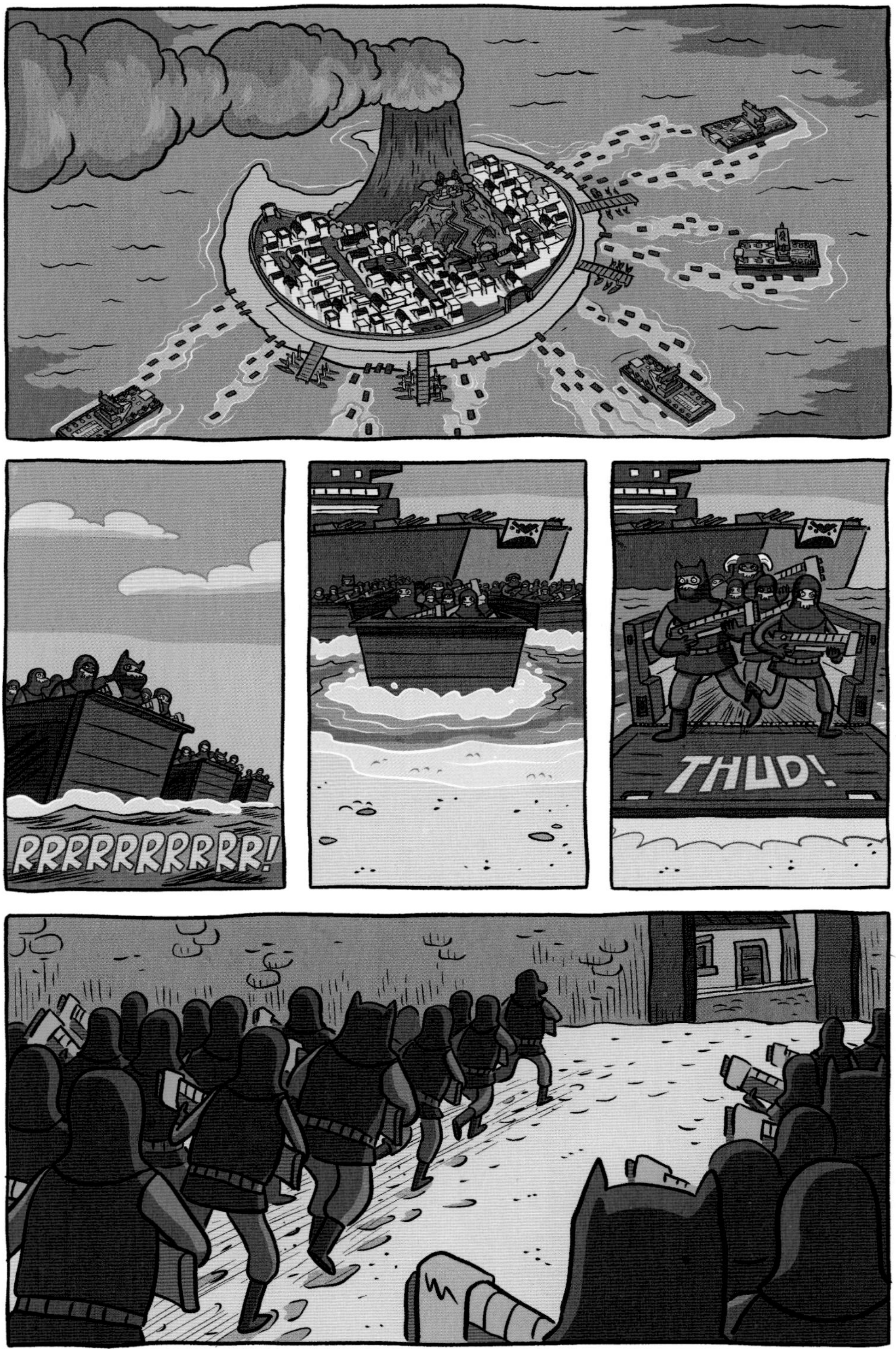
RRRRRRRRRR!
THUD!

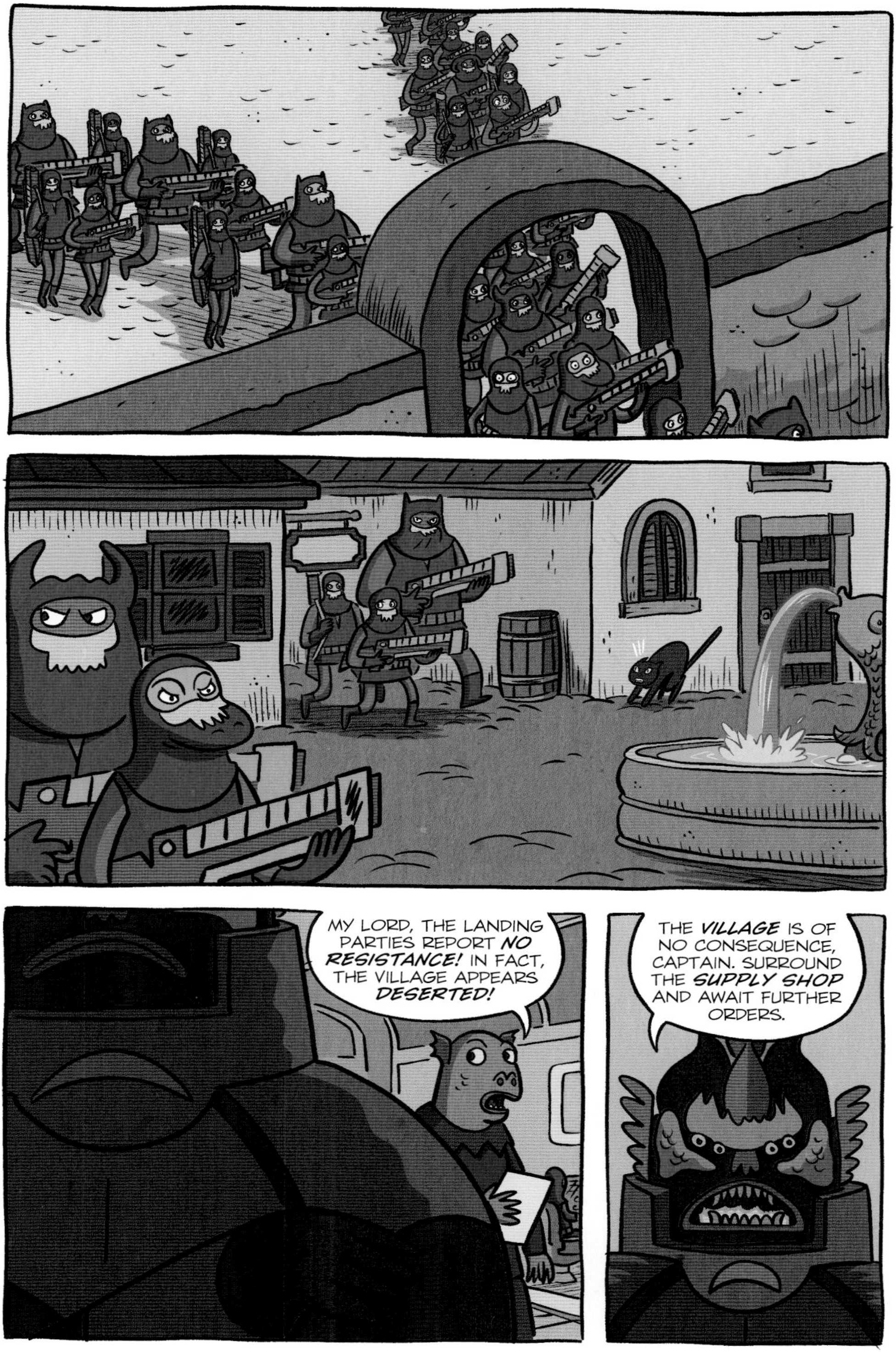
MY LORD, THE LANDING PARTIES REPORT NO RESISTANCE! IN FACT, THE VILLAGE APPEARS DESERTED!
THE VILLAGE IS OF NO CONSEQUENCE, CAPTAIN. SURROUND THE SUPPLY SHOP AND AWAIT FURTHER ORDERS.

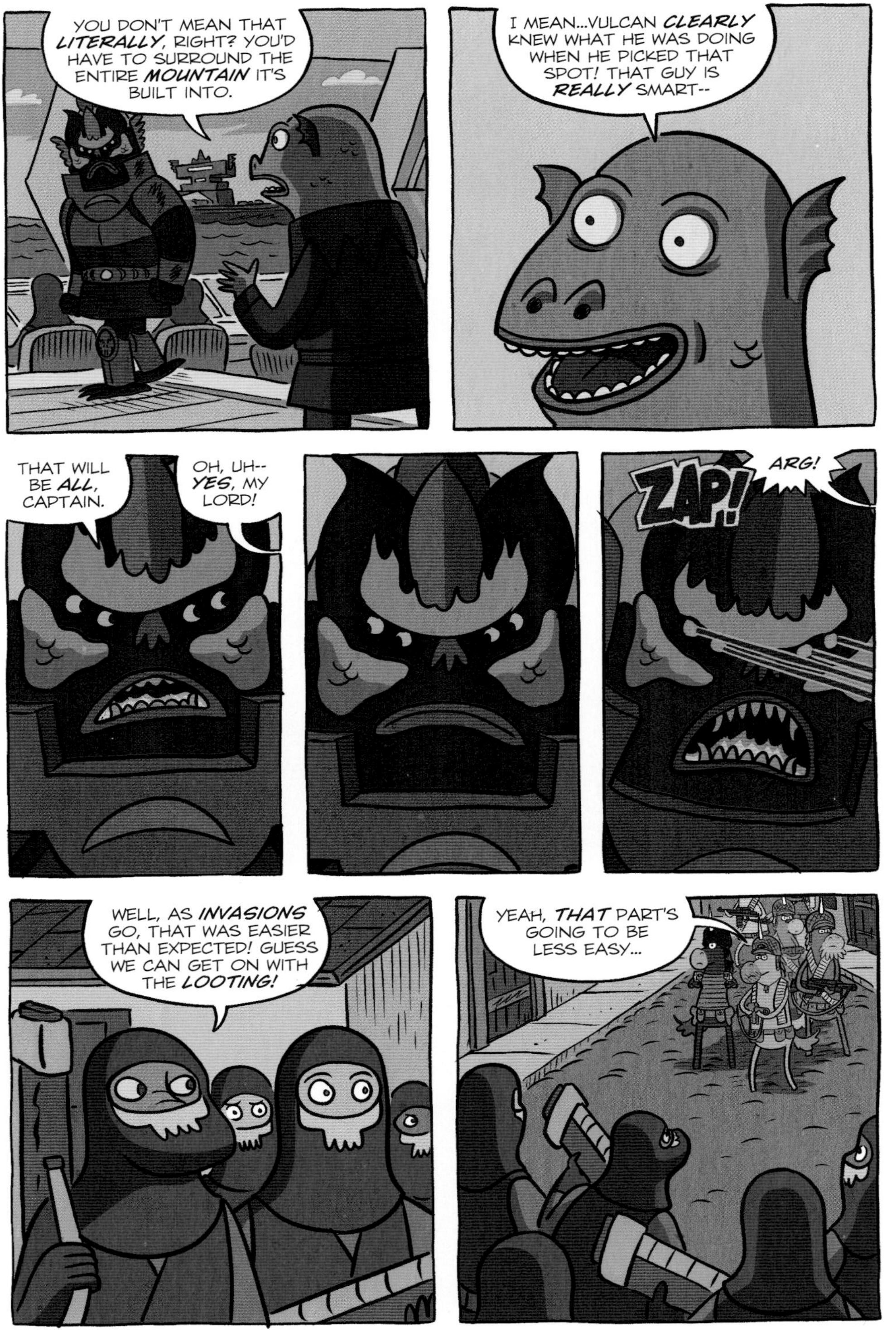
YOU DON'T MEAN THAT LITERALLY, RIGHT? YOU'D HAVE TO SURROUND THE ENTIRE MOUNTAIN IT'S BUILT INTO.
I MEAN...VULCAN CLEARLY KNEW WHAT HE WAS DOING WHEN HE PICKED THAT SPOT! THAT GUY IS REALLY SMART--
THAT WILL BE ALL, CAPTAIN.
OH, UH-- YES, MY LORD!
ZAP!
ARG!
WELL, AS INVASIONS GO, THAT WAS EASIER THAN EXPECTED! GUESS WE CAN GET ON WITH THE LOOTING!
YEAH, THAT PART'S GOING TO BE LESS EASY...

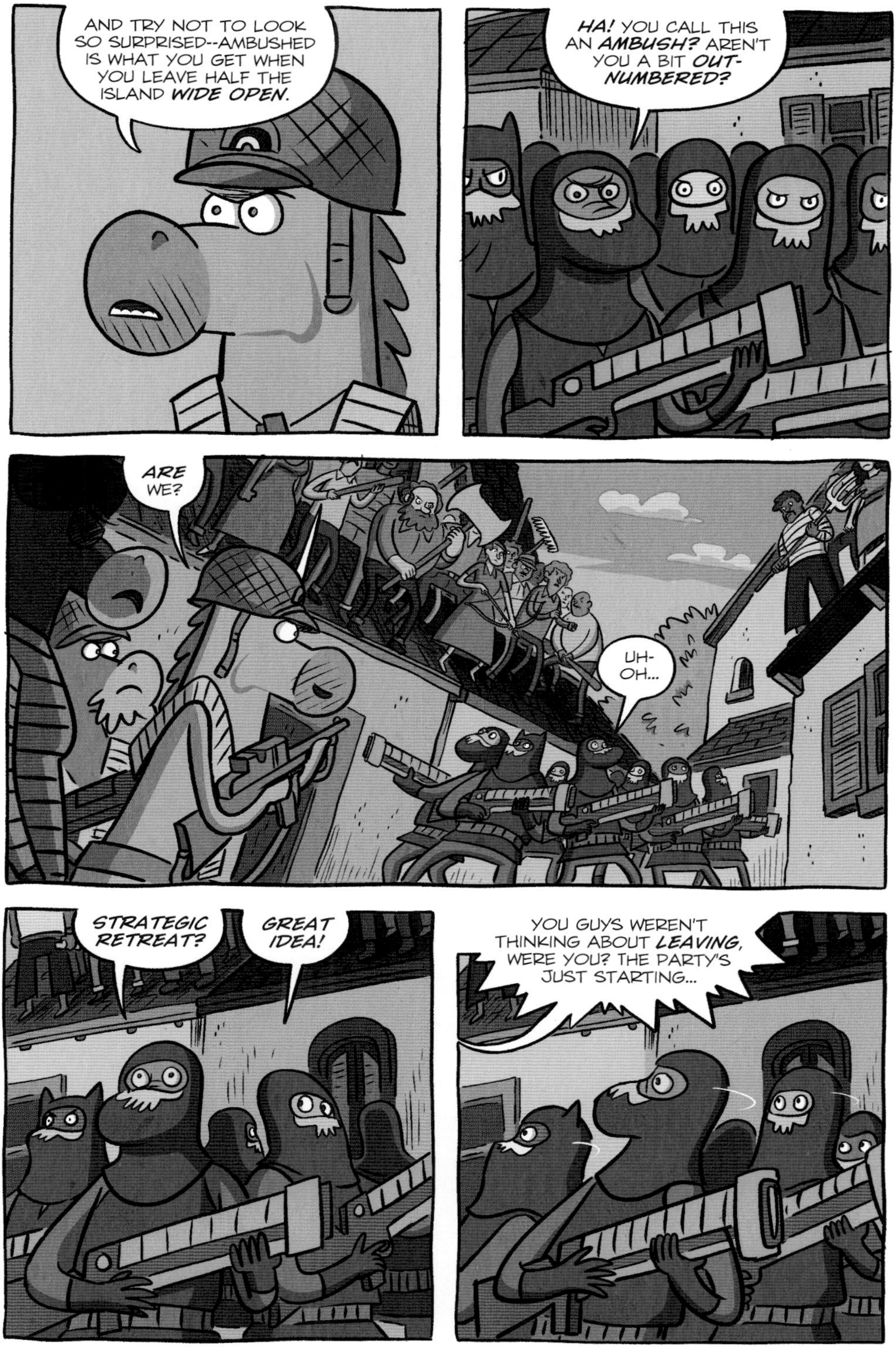
AND TRY NOT TO LOOK SO SURPRISED--AMBUSHED IS WHAT YOU GET WHEN YOU LEAVE HALF THE ISLAND **WIDE OPEN.**
HA! YOU CALL THIS AN **AMBUSH?** AREN'T YOU A BIT **OUT-NUMBERED?**
ARE WE?
UH-OH...
STRATEGIC RETREAT?
GREAT IDEA!
YOU GUYS WEREN'T THINKING ABOUT **LEAVING,** WERE YOU? THE PARTY'S JUST STARTING...

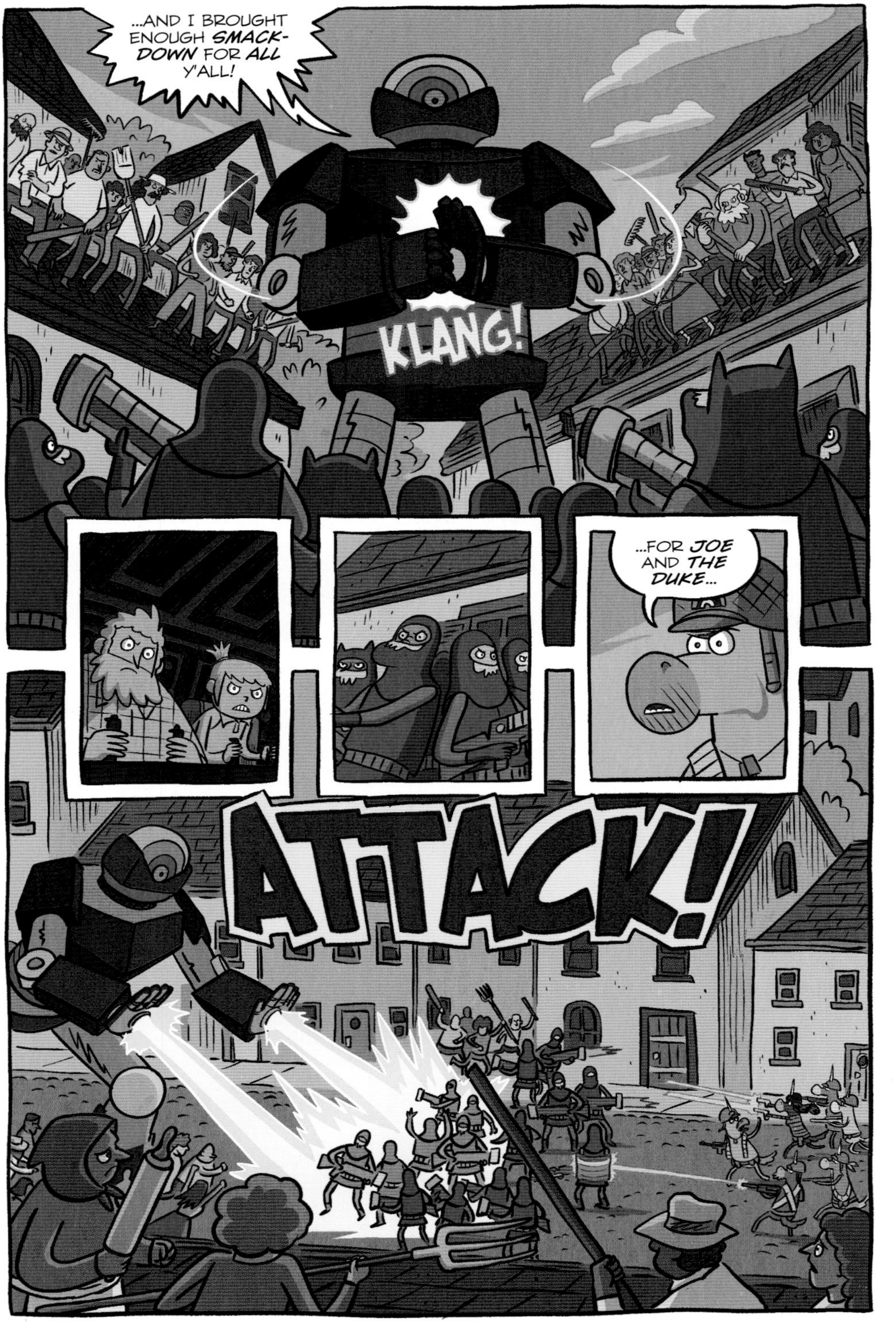
...AND I BROUGHT ENOUGH SMACK-DOWN FOR ALL Y'ALL!
KLANG!
...FOR JOE AND THE DUKE...
ATTACK!

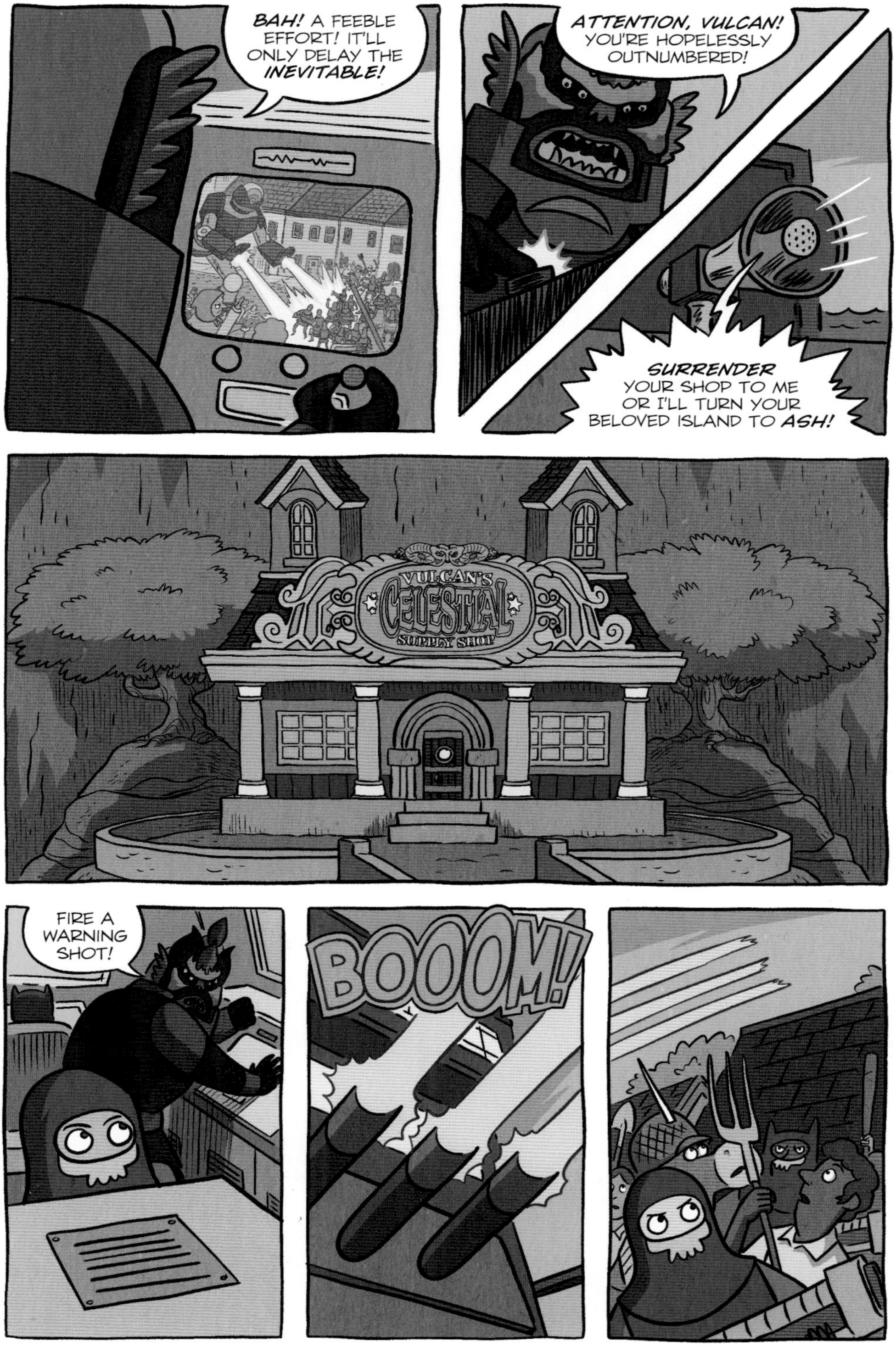

BAH! A FEEBLE EFFORT! IT'LL ONLY DELAY THE INEVITABLE!
ATTENTION, VULCAN! YOU'RE HOPELESSLY OUTNUMBERED!
SURRENDER YOUR SHOP TO ME OR I'LL TURN YOUR BELOVED ISLAND TO ASH!
VULCAN'S CELESTIAL SUPPLY SHOP
FIRE A WARNING SHOT!
BOOOM!

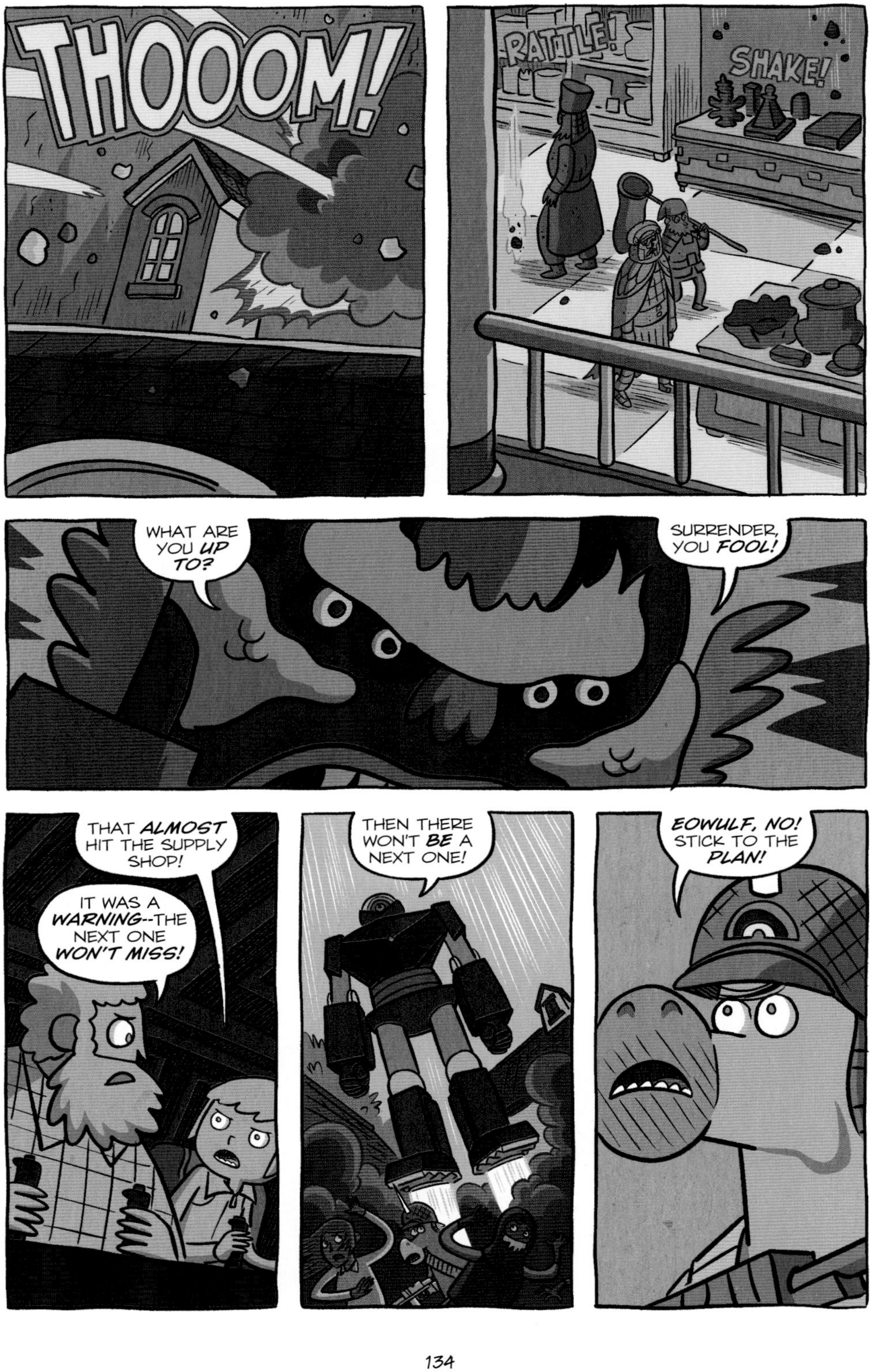
THOOOM!
RATTLE!
SHAKE!
WHAT ARE YOU UP TO?
SURRENDER, YOU FOOL!
THAT ALMOST HIT THE SUPPLY SHOP!
IT WAS A WARNING--THE NEXT ONE WON'T MISS!
THEN THERE WON'T BE A NEXT ONE!
EOWULF, NO! STICK TO THE PLAN!

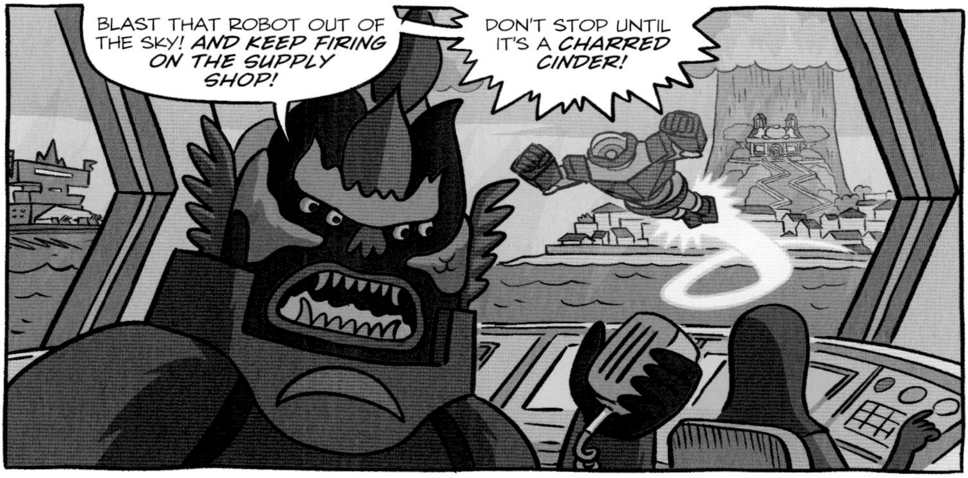
BLAST THAT ROBOT OUT OF THE SKY! AND KEEP FIRING ON THE SUPPLY SHOP!
DON'T STOP UNTIL IT'S A CHARRED CINDER!

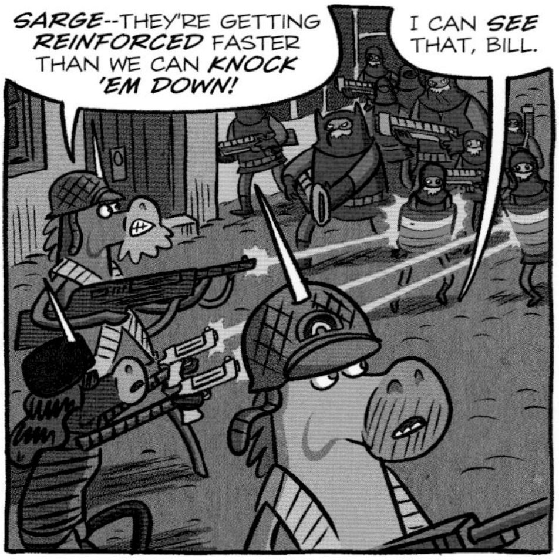
SARGE--THEY'RE GETTING REINFORCED FASTER THAN WE CAN KNOCK 'EM DOWN!
I CAN SEE THAT, BILL.

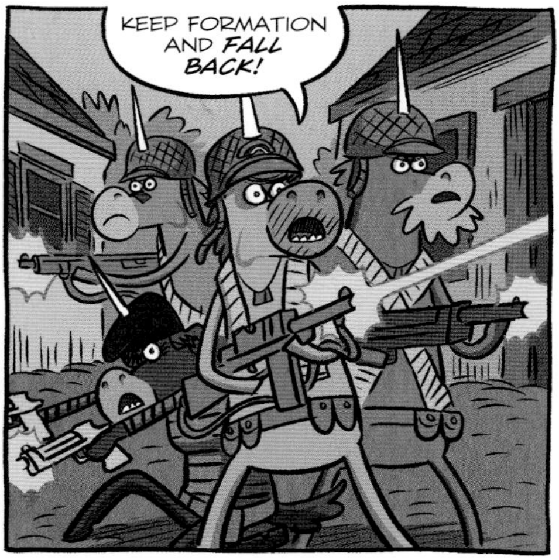
KEEP FORMATION AND FALL BACK!

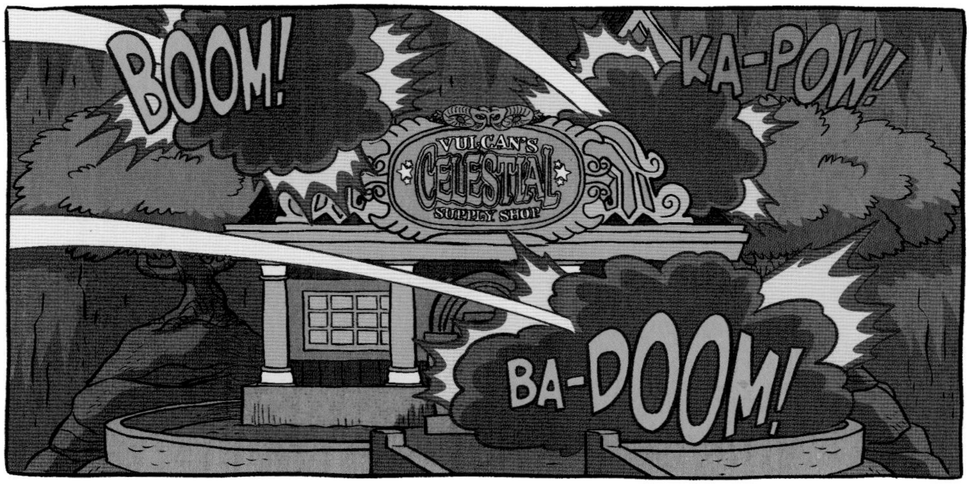
BOOM!
KA-POW!
VULCAN'S CELESTIAL SUPPLY SHOP
BA-DOOM!

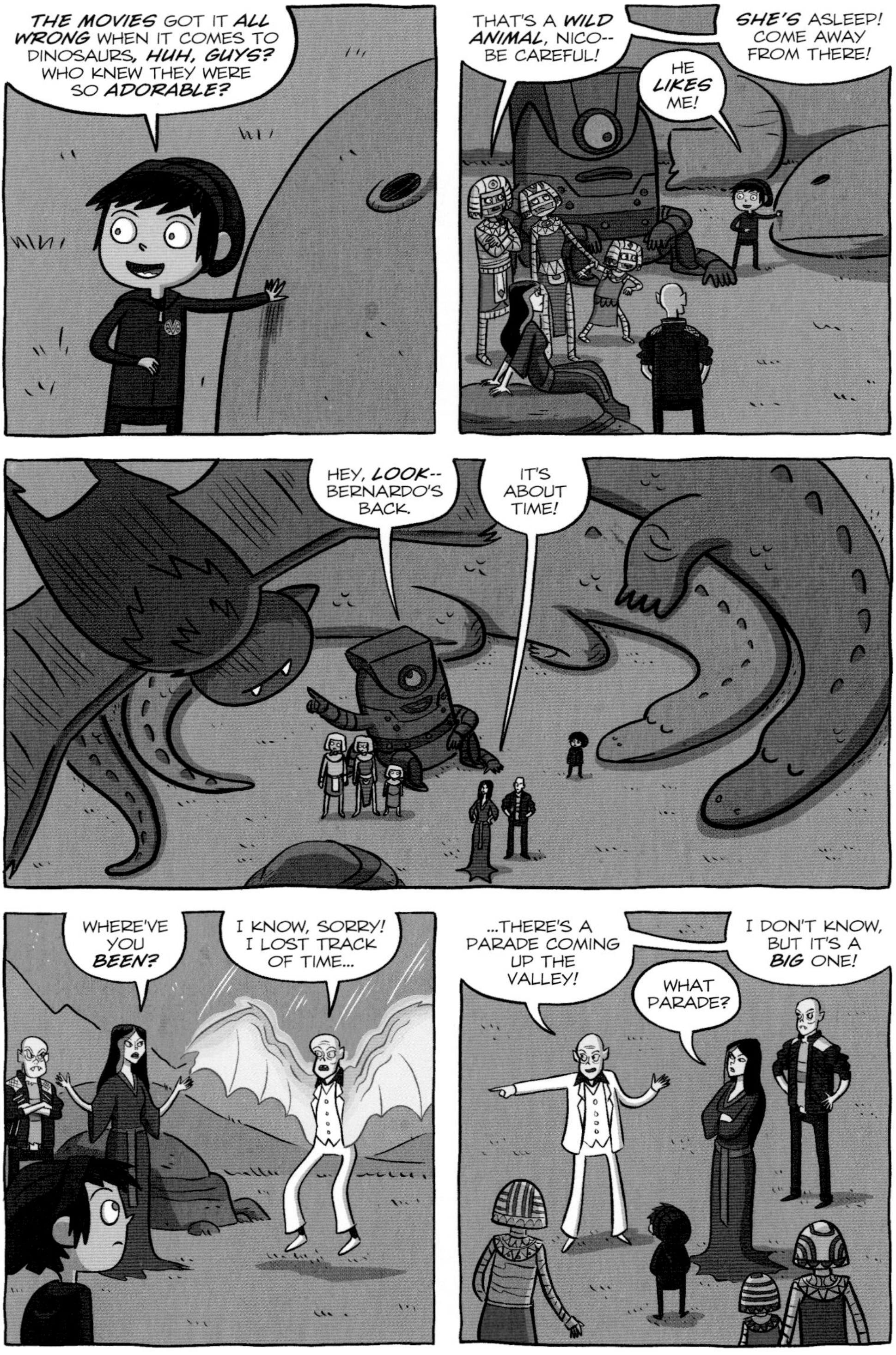

THE MOVIES GOT IT ALL WRONG WHEN IT COMES TO DINOSAURS, HUH, GUYS? WHO KNEW THEY WERE SO ADORABLE?
THAT'S A WILD ANIMAL, NICO-- BE CAREFUL!
SHE'S ASLEEP! COME AWAY FROM THERE!
HE LIKES ME!
HEY, LOOK-- BERNARDO'S BACK.
IT'S ABOUT TIME!
WHERE'VE YOU BEEN?
I KNOW, SORRY! I LOST TRACK OF TIME...
...THERE'S A PARADE COMING UP THE VALLEY!
I DON'T KNOW, BUT IT'S A BIG ONE!
WHAT PARADE?

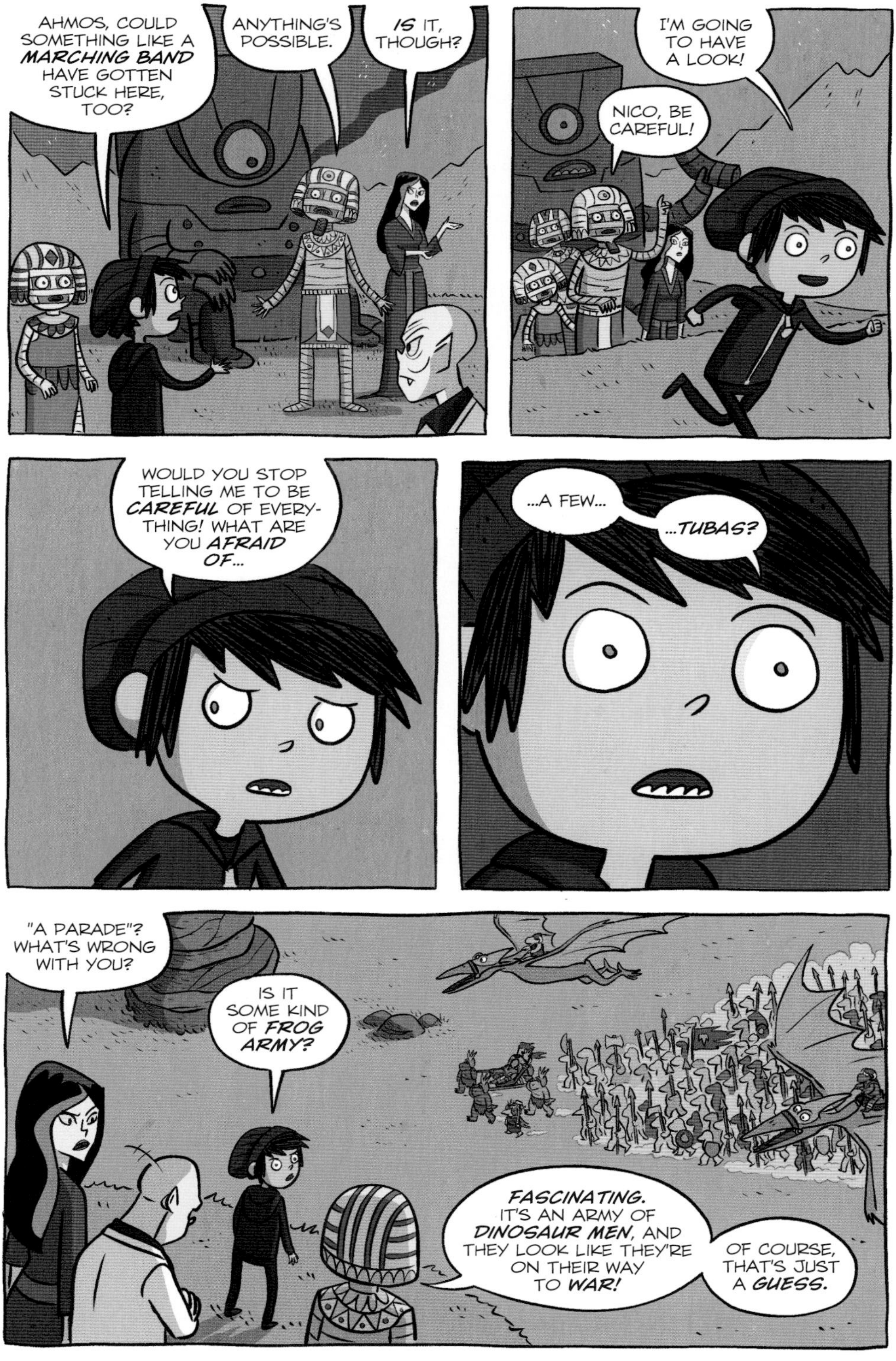
AHMOS, COULD SOMETHING LIKE A MARCHING BAND HAVE GOTTEN STUCK HERE, TOO?
ANYTHING'S POSSIBLE.
IS IT, THOUGH?
I'M GOING TO HAVE A LOOK!
NICO, BE CAREFUL!
WOULD YOU STOP TELLING ME TO BE CAREFUL OF EVERY-THING! WHAT ARE YOU AFRAID OF...
...A FEW...
...TUBAS?
"A PARADE"? WHAT'S WRONG WITH YOU?
IS IT SOME KIND OF FROG ARMY?
FASCINATING. IT'S AN ARMY OF DINOSAUR MEN, AND THEY LOOK LIKE THEY'RE ON THEIR WAY TO WAR!
OF COURSE, THAT'S JUST A GUESS.

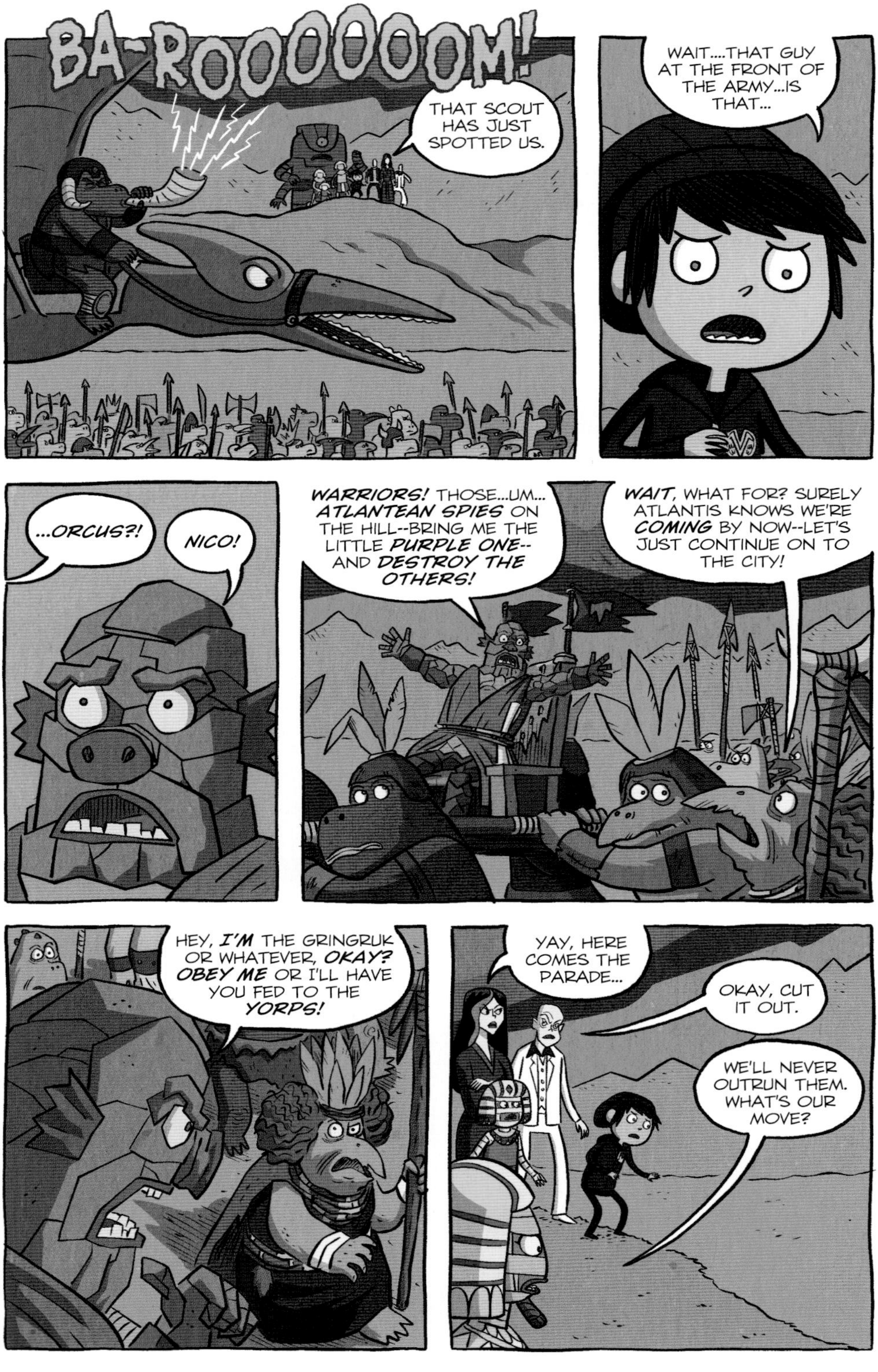
BA-ROOOOOOM!
THAT SCOUT HAS JUST SPOTTED US.
WAIT....THAT GUY AT THE FRONT OF THE ARMY...IS THAT...
...ORCUS?!
NICO!
WARRIORS! THOSE...UM... ATLANTEAN SPIES ON THE HILL--BRING ME THE LITTLE PURPLE ONE-- AND DESTROY THE OTHERS!
WAIT, WHAT FOR? SURELY ATLANTIS KNOWS WE'RE COMING BY NOW--LET'S JUST CONTINUE ON TO THE CITY!
HEY, I'M THE GRINGRUK OR WHATEVER, OKAY? OBEY ME OR I'LL HAVE YOU FED TO THE YORPS!
YAY, HERE COMES THE PARADE...
OKAY, CUT IT OUT.
WE'LL NEVER OUTRUN THEM. WHAT'S OUR MOVE?

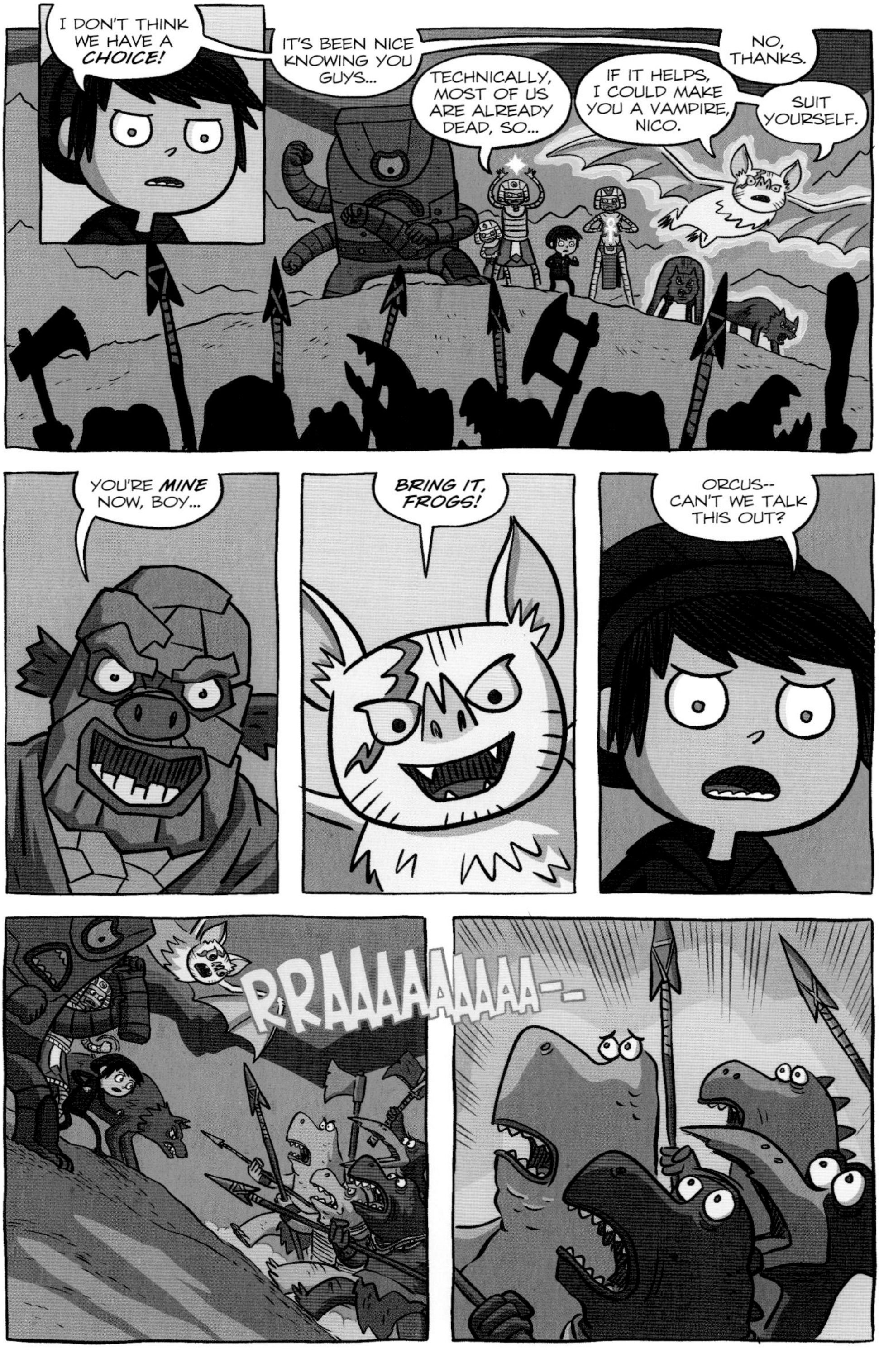
I DON'T THINK WE HAVE A CHOICE!
IT'S BEEN NICE KNOWING YOU GUYS...
TECHNICALLY, MOST OF US ARE ALREADY DEAD, SO...
IF IT HELPS, I COULD MAKE YOU A VAMPIRE, NICO.
NO, THANKS.
SUIT YOURSELF.
YOU'RE MINE NOW, BOY...
BRING IT, FROGS!
ORCUS-- CAN'T WE TALK THIS OUT?
RRAAAAAAAAA--

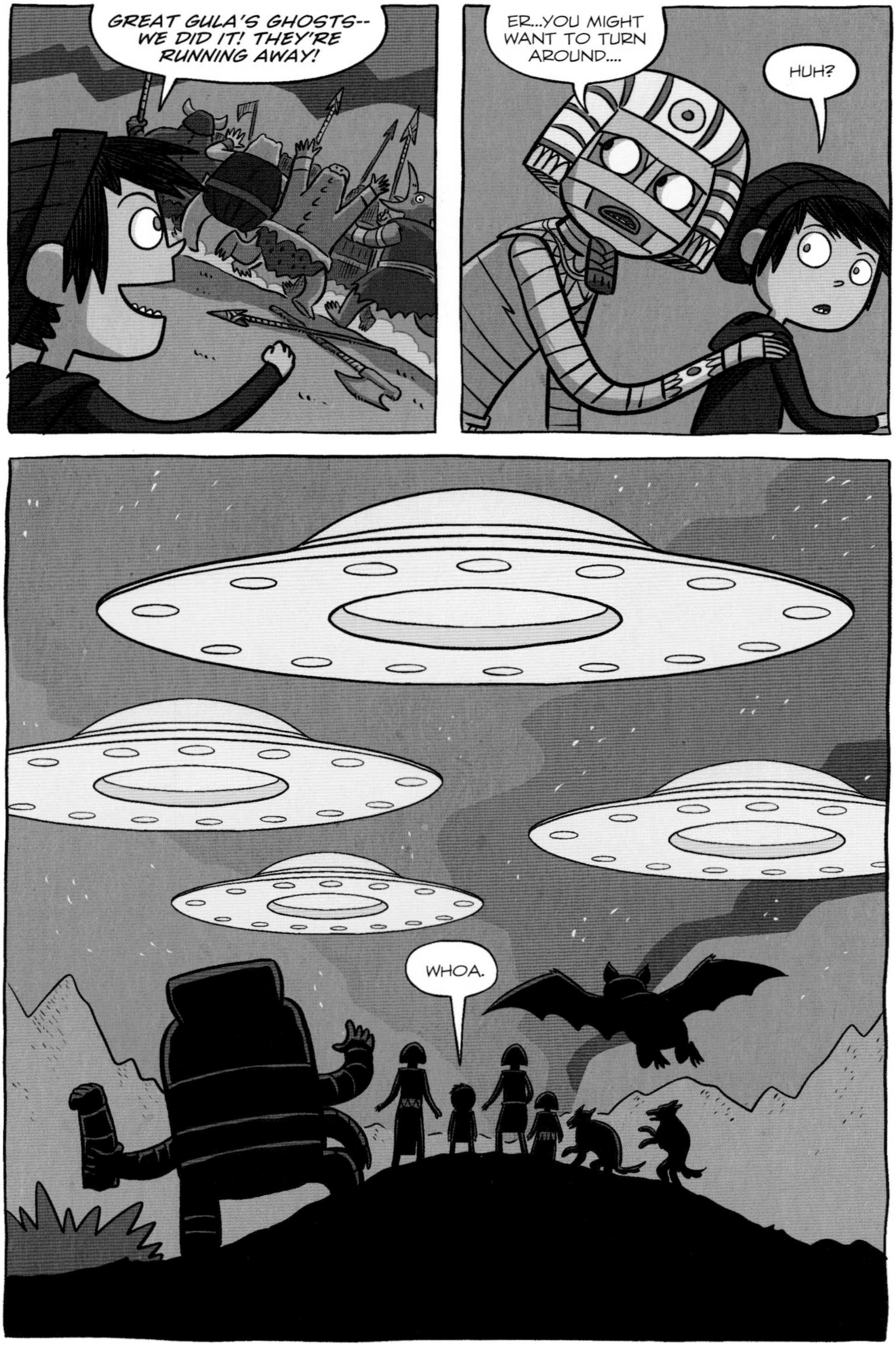
GREAT GULA'S GHOSTS-- WE DID IT! THEY'RE RUNNING AWAY!
ER...YOU MIGHT WANT TO TURN AROUND....
HUH?
WHOA.

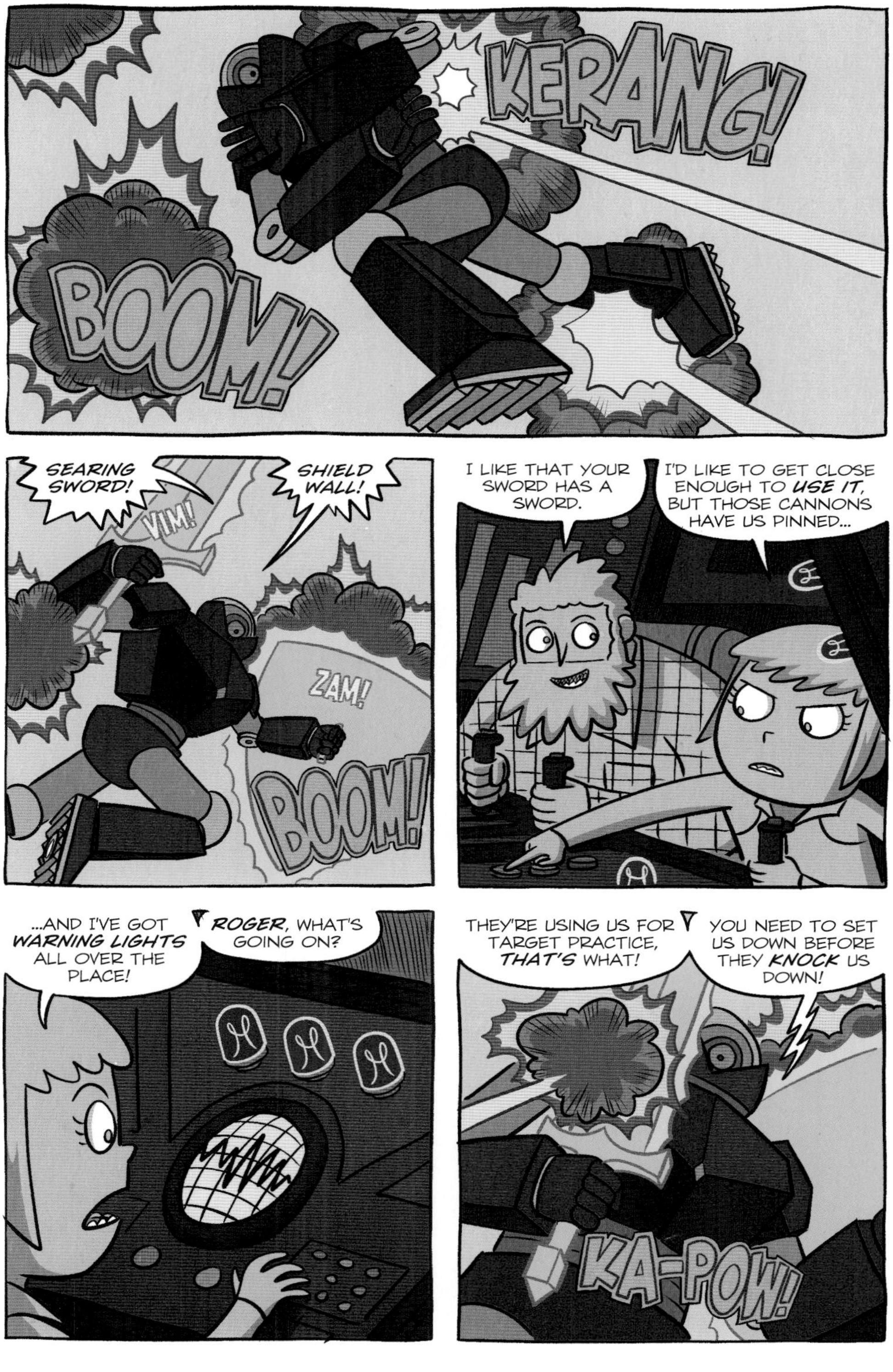
KERANG!
BOOM!
SEARING SWORD!
VIM!
SHIELD WALL!
ZAM!
BOOM!
I LIKE THAT YOUR SWORD HAS A SWORD.
I'D LIKE TO GET CLOSE ENOUGH TO ***USE IT***, BUT THOSE CANNONS HAVE US PINNED...
...AND I'VE GOT ***WARNING LIGHTS*** ALL OVER THE PLACE!
ROGER, WHAT'S GOING ON?
THEY'RE USING US FOR TARGET PRACTICE, ***THAT'S*** WHAT!
YOU NEED TO SET US DOWN BEFORE THEY ***KNOCK*** US DOWN!
KA-POW!

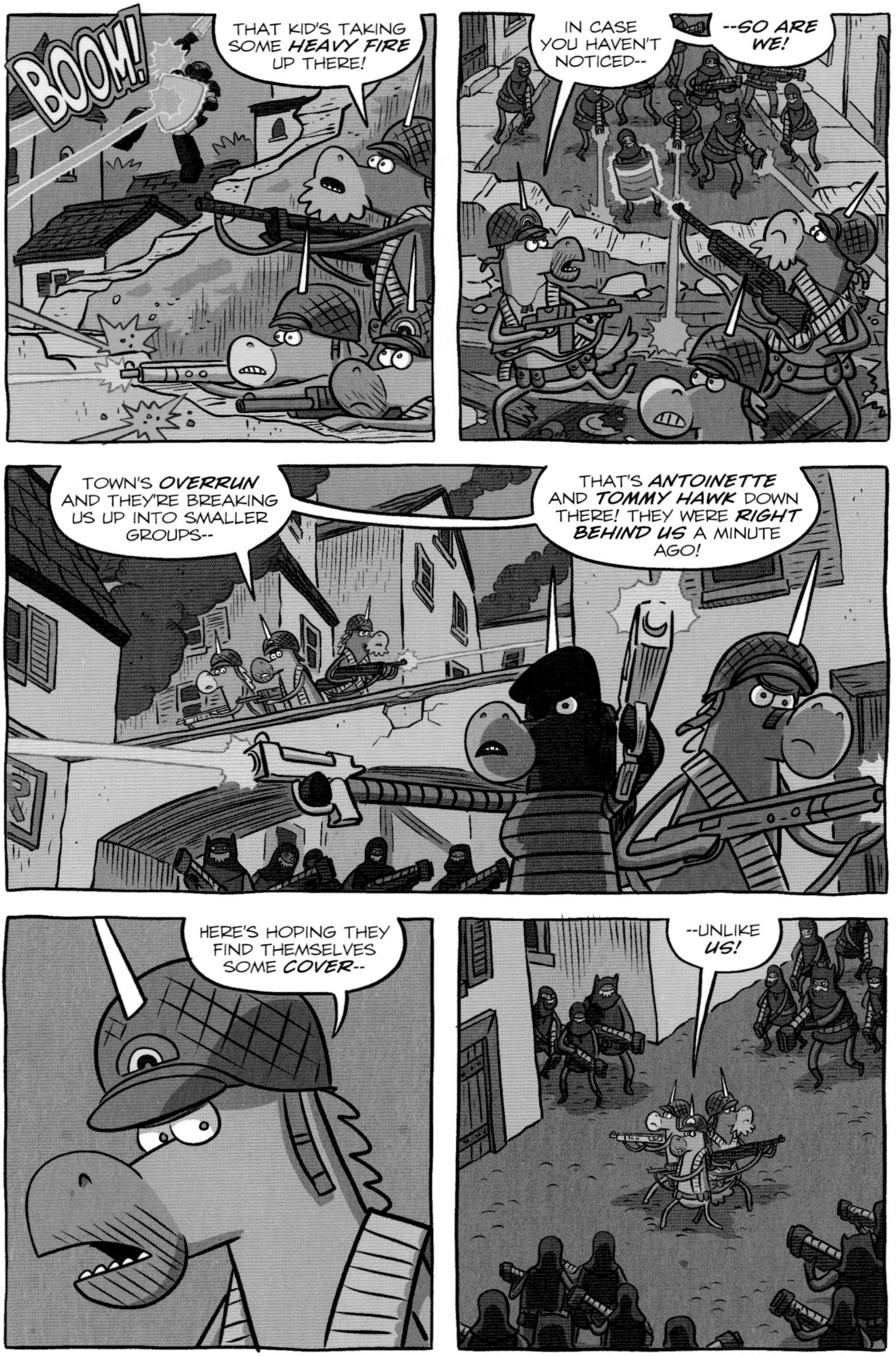
BOOM!
THAT KID'S TAKING SOME HEAVY FIRE UP THERE!
IN CASE YOU HAVEN'T NOTICED--
--SO ARE WE!
TOWN'S OVERRUN AND THEY'RE BREAKING US UP INTO SMALLER GROUPS--
THAT'S ANTOINETTE AND TOMMY HAWK DOWN THERE! THEY WERE RIGHT BEHIND US A MINUTE AGO!
HERE'S HOPING THEY FIND THEMSELVES SOME COVER--
--UNLIKE US!

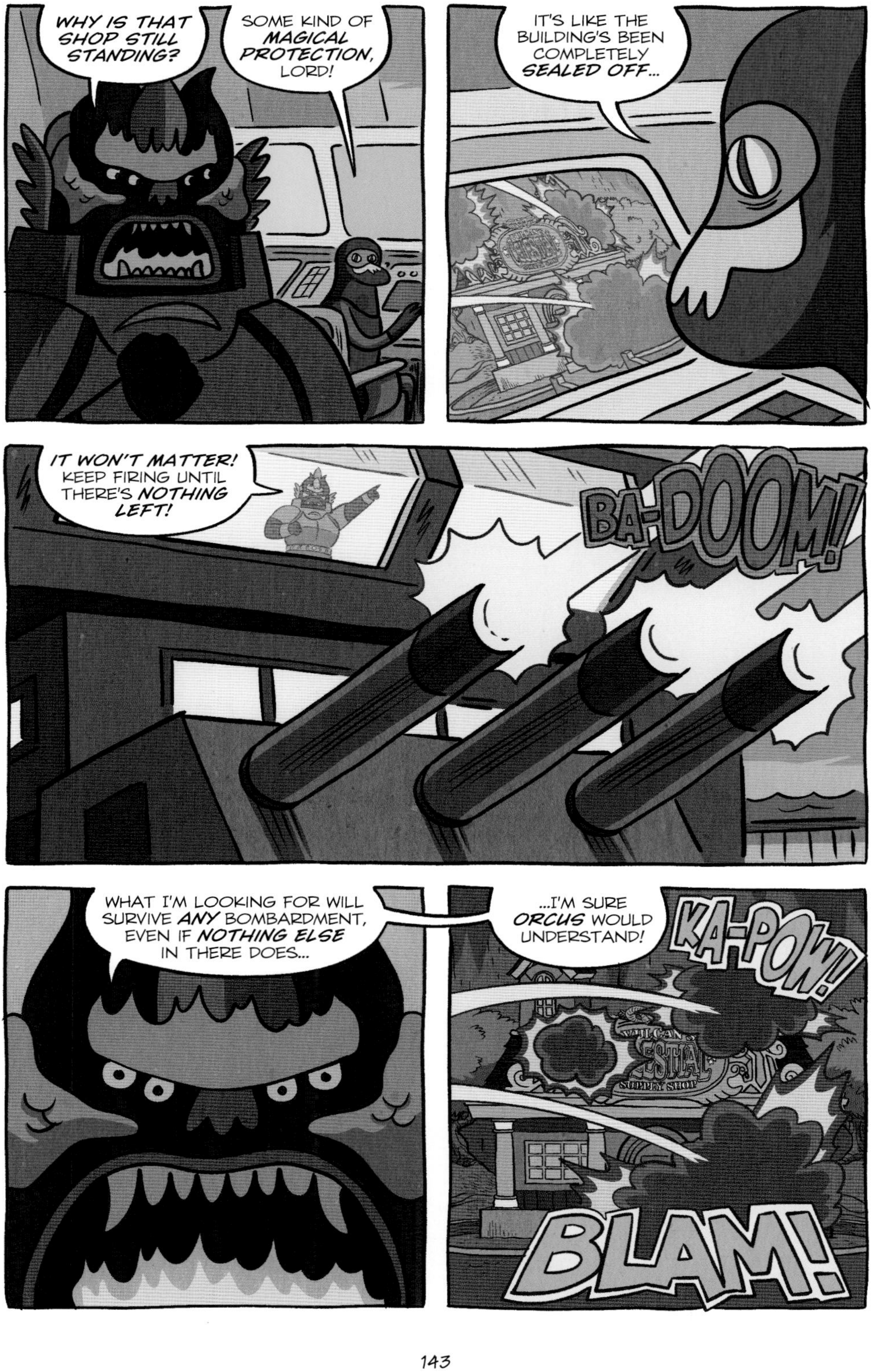
WHY IS THAT SHOP STILL STANDING?
SOME KIND OF MAGICAL PROTECTION, LORD!
IT'S LIKE THE BUILDING'S BEEN COMPLETELY SEALED OFF...
IT WON'T MATTER! KEEP FIRING UNTIL THERE'S NOTHING LEFT!
BA-DOOOM!!
WHAT I'M LOOKING FOR WILL SURVIVE ANY BOMBARDMENT, EVEN IF NOTHING ELSE IN THERE DOES...
...I'M SURE ORCUS WOULD UNDERSTAND!
KA-POW!!
SUPPLY SHOP
BLAM!

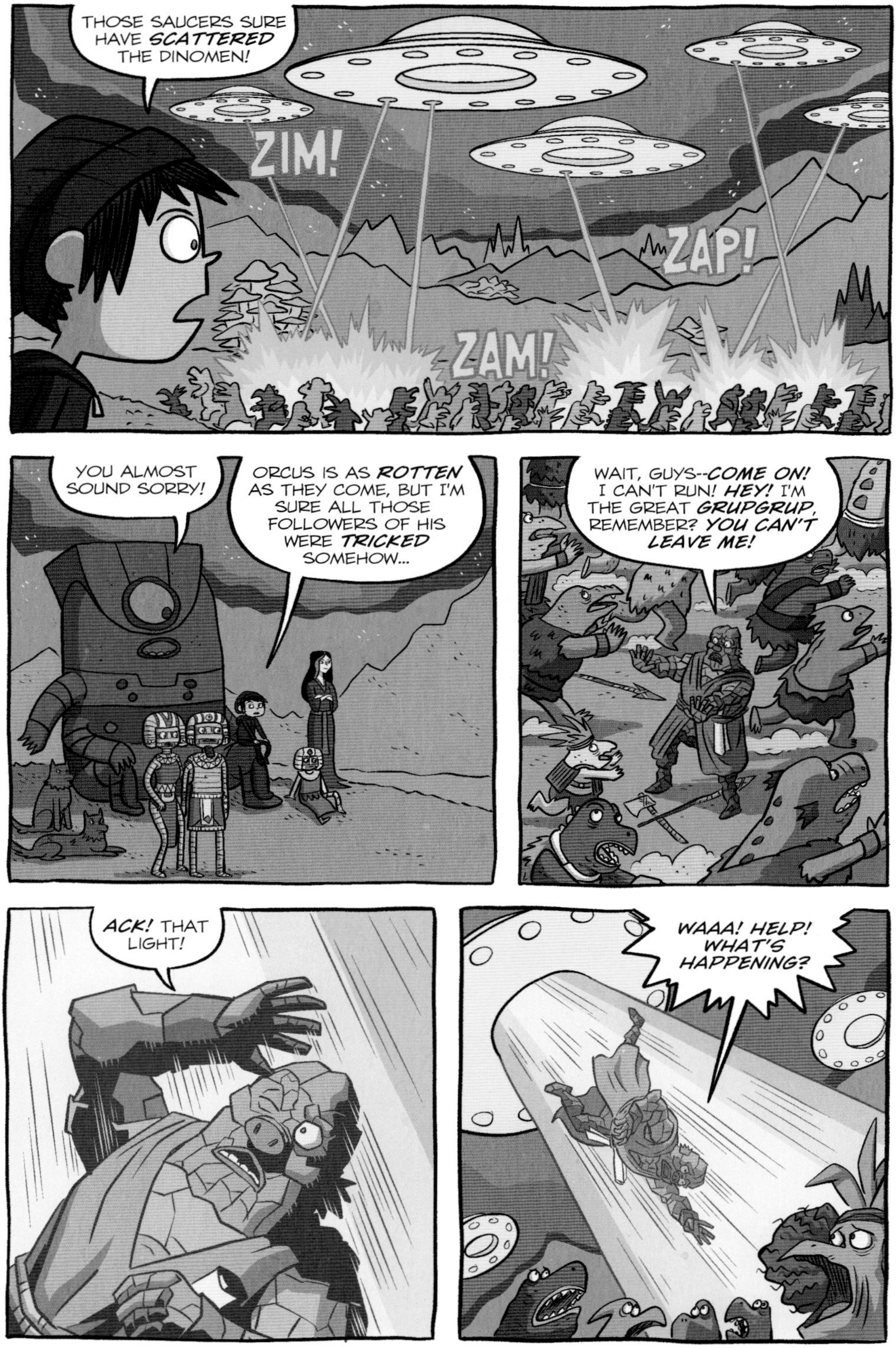
THOSE SAUCERS SURE HAVE **SCATTERED** THE DINOMEN!
ZIM!
ZAP!
ZAM!
YOU ALMOST SOUND SORRY!
ORCUS IS AS **ROTTEN** AS THEY COME, BUT I'M SURE ALL THOSE FOLLOWERS OF HIS WERE **TRICKED** SOMEHOW...
WAIT, GUYS--**COME ON!** I CAN'T RUN! **HEY!** I'M THE GREAT **GRUPGRUP**, REMEMBER? **YOU CAN'T LEAVE ME!**
ACK! THAT LIGHT!
WAAA! HELP! WHAT'S HAPPENING?

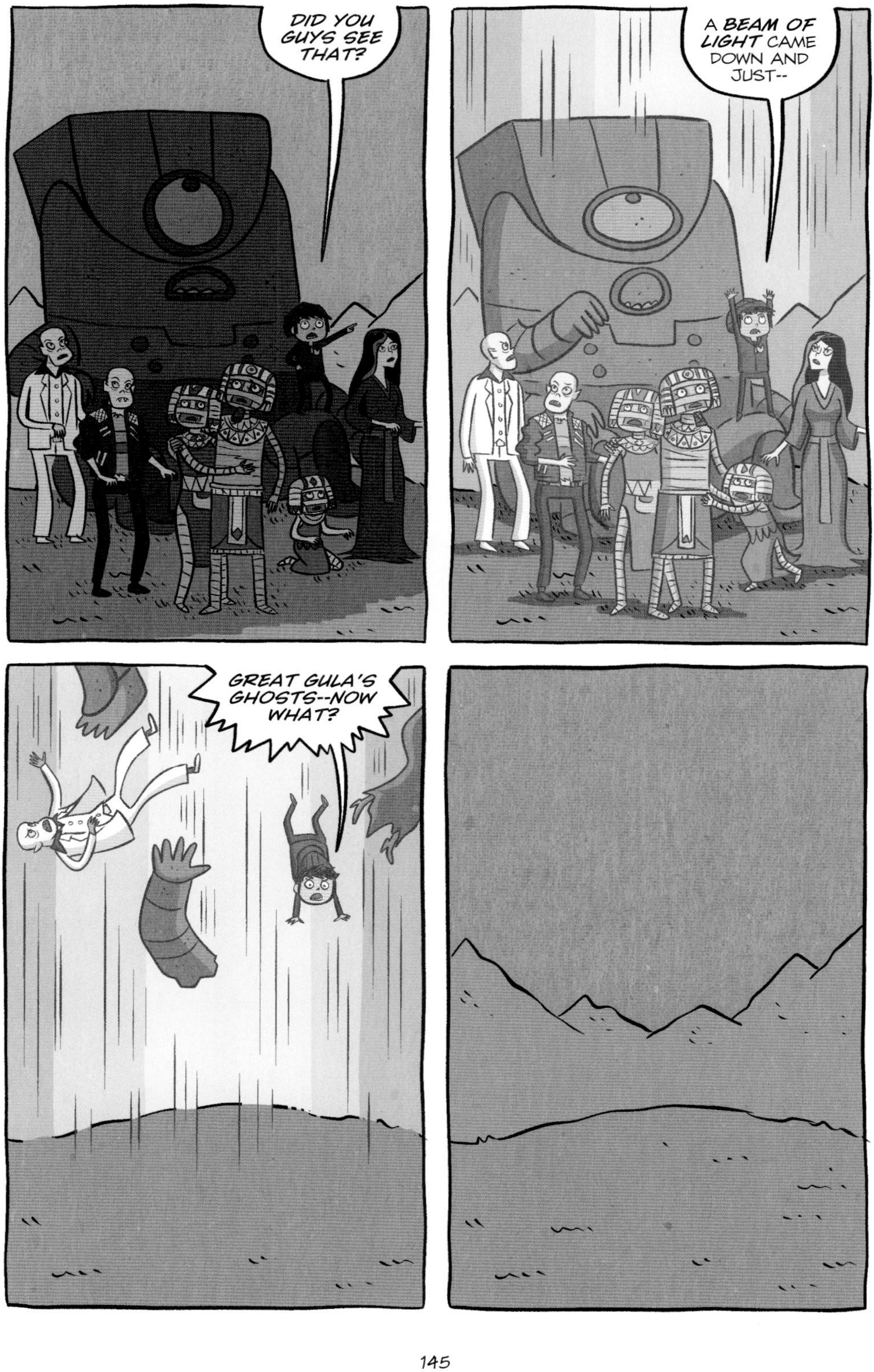
DID YOU GUYS SEE THAT?
A BEAM OF LIGHT CAME DOWN AND JUST--
GREAT GULA'S GHOSTS--NOW WHAT?

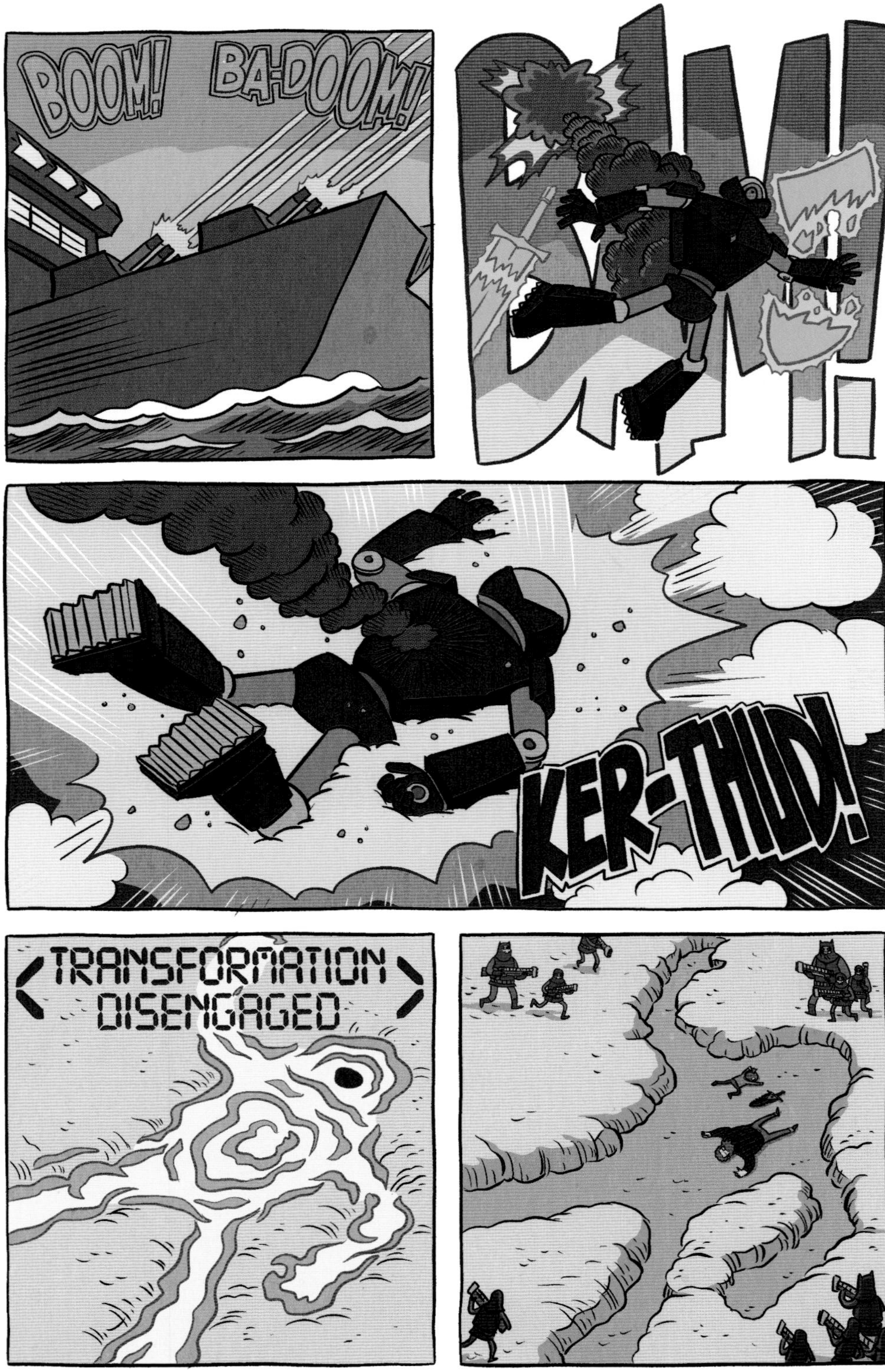
BOOM! BA-DOOM!
KER-THUD!
TRANSFORMATION DISENGAGED

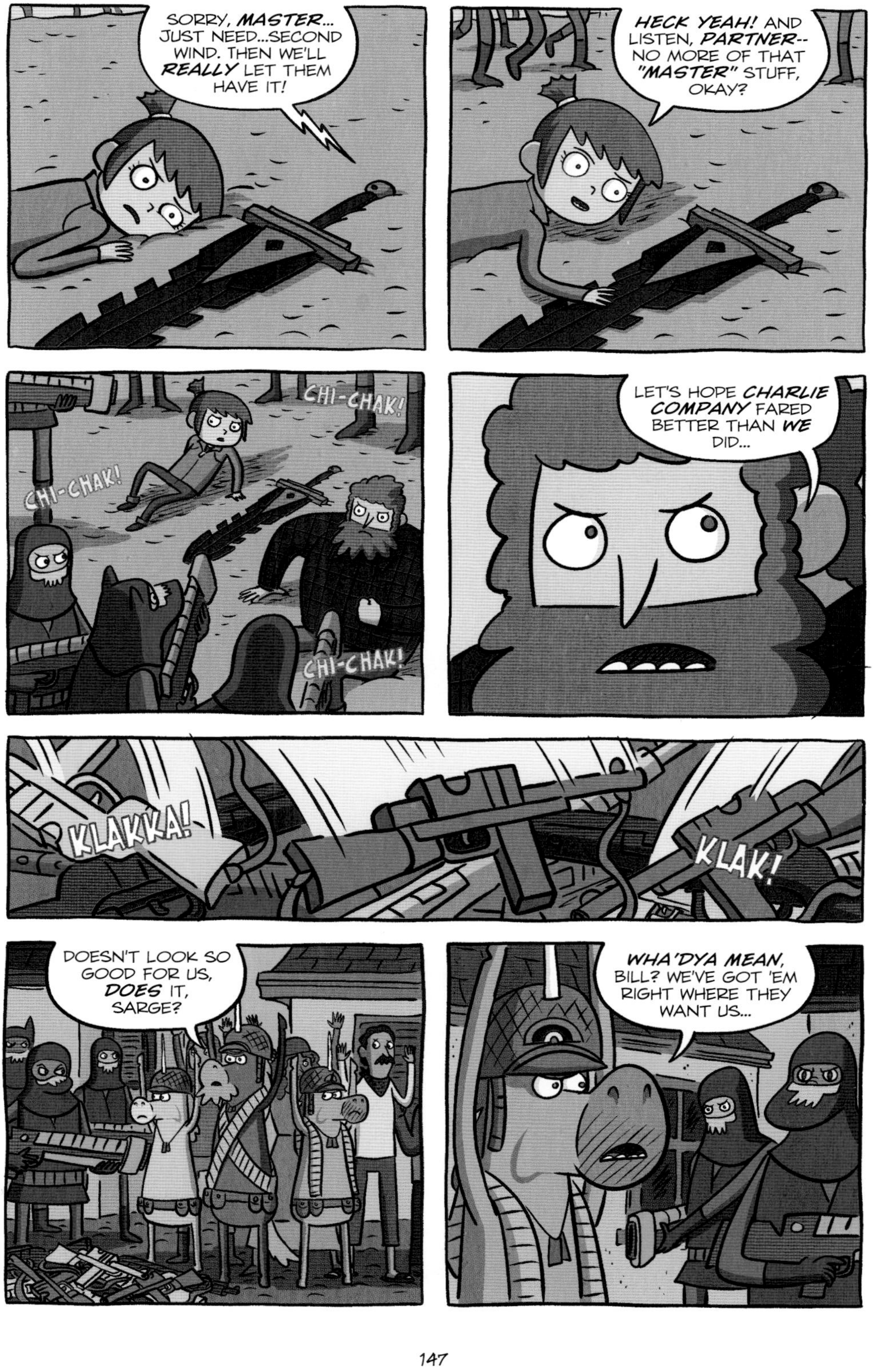
SORRY, MASTER... JUST NEED...SECOND WIND. THEN WE'LL REALLY LET THEM HAVE IT!
HECK YEAH! AND LISTEN, PARTNER-- NO MORE OF THAT "MASTER" STUFF, OKAY?
CHI-CHAK!
CHI-CHAK!
CHI-CHAK!
LET'S HOPE CHARLIE COMPANY FARED BETTER THAN WE DID...
KLAKKA!
KLAK!
DOESN'T LOOK SO GOOD FOR US, DOES IT, SARGE?
WHA'DYA MEAN, BILL? WE'VE GOT 'EM RIGHT WHERE THEY WANT US...

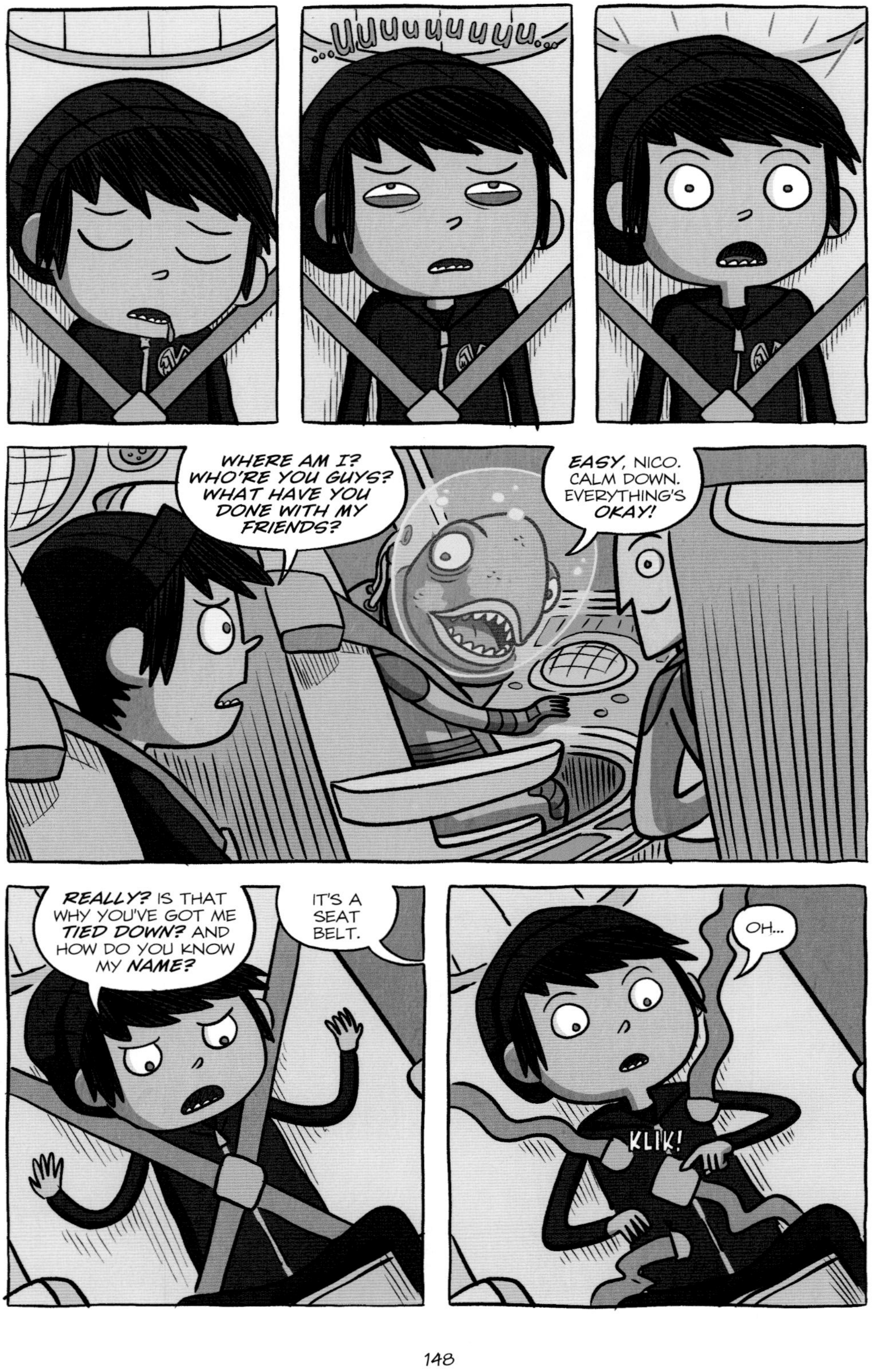
...UUUUUUUUUU...
WHERE AM I? WHO'RE YOU GUYS? WHAT HAVE YOU DONE WITH MY FRIENDS?
EASY, NICO. CALM DOWN. EVERYTHING'S OKAY!
REALLY? IS THAT WHY YOU'VE GOT ME TIED DOWN? AND HOW DO YOU KNOW MY NAME?
IT'S A SEAT BELT.
OH...
KLIK!

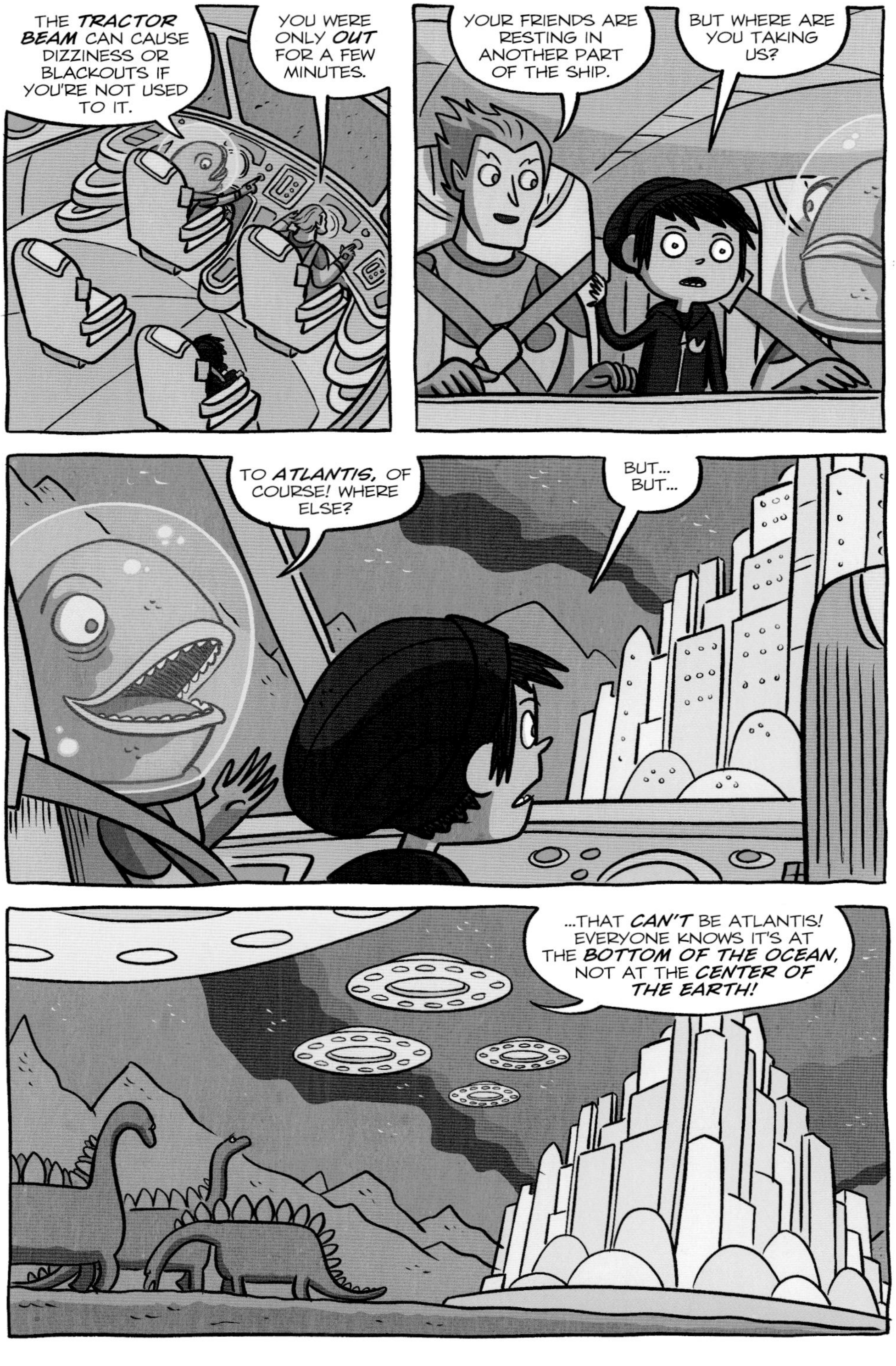
THE *TRACTOR BEAM* CAN CAUSE DIZZINESS OR BLACKOUTS IF YOU'RE NOT USED TO IT.
YOU WERE ONLY *OUT* FOR A FEW MINUTES.
YOUR FRIENDS ARE RESTING IN ANOTHER PART OF THE SHIP.
BUT WHERE ARE YOU TAKING US?
TO *ATLANTIS,* OF COURSE! WHERE ELSE?
BUT... BUT...
...THAT *CAN'T* BE ATLANTIS! EVERYONE KNOWS IT'S AT THE *BOTTOM OF THE OCEAN,* NOT AT THE *CENTER OF THE EARTH!*

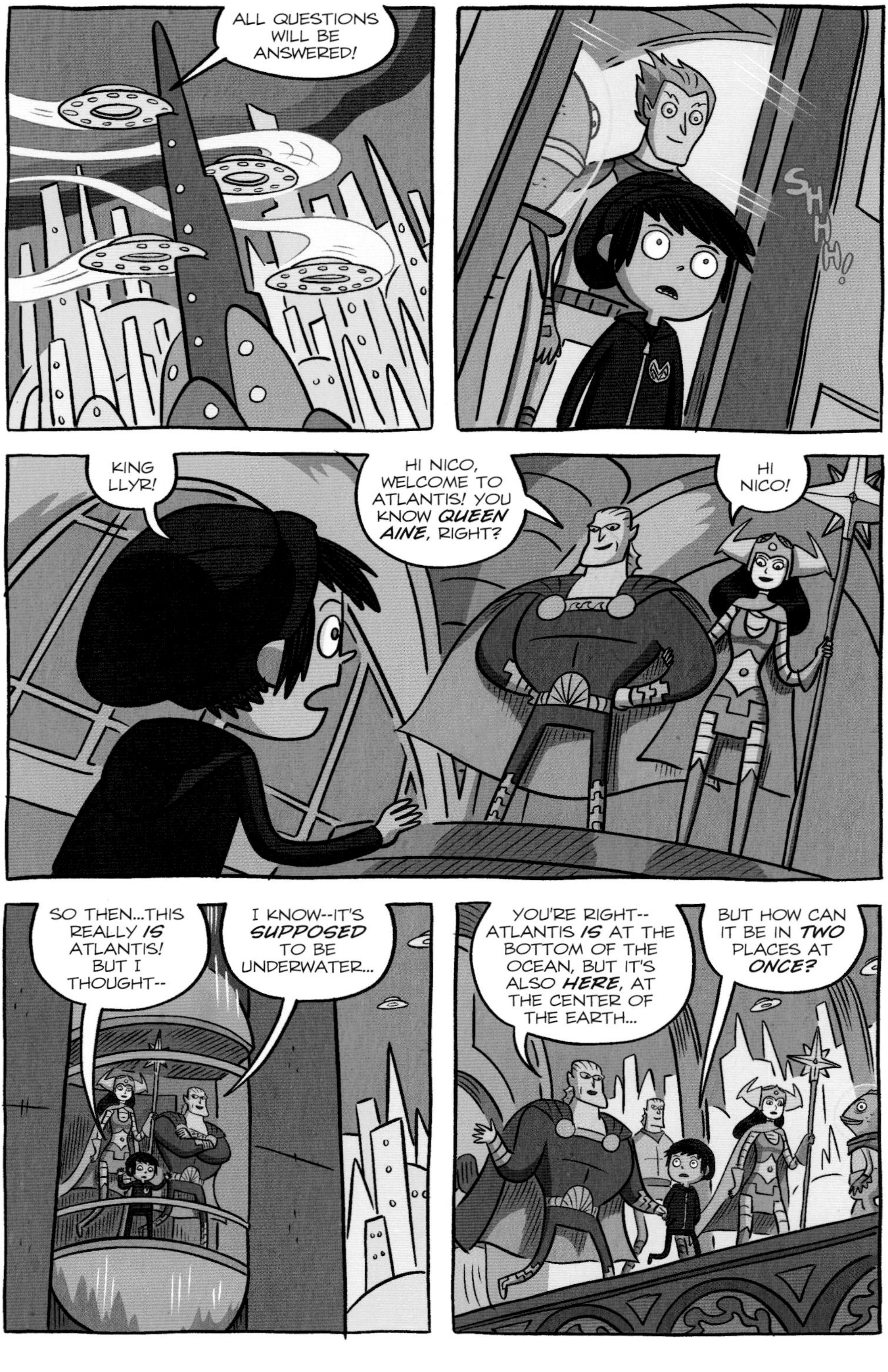
ALL QUESTIONS WILL BE ANSWERED!
SHHHH!
KING LLYR!
HI NICO, WELCOME TO ATLANTIS! YOU KNOW QUEEN AINE, RIGHT?
HI NICO!
SO THEN...THIS REALLY IS ATLANTIS! BUT I THOUGHT--
I KNOW--IT'S SUPPOSED TO BE UNDERWATER...
YOU'RE RIGHT--ATLANTIS IS AT THE BOTTOM OF THE OCEAN, BUT IT'S ALSO HERE, AT THE CENTER OF THE EARTH...
BUT HOW CAN IT BE IN TWO PLACES AT ONCE?

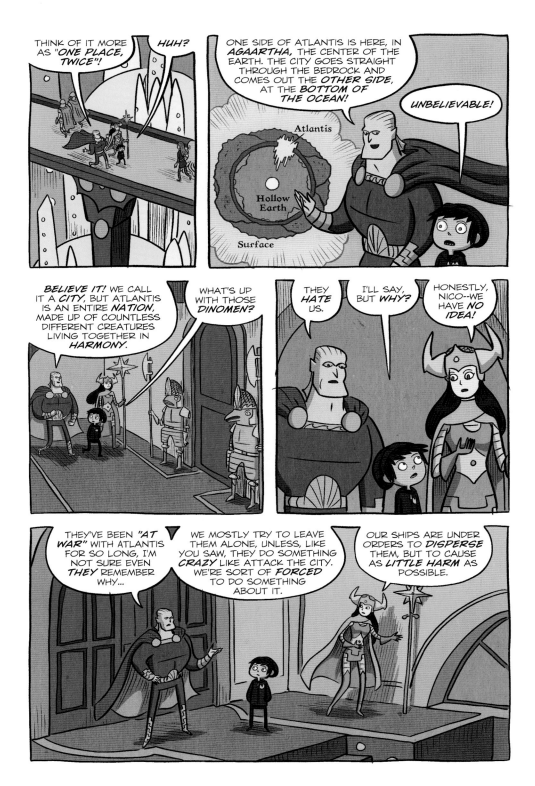

THINK OF IT MORE AS "ONE PLACE, TWICE"!

HUH?

ONE SIDE OF ATLANTIS IS HERE, IN AGAARTHA, THE CENTER OF THE EARTH. THE CITY GOES STRAIGHT THROUGH THE BEDROCK AND COMES OUT THE OTHER SIDE, AT THE BOTTOM OF THE OCEAN!

UNBELIEVABLE!

Atlantis

Hollow Earth

Surface

BELIEVE IT! WE CALL IT A CITY, BUT ATLANTIS IS AN ENTIRE NATION, MADE UP OF COUNTLESS DIFFERENT CREATURES LIVING TOGETHER IN HARMONY.

WHAT'S UP WITH THOSE DINOMEN?

THEY HATE US.

I'LL SAY, BUT WHY?

HONESTLY, NICO--WE HAVE NO IDEA!

THEY'VE BEEN "AT WAR" WITH ATLANTIS FOR SO LONG, I'M NOT SURE EVEN THEY REMEMBER WHY...

WE MOSTLY TRY TO LEAVE THEM ALONE, UNLESS, LIKE YOU SAW, THEY DO SOMETHING CRAZY LIKE ATTACK THE CITY. WE'RE SORT OF FORCED TO DO SOMETHING ABOUT IT.

OUR SHIPS ARE UNDER ORDERS TO DISPERSE THEM, BUT TO CAUSE AS LITTLE HARM AS POSSIBLE.

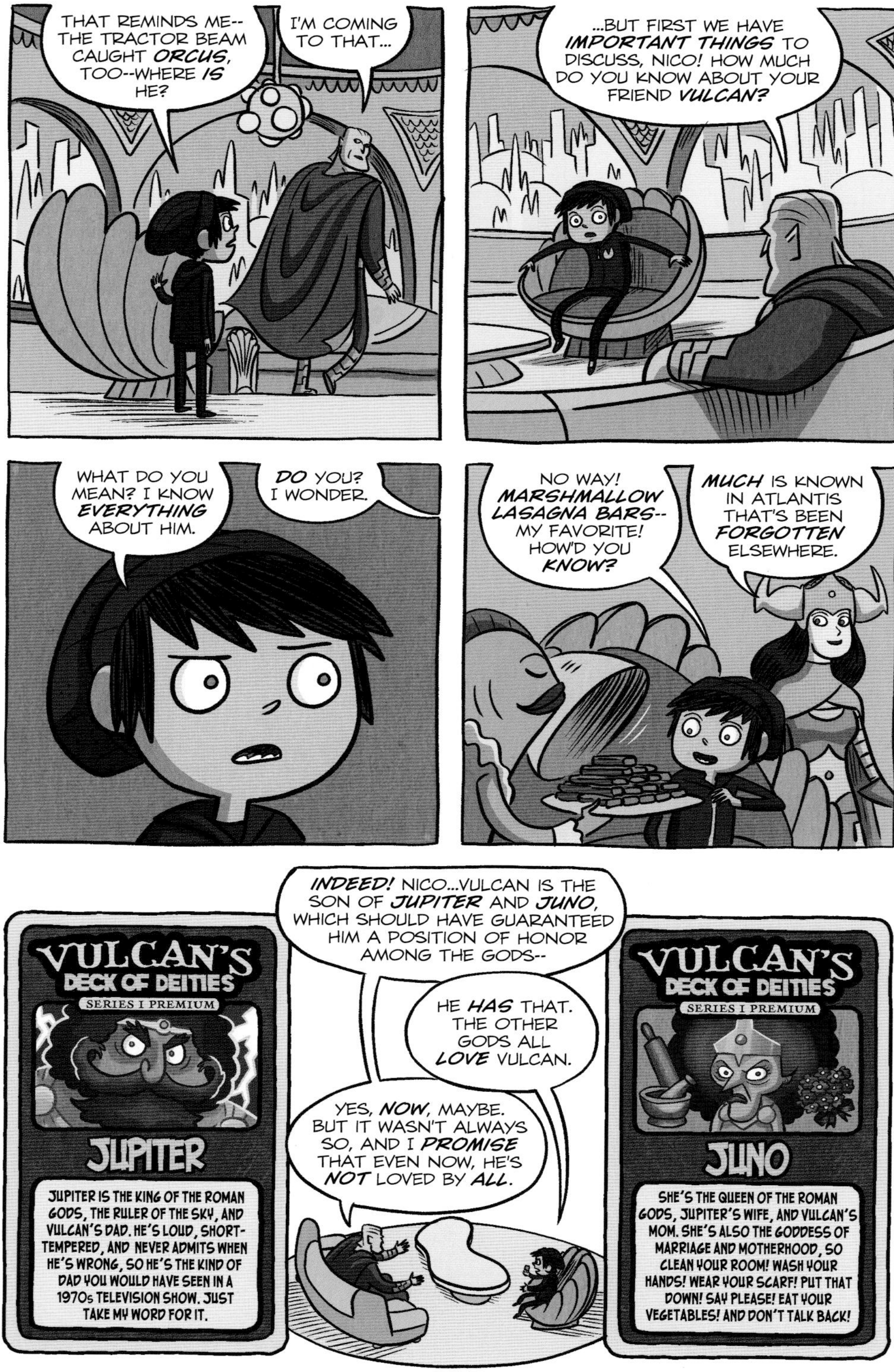
THAT REMINDS ME--THE TRACTOR BEAM CAUGHT ORCUS, TOO--WHERE IS HE?
I'M COMING TO THAT...
...BUT FIRST WE HAVE IMPORTANT THINGS TO DISCUSS, NICO! HOW MUCH DO YOU KNOW ABOUT YOUR FRIEND VULCAN?
WHAT DO YOU MEAN? I KNOW EVERYTHING ABOUT HIM.
DO YOU? I WONDER.
NO WAY! MARSHMALLOW LASAGNA BARS--MY FAVORITE! HOW'D YOU KNOW?
MUCH IS KNOWN IN ATLANTIS THAT'S BEEN FORGOTTEN ELSEWHERE.
INDEED! NICO...VULCAN IS THE SON OF JUPITER AND JUNO, WHICH SHOULD HAVE GUARANTEED HIM A POSITION OF HONOR AMONG THE GODS--
HE HAS THAT. THE OTHER GODS ALL LOVE VULCAN.
YES, NOW, MAYBE. BUT IT WASN'T ALWAYS SO, AND I PROMISE THAT EVEN NOW, HE'S NOT LOVED BY ALL.
VULCAN'S DECK OF DEITIES
SERIES I PREMIUM
JUPITER
JUPITER IS THE KING OF THE ROMAN GODS, THE RULER OF THE SKY, AND VULCAN'S DAD. HE'S LOUD, SHORT-TEMPERED, AND NEVER ADMITS WHEN HE'S WRONG, SO HE'S THE KIND OF DAD YOU WOULD HAVE SEEN IN A 1970s TELEVISION SHOW. JUST TAKE MY WORD FOR IT.
VULCAN'S DECK OF DEITIES
SERIES I PREMIUM
JUNO
SHE'S THE QUEEN OF THE ROMAN GODS, JUPITER'S WIFE, AND VULCAN'S MOM. SHE'S ALSO THE GODDESS OF MARRIAGE AND MOTHERHOOD, SO CLEAN YOUR ROOM! WASH YOUR HANDS! WEAR YOUR SCARF! PUT THAT DOWN! SAY PLEASE! EAT YOUR VEGETABLES! AND DON'T TALK BACK!

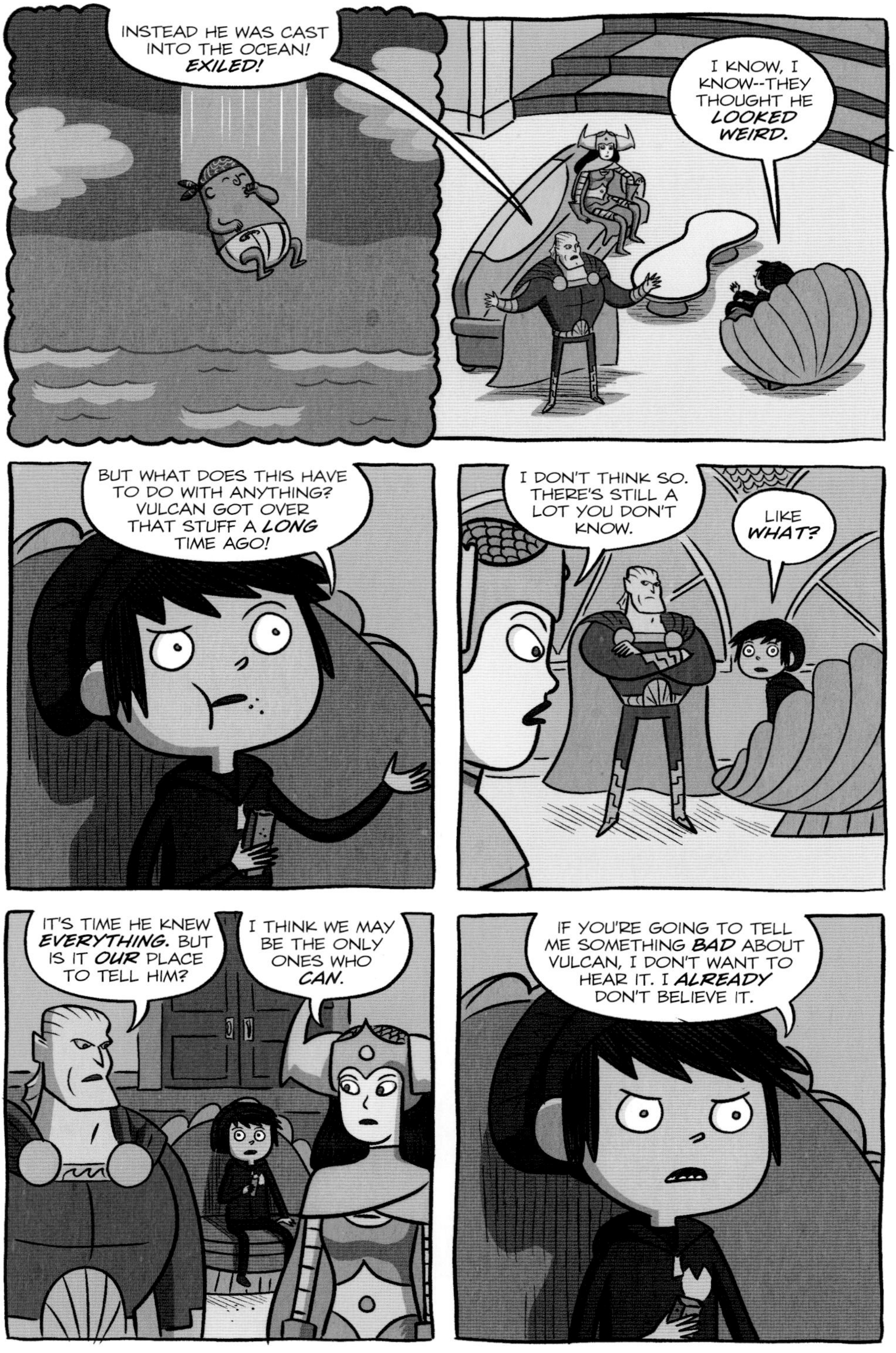
INSTEAD HE WAS CAST INTO THE OCEAN! EXILED!
I KNOW, I KNOW--THEY THOUGHT HE LOOKED WEIRD.
BUT WHAT DOES THIS HAVE TO DO WITH ANYTHING? VULCAN GOT OVER THAT STUFF A LONG TIME AGO!
I DON'T THINK SO. THERE'S STILL A LOT YOU DON'T KNOW.
LIKE WHAT?
IT'S TIME HE KNEW EVERYTHING. BUT IS IT OUR PLACE TO TELL HIM?
I THINK WE MAY BE THE ONLY ONES WHO CAN.
IF YOU'RE GOING TO TELL ME SOMETHING BAD ABOUT VULCAN, I DON'T WANT TO HEAR IT. I ALREADY DON'T BELIEVE IT.

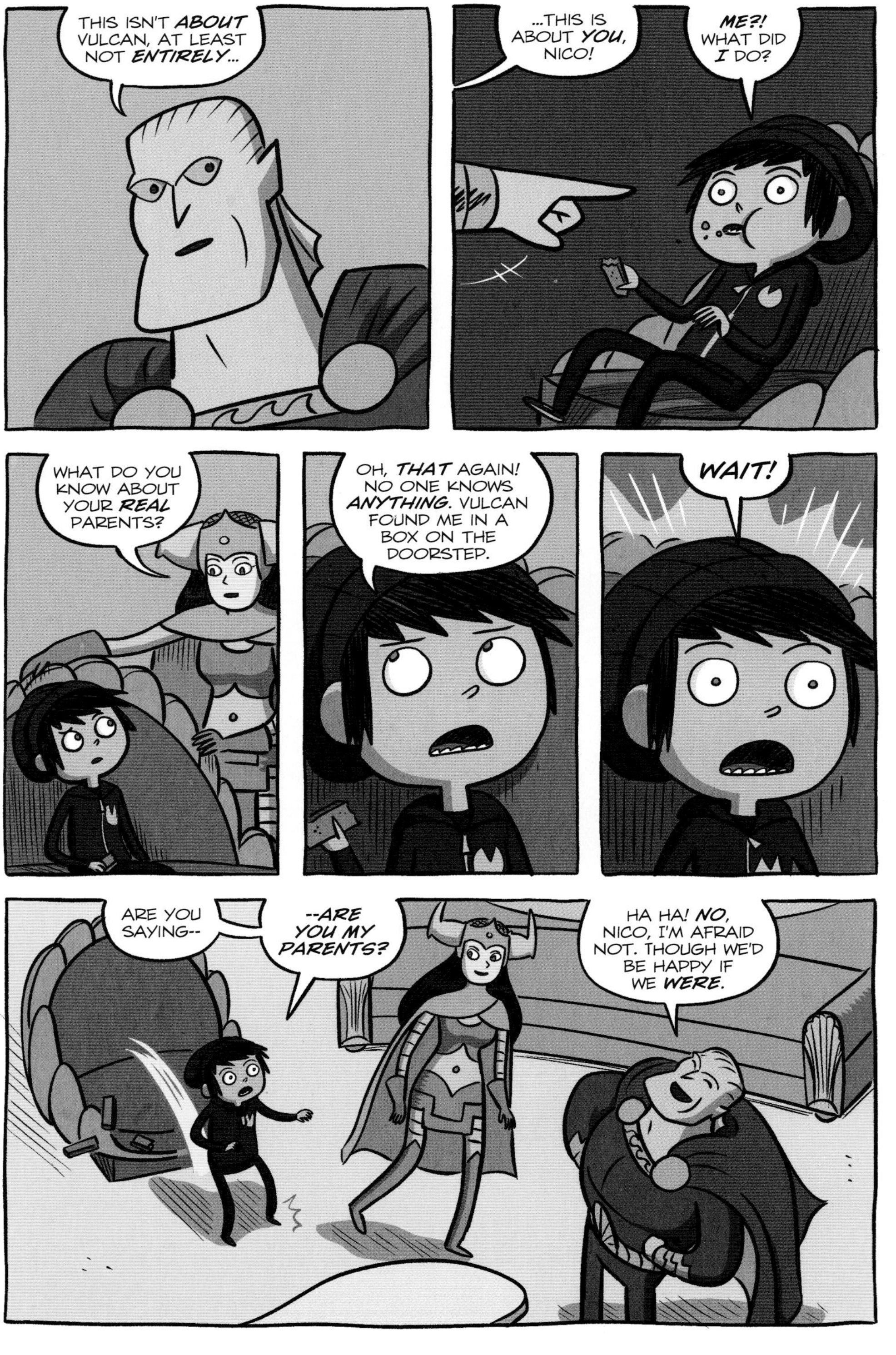
THIS ISN'T ABOUT VULCAN, AT LEAST NOT ENTIRELY...
...THIS IS ABOUT YOU, NICO!
ME?! WHAT DID I DO?
WHAT DO YOU KNOW ABOUT YOUR REAL PARENTS?
OH, THAT AGAIN! NO ONE KNOWS ANYTHING. VULCAN FOUND ME IN A BOX ON THE DOORSTEP.
WAIT!
ARE YOU SAYING--
--ARE YOU MY PARENTS?
HA HA! NO, NICO, I'M AFRAID NOT. THOUGH WE'D BE HAPPY IF WE WERE.

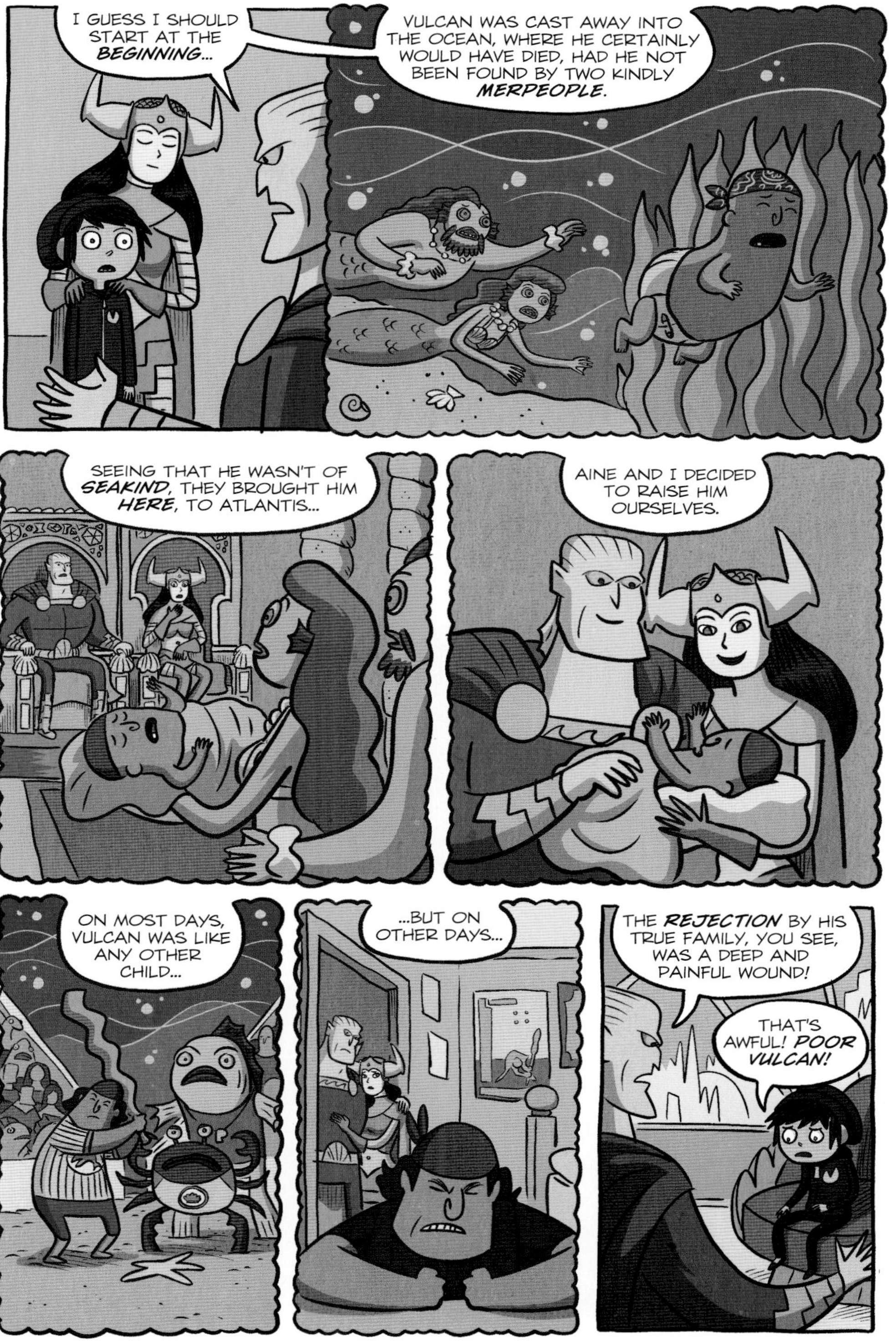
I GUESS I SHOULD START AT THE *BEGINNING*...
VULCAN WAS CAST AWAY INTO THE OCEAN, WHERE HE CERTAINLY WOULD HAVE DIED, HAD HE NOT BEEN FOUND BY TWO KINDLY *MERPEOPLE*.
SEEING THAT HE WASN'T OF *SEAKIND*, THEY BROUGHT HIM *HERE*, TO ATLANTIS...
AINE AND I DECIDED TO RAISE HIM OURSELVES.
ON MOST DAYS, VULCAN WAS LIKE ANY OTHER CHILD...
...BUT ON OTHER DAYS...
THE *REJECTION* BY HIS TRUE FAMILY, YOU SEE, WAS A DEEP AND PAINFUL WOUND!
THAT'S AWFUL! *POOR VULCAN!*

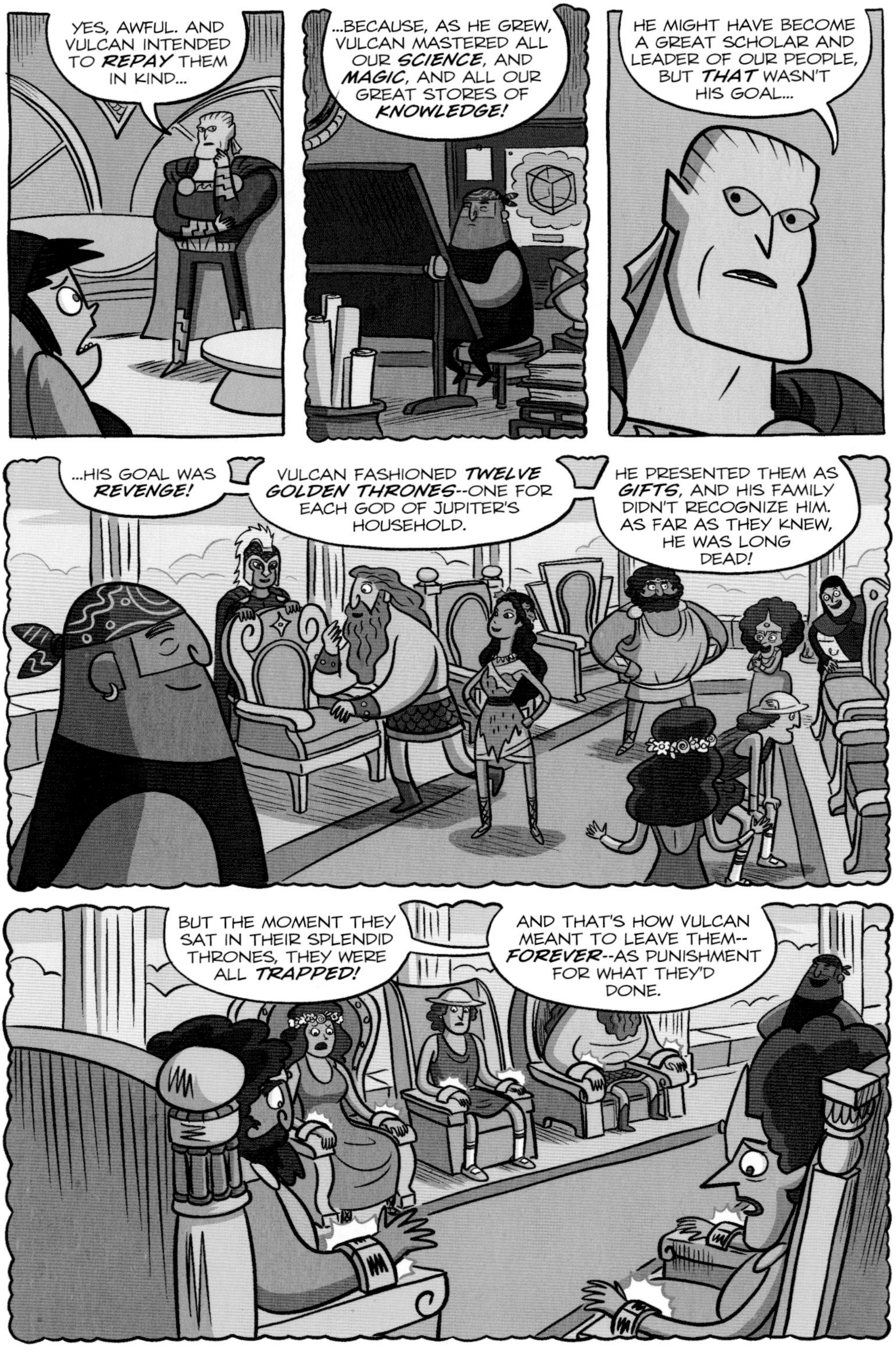
YES, AWFUL. AND VULCAN INTENDED TO REPAY THEM IN KIND...
...BECAUSE, AS HE GREW, VULCAN MASTERED ALL OUR SCIENCE, AND MAGIC, AND ALL OUR GREAT STORES OF KNOWLEDGE!
HE MIGHT HAVE BECOME A GREAT SCHOLAR AND LEADER OF OUR PEOPLE, BUT THAT WASN'T HIS GOAL...
...HIS GOAL WAS REVENGE!
VULCAN FASHIONED TWELVE GOLDEN THRONES--ONE FOR EACH GOD OF JUPITER'S HOUSEHOLD.
HE PRESENTED THEM AS GIFTS, AND HIS FAMILY DIDN'T RECOGNIZE HIM. AS FAR AS THEY KNEW, HE WAS LONG DEAD!
BUT THE MOMENT THEY SAT IN THEIR SPLENDID THRONES, THEY WERE ALL TRAPPED!
AND THAT'S HOW VULCAN MEANT TO LEAVE THEM--FOREVER--AS PUNISHMENT FOR WHAT THEY'D DONE.

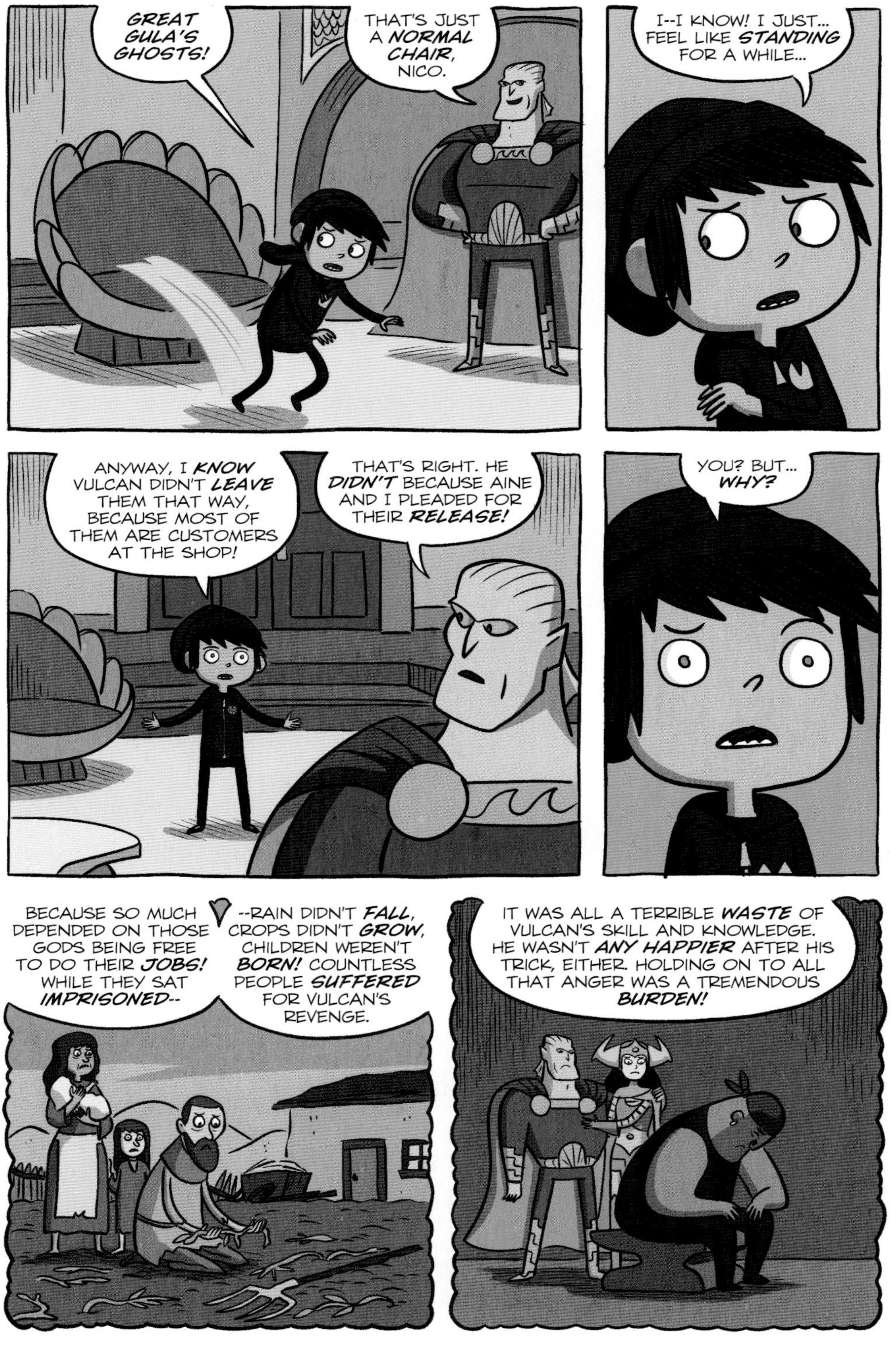
GREAT GULA'S GHOSTS!
THAT'S JUST A NORMAL CHAIR, NICO.
I--I KNOW! I JUST... FEEL LIKE STANDING FOR A WHILE...
ANYWAY, I KNOW VULCAN DIDN'T LEAVE THEM THAT WAY, BECAUSE MOST OF THEM ARE CUSTOMERS AT THE SHOP!
THAT'S RIGHT. HE DIDN'T BECAUSE AINE AND I PLEADED FOR THEIR RELEASE!
YOU? BUT... WHY?
BECAUSE SO MUCH DEPENDED ON THOSE GODS BEING FREE TO DO THEIR JOBS! WHILE THEY SAT IMPRISONED--
--RAIN DIDN'T FALL, CROPS DIDN'T GROW, CHILDREN WEREN'T BORN! COUNTLESS PEOPLE SUFFERED FOR VULCAN'S REVENGE.
IT WAS ALL A TERRIBLE WASTE OF VULCAN'S SKILL AND KNOWLEDGE. HE WASN'T ANY HAPPIER AFTER HIS TRICK, EITHER. HOLDING ON TO ALL THAT ANGER WAS A TREMENDOUS BURDEN!

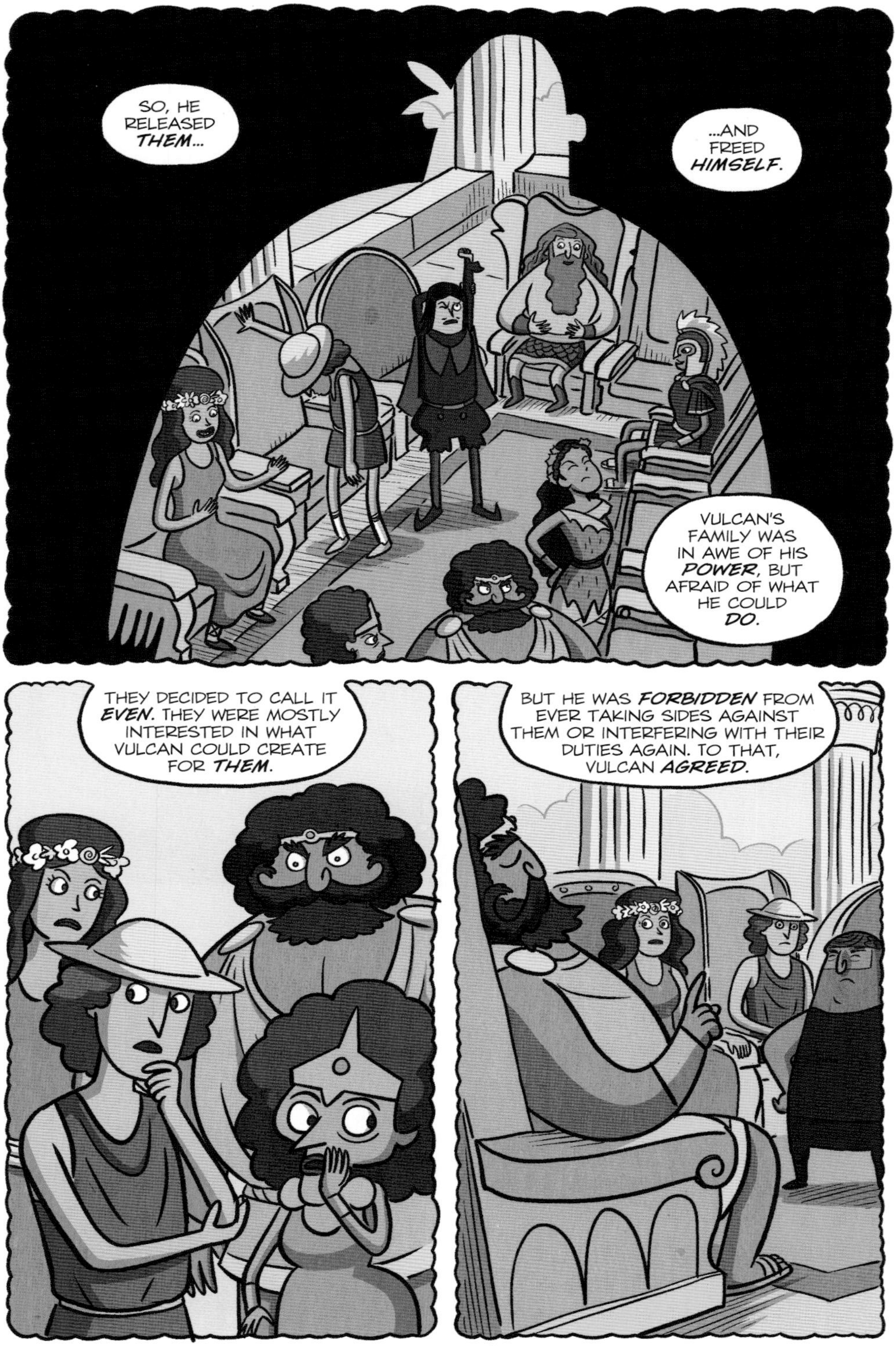
SO, HE RELEASED THEM...
...AND FREED HIMSELF.
VULCAN'S FAMILY WAS IN AWE OF HIS POWER, BUT AFRAID OF WHAT HE COULD DO.
THEY DECIDED TO CALL IT EVEN. THEY WERE MOSTLY INTERESTED IN WHAT VULCAN COULD CREATE FOR THEM.
BUT HE WAS FORBIDDEN FROM EVER TAKING SIDES AGAINST THEM OR INTERFERING WITH THEIR DUTIES AGAIN. TO THAT, VULCAN AGREED.

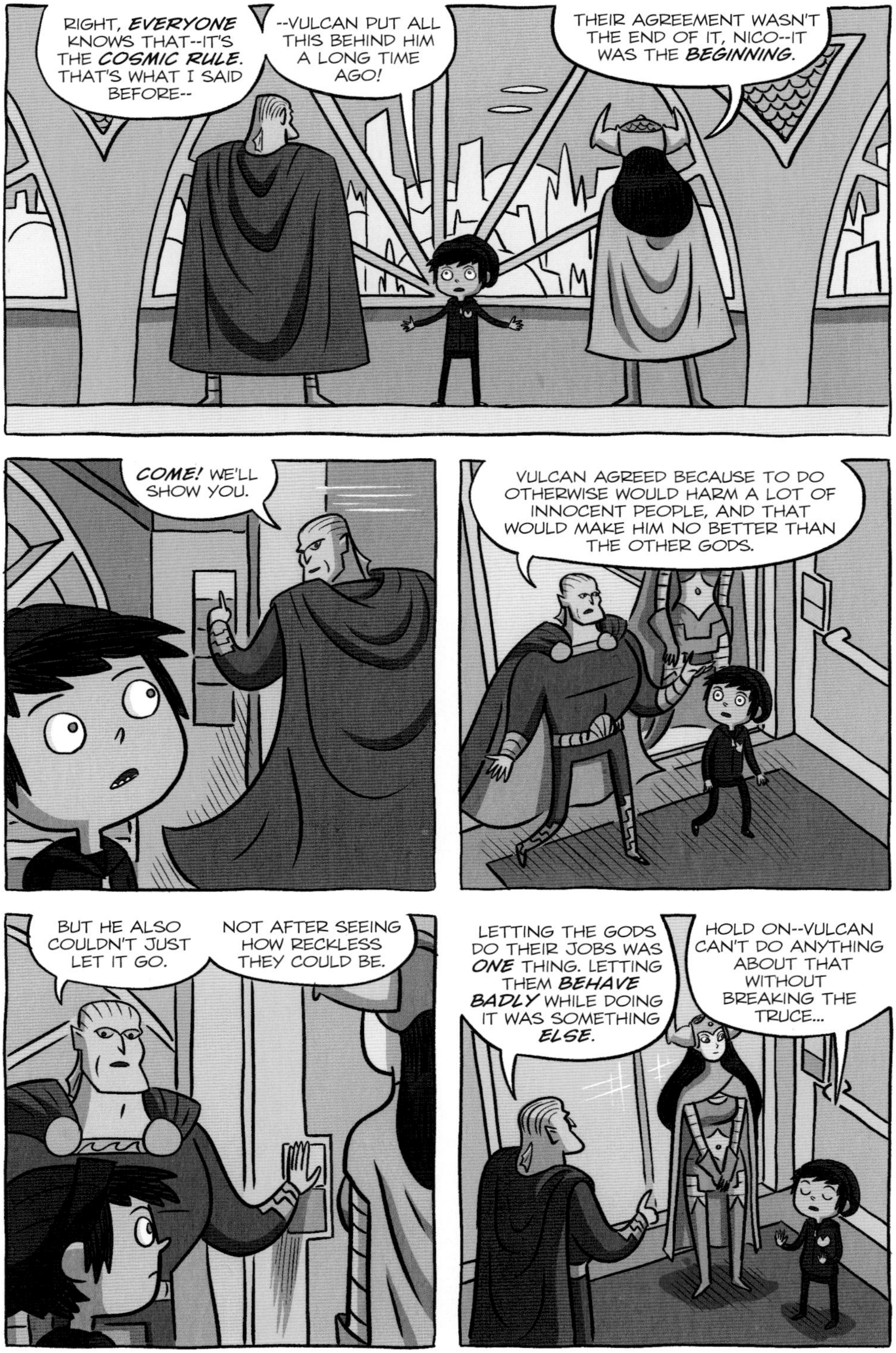
RIGHT, EVERYONE KNOWS THAT--IT'S THE COSMIC RULE. THAT'S WHAT I SAID BEFORE--
--VULCAN PUT ALL THIS BEHIND HIM A LONG TIME AGO!
THEIR AGREEMENT WASN'T THE END OF IT, NICO--IT WAS THE BEGINNING.
COME! WE'LL SHOW YOU.
VULCAN AGREED BECAUSE TO DO OTHERWISE WOULD HARM A LOT OF INNOCENT PEOPLE, AND THAT WOULD MAKE HIM NO BETTER THAN THE OTHER GODS.
BUT HE ALSO COULDN'T JUST LET IT GO.
NOT AFTER SEEING HOW RECKLESS THEY COULD BE.
LETTING THE GODS DO THEIR JOBS WAS ONE THING. LETTING THEM BEHAVE BADLY WHILE DOING IT WAS SOMETHING ELSE.
HOLD ON--VULCAN CAN'T DO ANYTHING ABOUT THAT WITHOUT BREAKING THE TRUCE...

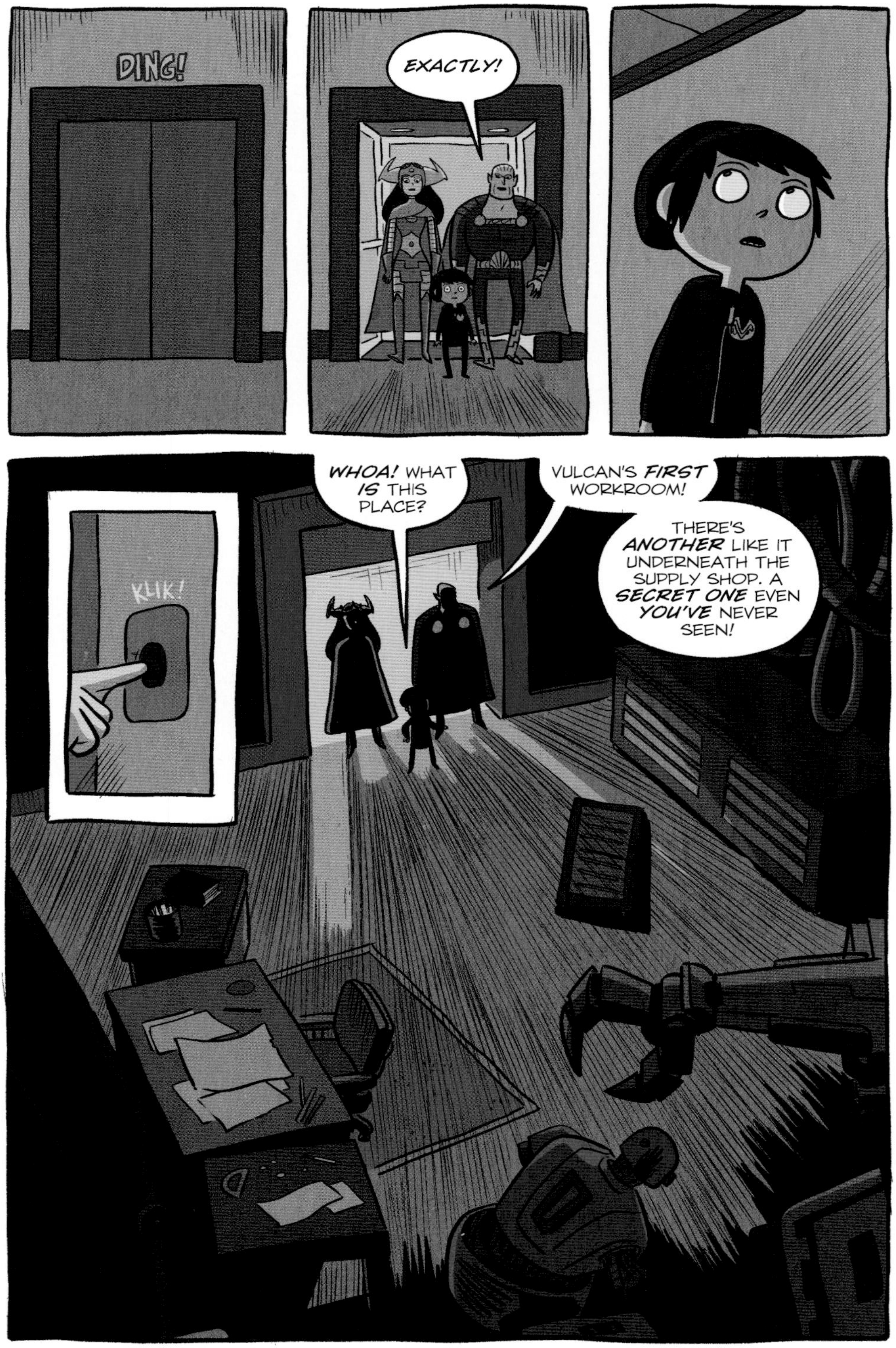
DING!
EXACTLY!
KLIK!
WHOA! WHAT IS THIS PLACE?
VULCAN'S FIRST WORKROOM!
THERE'S ANOTHER LIKE IT UNDERNEATH THE SUPPLY SHOP. A SECRET ONE EVEN YOU'VE NEVER SEEN!

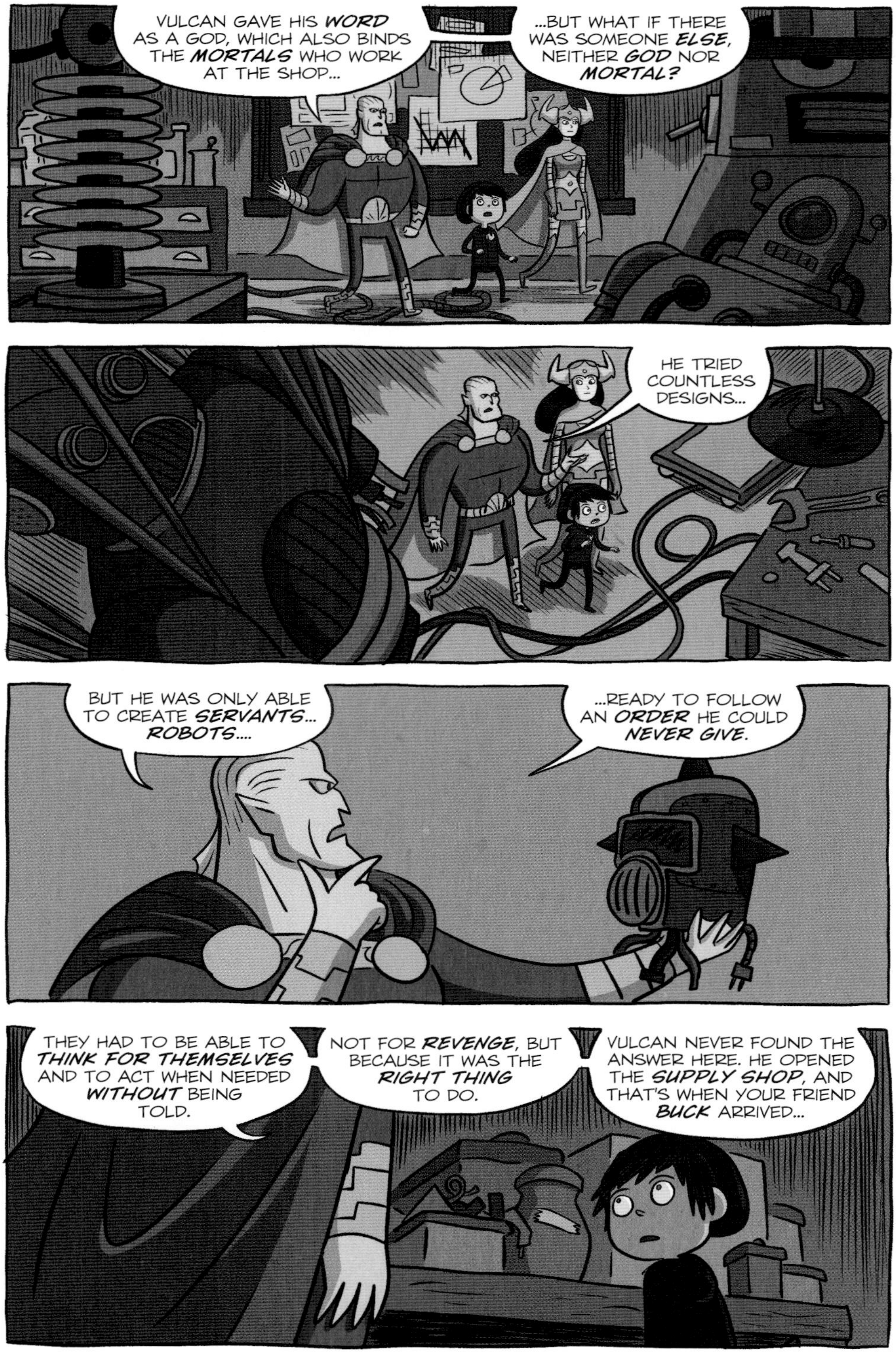
VULCAN GAVE HIS WORD AS A GOD, WHICH ALSO BINDS THE MORTALS WHO WORK AT THE SHOP...
...BUT WHAT IF THERE WAS SOMEONE ELSE, NEITHER GOD NOR MORTAL?
HE TRIED COUNTLESS DESIGNS...
BUT HE WAS ONLY ABLE TO CREATE SERVANTS... ROBOTS....
...READY TO FOLLOW AN ORDER HE COULD NEVER GIVE.
THEY HAD TO BE ABLE TO THINK FOR THEMSELVES AND TO ACT WHEN NEEDED WITHOUT BEING TOLD.
NOT FOR REVENGE, BUT BECAUSE IT WAS THE RIGHT THING TO DO.
VULCAN NEVER FOUND THE ANSWER HERE. HE OPENED THE SUPPLY SHOP, AND THAT'S WHEN YOUR FRIEND BUCK ARRIVED...

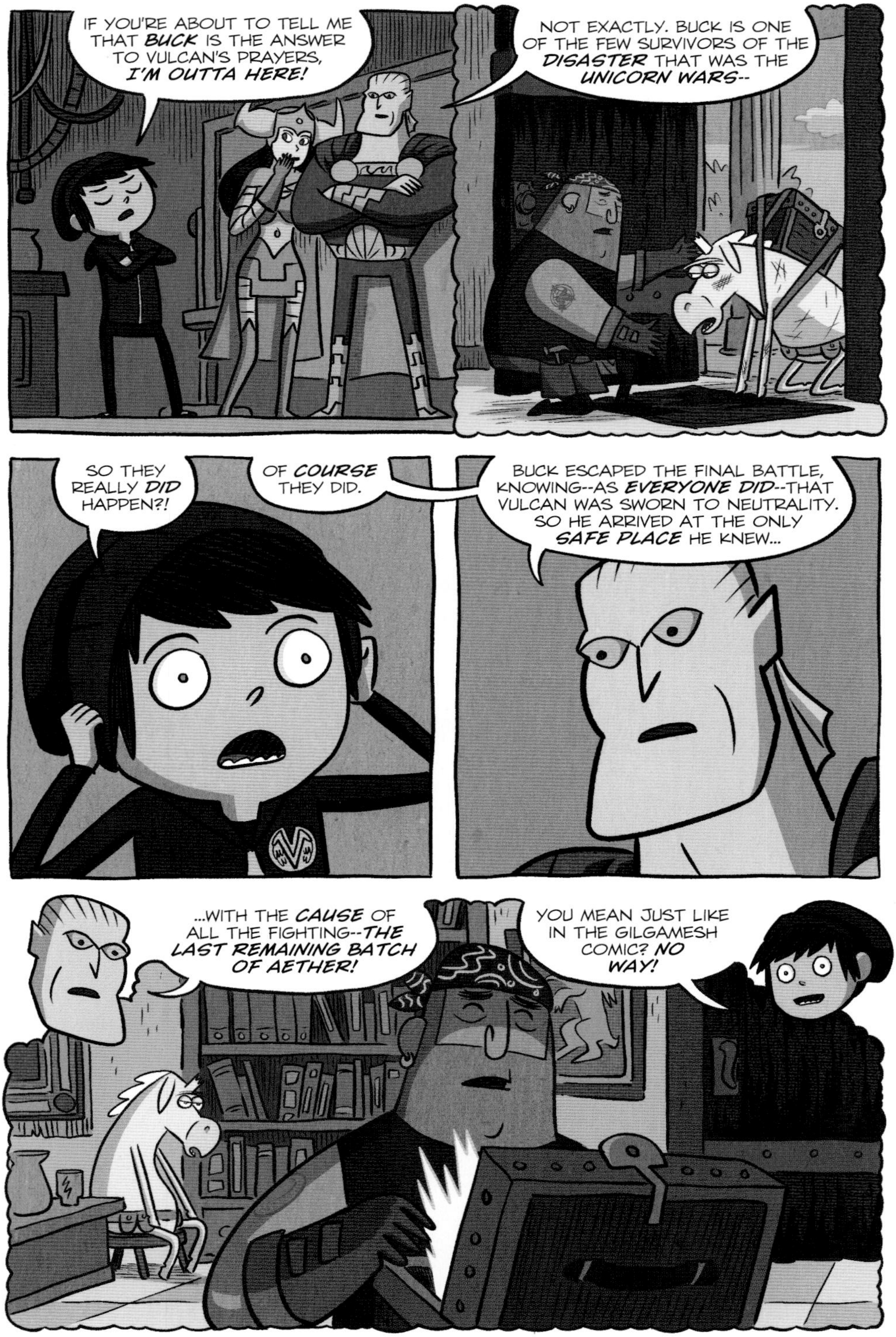
IF YOU'RE ABOUT TO TELL ME THAT BUCK IS THE ANSWER TO VULCAN'S PRAYERS, I'M OUTTA HERE!
NOT EXACTLY. BUCK IS ONE OF THE FEW SURVIVORS OF THE DISASTER THAT WAS THE UNICORN WARS--
SO THEY REALLY DID HAPPEN?!
OF COURSE THEY DID.
BUCK ESCAPED THE FINAL BATTLE, KNOWING--AS EVERYONE DID--THAT VULCAN WAS SWORN TO NEUTRALITY. SO HE ARRIVED AT THE ONLY SAFE PLACE HE KNEW...
...WITH THE CAUSE OF ALL THE FIGHTING--THE LAST REMAINING BATCH OF AETHER!
YOU MEAN JUST LIKE IN THE GILGAMESH COMIC? NO WAY!

WAY.

WHAT DID VULCAN DO? HE *HID* IT, RIGHT?

THAT'S RIGHT.

HE HID IT.

ORCUS!

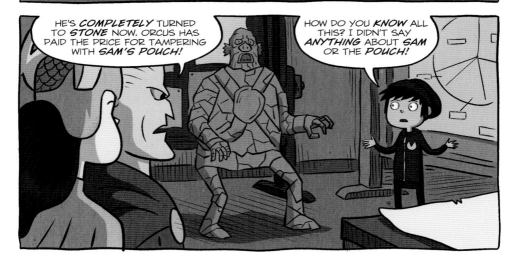

HE'S *COMPLETELY* TURNED TO *STONE* NOW. ORCUS HAS PAID THE PRICE FOR TAMPERING WITH *SAM'S POUCH!*

HOW DO YOU *KNOW* ALL THIS? I DIDN'T SAY *ANYTHING* ABOUT *SAM* OR THE *POUCH!*

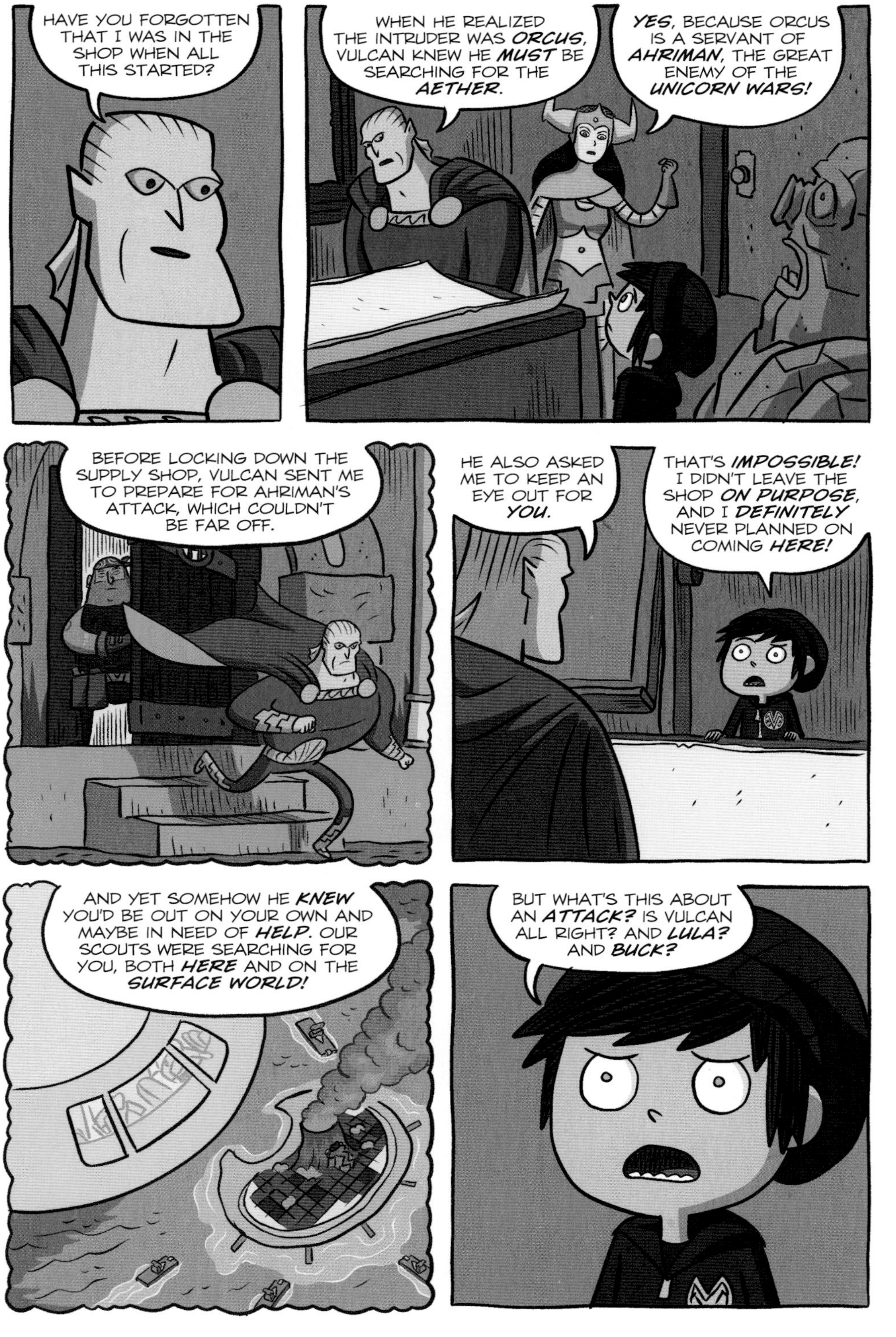
HAVE YOU FORGOTTEN THAT I WAS IN THE SHOP WHEN ALL THIS STARTED?
WHEN HE REALIZED THE INTRUDER WAS ORCUS, VULCAN KNEW HE MUST BE SEARCHING FOR THE AETHER.
YES, BECAUSE ORCUS IS A SERVANT OF AHRIMAN, THE GREAT ENEMY OF THE UNICORN WARS!
BEFORE LOCKING DOWN THE SUPPLY SHOP, VULCAN SENT ME TO PREPARE FOR AHRIMAN'S ATTACK, WHICH COULDN'T BE FAR OFF.
HE ALSO ASKED ME TO KEEP AN EYE OUT FOR YOU.
THAT'S IMPOSSIBLE! I DIDN'T LEAVE THE SHOP ON PURPOSE, AND I DEFINITELY NEVER PLANNED ON COMING HERE!
AND YET SOMEHOW HE KNEW YOU'D BE OUT ON YOUR OWN AND MAYBE IN NEED OF HELP. OUR SCOUTS WERE SEARCHING FOR YOU, BOTH HERE AND ON THE SURFACE WORLD!
BUT WHAT'S THIS ABOUT AN ATTACK? IS VULCAN ALL RIGHT? AND LULA? AND BUCK?

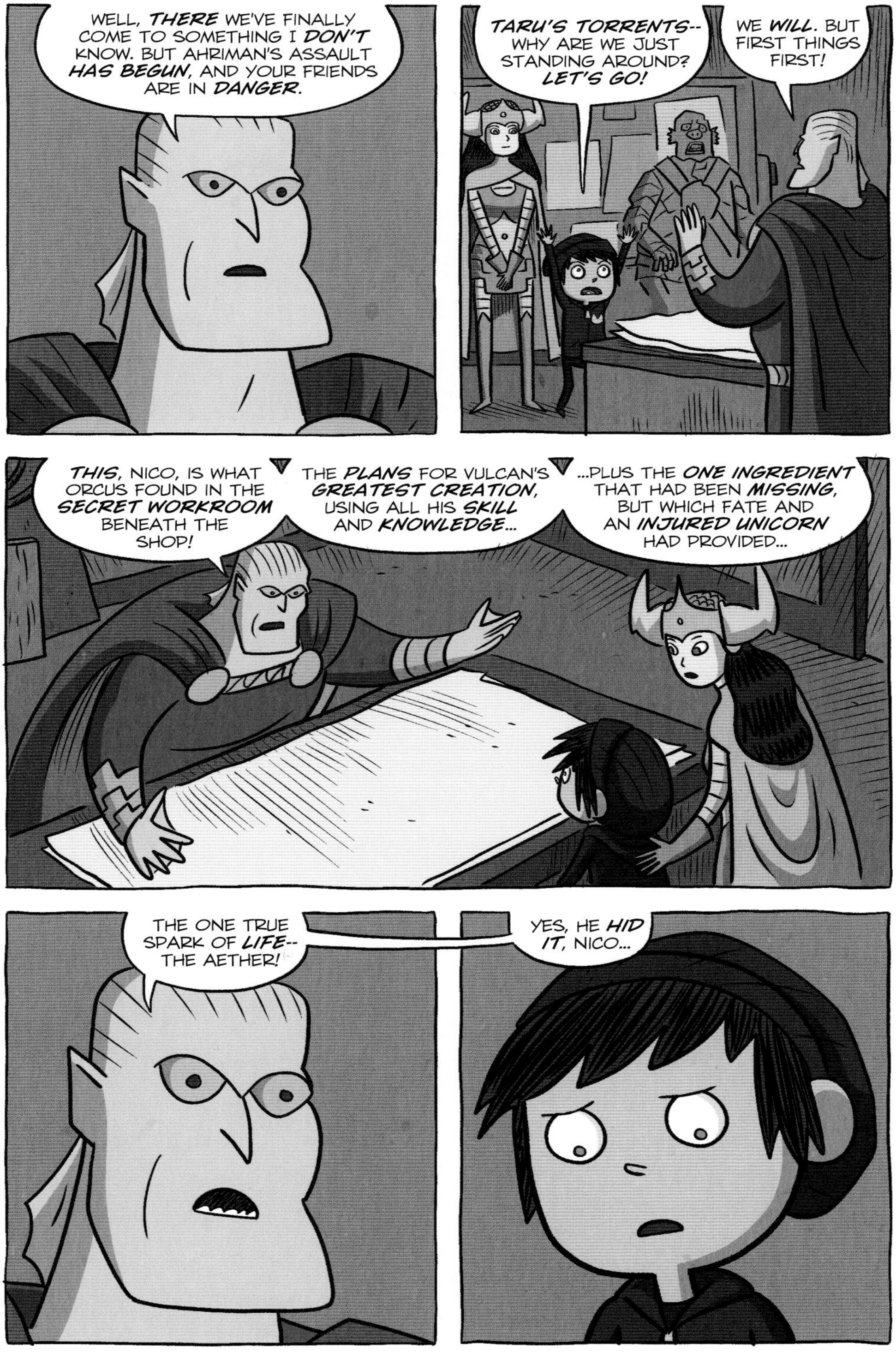
WELL, THERE WE'VE FINALLY COME TO SOMETHING I DON'T KNOW. BUT AHRIMAN'S ASSAULT HAS BEGUN, AND YOUR FRIENDS ARE IN DANGER.
TARU'S TORRENTS-- WHY ARE WE JUST STANDING AROUND? LET'S GO!
WE WILL. BUT FIRST THINGS FIRST!
THIS, NICO, IS WHAT ORCUS FOUND IN THE SECRET WORKROOM BENEATH THE SHOP!
THE PLANS FOR VULCAN'S GREATEST CREATION, USING ALL HIS SKILL AND KNOWLEDGE...
...PLUS THE ONE INGREDIENT THAT HAD BEEN MISSING, BUT WHICH FATE AND AN INJURED UNICORN HAD PROVIDED...
THE ONE TRUE SPARK OF LIFE-- THE AETHER!
YES, HE HID IT, NICO...

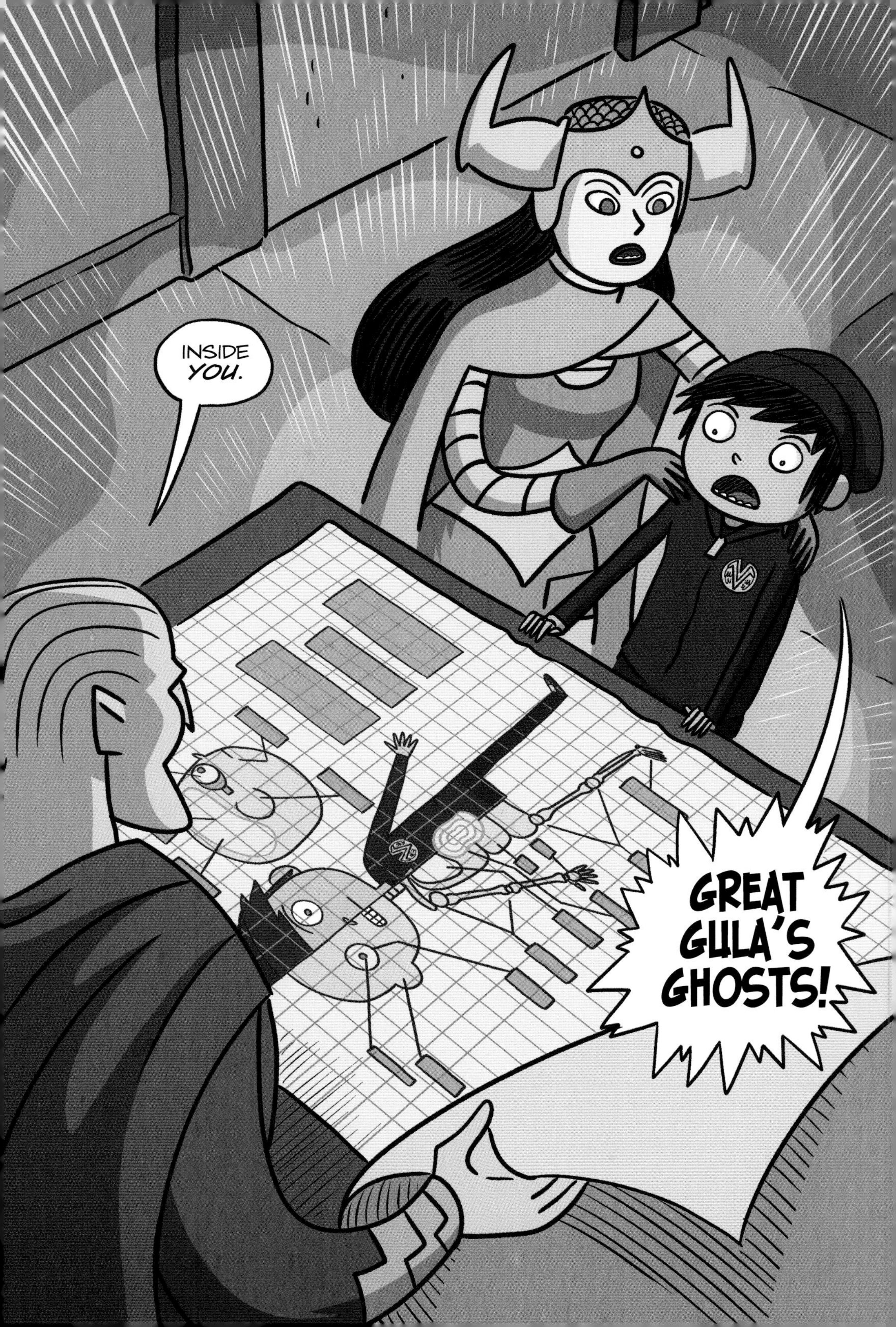
INSIDE *YOU*.
GREAT GULA'S GHOSTS!

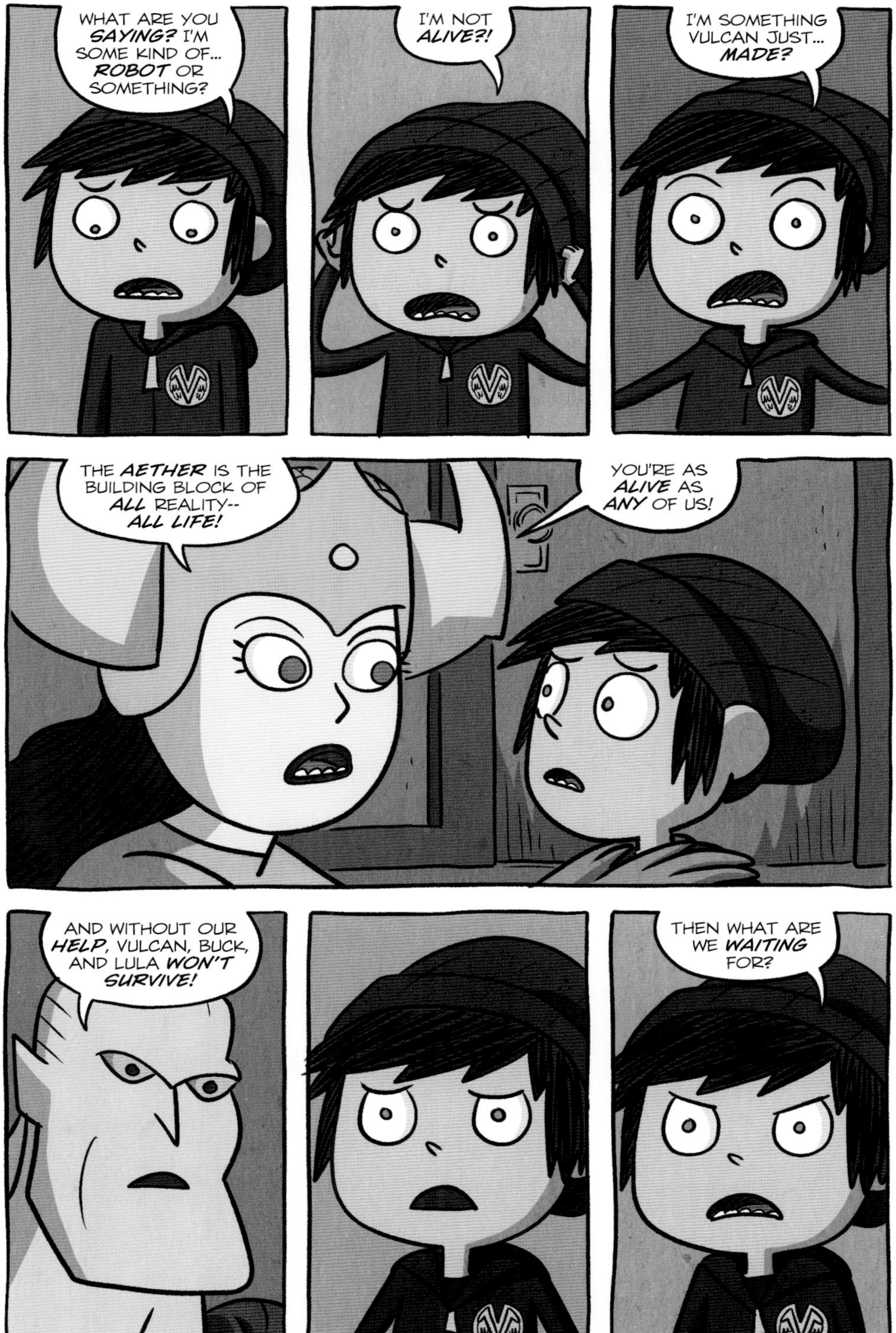
WHAT ARE YOU SAYING? I'M SOME KIND OF... ROBOT OR SOMETHING?
I'M NOT ALIVE?!
I'M SOMETHING VULCAN JUST... MADE?
THE AETHER IS THE BUILDING BLOCK OF ALL REALITY-- ALL LIFE!
YOU'RE AS ALIVE AS ANY OF US!
AND WITHOUT OUR HELP, VULCAN, BUCK, AND LULA WON'T SURVIVE!
THEN WHAT ARE WE WAITING FOR?

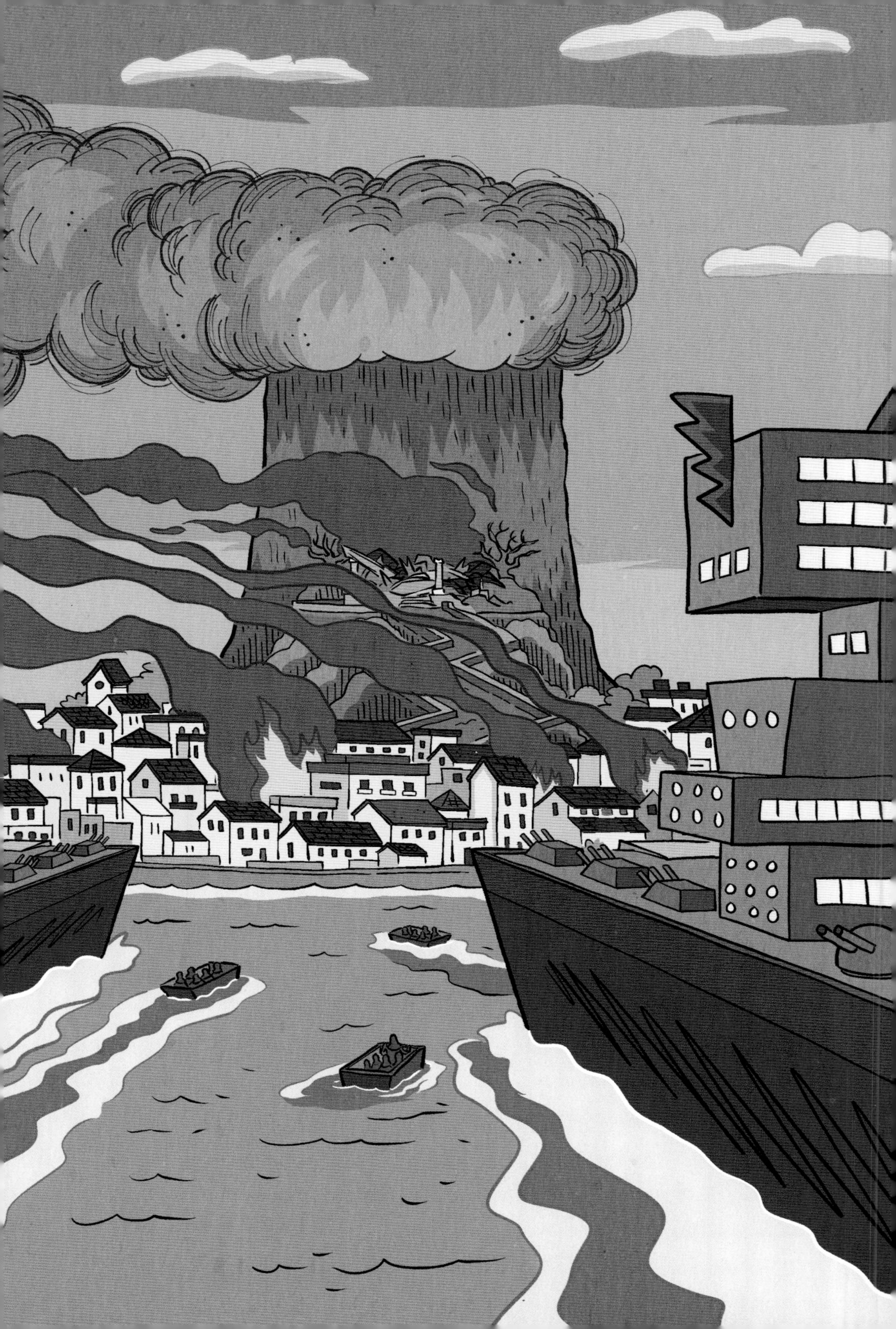

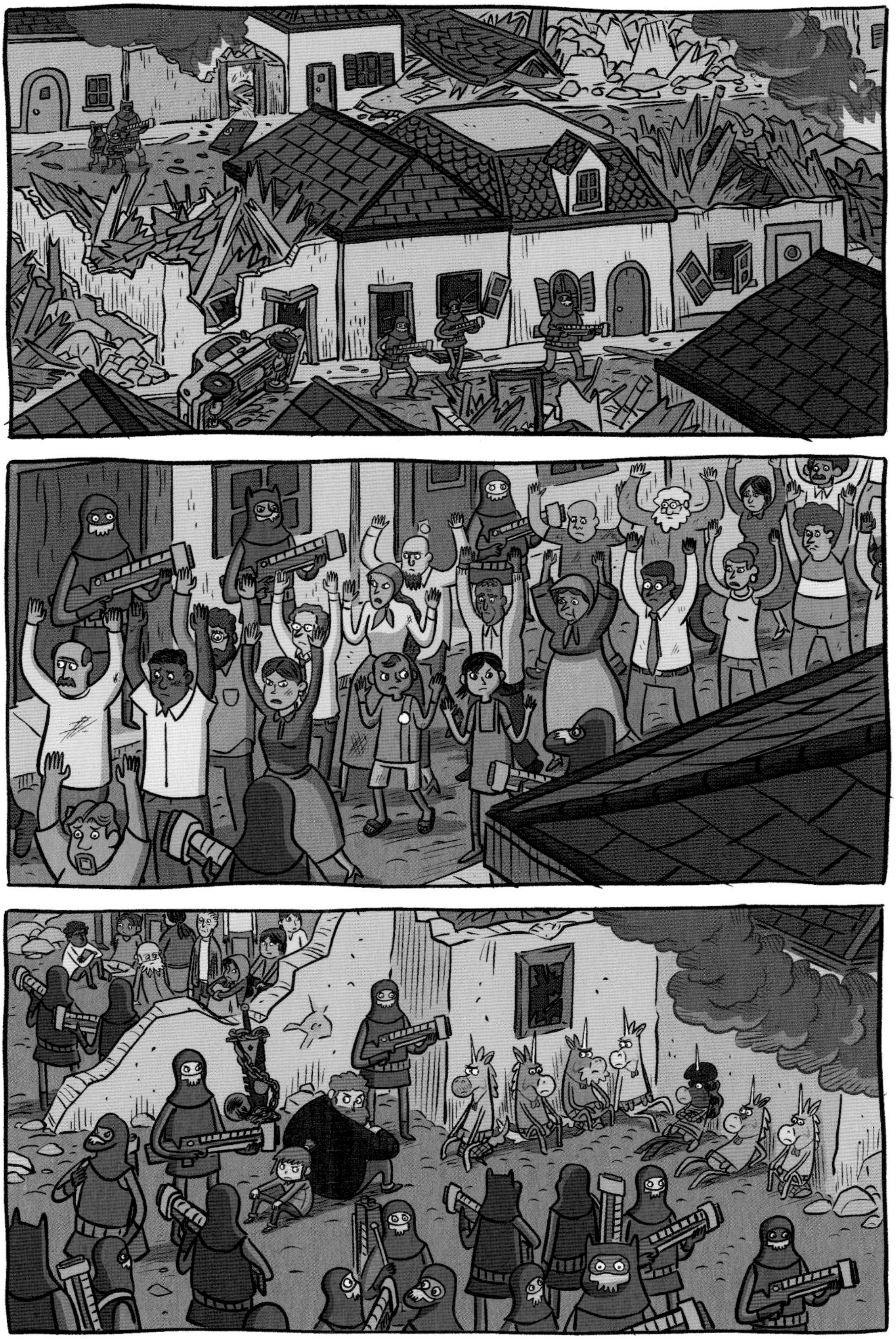

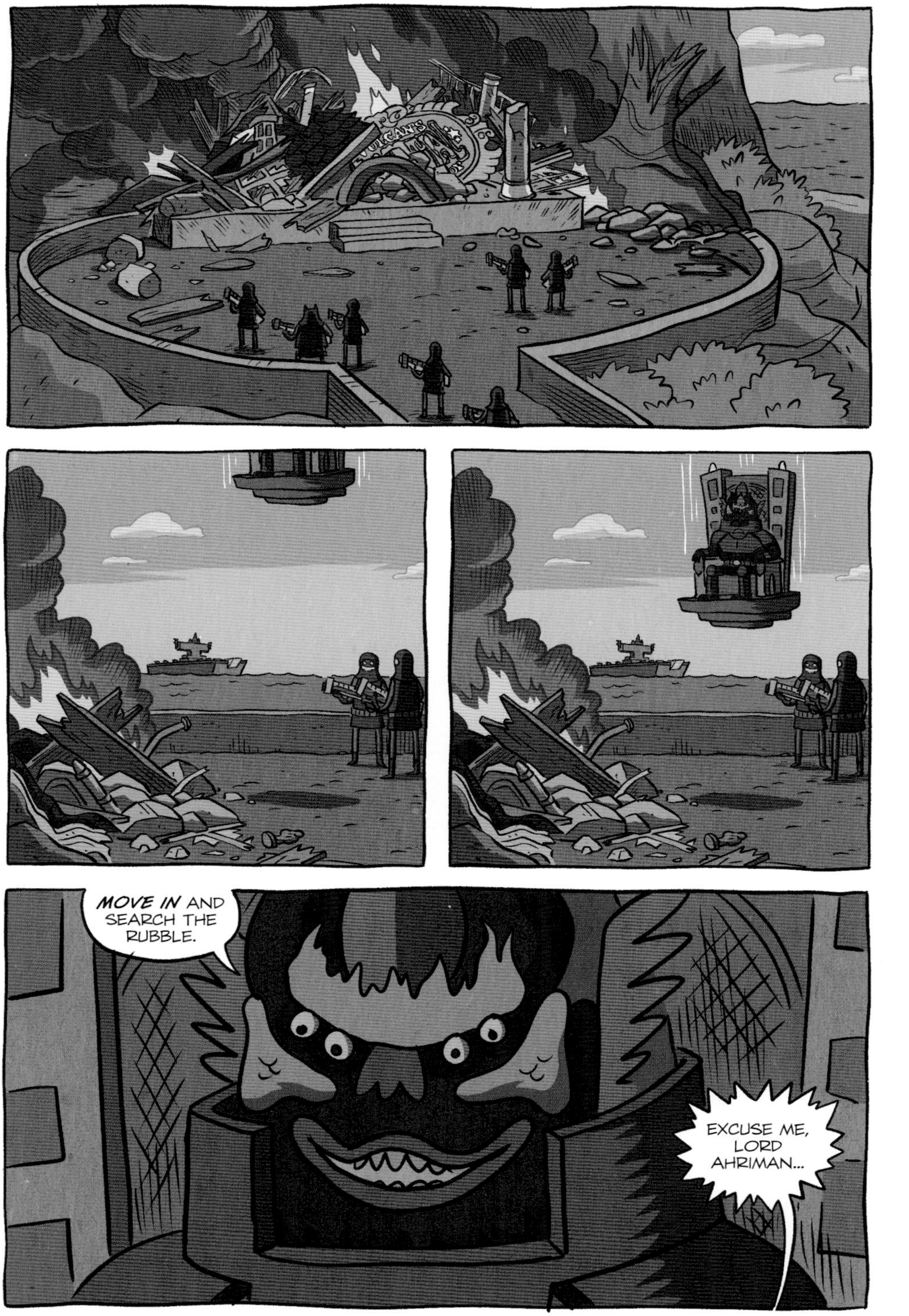
MOVE IN AND SEARCH THE RUBBLE.
EXCUSE ME, LORD AHRIMAN...

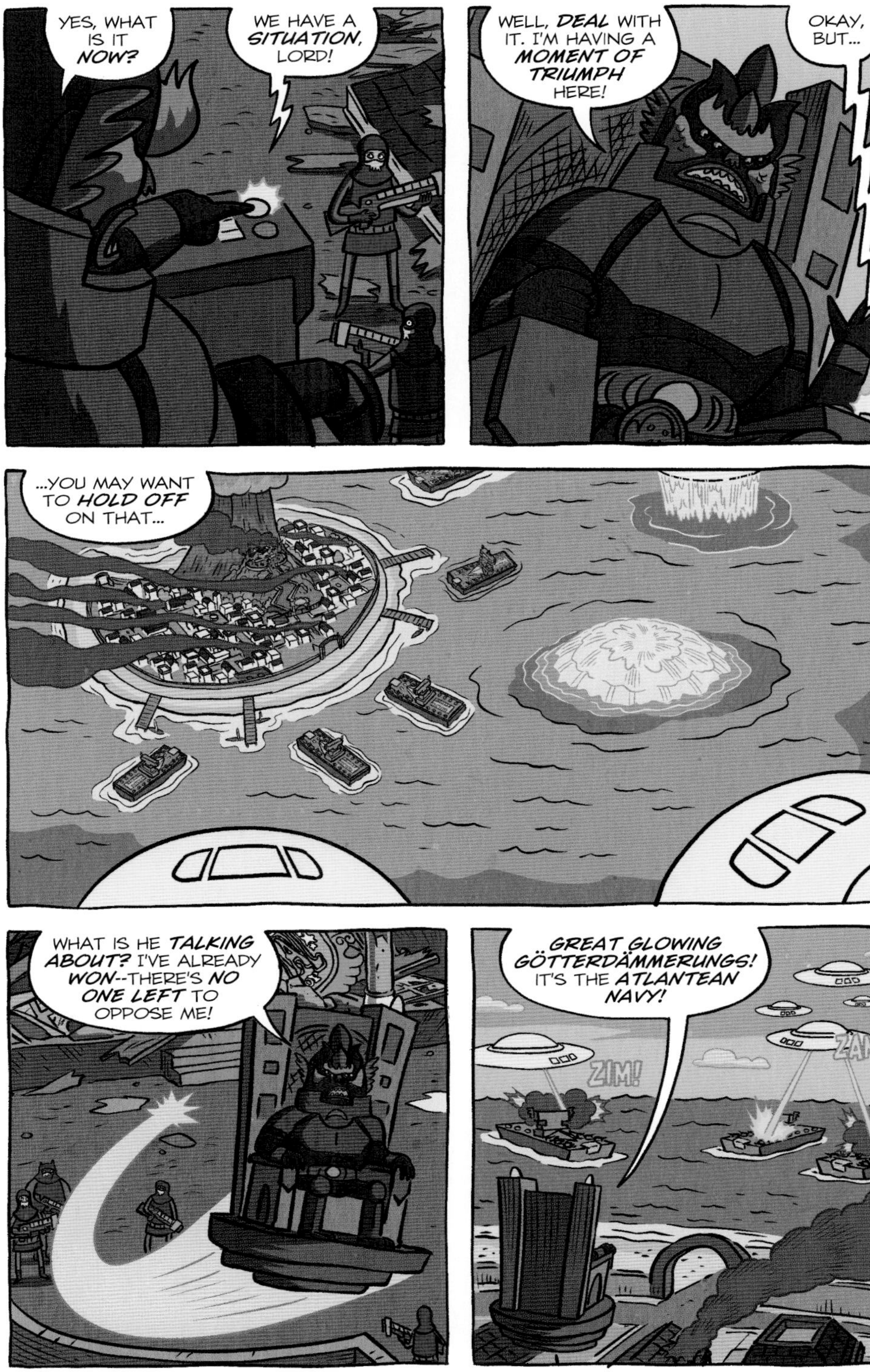
YES, WHAT IS IT NOW?
WE HAVE A SITUATION, LORD!
WELL, DEAL WITH IT. I'M HAVING A MOMENT OF TRIUMPH HERE!
OKAY, BUT...
...YOU MAY WANT TO HOLD OFF ON THAT...
WHAT IS HE TALKING ABOUT? I'VE ALREADY WON--THERE'S NO ONE LEFT TO OPPOSE ME!
...GREAT GLOWING GÖTTERDÄMMERUNGS! IT'S THE ATLANTEAN NAVY!
ZIM!
ZAM!

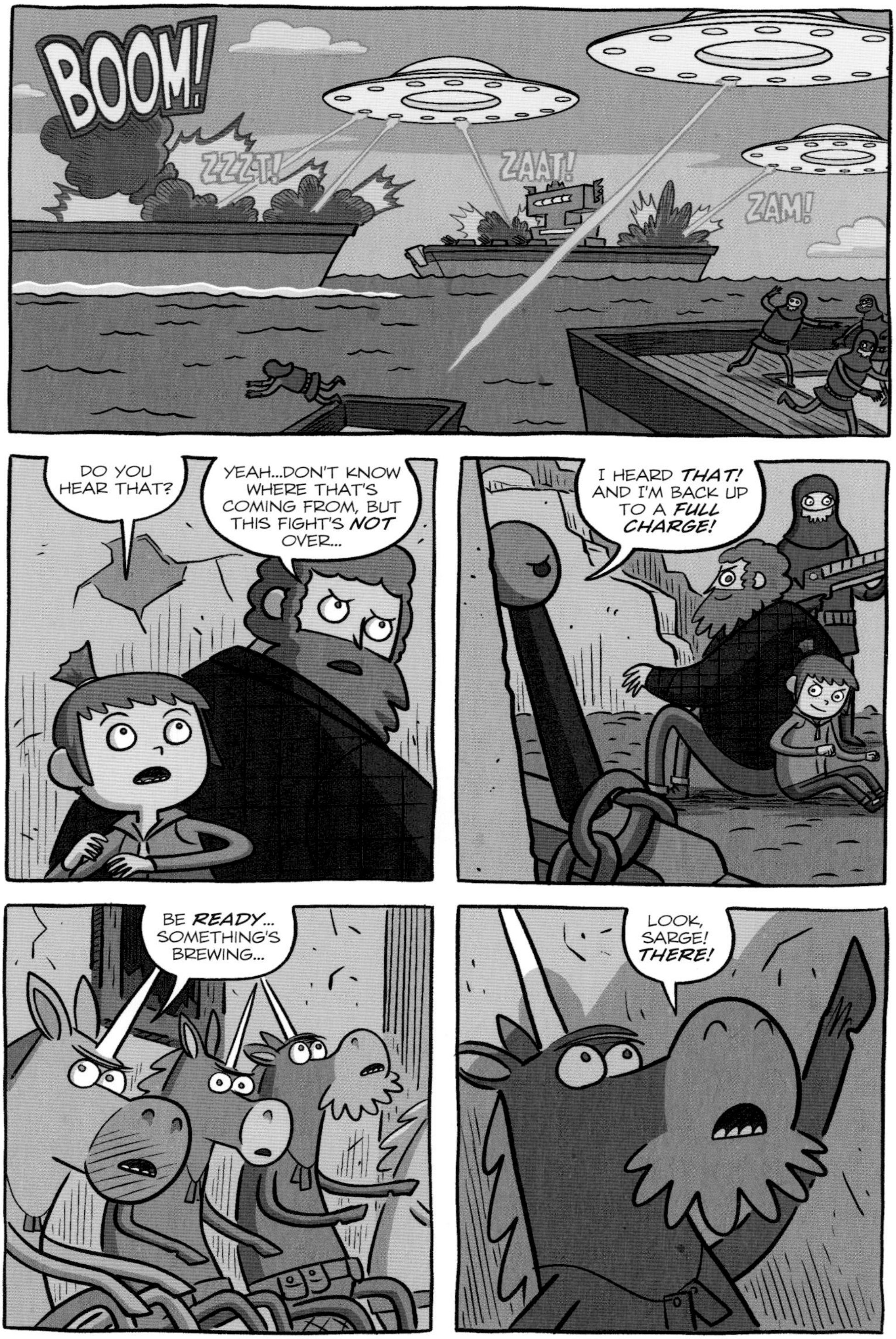
BOOM!
ZZZT!
ZAAT!
ZAM!
DO YOU HEAR THAT?
YEAH...DON'T KNOW WHERE THAT'S COMING FROM, BUT THIS FIGHT'S NOT OVER...
I HEARD THAT! AND I'M BACK UP TO A FULL CHARGE!
BE READY... SOMETHING'S BREWING...
LOOK, SARGE! THERE!

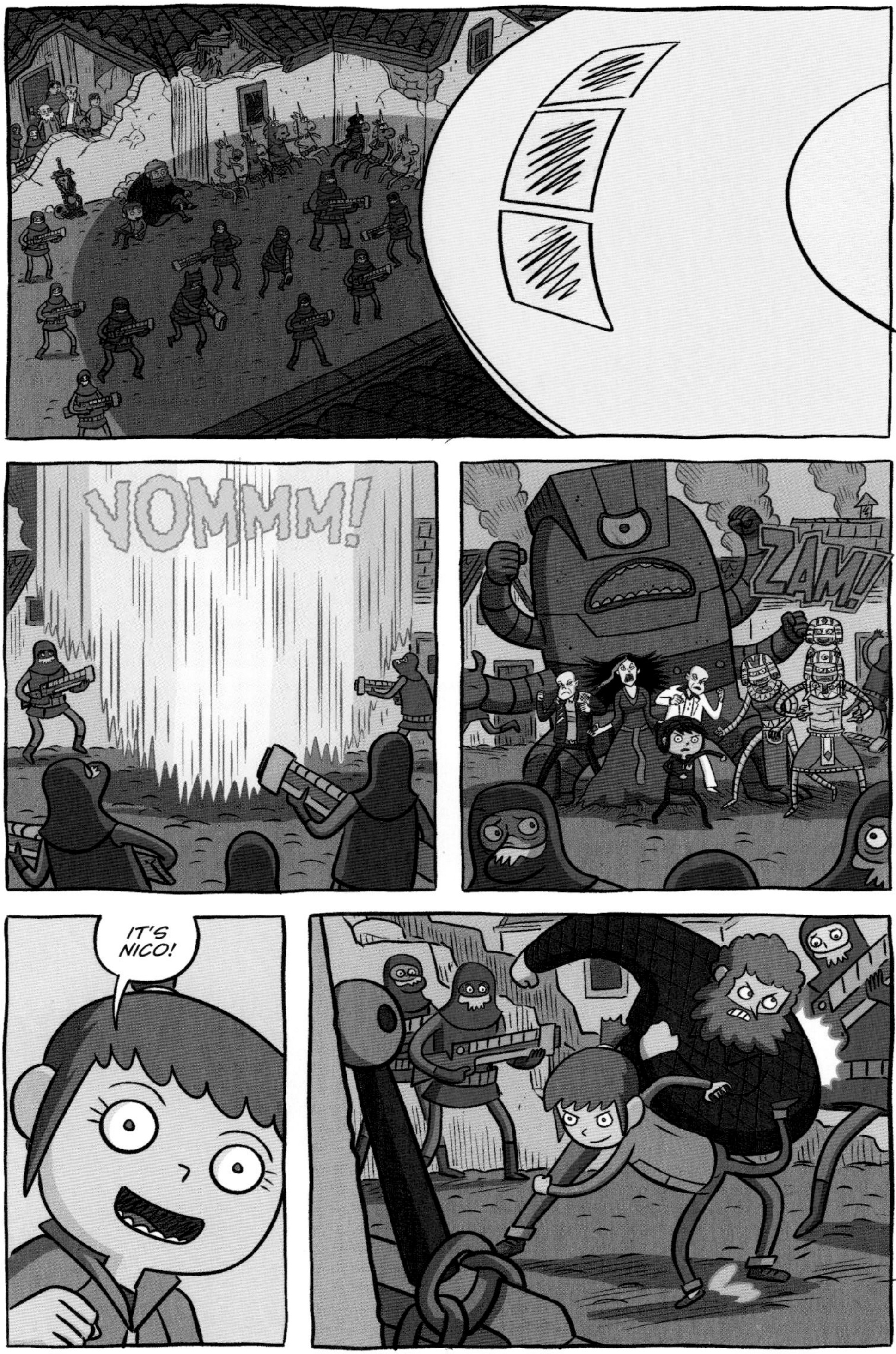
VOMMM!
ZAM!
IT'S NICO!

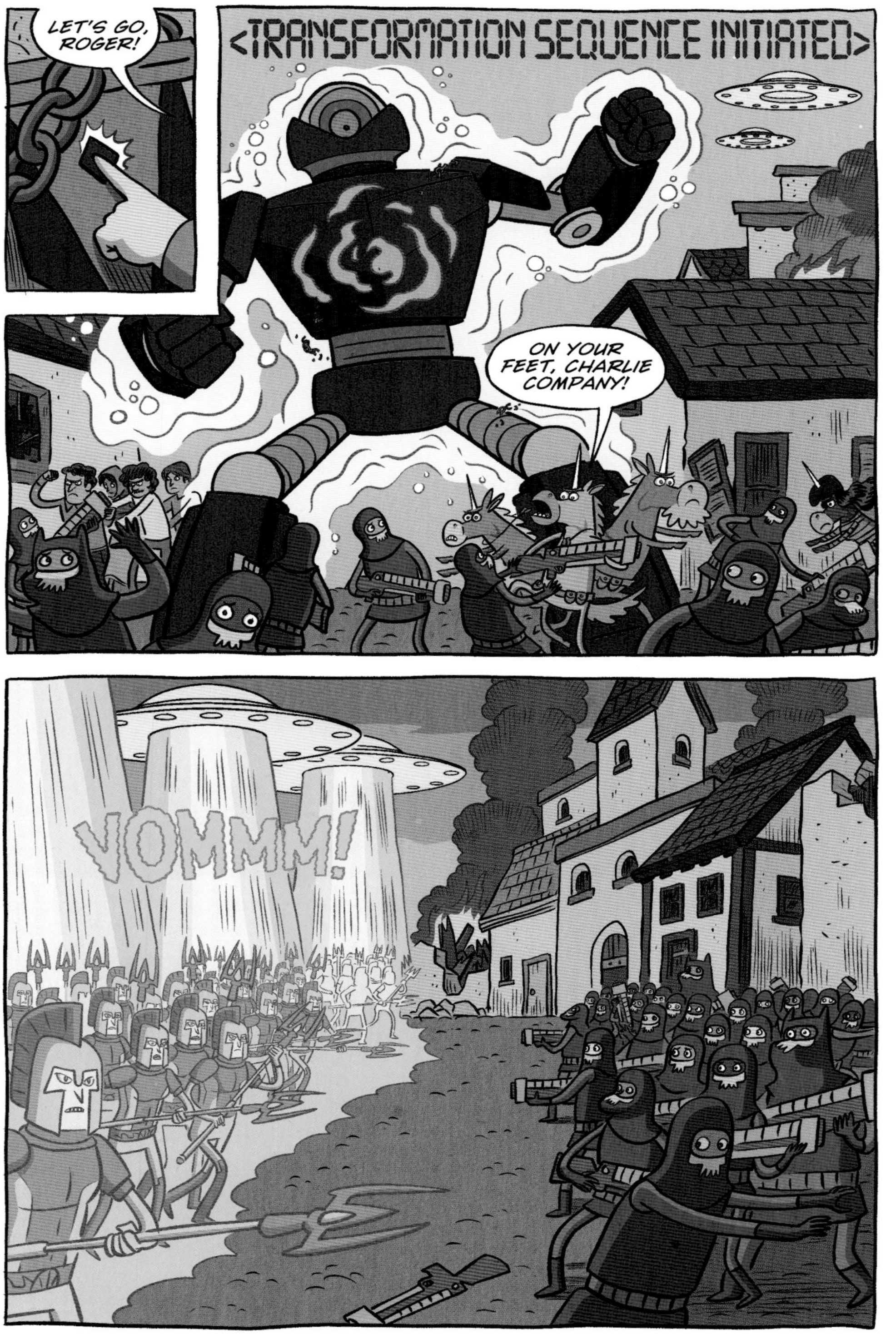
LET'S GO, ROGER!
<TRANSFORMATION SEQUENCE INITIATED>
ON YOUR FEET, CHARLIE COMPANY!
VOMMM!

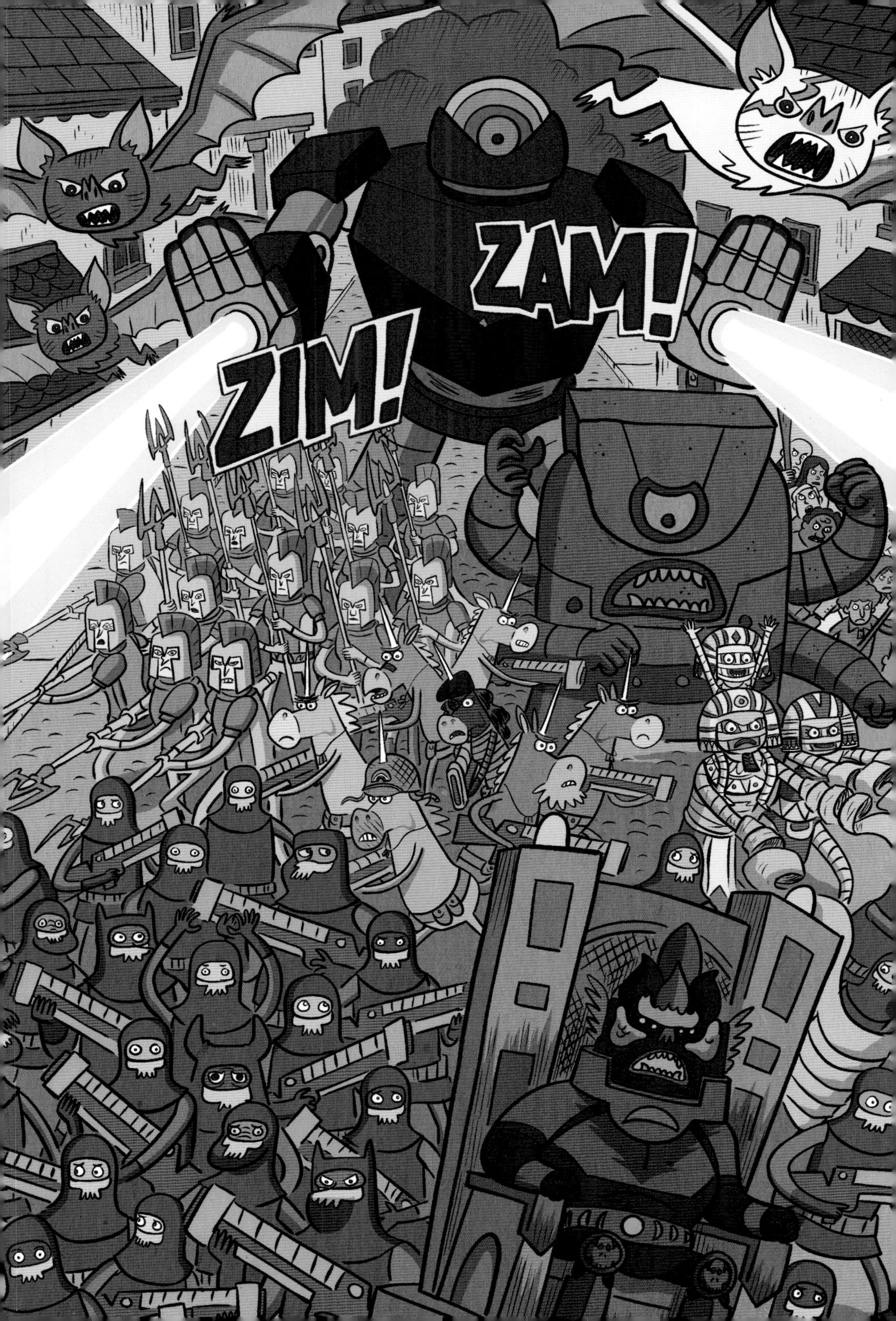
ZAM!
ZIM!

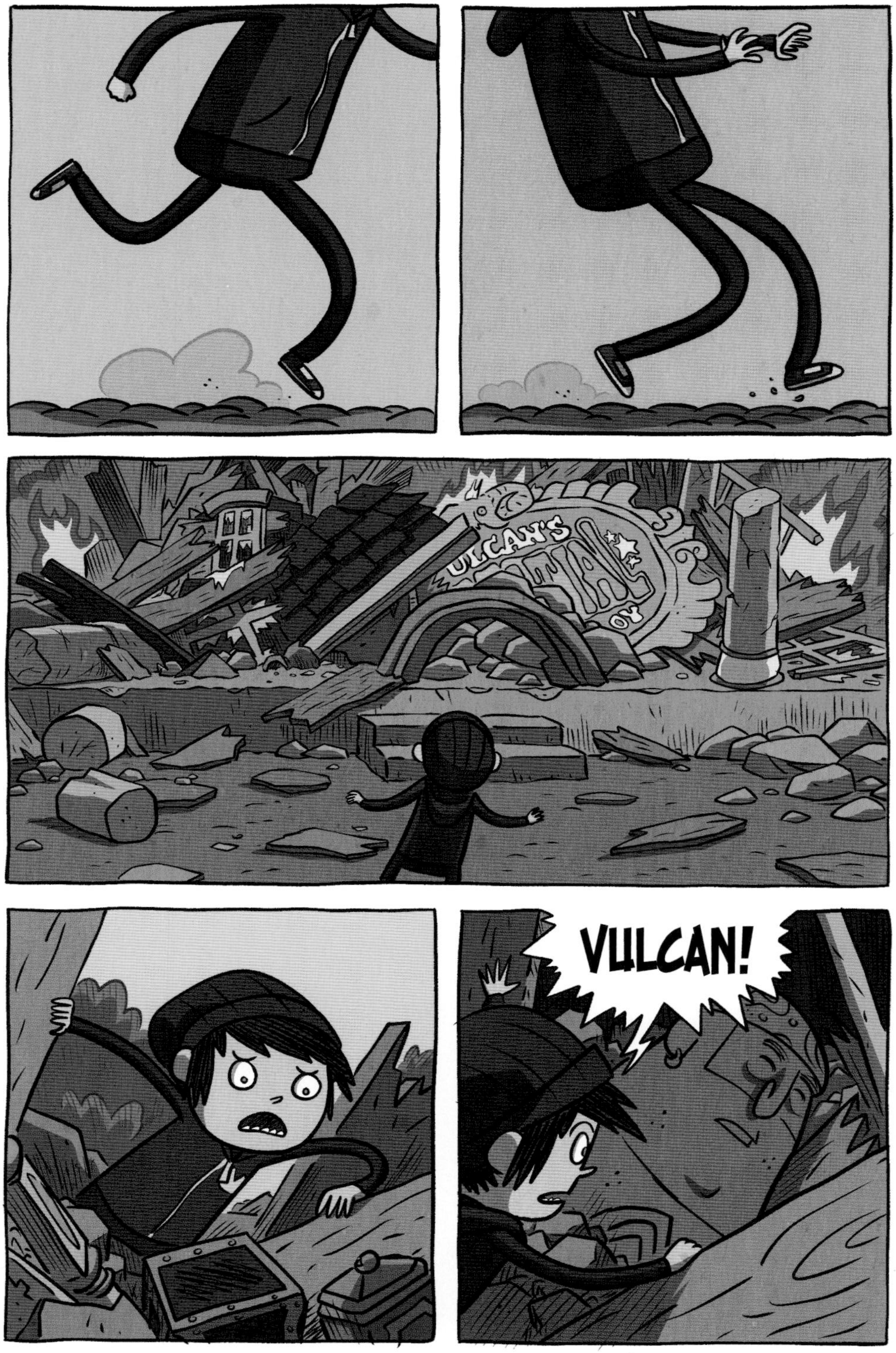
VULCAN!

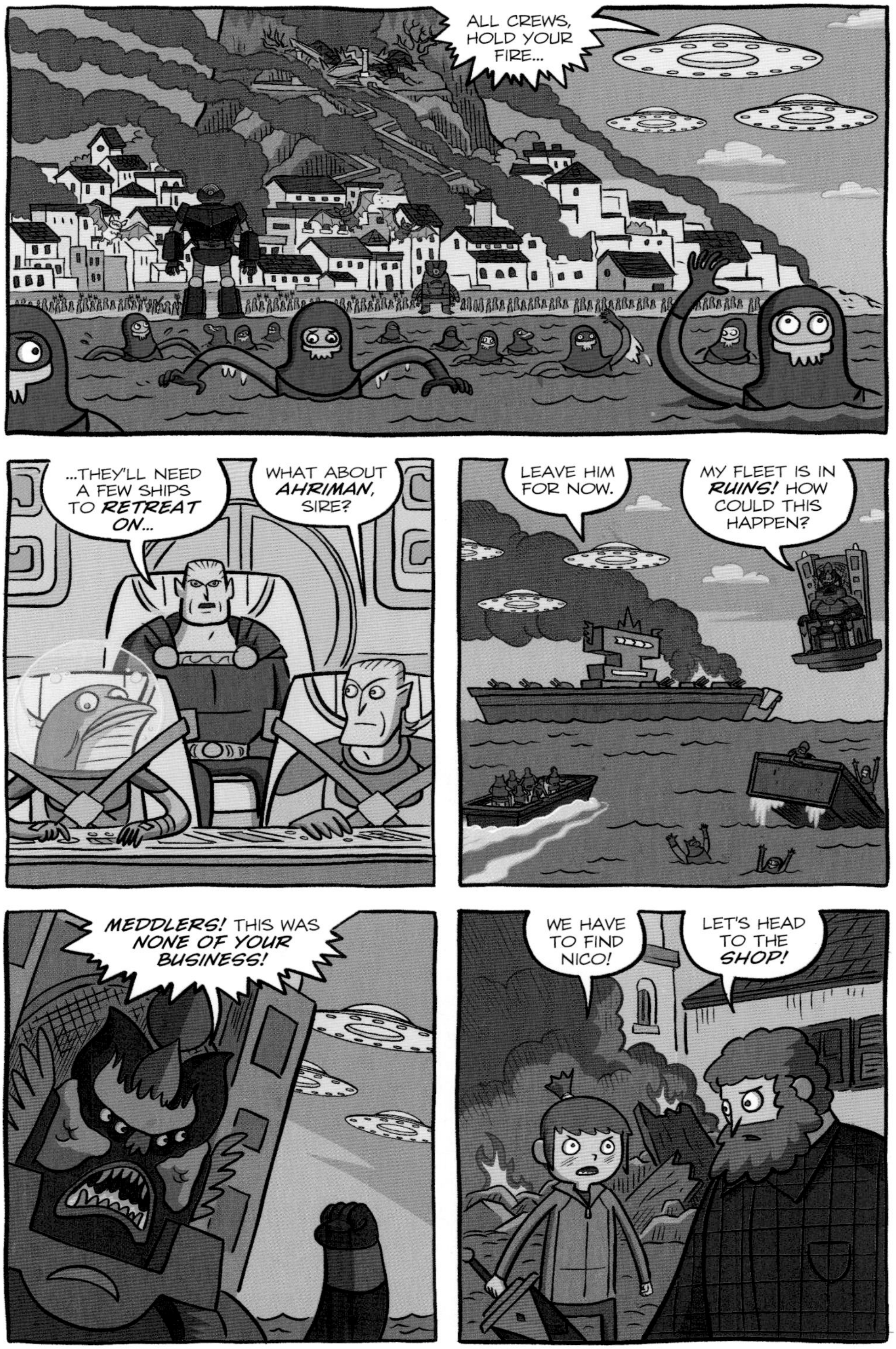
ALL CREWS, HOLD YOUR FIRE...
...THEY'LL NEED A FEW SHIPS TO **RETREAT ON...**
WHAT ABOUT **AHRIMAN,** SIRE?
LEAVE HIM FOR NOW.
MY FLEET IS IN **RUINS!** HOW COULD THIS HAPPEN?
MEDDLERS! THIS WAS **NONE OF YOUR BUSINESS!**
WE HAVE TO FIND NICO!
LET'S HEAD TO THE **SHOP!**

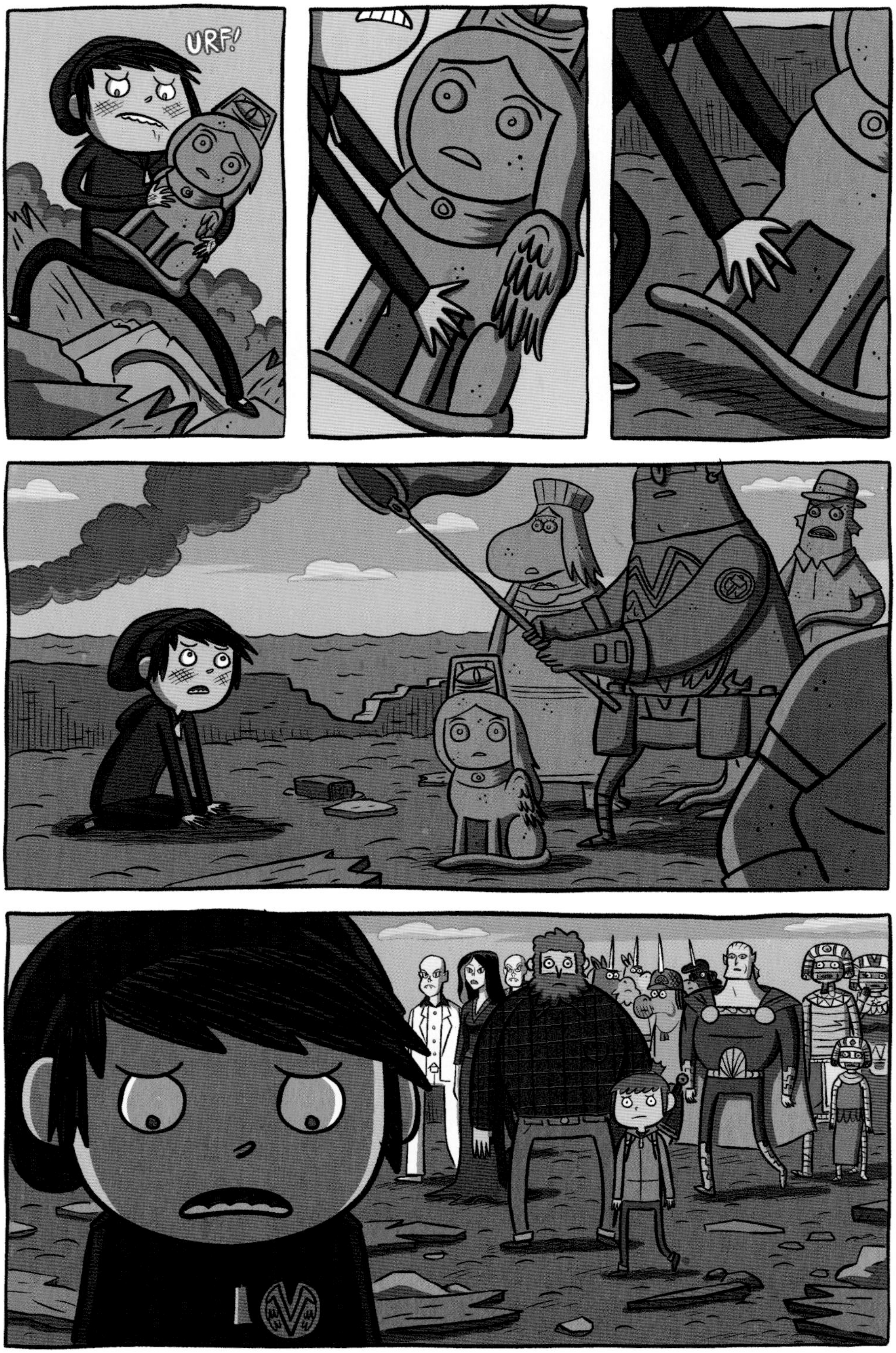
URF!

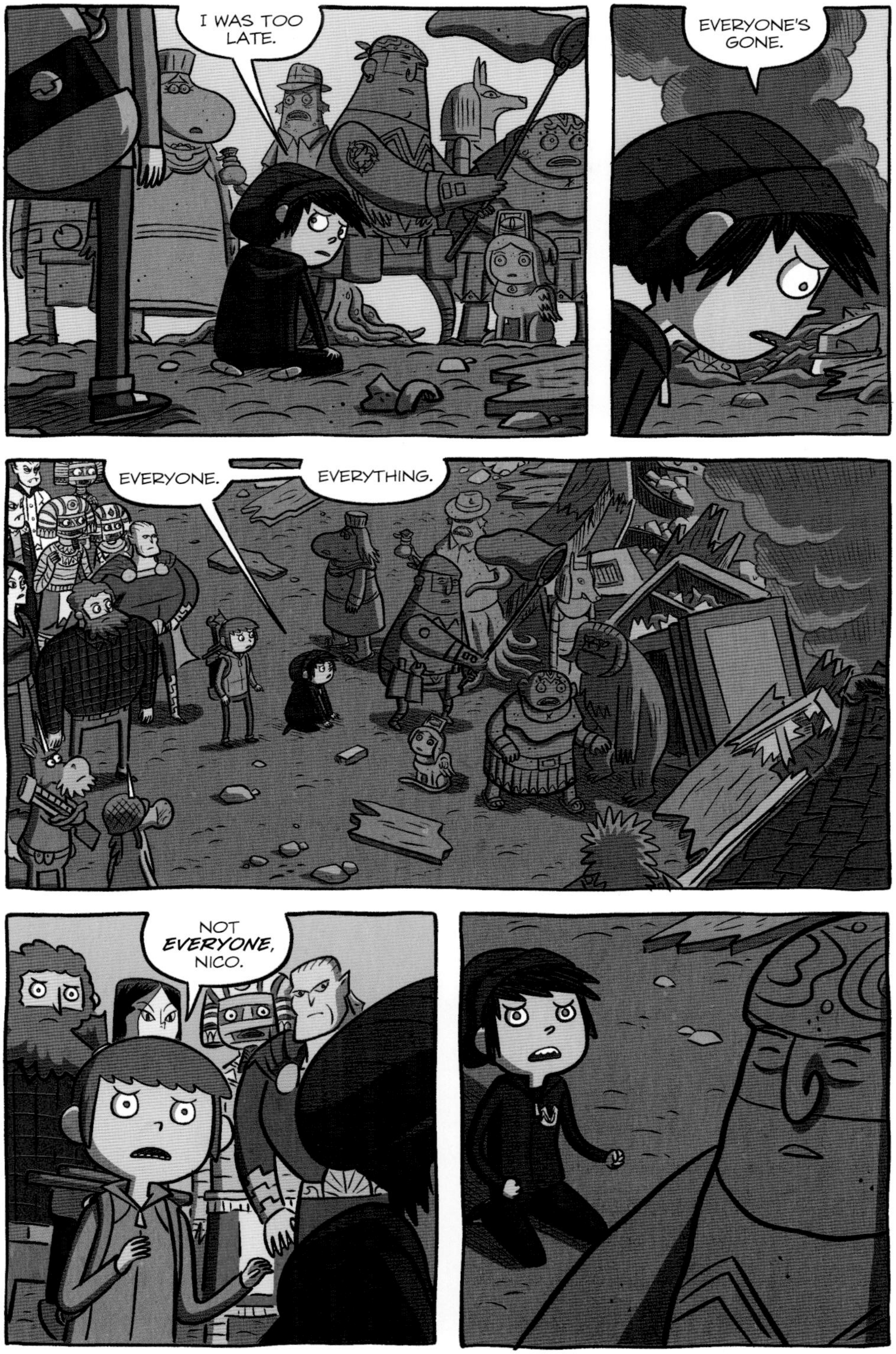
I WAS TOO LATE.
EVERYONE'S GONE.
EVERYONE.
EVERYTHING.
NOT *EVERYONE,* NICO.

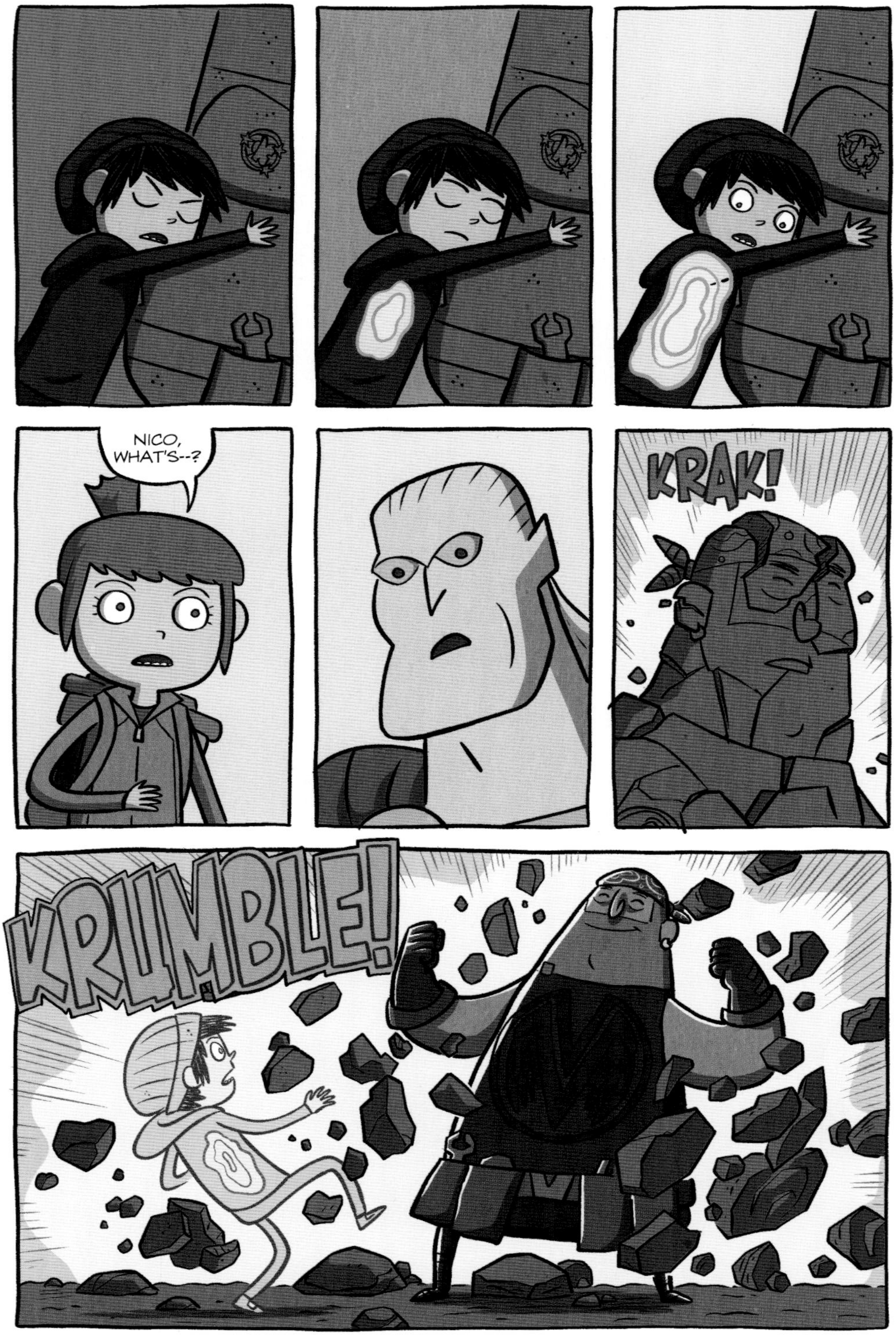
NICO, WHAT'S--?
KRAK!
KRUMBLE!

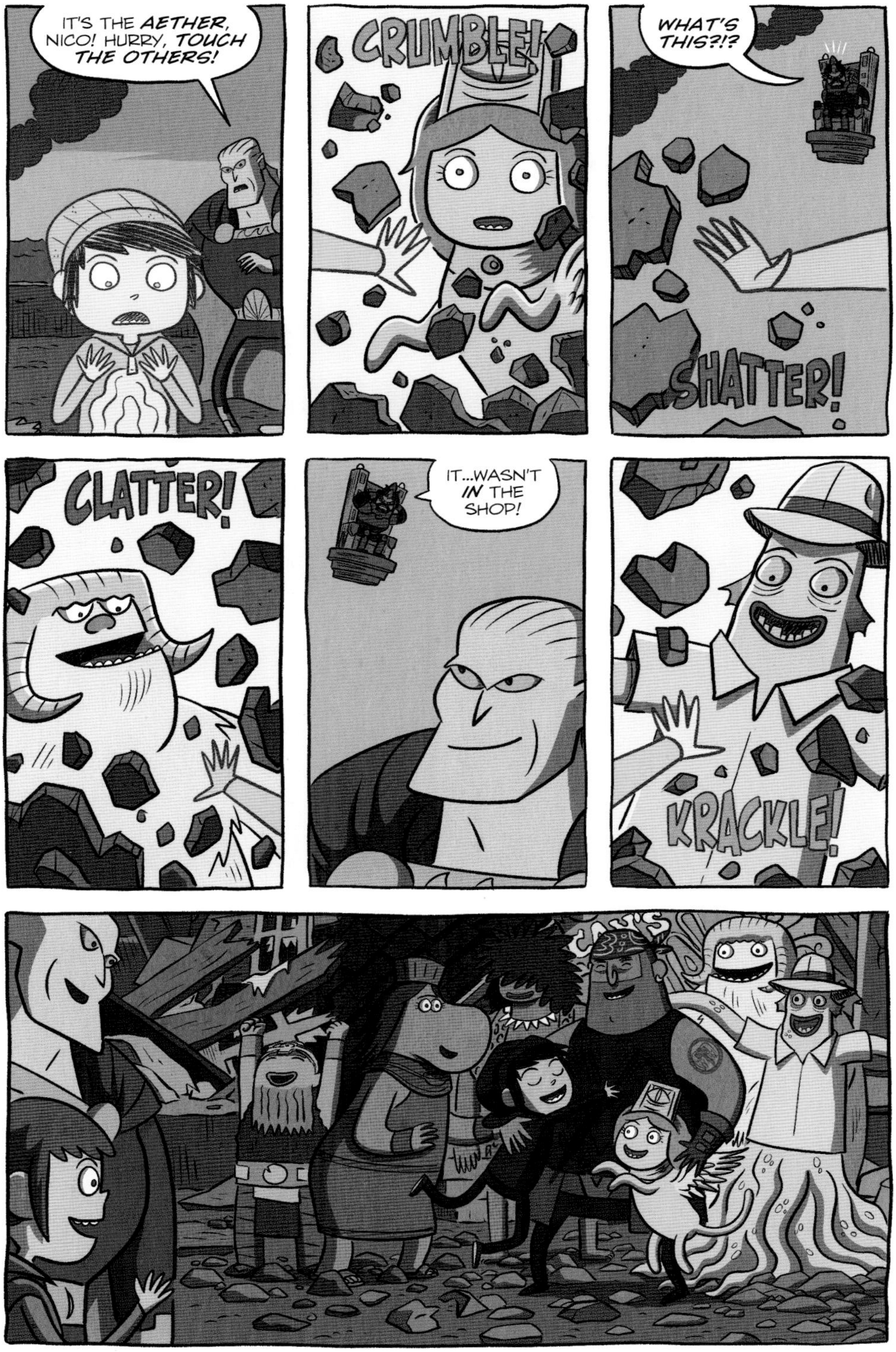

IT'S THE AETHER, NICO! HURRY, TOUCH THE OTHERS!
CRUMBLE!
WHAT'S THIS?!?
SHATTER!
CLATTER!
IT...WASN'T IN THE SHOP!
KRACKLE!

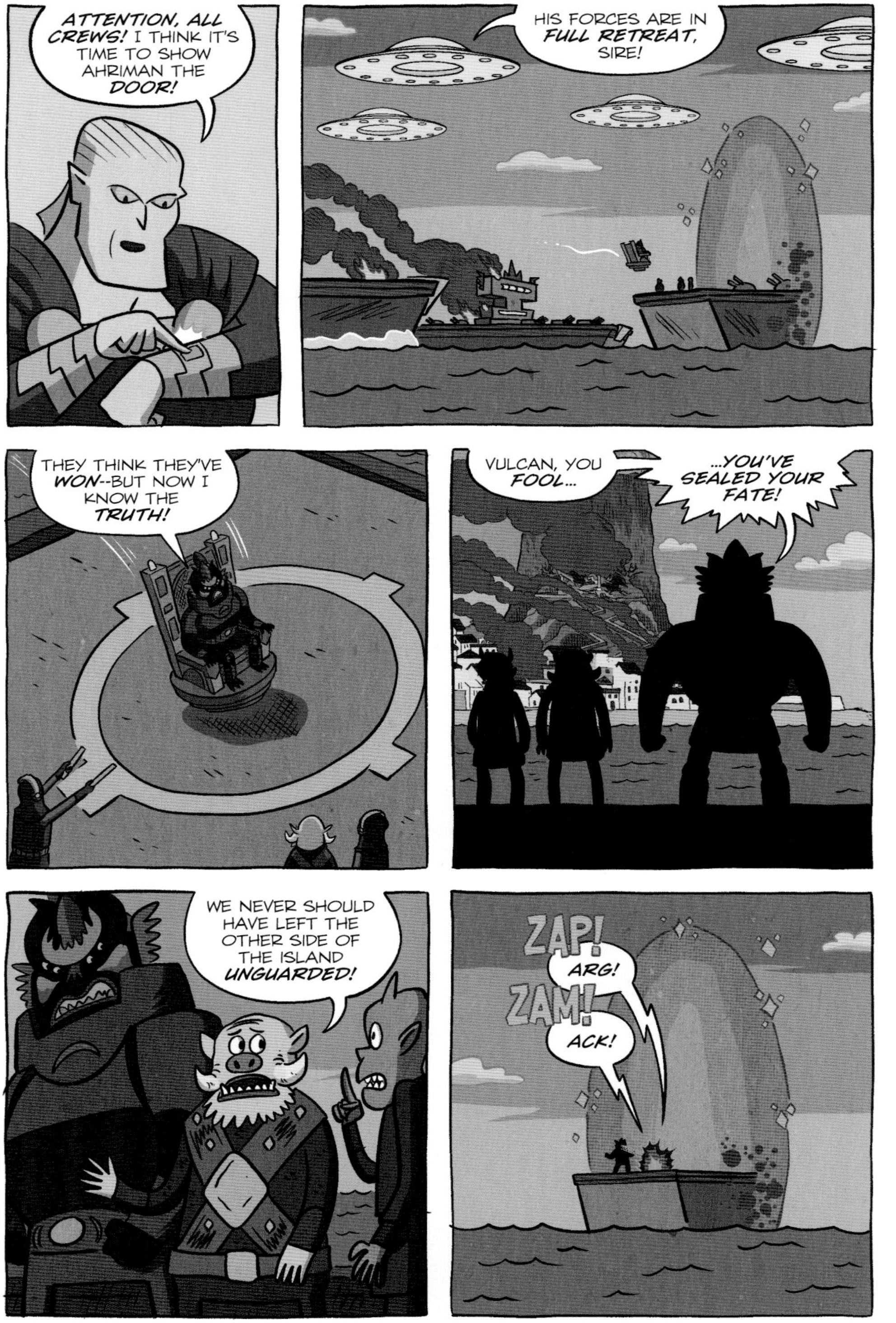
ATTENTION, ALL CREWS! I THINK IT'S TIME TO SHOW AHRIMAN THE DOOR!
HIS FORCES ARE IN FULL RETREAT, SIRE!
THEY THINK THEY'VE WON--BUT NOW I KNOW THE TRUTH!
VULCAN, YOU FOOL...
...YOU'VE SEALED YOUR FATE!
WE NEVER SHOULD HAVE LEFT THE OTHER SIDE OF THE ISLAND UNGUARDED!
ZAP!
ARG!
ZAM!
ACK!

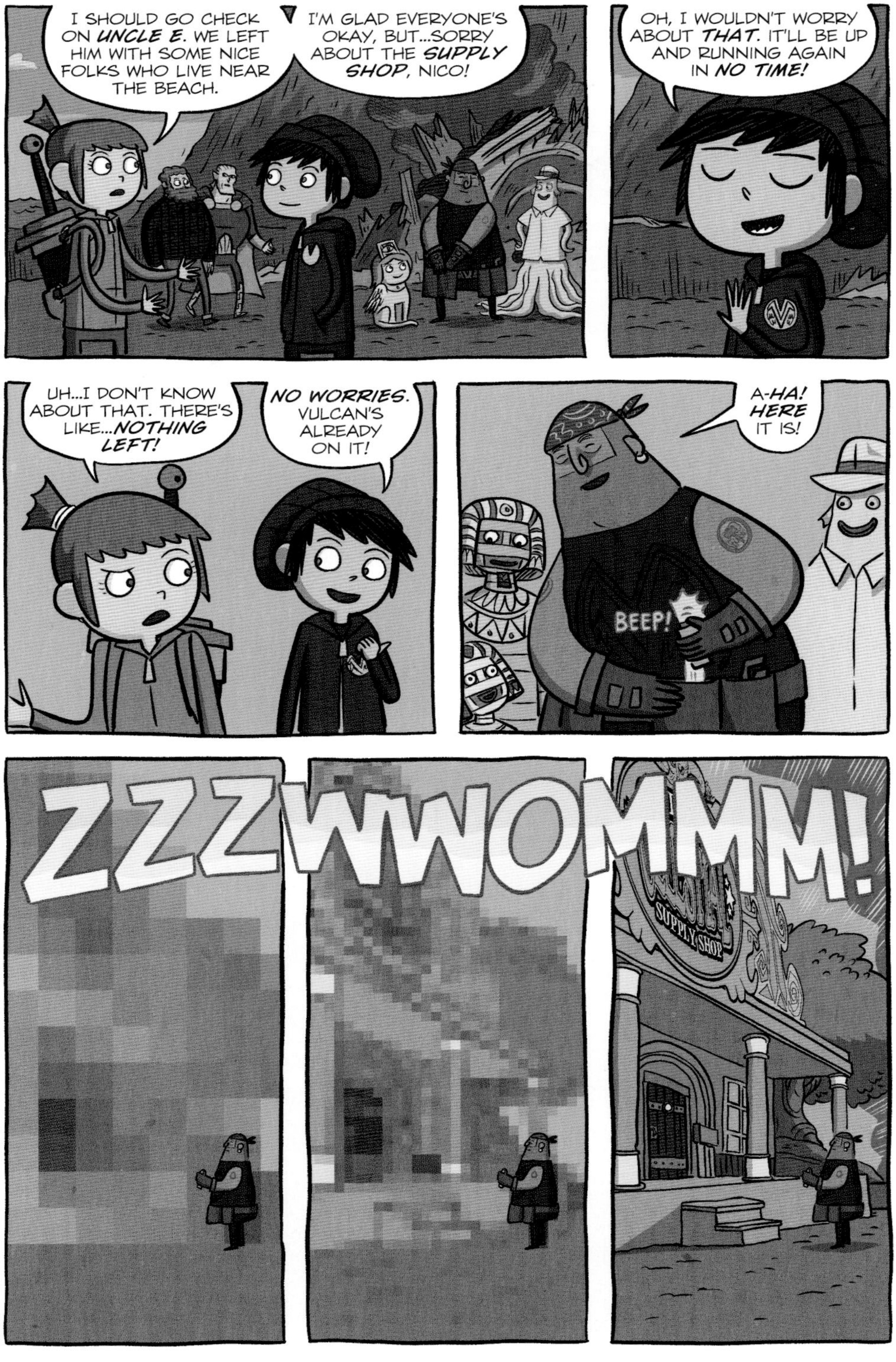

I SHOULD GO CHECK ON UNCLE E. WE LEFT HIM WITH SOME NICE FOLKS WHO LIVE NEAR THE BEACH.
I'M GLAD EVERYONE'S OKAY, BUT...SORRY ABOUT THE SUPPLY SHOP, NICO!
OH, I WOULDN'T WORRY ABOUT THAT. IT'LL BE UP AND RUNNING AGAIN IN NO TIME!
UH...I DON'T KNOW ABOUT THAT. THERE'S LIKE...NOTHING LEFT!
NO WORRIES. VULCAN'S ALREADY ON IT!
A-HA! HERE IT IS!
BEEP!
ZZZWWOMMM!
SUPPLY SHOP

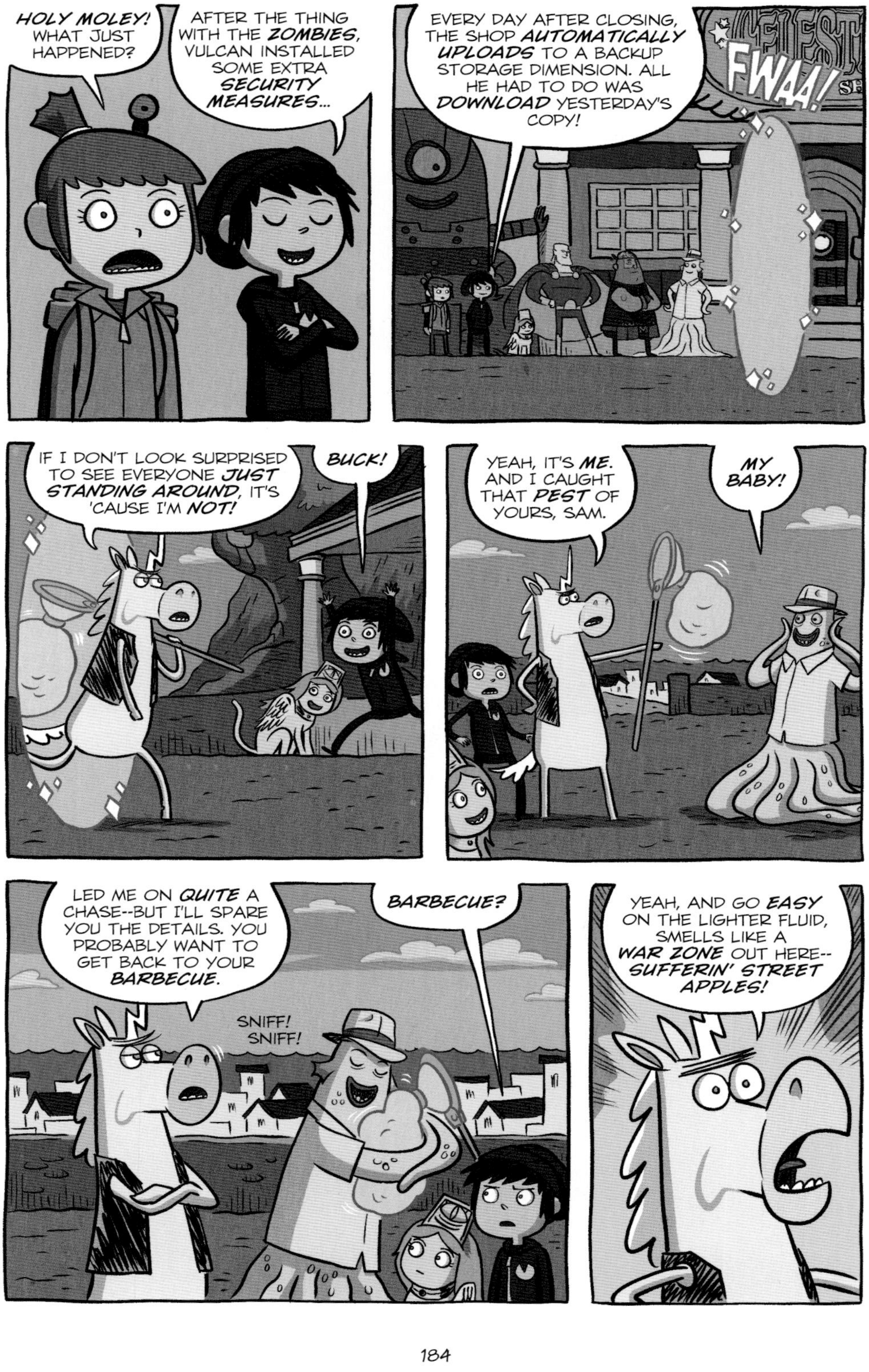
HOLY MOLEY! WHAT JUST HAPPENED?
AFTER THE THING WITH THE ZOMBIES, VULCAN INSTALLED SOME EXTRA SECURITY MEASURES...
EVERY DAY AFTER CLOSING, THE SHOP AUTOMATICALLY UPLOADS TO A BACKUP STORAGE DIMENSION. ALL HE HAD TO DO WAS DOWNLOAD YESTERDAY'S COPY!
FWAA!
IF I DON'T LOOK SURPRISED TO SEE EVERYONE JUST STANDING AROUND, IT'S 'CAUSE I'M NOT!
BUCK!
YEAH, IT'S ME. AND I CAUGHT THAT PEST OF YOURS, SAM.
MY BABY!
LED ME ON QUITE A CHASE--BUT I'LL SPARE YOU THE DETAILS. YOU PROBABLY WANT TO GET BACK TO YOUR BARBECUE.
SNIFF! SNIFF!
BARBECUE?
YEAH, AND GO EASY ON THE LIGHTER FLUID, SMELLS LIKE A WAR ZONE OUT HERE-- SUFFERIN' STREET APPLES!

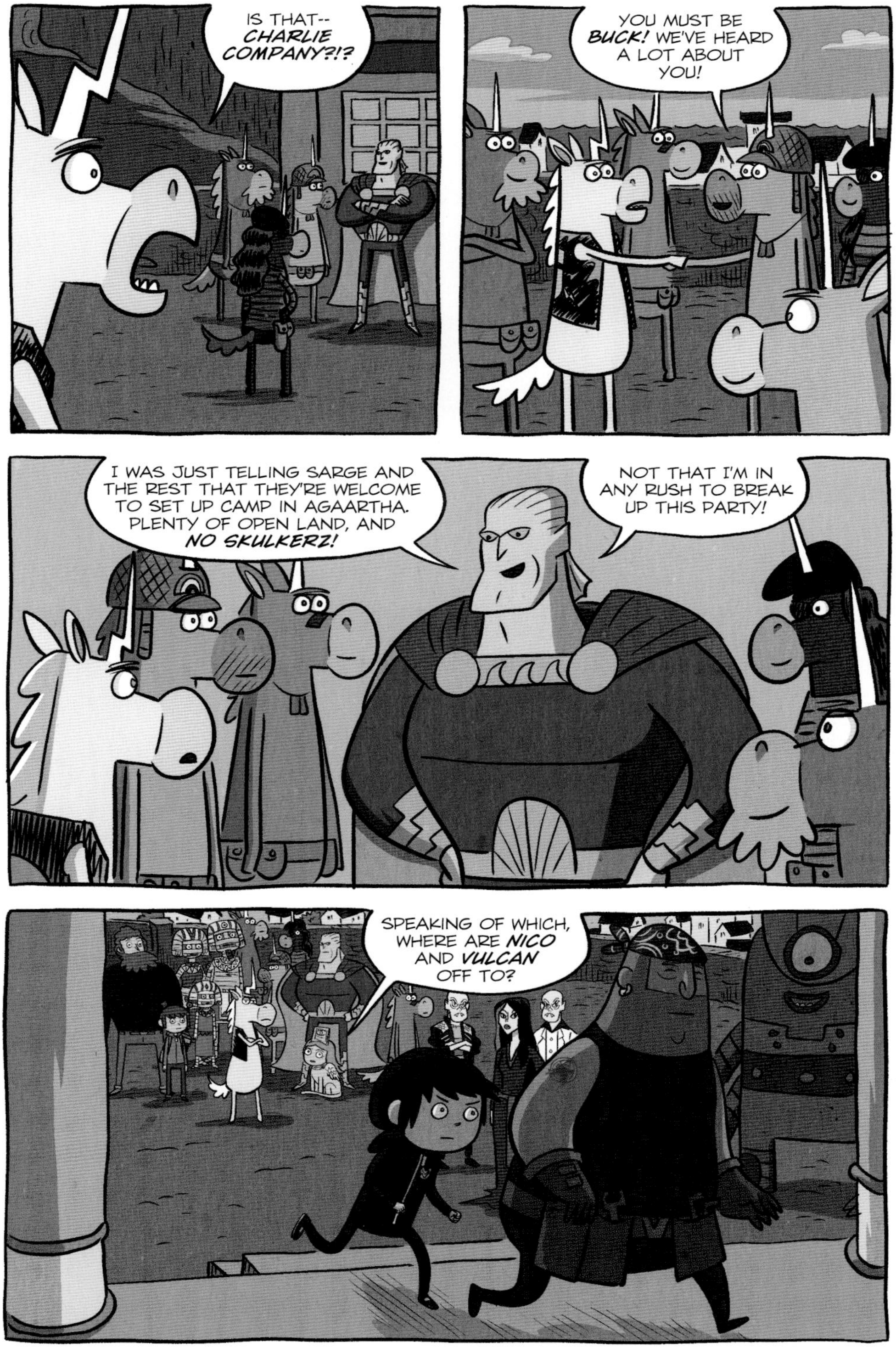
IS THAT--
CHARLIE COMPANY?!?
YOU MUST BE **BUCK!** WE'VE HEARD A LOT ABOUT YOU!
I WAS JUST TELLING SARGE AND THE REST THAT THEY'RE WELCOME TO SET UP CAMP IN AGAARTHA. PLENTY OF OPEN LAND, AND **NO SKULKERZ!**
NOT THAT I'M IN ANY RUSH TO BREAK UP THIS PARTY!
SPEAKING OF WHICH, WHERE ARE **NICO** AND **VULCAN** OFF TO?

Epilogue

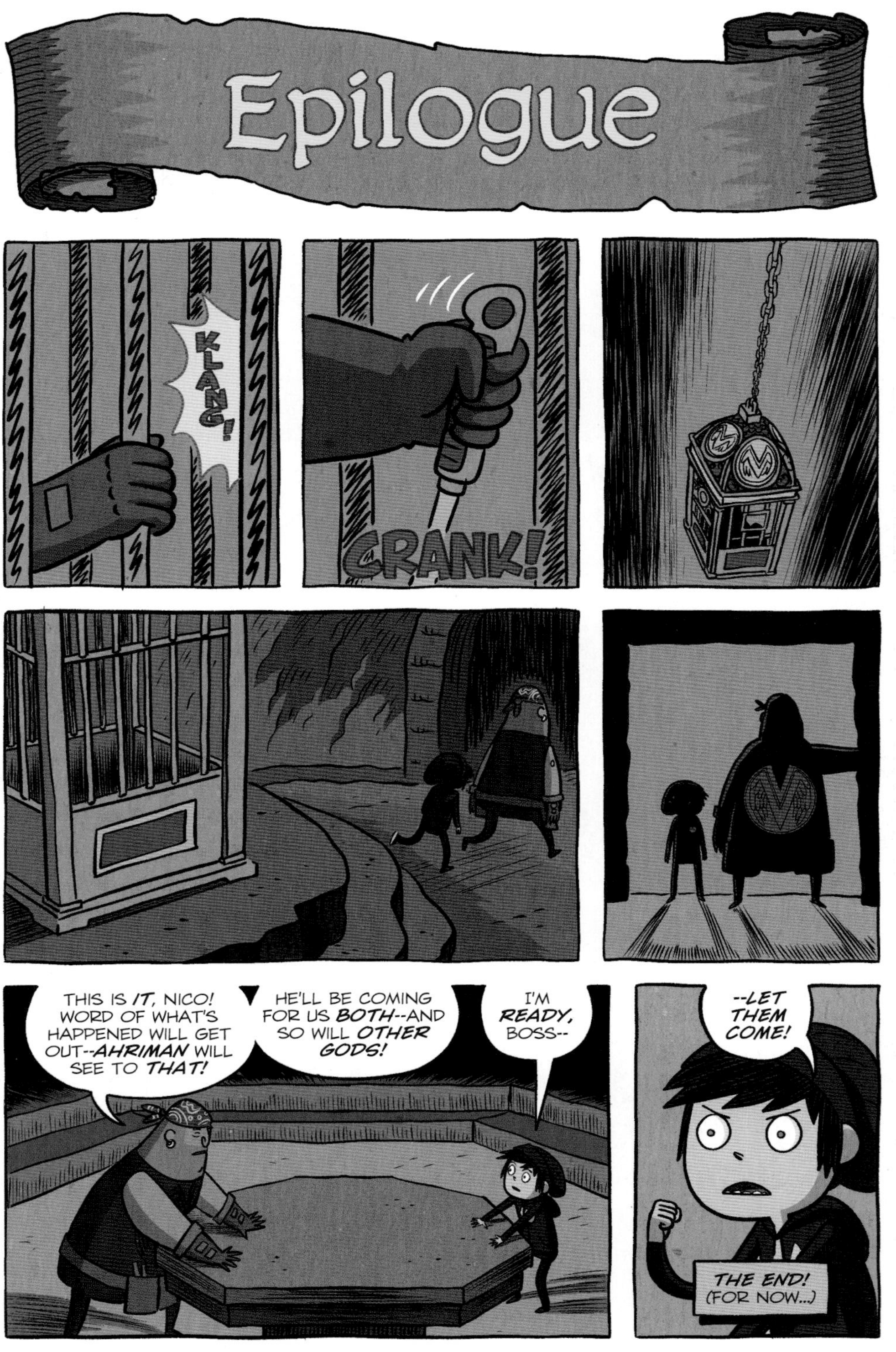
KLANG!
CRANK!
THIS IS *IT*, NICO! WORD OF WHAT'S HAPPENED WILL GET OUT--*AHRIMAN* WILL SEE TO *THAT!*
HE'LL BE COMING FOR US *BOTH*--AND SO WILL *OTHER GODS!*
I'M *READY,* BOSS--
--LET THEM COME!
THE END! (FOR NOW...)

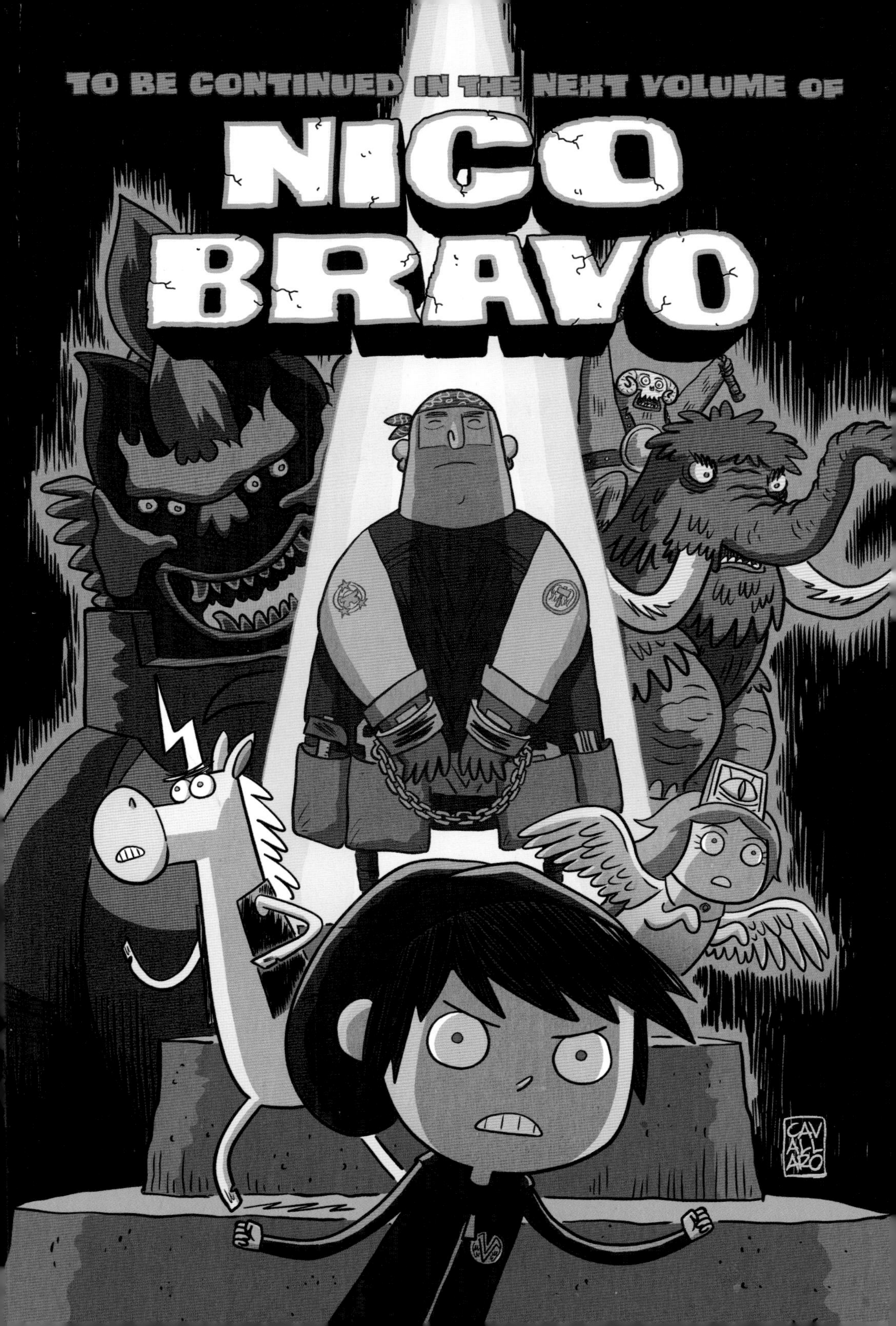
TO BE CONTINUED IN THE NEXT VOLUME OF
NICO BRAVO
CAVALLARO

THANK YOU

GIORGIA & FRANK CAVALLARO, PAUL CAVALLARO & FAMILY,
ANNA WINCHOCK & FAMILY, LISA NATOLI, NICK ABADZIS,
ANDREW ARNOLD, KIRK BENSHOFF, J.M. DEMATTEIS,
KRISTIN DULANEY, SCOTT FRIEDLANDER, MOLLY JOHANSON,
JEREMY LAWSON, SUNNY LEE, GEORGE O'CONNOR,
BEN SHARPE, MARK SIEGEL, GABE SORIA, ED STECKLEY,
NICOLE SWIFT, KIARA VALDEZ, SARA VARON,
CARYN WISEMAN AT ANDREA BROWN LITERARY AGENCY,
AND THE NATIONAL CARTOONISTS SOCIETY.